The Honduran Plot

A Novel

By

Horton Prather

Basswood
Cove
Publishing

Horton Prather

The Honduran Plot

Published by: Basswood Cove Publishing, Buford, Georgia

ISBN-13: 978-0-9899349-0-9 (paperback)
978-0-9899349-1-6 (e-book)

Library of Congress Control Number: 2013917526

For more information visit the website: www.hortonprather.com or e-mail the author at horton@hortonprather.com.

Cover Design by: Horton Prather
Cover Photograph: *Cruz de Chatarra* (Cross of Scrap) This beautiful cross sits on a hilltop near Santa Ana, Morazán, Honduras. The artist and builder created it from scrap automobile parts, to symbolize the idea that God, the ultimate artist, can create a thing of beauty from a worthless, broken and worn out life.

Horton Prather

DEDICATION

This book is dedicated to my seven grandchildren. I love each of
you for the unique qualities God has given you.
– Papa

Horton Prather

ACKNOWLEGMENTS

Many people were instrumental in producing this novel. While the plot and words are products of the author's imagination, many others helped those words come to life.

My sincere thanks go to my wife, Vivian Prather, for critique, editing, and navigating the twists and turns of the plot. She also helped an emotionally challenged engineer gain awareness of the feelings and reactions of the characters. I am grateful for her love and encouragement.

Thanks also to the reviewers of the first draft (originally entitled Honduran Awakening) who provided corrections, suggestions, and other useful critique. They are, in no particular order; John Clovis, Lewis (Buzz) Gibbs, Sue Church, and Vivian Prather. Thanks also go to Daryle Geyer, Vivian Prather, and Jennifer McLain for review and editing of the final draft. My apologies to anyone else who I forgot to mention.

I appreciate the members of Northeast Georgia Writers and the Writers Roundtable critique group, who provided encouragement, suggestions, insights, a sharp eye for errors, and advice on the cover.

The original inspiration for this novel began when the youth group from Campus Church of Christ in Norcross, Georgia shared their experiences from a mission trip to Honduras. My imagination was captured by people living in the large municipal dump in the hills northwest of Tegucigalpa, the capital city of Honduras. Thanks to Jeff Hubright for helping arrange travel to Honduras so I could see it for myself.

I am amazed at the dedication of the many Christian missionaries who dedicate their time, effort, money, and love to help the people living in poverty in Honduras. This is what brought my protagonist, Jake Grayson, to Honduras on a mission trip—a mission trip that changed his life.

My thanks and admiration go to Marc and Terri Tindall for their gracious hospitality during my research trip to Honduras in 2011. Marc and Terri are truly an inspiration to all who know of their efforts in

Honduras. Rather than enjoy a comfortable upper class retirement, Marc and Terry chose to spread God's love to those in need.

They founded *Casa de Esperanza* ("House of Hope") where they show the love of Jesus Christ by raising and caring for a number of Honduran children. They also host numerous mission teams who do amazing things. These teams feed people living in the Tegucigalpa dump, build houses, churches, school buildings, and feeding centers for children. Marc, Terri and the mission teams do many other things—there isn't enough room here to list everything these servants of the Lord are doing to improve the condition of the desperately poor.

You can find more about their work through Marc Tindall's posts on Facebook or Terri Tindall's blog: http://terriltindall.blogspot.com. Contributions can be sent to Honduras Hope, P.O. Box 4222, Columbus, MS 39705.

Thanks also to Luis Estrada for driving me to many locations in, and around, Tegucigalpa. Luis explained many things and helped me pick locales for several scenes in the book. He also graciously agreed to let me use his name for one of the fictional characters.

I would also like to recognize Pastor Jeony Ordonez of *Amor, Fey y Esperanza* ("Love, Faith and Hope")—the school which provides education for the children of the garbage dump. Pastor Jeony was instrumental in founding AFE, with the idea that, through education, these children might be given a better chance in life. His story was another inspiration at the beginning of the writing process. For more information on AFE see: http://afehonduras.blogspot.com.

A portion of the author's proceeds will be dedicated to support of the important work of Marc and Terri Tindall, and also the AFE School.

My thanks also go to the Consulate General of Honduras in Atlanta, Georgia for their hospitality and time taken to answer my many questions. Also thanks to Mike Escarra for his work in establishing Networking Honduras, Inc. to better coordinate NGOs (Non-Governmental Organizations) with the Honduran government.

Lastly, and most importantly, I would like to thank God for his enduring love, blessings, and mercy. Without Him all my efforts would be meaningless.

Consider it pure joy, my brothers and sisters, whenever you face trials of many kinds, because you know that the testing of your faith produces perseverance. Let perseverance finish its work so that you may be mature and complete, not lacking anything.

– James 1: 2-4

Horton Prather

Chapter 1

Jake Grayson sat back in frustration, rubbing his tired eyes. Ruben's decision to stay in Honduras had distracted him once again. *What is going on with Ruben? He's throwing his future away, staying down there.*

The engineering lab was now filled with the sound of students talking, joking, and occasionally a groan of dismay when sparks flew. Jake slapped his face in an effort to come alert. The long night of checking circuit boards and debugging programs had proved fruitless. His thoughts constantly returning to his friend's rash abandonment of reality hadn't helped matters either. He needed to concentrate—had to impress the Intelibotics guy—his career depended on it. It was already Friday morning, and only a few hours left until the demonstration.

Jake sighed and returned to the lighted magnifier, resuming his search, determined to find the problem. Concentrate! It had to be in this board—nothing else made sense. The view through the lens reminded Jake of a miniature cityscape. Electronic chips resembled buildings strewn across a circuit-board landscape, connected by copper-trace streets. Finally! A shiny, round ball of solder glittered in the fluorescent light, caught between two of the tiny copper traces. There it was—the short circuit that was plaguing the control board for "Arvie," his Autonomous Robotic Vehicle.

As he reached for a pair of tweezers, Jake felt a vibration from his pocket and heard the swelling sound of the Aggie Fight Song. He pulled out the cell phone and looked at the screen. *Mom.* Should he answer it? Yeah, he needed a break anyway.

"Hi Mom. Listen, I'm kinda tied up right now. Call you back?"

"Jake, you have to do something about Ruben. Talk some sense into him! His mother just called. Crying. Won't even call her back now … his phone just goes directly to voice mail."

Jake tried to reassure her. "Listen Mom, I know Mrs. Avila is upset, but Ruben has decided to stay. I've been texting him … tried to persuade him … told him he's making a mistake."

"Texting him? Why don't you actually call and talk to him? I don't understand all you kids, always texting!"

He wasn't a kid, and the texting conversation had been an ongoing thing. Jake didn't want to rehash either of these old arguments—he could tell she was upset. Ruben's mom and dad were his parent's best friends, and Jake and Ruben had been friends since the third grade.

"Mom, you know Ruben. Determined to do what he thinks is right … he won't change his mind. He's been going down there every summer since we went on the mission trip in 2009, so he knows his way around. Besides, he gets along with everybody and has good judgment. He'll be OK."

So why have I been so distracted about it? He had been reading Juanita's blog and knew things weren't going well in Honduras, that's why. But he didn't need to worry Mom with that.

"Look Mom, I have to go…"

He reached for the tweezers while he listened to his mother's response. Holding the phone to his ear, he again looked for the solder ball he had spotted. *What did she say?* It was no use—he just wasn't good at multitasking. Jake dropped the tweezers on the workbench.

"Yeah, I know 'that Juanita girl,' as Mrs. Avila calls her, is part of the problem. Ruben says he loves her, and he's staying in Honduras. But there's more to it than that … he thinks that he needs to stay and protect her."

Well, so much for not worrying her. He could hear the concern in her rising voice.

"No Mom, I don't think there's a serious problem. He just can't see leaving her alone. Maybe 'protect' is too strong a word. Just wants to be supportive. What kind of boyfriend would just up and leave if he really loves her?"

Jake finished reassuring his mother, hoping she could, in turn, reassure Mrs. Avila. He promised to actually call, not just text, Ruben, and disconnected. He had just picked up the tweezers again when the Aggie Fight Song sounded again. Jake slammed the tweezers down— annoyed that even if he didn't recognize the number on the screen, a compulsive urge always forced him to answer.

"What?"

There was a hesitation, and then a tentative female voice said, "Hello ... is this Jake Grayson?"

"Oh, sorry. Yeah ... who's this?"

"This is Leslie, from Dr. Borningfelter's office. He needs to see you right away."

Professor "Boring-fellow," what now? Dr. Phillip Borningfelter was Dean of the Electrical Engineering Department at Texas A&M University, and administered Jake's scholarship from Intelibotics Corporation, the premier electronics and robotics design firm in the United States.

"Uh, I'm kinda tied up right now," Jake said. "We're supposed to be meeting this afternoon with Dr. Strickland. Isn't that soon enough? ... Hello?"

Silence, then as Jake was about to speak again he heard, "Good morning Mister Grayson. Leslie said you were on the line."

"Uh, yes sir. She said something about you wanting to see me?"

"Indeed, there has been a change of plans. Dr. Strickland is already here. He needs to be back at company headquarters this afternoon for an emergency board meeting, so we need for you to come give your presentation. Then we will accompany you back to the laboratory for the demonstration."

"But ..."

"Afterwards, I hope you can join us in the Faculty Dining Room for lunch before he has to catch his flight to Atlanta."

"Uh, well I had planned on this afternoon for ..."

"Of course, of course," Dr. Borningfelter interrupted. "That is the way it always is, isn't it? Plans always have to be amended. Come on up now and we will get started."

"Uh, well sir, there's a problem ..." Jake said, "... Dr. Borningfelter? Sir?" Silence.

He hung up on me! Jake closed his eyes and shook his head. He had been so focused on the intermittent problem with "Arvie," and trying to reason with Ruben, that he had procrastinated on his Power Point presentation. Now nothing was ready! *Could this morning get any worse?*

■■■

Jake entered the reception area of Dr. Borningfelter's office. As he closed the door behind him, Leslie looked up from her laptop and said, "Go right in, they're waiting for you."

"OK," Jake said, running his fingers through his hair and trying to get the cowlick in back to lie down. He started for the closed office door.

"Wait!" Leslie said. "Give me the flash drive for your presentation and I'll queue it up on the computer in the conference room."

"Uh, well, that's the problem," Jake mumbled. "I'll have to explain to them …" He knocked on the office door and went in before Leslie could say anything more.

Dr. Borningfelter sat behind his expansive mahogany desk, his back to a large window which looked out over the live-oak trees on the campus of Texas A&M University. Jake wondered why the man would turn his back on such an expansive view, and then realized that the professor was more concerned about presenting an impressive image to anyone entering his office. Dr. Strickland, Vice-president of Advanced Development for Intelibotics Corporation, sat on a small couch on the right side of the room.

"Come in Mister Grayson," Borningfelter said, waving a manicured hand toward a chair situated partly between the desk and couch. "Have a seat for a moment before we go into the conference room for your presentation."

My presentation. Yeah, maybe I should have just brought whatever I had anyway. Jake took a seat, smiled and glanced nervously from one man to the other. "Uh, I guess I'm a little surprised that the meeting got changed."

Dr. Strickland smiled and said, "My fault, Jake. There is a problem back at the plant and I have to fly back to Atlanta this afternoon. I called Phillip last night from L.A. and he suggested we could meet this morning rather than cancel."

Last night! Thanks for the warning Doctor B!

Jake explained about the technical problems the vehicle had, and eventually admitted that neither the presentation nor the demonstration was ready. Red faced, he insisted that with just a few hours more time he could have put on an impressive demonstration. More difficult to explain was the fact that the Power Point presentation was incomplete. He emphasized that it wasn't worth showing without performance data from the ARV—it all needed to be shown together to get the whole picture.

As he finished his hurried explanations, Jake could detect traces of skepticism on the face of both men. Well, had he been in their place, he wasn't sure he would have bought the story either. Thank goodness they weren't aware of his preoccupation over Ruben. He still couldn't believe Ruben would choose to miss the start of his senior year at the University of Texas, Pan American. How could he be so foolish?

At the end of the meeting Dr. Strickland seemed to try putting Jake at ease, but also warned, "Jake, I understand how these things happen. It is entirely my fault that the meeting got moved up—it couldn't be helped. This was just a progress assessment, so it's not the end of the world."

"Thank you, sir. I'll be ready next time."

"The next steps are critical, however. There is extreme competition for the graduate school scholarships and the co-op placements we offer. Because of the economic climate, there is only one co-op position at our Advanced Development Laboratory next semester. Personally, I'd like to see you get it, but you are in a head-to-head competition with Jason Lee at the University of Texas."

Head-to-head competition! He was in a two man race. This was much better than he thought. Earlier phases of the ongoing competition had been with other strong competitors.

"I appreciate your support, Dr. Strickland. I'm very interested in a position with Intellibotics, and will do my best not to disappoint you."

"You have to have an impressive demonstration of your ARV and a complete analysis of the design. You have only one month until the formal judging."

One month, he could do that—he hoped. There was still so much to be done and Arvie wasn't even working yet, then there would be testing, analysis of performance and comparison to theoretical models. And what if it didn't work right?

He had to call Barbara and cancel their date for Friday night. He really wanted to see her, but it was eighty miles to Waco—a date would take up all afternoon and evening—no time for that. His career depended on acing the competition. *She was not going to be happy!*

Chapter 2

The Friday night crowd filled *Carnitas,* a popular grill restaurant in Tegucigalpa, Honduras. The sizzle and smells from the open wood-fired grill near the entrance wafted through the open air seating area, carried by a gentle evening breeze. Juanita Perez stared at her plate, ignoring the bustle around her, willing the queasy feeling in her stomach to subside. The festive atmosphere was wasted on her.

She ignored her boyfriend, Ruben, sitting across the table, her attention turned inward. Maybe she should not have been so outspoken in her Princess Maya internet blog, railing against violence and corruption that still plagued the Honduran government. Was she being watched? In the past few days she had seen two men who appeared to be observing her.

As if thoughts had made him materialize, she looked up and her attention was drawn to a tall man with long black hair. He was staring at her! Was he the one who had been with the muscular creepy guy? As her eyes locked onto his he looked quickly away. She struggled to take a breath and her hand shook. Her fork clattered onto her plate.

"Babe, what's wrong?" Ruben said.

"What?" She rubbed her eyes, trying to keep from crying, ashamed to let Ruben see her apprehension. "That guy was watching me ... I think he might be one of the men following me!"

"Where? What guy?" Ruben scanned the room.

"The tall guy ... long hair ... by the grill," she muttered, glancing quickly toward the grill. "There! He's staring again."

Ruben looked toward the man and rose from his chair.

"Wait! What are you doing?" she said as he left the table.

She gaped in horror as he stalked toward the grill and approached the long haired man. She held her breath. If something happened to Ruben, she could never forgive herself. These guys were dangerous. She didn't think Ruben really understood, having been brought up in the United States.

But wait, what was going on? The long haired man stood up, smiling and shaking Ruben's hand. They both looked over at her and the man said something. Ruben punched him lightly in the shoulder and they laughed again. Then Ruben was returning to the table.

"What was that?" she said when he got back and sat down.

"I thought he looked familiar. That's Fredrik, brother of the guy who cooks on the grill here. He was plenty embarrassed, for sure, that I had caught him checking you out."

"Checking me out?"

"Babe, what do you expect? You are one hot woman. I can't really blame the guy. Heck, it happens every time we go out that some guy is sure to take a look. I'm the envy of all the guys."

Her face flushed, and this time she couldn't hold back the tears. "I'm sorry. Those guys who followed me the past few days—they've got me scared." A shudder ran up her back at the memory.

Ruben reached across the table and took her hand. "I know you're worried, but you can't be sure they were really following you. And Fredrik doesn't fit your description."

"They were following me!" Why did Ruben always try to be so reasonable? "And one of them was tall. Why do you keep trying to tell me not to worry?" She sat back crossing her arms over her chest, glaring through teary eyes at the hurt expression on Ruben's face.

"Uh…" Ruben hesitated, evidently trying to find the right words. "Babe, I'm sorry! I do believe you. I just want to be … uh … reassuring. Trying to calm you down a little bit. You have been sort of rattled today, for sure. Come on, eat, your food's getting cold."

She uncrossed her arms. "OK … I'm probably just being paranoid, but Amélia scared me this afternoon with all that talk about disappearances, and criminals from the old regimes. 'Like roaches hiding in the cracks of the government,' is how she termed it."

Despite her worry, she smiled at Ruben. Somehow he could always make her smile. Ruben's tall good looks, dark wavy hair, and liquid brown eyes—what a contrast from the coarse appearance of the creepy, rheumy eyed man that had first spooked her. Juanita observed the concern in Ruben's eyes, and made an effort to eat a few bites.

"Amélia wants you to keep up your *'Princesa Maya'* blog," Ruben said. "That's what has you so upset, for sure."

"*Por supuesto* (of course.)" Ruben could always read her mood, and was always perceptive. "Someone doesn't like the things I am blogging. That piece about corruption in the government, maybe even drug smuggling, must have hit a nerve."

"Yeah, but following you? Seems a little extreme."

Juanita frowned, trying to think through the implications. "Maybe they think I know who is involved. But how could they even know about me?"

"Well, they can't know for sure. I think you should keep up the blog … just be careful. You're getting really popular now with the university students, and I've even heard that the *'Princesa'* is followed by some high school kids."

"Maybe something more is going on. There has been corruption and drugs for a long time … must be more than that."

Ruben pointed across the table with his loaded fork. "Well gee, babe … in a Central American country … somebody's probably trying to overthrow the country!"

"Be serious, Ruben. Maybe I should dig a little deeper … find out if there's more than meets the eye. Maybe publicize some of the disappearances and connections in the blog to see if anything pops up."

Should she keep up the blog? Amélia thought so, and she didn't want to let her down. "Even if someone suspects me … you're right … can't know for sure. I'll just keep going about my normal activities for a while. Won't use the bookstore computer, or the one at the office in the parsonage."

"Don't let Amélia push you into this if you don't want to do it," Ruben said.

"I'm not … I'm as determined as she is. I can use the university library or an internet café. The blog site should protect my real identity, so I should be OK." She wished she felt as confident as she sounded.

"I love dating a woman of mystery and beauty." Ruben smiled and reached across the table to squeeze her hand. "Now eat."

They finished their meal, left the restaurant, and walked hand-in-hand down the sidewalk, past the colorful murals across from the National Stadium. Juanita heard the roar of an engine behind her and caught her breath as a black van screeched to a halt beside them. Two armed men jumped out and were on them before she could react.

It's them! The startled thought came to Juanita as the tall creep who had been following her clubbed Ruben with the butt of a rifle. The other man grabbed her, her cry for help muffled by his hand covering her mouth. She tasted sweat and blood as she bit his hand, and felt a surge of hope at his startled curse. Then he punched her. Blinding pain shot through her head and her knees sagged. Suddenly everything was a dizzy whirl as she flew through the air, into the open door of the van. Her breath was knocked out when Ruben's limp body landed on top of her. Her vision dimmed as she heard the sounds of doors slamming, engine roaring, and tires screeching.

Chapter 3

Colonel Manuel Fuentes, dressed in civilian clothes, approached a Gulfstream G200 business jet idling on a taxi way at the south end of Toncontin airport in Tegucigalpa. Except for the required tail numbers, which he knew were registered to an obscure Venezuelan oil company, the plane was unmarked. He smiled in admiration of the beautiful aircraft as he boarded.

Inside the cabin he found Enrique Salas, already seated, and taking a cocktail from the attractive stewardess. Fuentes frowned at the sight of the older man, overweight, sweating, and fidgeting. He looked at the stewardess approaching him—a much better sight.

"May I take your coat sir?" she asked. "And maybe you would like something to drink."

"Yes, thank you," Fuentes said, removing his coat. "Jack Daniels, over ice, a double."

He sat across the aisle and appraised Salas. "Is something wrong Enrique?"

Salas hesitated, "I ... I just don't know what I'd say if President Lobo found out about this trip. How could I explain it?"

"Don't worry. He's not going to find out. I have everything accounted for," Fuentes said. *How did this pendejo (coward) get to be the Director of Intelligence for the President of Honduras?*

True, it would be disastrous if anyone discovered they were being whisked away for a secret meeting. But Salas had known the risks involved when they agreed to the meeting. Fuentes, as Director of S&I, the Ministry of Security and Intelligence for the government of Honduras, had to work closely with Salas. It galled him that he had to report to this man on intelligence matters. Fuentes had risen through the ranks due to his skill, whereas this man, a political appointee—well, who knew what he had really done to get the president's approval? Perhaps it was best that the man wasn't too competent, otherwise he would be more difficult to manipulate.

The Honduran Plot

"What we should be worried about is how General Velasquez will react to your failure to initiate a political crisis in Honduras," Fuentes said.

■■■

That evening they dined at the Miraflores Palace, the official workplace of the President of Venezuela. Fuentes admired President Chavez, and wished he were present, but he was still in Cuba undergoing cancer treatments. Instead, they were hosted by General Rafael Velasquez, the top political strategist of Venezuela, and military advisor to Hugo Chavez. As Velasquez pontificated on his vision of the future for Central America, Cuba and Venezuela, Fuentes noticed that Salas was listening with rapt attention.

"These are grand plans," Salas said when there was a pause in the monologue. "I am pleased that you have taken us into your confidence, and we will do all that is in our power to assist you."

Fuentes rolled his eyes, and sighed. He had helped Chavez and Velasquez cultivate a relationship with Salas over the previous four years, telling them that Salas could be a clandestine channel of information and influence in the Honduran government. Had he made the correct choice? Salas seemed so ineffective in promoting their goal, always choosing the path of safety rather than bold political action. His obvious pandering to Velasquez was embarrassing.

Finally the meal was over and they retired to the spacious central patio of the palace. General Velasquez lit a Cuban cigar and exhaled a fragrant cloud of smoke. As they savored the quality of cigars, the General broke the silence. "Do you remember the last time we met here? It was over three years ago and our plans have gone nowhere!"

Here it comes. Fuentes frowned at the reprimand, although it was not unexpected. He held his silence, waiting to see what happened.

"I remember it well," Salas said. "It was shortly before President Zelaya had scheduled his referendum. Since then we have had difficulties."

"That's right," Velasquez said. "Zelaya mishandled the whole thing and got himself expelled from the country. President Chavez had worked with other Latin American leaders to establish ALBA to counter United States trade and security policies. I initially thought President Zelaya could bring Honduras along, but he miscalculated. By the spring of 2009 I could see it coming. That is why I told you, at that last meeting, to distance yourselves from Zelaya."

The General ground out the stub of his cigar, jamming it repeatedly into the bottom of a nearby ashtray. "I expected both of you to work together to develop an alternative plan. What progress have you made? None! We need to bring Honduras into the grand alliance of socialist countries of Central and South America! Instead, things are drifting the other way and the United States is having more influence in Honduras."

Fuentes still kept silent, but Salas reacted to the reprimand. "Sir, we have managed to remain connected to the inner workings of the government. As Director of Intelligence, I have tried to exert influence in Congress and on President Lobo's staff members. It just takes time."

"We don't have time! Things need to be resolved quickly. The Hugo Chavez is failing due to cancer, and has lost much of his aggressive nature."

He paused for a moment, as if considering what he wanted to say. Then pointing at them he said, "We have to take aggressive action! I have made agreements with Cuba, with Raul Castro directly, for an alliance that will greatly expand our sphere of influence in the Western Hemisphere." Standing, he dismissed them by saying, "Make something happen!"

As they prepared to leave, Fuentes saw Velasquez motion with his head toward the fountain at the center of the patio. Salas was busy stuffing his useless papers, timid ineffective plans, into his briefcase.

Fuentes joined Velasquez at the fountain. "Yes sir?"

"Let me speak to you in private for a moment," Velasquez said. "I've been pleased with the way you have helped with our recent 'logistics problems.' Rodriguez is making another pickup in Columbia enroute to bring some oilfield equipment to Toncontin. He will have some packages for you on Monday."

"I appreciate your confidence in me sir."

"Good, make sure that you continue to earn it. Now, as for making something happen politically, I'm depending on you to push things with some sort of incident. We can't wait much longer for Salas to do something with political maneuvering. Understand?"

Fuentes smiled and assured him, "Perfectly sir; don't worry, I'm still working on the problem without Director Salas' knowledge. As my clandestine troops crack down on protests, the government gets blamed and things become less stable. Salas and the others can't understand why people don't believe their denials. Things should break soon. I won't let you down—on either thing."

Chapter 4

The Texas Aggie Fight Song issuing from Jake Grayson's cell phone woke him from a deep sleep. His hand groped the bedside table top until it located the offending instrument, and answered it with a mumbled, "H'lo."

"Jake, I'm glad you answered," his mother said. "I was afraid you would have your phone off because you were in church. I was going to leave a message."

Jake closed his eyes and struggled to find an acceptable response. Except during summers, when he went with his parents, he hadn't gone to church in three years. Maybe he should tell her about the disaster of Friday's meeting with the Intelibotics guy, or his argument with Barbara James when he broke their date last night. Well, those weren't really good excuses were they, and besides, it would just worry her.

"Uh ... didn't go this morning. What's up?"

"Ruben is missing! His mother just called me as we were leaving for church. She's beside herself with worry."

As Jake's head cleared, his mother filled him in on what little she knew. After promising to do something—he really didn't know what—Jake sat on the edge of his bed, thinking.

Why hadn't he seen something like this coming? He should have been more forceful in his efforts to convince Ruben to come back. No, that would have never worked, Ruben probably was more aware of the dangers than anyone.

Could it be that Ruben and Juanita had just run off? Maybe they eloped without telling anyone. He dismissed that thought almost as soon as it had popped into his mind. Ruben had always been the responsible one, and seemed mature beyond his years. *And he was always getting me into something that I wasn't sure how to handle.* Well, he sure didn't know how to handle this.

Jake paced the floor and stared out the window of his dorm room. What should he do, if anything? There didn't seem to be much he could do. The Honduran National Police and the U.S. Embassy had both been notified. So far, little was known about what might have happened. There wasn't anything he could do.

No, you're Ruben's best friend—you have to do something!

Jake stopped in mid-stride. The thought had been almost like an audible voice speaking to him. *Weird.*

But what could he do? He could at least make some calls—that's what he could do! Of all the Hondurans he had met on that mission trip three years before, Raul Salas was the one who had really befriended him—and he also might be his best bet for getting good information.

Raul's father was Enrique Salas, the Director of Intelligence on the staff of the President of Honduras. Maybe Raul could use his father's influence to help find Ruben and Juanita. Jake dug through his desk drawer and found Raul's number. He punched it into his cell phone, he wondered if he had international free calling. Probably not—might be an expensive call.

"*Hola. ¿quien habla?*" Raul answered.

Jake mentally translated, "Hello. Who's speaking?"

"Raul, it's me, Jake Grayson—Ruben's friend."

"*Jake! ¿Que Tal?* (What's up?) Been a long time."

"Ruben and Juanita ... do you know what happened?"

"No ... what do you mean?" Raul said.

Jake told him everything he knew, which wasn't much. Raul agreed to find out what he could. He would get his father's help to find out the latest information.

A couple of hours later, Raul called back and told Jake that Ruben and Juanita had last been seen Thursday night at *Carnitas*, across from the National Stadium. Some people there had reported a commotion outside right after the two left, but nobody had actually seen anything. Since then, there had been no word from them, and the old parsonage where Ruben had been staying was empty.

The only reason anyone knew they were missing was because of Mrs. Avila. When she couldn't get in touch with Ruben on Friday, she called Juan Zamora, the pastor of the church, and Luis Estrada, a friend of Juanita's.

"Lots of strange and terrible things going on down here," Raul said to Jake, "rumors of beatings, kidnappings, and death squads. It worries me."

"I know," Jake said, "I've been reading the Princess Maya blog—or at least trying to. My Spanish still isn't good enough to understand everything she says."

"You know about that?" Raul asked. "You know Juanita is *la princesa*?"

"Yeah, Ruben clued me in and got me to reading it. But I still don't understand what's really happening down there."

"I don't know if anyone does," Raul said. "Weird thing is both people who had supported Zelaya's return, and those who protested against it, have been targeted by these thugs."

"Zelaya?" Jake said. "He was thrown out back in 2009. What does that have to do with anything now?"

"Well, a lot of people called it a coup and wanted him to return. I know … I was one of them. Found myself on the opposite side of the protests from Juanita and Luis. Anyway, even though things calmed down after Pepe Lobo was formally elected there has been a lot of political strife and mudslinging between the left wing and right wing parties. Now it's gotten worse again, but the situation is confused."

"I don't think I ever understand all the emotional, crazy Central American politics," Jake said. "And why anyone would go after Ruben and Juanita?"

"Maybe the blog."

"I can't see that. Isn't it sort of a student protest thing at the university? Most people don't consider that something that would get someone kidnapped."

"Maybe not there, but this is Honduras. You said it yourself, 'crazy Central American politics.' No, not just politics, she has been talking about drug smuggling too."

"You think drug dealers got them?" Jake felt a shiver run down his back. That would mean they were probably dead! He didn't want to think about that.

Raul's answer surprised him. "I'm beginning to think someone in the government might be behind a lot of the violence—and maybe drug smuggling too." He hesitated, and then added, "But my father denies that the government is doing any of those things."

"Do you believe him?" Jake asked.

"I guess," Raul said, "but I don't know. Maybe something else is going on. My dad seems stressed out. Like there's some sort of problem, and he's not telling me everything …"

"Even if somebody in the government was involved in drugs, what about all that other stuff?" Jake said. "You talked about beatings and kidnappings—stuff like that. It doesn't make a lot of sense that the government would do those things."

"Yeah, I know. That's why I said it was strange. But the rumors are that a lot of this stuff is being done by government soldiers."

"So where does that leave us?" Jake asked.

"I don't know, but I've got an idea."

"What?"

"Well … you could look at a website my dad uses … maybe get access to the government files. You know a lot about that stuff don't you?"

"Some," Jake said. Where was this going? *Holy cow—he was talking about hacking!*

"I've been trying to find out what's going on down here, so last week I found a list of passwords Dad uses to get into the S&I computer …"

"S&I?" Jake interrupted.

"Oh," Raul said, "it's the Ministry of Security and Intelligence. Sort of like your FBI or CIA, but run by the military. Anyway, I got in using his passwords, but I can't make much sense of the website."

This was nuts. "Wait Raul, 'sort of like the CIA,' and you want me to hack into their website?"

"Hack? Oh, no Jake, it's not like that. I told you, I've got my dad's passwords. It wouldn't be like you were breaking in or anything."

"They might not think so."

"They wouldn't even know, man. You would have the passwords. Besides, what are they going to do if they did find out? They're not going to come up there and get you."

Jake thought about what Raul was telling him. Maybe it was a way he could help, if there were any clues there.

"I could try," Jake said. "Should be able to access it through the internet from here. E-mail the information you have and details about what things you have tried. I've got some tools on the computer at the Electrical Engineering Lab that might help me."

The conversation with Raul hadn't shed much light on things. He hadn't seriously considered that the violence down there might be directed at Ruben and Juanita. The idea that he could find something in the government file seemed like a long shot. But, at least he would be taking some action.

Jake had also forgotten about Luis Estrada—maybe he might have some ideas, but he didn't have any contact information. Well, he could try that later. Jake's thoughts returned to Ruben and Juanita. *Were they even still alive?*

Chapter 5

Jake looked around the electronics lab, deserted on late Sunday night, with its disarray of workbenches cluttered with circuit boards, test equipment, parts, and wires. Normally he felt calm and assured here, it was his element, but he couldn't capture that feeling tonight. Almost midnight, and he couldn't penetrate the Honduran Ministry of Security and Intelligence website beyond the publically accessible pages. *And I can't read half of that! My Spanish is so lousy!*

Jake puzzled over the list of passwords Raul had e-mailed to him, looking for something he had missed. He re-read Raul's description of secure pages of the site he had managed to find. Why couldn't he do the same thing? The passwords on his Android phone blurred as Jake lost focus—he didn't even notice.

His mind wandered off to scenarios of Ruben lying bloody along the side of a road, or maybe in a prison cell, or … and what about Barbara? He could understand that she got a little upset when he cancelled their date Saturday. But she should have been glad he came to Baylor this afternoon to see her. Instead, she blew a gasket because he had to leave early to get back to the lab! She doesn't understand how important this …

He snapped out of it. He must really be exhausted for his mind to wander like that. Better get back to the dorm to get some sleep.

■■■

Monday morning Jake skipped classes, and went back to the lab so he could probe the site using the lab's software tools, powerful computer and high speed internet connection. After a good night's sleep, he hoped to attack the problem with a clear head. Maybe he could find something he had missed the night before. Still, after an hour of poking around, none of the passwords would work. He had been tired last night, but apparently that wasn't the only problem.

Mapping and profiling the site hadn't done much good either. This was a bigger challenge than he had anticipated, but he wasn't going to let this defeat him so easily. Time to go back to the books—he needed to find another way in.

"OK, here's the thing," Jake explained that afternoon when he called Raul, "from my computer the only pages accessible were the public pages. I couldn't even log in."

"But you had the password. I told you which one got me in."

"Nothing would work for me. Not with any of your father's passwords. But you used them to log in to the S&I website from your dad's home computer … right?"

"Yeah," Raul said. "Oh, wait a minute! I forgot to tell you. I tried to use my laptop, and it wouldn't work either. I had to use my dad's computer in his study."

Jake grimaced. "Now you tell me!"

"I'm sorry Jake," Raul said. "After my laptop couldn't log in, I thought there might be some problem with it … a software incompatibility or something. So, I tried my dad's computer and it worked fine, but I found part of the site that was secure and inaccessible, and none of Dad's passwords work. When we talked, I thought maybe you could do better than me. I guess I forgot about my laptop not working."

"That's OK, it wasn't a bad idea," Jake said. He wished he hadn't been so abrupt with his response to this new twist.

"So what now?"

"When the easy way … with passwords … doesn't work, we have to consider it like any other clandestine penetration."

"You mean real hacking? You know how to do that?"

"Well, I've studied a lot of the methods. You need to know how it's done to protect your own systems these days."

Raul answered softly, "But … what you said before … it's the government … that could be dangerous."

Jake had revised his opinion on that after being foiled in his attempts. He had spent the rest of the morning and early afternoon reviewing the software tools and methods. Stubborn when faced with a technical challenge, Jake hated to admit defeat.

"It's like you said yesterday … what are they going to do? I'm thousands of miles away in another country. And I can try to make sure it's untraceable."

"If you're willing to try," Raul said, "sure, go for it."

Jake terminated the call and smiled to himself. OK, time to do it the hard way. He was ready for the challenge!

The Honduran Plot

But first he needed to make sure no one could trace his probing back to him. He clicked on the "Torbutton" in the bottom right corner of his Firefox browser, and then connected to Tor's check website. Back came the message, "Congratulations. You are using Tor." Now he could surf the internet anonymously, using a series of "onion routers" that masked his identity. Jake began his probing of the Honduran Ministry of Intelligence website. Making sure to run his scans through the Tor network, he used Nmap to scan for the most common ports that might be open to exploitation on their host computer.

Two hours and four cups of coffee later, Jake had had enough. He had probed for all specific vulnerabilities he could think of. Even with help from a graduate student he knew who was in the lab that afternoon, he couldn't break the safeguards. This thing was locked up tight.

He called Raul back. "It's no-go on the hacking thing. I tried everything I knew to do, but couldn't get in."

"Can you get some help? Maybe someone who's a real expert?" Raul asked.

"I had help from a guy who knows a lot more than me. I don't think anything else will work here."

"So there isn't anything we can do?"

Jake thought for a moment. "There's something about your dad's home computer ... if I used your dad's computer to get past the firewall ... but, no ... that won't work, I'd have to be down there ..."

"That is a great idea!" Raul said.

"What?"

"For you to come down here," Raul said.

"No! I was just mumbling ... thinking to myself," Jake said, sitting up straight and suddenly breathing hard. "Can't do that. Too much going on ... just started the semester ... big project too ..." He ran out of words.

"Jake, you should really come anyway. We need to find them, and it's the only way I can think of to start. I don't know what to do on my own."

"We don't even know there's anything on the website," Jake said, "or even if the government is involved." He knew that he was struggling to talk himself out of the idea. "Look, we don't have to get into it right now. It's just a hunch I had ... might not even be right. Let me think about it, OK?"

"OK, you know best," Raul said. "But even if the computer thing didn't work out, I think it would be great if you came down. Maybe we can still make some progress on finding them."

That idea really didn't make a lot of sense to Jake. Missing person reports had been filed, the police had been alerted, even the American Embassy had made inquiries, but there were no clues as to Ruben's whereabouts. Why should Jake think he and Raul could accomplish something more than all the other efforts?

Then the realization came to him. Computers or no computers, he would have to go back to Honduras to get the answers, or have any hope of finding out what happened to Ruben. A shiver ran down his back. Something was nudging him to find his friend. The thought kept running through his mind, *Ruben needs me ... I need to go.* Was this a sign?

Chapter 6

The unmarked Gulfstream G200 touched down at Toncontin International Airport and taxied to a metal roofed concrete pad south of the main terminal. Manuel Fuentes, in civilian clothes, watched through the smeared glass window of the customs office as the plane's engines wound down and silence returned. His tension grew as the aircraft's door opened, lowering stairs to the tarmac. He had met this plane many times before, but this time more was at stake.

Fuentes recognized Rodriguez as soon as his shadowed form darkened the doorway. Dressed in jeans and a sports jacket over a black T-shirt, the man descended the stairs, as graceful as a large panther. Fuentes only knew the man's last name, and he wasn't even sure if that was real. Rodriguez must hold some sort of influential position but he had no identifiable title or military rank. Fuentes had been introduced to him personally by General Velasquez, on one of the clandestine visits that he and Salas had made to Venezuela.

Fuentes left the dingy office and strode quickly to the plane. He wiped his sweaty hands on his slacks, and then held out his right hand. *"Bienvenido, Señor Rodriguez"*

"Hola, Coronel Fuentes," Rodriguez said, with a knowing glance at his outstretched hand, before shaking it. "Isn't it unusual for the head of Security and Intelligence to personally be on hand to inspect a shipment of oilfield equipment?"

Fuentes wanted to knock the smirk from the man's face. But instead, he forced a smile. "A good Director sometimes makes surprise inspections of his men in the field. But I imagine you are aware of that."

"My men always do exactly as I instruct them, whether or not I am there." Rodriguez raised his hand, and immediately two men descended the stairs, wrestling with a large sized crate which prominently displayed an oil-rig logo and manufacturer's name. They set it on the ground and returned to the plane to repeat the process. Fuentes silently watched as they unloaded three more of the large boxes. The two men unloading these things looked strong and hard. They were almost interchangeable, with their close cropped hair and muscular builds, identically dressed in camouflage pants and tight black tee shirts.

Fuentes signaled his man, who was waiting with the customs inspector and a truck driver near the office door. While they began opening the crates for inspection he turned back to Rodriguez.

"Where do you want the other crate?" Rodriguez asked. By this time the two men were bringing another smaller crate out of the airplane.

Fuentes nodded his head toward a grassy area just south of the tarmac, which contained several faded green cargo containers. "No different than before. Have your men put it in the open container over there."

The two men delivered the crate and then went over to assist the truck driver in loading the four large crates onto a flatbed truck. The S&I agent and the customs inspectors were returning to the office.

When they were alone Fuentes said, "Let's see what you have brought me."

They entered the faded green container and Rodriguez pried the top off the crate, revealing packages of cocaine wrapped in plastic. Rodriguez spoke as Fuentes examined the packages, "This new arrangement is probably four times what you have been handling. I have personally checked the quality when I picked up the shipment in Colombia."

"Excellent," Fuentes replied. "I have the money right here in this briefcase." He handed over the briefcase, trusting Rodriguez. Their future was linked, too much at stake for either to jeopardize it. Besides, hadn't Velasquez vouched for him? Fuentes knew that Rodriguez carried out operations for Velasquez in Colombia, where he dealt with the FARC rebels, trading weapons for drugs.

"Listen Fuentes," Rodriguez said, "we vouched for you with the Mexicans and have made you a key link in the new supply chain. Don't let us down."

Fuentes stared at him. Despite his nervousness, he resolved not to show any weakness or deference to this man. "I am a key link in the supply chain because it was me who could solve your problems. Don't forget that."

"I know. I'm not trying to disrespect you," Rodriguez replied. "I agreed with Velasquez when he said you were ambitious and could be a good partner. We both need to make this work out. My *grupo* has lost two aircraft in *La Mosquitia* just this past month."

Fuentes swallowed. *Agreed with Velasquez—were they on a more equal basis than he had thought?* He was determined to make this expanded arrangement work. The Venezuelan's problems were the perfect opportunity for him.

Honduras was a key stop in the drug route from Colombia and Venezuela to Mexico and the United States. The vast undeveloped territory of the *La Mosquitia* district in the northeast tip of Honduras was used to hide planes, and confuse efforts by the government to track drug flights. The drug smugglers could make a clearing and fly in a plane. Once it was camouflaged it was difficult to find in the uncharted territory. The plane could be refueled and repainted, given new registration numbers, or just delayed to an unknown flight date and time to confuse efforts by the authorities to interdict them. Lately though, with help from U.S. Air Force and DEA resources stationed at Palmerola Air Base near Comayagua, the authorities were having more success in tracking these flights and locating their hiding places. More and more they were succeeding in putting a crimp in the drug traffic.

"I know my friend," Fuentes replied. "That is why I mentioned the possibility of this alternate trade route to General Velasquez. I thought he might be able to pass the word to the appropriate people. Now we will help each other."

"I agree … if we can assure the security and secrecy we need."

"*No te preocupes* (don't worry)" Fuentes assured him. "I control a cadre of key government officials who can create and authorize all kinds of documents to make our flights to Mexico appear to be legitimate commercial or government flights. We have been doing this for a while now. Our Mexican contacts can't be involved in this though; yours will have to be able to handle the customs officials in Mexico."

Rodriguez laughed, "That shouldn't be a problem. They have been doing that for years. The real risk will be rivalry between the cartels we have been using and your people there in Mexico and the U.S."

"Well, we just have to have enough supply to keep them both happy. I wouldn't want to have to choose between them," Fuentes said.

Fuentes was excited to be cut in on this expanded drug trade; it would make him fantastically rich and assure control of his secret power base in Honduras. He already had developed a distribution network to smuggle the drugs into the U.S. through street gangs that operated in both countries.

Los Angeles was a refuge for many Hondurans who fled from the violence and conflict that raged in Central America during the 1980s. Conditions there spawned many street gangs. The violence and drug culture of these gangs led to many arrests and deportation of gang members back to their home countries. They brought the gang culture back with them; rap music, tattoos, baggy clothing, hand signs, and crime. Joining with criminal networks, drug lords and corrupt police, they became even more dangerous. As a result of the Honduran government's efforts to control the gangs, many found their way back to the U.S.

For Fuentes, this linkage between gang members in Honduras and the U.S. created the perfect distribution network. From his position in the Honduran Ministry of Defense, he was able to use police contacts to have certain gang members released from jail, or protected from arrest; then he recruited them. With the more violent police and gang members as his enforcement crew he kept the organization in line. When the drugs began to flow—from Columbia to Fuentes, then smuggled into the U.S., either through Mexico or directly, and then distributed by the gangs— there was a generous profit at each step along the way. Now it would just get better.

There was another benefit for Fuentes. The vast amounts of money, violent gang members at his command, and corrupt police under his influence all combined to give him a power base, a secret army that he could use against his enemies. All of this would be made stronger by this expanded arrangement with Velasquez and Rodriguez. Even Enrique Salas, though he was taking advice from Velasquez, had no idea of the secret manipulations that were going on right under his nose.

Chapter 7

Jake gazed out of the airplane window at the puffy clouds hovering over the blue expanse of the Gulf of Mexico, listening to the muted roar of the jet engines. He swirled the ice in his glass of Coke. His stomach was queasy, but the Coke hadn't helped. What impulse had spurred him into frantic action? It was all the fault of that small voice in his head that had said, *"You can't just abandon Ruben down there—he needs you. Go do something!"*

Had he made a catastrophic mistake? It seemed like it now, as he had time to sit and reflect. He stared at the water, remembering the frenetic activities of the past week

■■■

By Monday afternoon he had finally made the decision; he would definitely go. At the lab he loaded copies of every hacking tool he could think of onto the hard drive of his laptop, transferring almost all of the other files into "cloud" storage to make room. Then he had almost given old Borningfelter a stroke—the professor couldn't believe he would ruin his chances with Intelibotics to go on a "fool's errand." But, in the end, he had approved Jake's withdrawal from classes with an "incomplete" instead of a failing grade.

Barbara was another matter—when he called her to explain his decision she had exploded. "You are throwing away your future—our future!" she screamed into the phone, just before the line went dead. Since then, all Jake got was voice-mail when he called her. Would she ever talk to him again?

Tuesday morning he packed a few things and drove to his home in McAllen, Texas. His stomach churned and he felt nauseous. Maybe I'm coming down with a virus, the flu, or something he thought, until he realized it was the loathing of having to go back to Honduras.

That afternoon he got home and told his mother about his plans.

"Jake, this is crazy!" his mother said.

"I know," Jake admitted. "But I have to do something. No one else seems to be finding them."

"Your dad won't stand for it."

"Well, he might—if you help me convince him," Jake said.

"Me? How can you ask that? I can't believe you would even think such a thing," she said. "You'll fail all your classes … besides … who knows how long you'd have to be there? And where would you stay?"

"Listen Mom, the semester just started. I dropped the classes without failing … just got an incomplete …"

"If you do that …"

"Mom, it's done!" Jake said. "I already withdrew."

"Oh," his mother sighed, looking crestfallen.

"Remember Pastor Juan Zamora?" Jake said. "He was our host on the mission trip three years ago. Well, he said I could stay in the old church parsonage. They don't use it anymore and that's where Ruben has been staying. His stuff is still there."

They talked for the rest of the afternoon and she had finally agreed to help convince Jake's father that the trip was necessary.

Jake waited for his father to come home from the hardware store, thinking that would be the best time to broach the idea of the trip. His father seemed surprised to find Jake at home.

"Jake! What's wrong? Why are you here?" His father looked quizzically at Jake, and then to his wife who stood silently, looking downward. "What's going on?"

Jake spent a few moments explaining the situation to his father, and then received the surprise of his life.

"You boys were always so close, growing up," Jake's father said, "that I think of Ruben as part of the family. You go down there and do what you can to find him."

His mother cried then, but his father comforted her.

"Shhh … it will be alright. Jake will be careful. He is a man now and has to do what he thinks is right. Let's stop right now and say a prayer for God to bless this trip, and to protect both Ruben and Jake."

As his father prayed, Jake wondered how much difference it would make. God didn't always answer prayers—Jake had seen that. But the prayer seemed to have an effect on his mom. She calmed down and even smiled when she hugged Jake with a strong embrace.

"You go find Ruben," she whispered in his ear. "I'll go call Mrs. Avila and tell her you are going."

They agreed that Jake would go to Honduras for two weeks. He would use his contacts there, particularly Raul Salas and his father, to find any information he could about Ruben and Juanita. Jake made no mention of the idea of hacking computers—he knew that they would never go for that. The next two days were spent in a rush of phone calls, bank transactions, ticket purchases, vaccinations, and packing. By Friday morning Jake was on his way.

■■■

Staring at the water below the airplane, Jake noticed they were passing some islands. They must be getting near the coast. Sure enough, the plane soon passed from ocean to land. *Feet dry!* Jake smiled, recalling his favorite video game—when he used to imagine he was a fighter pilot running bombing runs over North Vietnam. He loved those older war games, and remembered his grandfather regaling him with stories from the days when he flew the A-6 "Intruder" from a carrier in the Gulf of Tonkin.

As the aircraft descended through a layer of clouds it encountered turbulence. A sharp jolt startled Jake and he looked out his window again. He could see hills dotted with trees passing below him, and then the landscape filled with roads and houses as the plane approached the city. A thin layer of haze cast a brownish filter over the view of green hills and jumbled buildings passing below.

As it descended, the plane sank below the level of the mountain tops, banked sharply to the left and almost immediately dropped into the runway approach. Just before touchdown Jake was startled to see trees and houses on the hillside rushing past the tip of the wing. Interesting landing!

He deplaned, remembering his surprise at the modern and clean airport on his first trip. After hearing about the poverty of the country, Jake had been expecting something old and outdated. He passed through passport control and waited in baggage claim for his suitcase. Jake noted two men wearing dark blue uniforms, ball caps with *"POLICIA NACIONAL"* embroidered in bold yellow, and large pistols holstered in web belts, scanning the new arrivals.

Upon exiting the international baggage claim area, Jake looked around the modern terminal building and spotted Raul Salas waiting near the escalator.

"Jake, it's good to see you again," Raul said as he approached. "You all set to go?"

"Hi Raul," Jake said, shaking his hand. "I need to find the men's room and then get some money changed."

"Just go under the escalator and the restrooms are past the entrance on the right. Leave your bag here, I'll watch it. When you get back we'll get someone to exchange your dollars for Lempira."

Jake returned and said, "There wasn't much to eat on the flight. Maybe we could get some food."

They sat at a small table in the Espresso Americano and renewed their acquaintance, bringing each other up to speed on what had happened during the previous years.

"Are you still at UNAH, studying architecture?" Jake asked.

"Yeah, I'm getting my Master's Degree this year. Time for some big decisions."

"Like what?"

Raul said, "Deciding whether to get some experience with a large firm, or just to start out on my own."

"That would be a big step," Jake said. "Why would you try that?"

Raul replied, "I want to develop a class of affordable housing that would be functional and well built, despite the low cost. Maybe that is a way I can be a help to the people of my country. But, I don't think I can do that at a big firm."

"Sounds like a good plan," Jake said, "if you can make a living at it."

"Well, my family's pretty well off, and could help me get started. I may not make too much, but it's better than building grand villas and trying to get richer."

Jake couldn't imagine himself doing something like that. He planned to avoid risk in his career. There were awesome opportunities at Intelibotics Corporation. The graduate co-op program was very exclusive—he had qualified by winning a contest with his Autonomous Robotic Vehicle after high school—and his GPA at A&M since then had kept him eligible.

"… at Texas A&M?" he heard Raul say.

"What?" Jake said, startled out of his reverie. "My bad … must have zoned out there for a minute."

"That's OK," Raul said smiling. "I was just asking if you were still taking electrical engineering at Texas A&M."

"Oh, yeah," Jake said. Then he suddenly realized he wasn't still taking anything.

Oh, and I blew any chance with Intelibotics!

"I ... uh ...well, I had to drop classes to come down here. But I'm going to catch up ..." Jake's face flushed and he sat speechless.

Chapter 8

They left the airport and drove to the neighborhood of *La Vega* in Raul's white Toyota Tacoma truck. Jake said, "After we talked, I reviewed the news articles on violence and human rights violations in Honduras. A lot of people don't believe the government's denials."

"I know," Raul said. "There has been such a terrible history of corrupt government here that most people are very suspicious of them. Like I told you, I'm not sure what to believe."

"But your dad works for the government."

"Yeah, I know. He worked for Zelaya too, before he was kicked out."

"Why did they let your dad stay?"

"Remember when Zelaya came back after being kicked out, and holed up in the Brazilian embassy?"

"Yeah, vaguely," Jake said.

"My dad was really disillusioned by Zelaya's behavior. He threw his support in with the new government. Lobo kept him on because he knew the job. Anyway, he swears this stuff about government death squads and kidnappings isn't true. And, since President Lobo's election, it did calm down for a while. Now it's worse than ever."

"Do you really think someone in the government might have kidnapped Ruben and Juanita?" Jake said.

"Maybe," Raul said. "I think there might still be some pretty rough characters that will resort to violence. Besides, who else beside the government could get into the internet servers to take down Juanita's 'Princess Maya' blog?"

"They took it down?" Jake said.

"The day everyone realized Juanita and Ruben were missing the 'Princess Maya' blog site just ceased to exist. It's like it never existed. My dad said the ISP doesn't know what happened. Somebody got into their servers and deleted the whole thing."

"How long have you known Juanita wrote the 'Princess Maya' blog?" Jake asked.

The Honduran Plot

Raul said, "Oh, since before Zelaya got kicked out. Back then I believed in Zelaya, but the blog and student protest newsletter was against him. Yeah, I followed the blog online. Juanita and Luis Estrada tried to keep me from knowing about it, but I figured out that Juanita was 'Princess Maya' after reading it for a while. I was pretty sure that Luis Estrada and Amélia Ramirez were the ones doing a newsletter covering similar things. They never wanted to discuss politics, at least not while I was around. I think the only reason they tolerated me is because of Ramona. They are both close friends with her."

They arrived at the deserted parsonage across from Pastor Zamora's church, *Iglesia de las Flores*, or Church of the Flowers. The faded blue wall and rusty gate shielding the building looked even more dilapidated than Jake had remembered it. Raul led Jake inside and showed him the bedroom where he would stay.

"Get settled in," Raul said, handing Jake a key. "I've got a few things to do, and then I'll come back and take you to get something to eat. How would you like to go to Ramona's?"

"That would be great," Jake said, remembering the place from his mission trip.

Jake and Ruben had become friends with Raul then, and twice he had taken them there for dinner. It was one of the few good memories Jake had from that trip. Ramona was Raul's girlfriend, and a teacher at the school near the dump where Jake's mission group had served. Her father, the restaurant's owner, had named the place for her. When Raul took them the first time, they had met Ramona and her friends, Juanita Perez and Luis Estrada. Ruben really clicked with Juanita, and soon they had sat closely and talked quietly in Spanish, leaving Jake out of the conversation. He spent most of the time talking with Luis, who had a quirky sense of humor and joked about the others.

After Raul left, Jake tried to call Barbara—voice mail again. He sent her a text telling her that he had arrived safely, and that he loved her. *Still mad ... will even read it?*

He unpacked, washed up, and decided to look through Ruben's things. Maybe something would provide a clue. Ruben's suitcase was still there, but it was empty. Looking through the top drawer of the dresser, he found folded jeans, shirts, underwear, and socks. Then he noticed the digital camera, partially hidden by the pile of folded shirts.

Jake turned it on to review the pictures it contained. There were several tourist shots of the area, most having Juanita somewhere in the scene.

One was a good shot someone had taken of Ruben and Juanita, standing arm-in-arm with an impressive panorama of Tegucigalpa spread out behind them. The city sat upon rolling hills and was surrounded by higher mountains. The air was a little hazy with smog, but Jake could still see the green oval of the national stadium and the runway of the airport in the distance beyond it. He immediately recognized that it had been taken from the city park at the peak of the small mountain called El Picacho, probably from the foot of the huge statue of Jesus Christ, called *'Christo del Picacho'*, which overlooked the city. Jake was struck by how happy they looked.

Chapter 9

Scrolling through the pictures on the camera, Jake found several scenes from the dump, a large landfill just northwest of the city. As he looked at Ruben's pictures Jake's thoughts and feelings were taken back to the day he first encountered the dump.

■■■

It had been the first day of the mission trip, and Jake stood by Pastor Juan's old white van. Unease worked its way into Jake's consciousness as he gazed in amazement at the huge expanse of garbage and trash that was piled in the hills above Tegucigalpa. There were hills of trash everywhere he looked; it seemed to just go on and on. The smell was a strange mixture of odors, none of them pleasant. A steady stream of trash trucks and other vehicles brought the city's refuse, adding noise and dust to the odors and smoke that pervaded the area.

Jake watched as dozens of large birds circled while others picked through the garbage. He supposed that they must be some kind of buzzard. A group of children dressed in ragged and dirty clothes wandered around and picked through the garbage. Some even chased off buzzards to get scraps of edible food. He didn't think they could have been more than six or eight years old. While he watched, one of the boys said something and ran as another chased after him, both of them laughing and yelling. It seemed surprising that they were so carefree.

The adults rummaging through the trash were more subdued, but still talked and even joked as they rooted through the pile of trash dumped by the latest garbage truck. Most of them wore dark colored clothes with long sleeves, old work boots or sneakers, hoodies or ball caps, and a few had their faces covered with bandanas or knitted balaclavas, like ski masks. They all looked pretty dirty to Jake, but he guessed that was understandable considering they probably spent a lot of time picking through the trash. *How can they live like that?* To Jake it looked like a scene from Hell.

■■■

Jake continued scrolling through Ruben's pictures, still saddened by his memories of the dump. He found pictures of protest marches and

Jake recognized the Congress Building in downtown Tegucigalpa, perched in the air on large columns. In the photos soldiers with rifles appeared to be keeping protestors from coming near the building. Then he found two strange photos, showing a man with a pockmarked face and dark complexion near a faded green cargo container in a grassy area. The pictures were poorly lit and blurred— Jake guessed it was probably taken with the lens on maximum zoom setting. *What is that all about?*

Jake was interrupted by the screeching sound of the front gate protesting, followed by knocking on the front door. He put the camera away and went to open the door. It was Raul.

"Ready to go?"

"Sounds good to me," Jake said.

As they drove across town Jake watched shades of color passing by, houses of earth tones and bright pastels engaged his senses, despite the fading light. The angular juxtaposition of walls and bars and gates appealed to his engineering mind, but was marred by unruly spikes or coils of barbed wire topping the structures. Street vendors walked between lanes of traffic to sell fruit, water, or other goods. To his surprise, and unlike his last trip, Jake enjoyed the foreignness of the country, and he noted many similarities to the Mexican border towns.

When they passed under a bright yellow pedestrian crossover spanning the divided road Jake realized they were on the *Anilló Periférico*, the ring road around Tegucigalpa. Soon he spotted the *Basílica de Suyapa*, an imposing cathedral dominating a hillside.

"I remember that from before," Jake said. "We're pretty near the university now—right?"

Raul took the exit and said, "We're coming to it now. I thought we would swing through the campus. Do you remember the UNAH campus?"

"Yeah, vaguely," Jake said as he looked out the window. "Just saw it that first night you took Ruben and me to Ramona's."

"This is the largest university in Honduras; actually it's one of the largest in Central America. That building you see over there with the designs on the side is the Architectural building where I take most of my classes," Raul said. "Thought you might like to see it."

Raul turned onto *Bulevar Suyapa*, made a U-turn and pulled into a small shopping center behind a Dunkin' Donuts and a Pizza Hut. The shops, set behind white columns supporting a bright blue and yellow roofline, appeared closed. At the end of the shopping strip Jake could see the green glow of neon script spelling "Ramona's" in a window.

"Is Ramona going to be here?" Jake asked as they entered the restaurant.

"Not right now," Raul said. "But she may come by later. I told her you were in town."

Raul approached a young woman acting as greeter and requested a seat in the outdoor section. She grabbed menus and led them to a wrought iron fenced area covered by a large striped awning.

"I thought we could sit here rather than inside. It's a little more private."

They made small talk until a waiter had taken their order and left them alone.

Jake broke the silence. "I guess the first thing to do is to go over to your house, so you can show me how to log into the website."

"That might be a problem," Raul said. "We will have to do it when both my parents are away. My dad doesn't like me using his computer and usually keeps his study locked. I can get in ... made a copy of his key, but it would be hard to explain who you are, and why you're visiting."

"That's going to seriously limit what we can accomplish. I'm pretty sure we have to use your dad's computer."

"Maybe you couldn't get in because you weren't in Honduras," Raul said. "The government might restrict secure access from outside the country."

"I could try using my laptop from the parsonage. Maybe I don't have to be at your house," Jake said. "But that wouldn't be much different than what you tried with your laptop."

"Check anyway. Might have been my laptop, or the fact that I really didn't know what I was doing. If it doesn't work at the parsonage, then I'll come get you tomorrow afternoon," Raul said. "I know my dad has some kind of big meeting tomorrow. He told my mom he wouldn't be home until sometime that night. And she has some social thing in the afternoon, so we can use our house then if you need to."

Chapter 10

Jake woke up thinking about his dinner with Raul the previous night. Ramona had joined them after dinner, proudly showing Jake an engagement ring. They reminisced about the mission trip three years ago and talked about Ruben's and Juanita's growing romance. Jake was intrigued to learn that Ruben had plans to enroll at UNAH and finish his education there. His buddy hadn't told him that. As the evening wore on Jake lost interest in the thread of conversation. It had been a long day. After he was dropped back at the parsonage he went right to bed and slept late.

Sunlight was streaming through the barred window when Jake finally woke up. He sat on the edge of the bed and tried to call Barbara again—still got voice mail. This time he didn't bother leaving a message or sending a text. She was really being petty about this!

He should get online with his laptop to see if he could make progress. If not, he would have to wait until afternoon when they went to Raul's house. Maybe while the computer was booting up he should freshen up and brew some coffee.

Leaving the bedroom, he walked to the office to connect his laptop to the DSL modem. Jake opened the door to see the backside of an attractive female figure in tight jeans bent over the lowest drawer of a file cabinet.

"Oh!" she started. She spun to face him, one hand protectively clutched against her chest. "How did you get in here? What do you want?"

Jake stammered, "Nothing … I mean, I'm staying here."

She grabbed a letter opener from the nearby desk.

This was getting out of hand. He had to calm her down.

"Wait, calm down …I won't hurt you!"

She pointed the letter opener at him, her other hand clenched into a fist. "Who are you? What do you want?"

By this time Jake realized he knew her. He had better defuse the situation quickly.

"You know me! I'm Jake Grayson. Remember? ...uh ...Amalia? Three years ago. The mission trip?"

"Jake Grayson?" She waved the letter opener in his direction, her brows furrowing. Then they raised in surprise. "Jake! ... What? ... You scared me!"

Jake opened his mouth to speak. "I ..."

"What are you doing here? ... I mean in Honduras." The letter opener lowered slightly.

"I'm staying here," Jake said. "Pastor Juan said I could stay here."

Why did he feel like he had to defend himself? He hadn't done anything wrong. What was she doing here anyway? Raul hadn't mentioned her, neither had Pastor Juan.

Jake continued, "I didn't know anyone else was here. Sorry I startled you."

"It's OK. *No te preocupes*," She lowered the letter opener and unclenched her left hand.

"What?"

"Oh ... don't worry. I said 'don't worry' in Spanish."

"Oh ... yeah, I should have known that," Jake said. "My Spanish is a little rusty. I guess I need to practice getting it back." He hesitated, looking at her. "But what are you doing here? You're the last one I would have expected to be here ... at the church parsonage ... this church ..." His face flushed as the words died out.

To his surprise, she laughed. "Yeah, for someone who isn't sure there is a God, I seem to spend a lot of time at churches. And, by the way, my name is Amélia, not Amalia."

Jake wasn't sure what to say. This was awkward. Of all the people Jake had considered contacting in this quest, he had never considered Amalia—whoops, had to remember, it's Amélia. "Sorry about the name. I thought Spanish names used Amalia."

She was still smiling. "It's alright, Jake ...common mistake. My grandfather was Brazilian, and I am named after Princess Maria Amélia of Brazil."

So she's named after a princess. Jake tried to think of some rejoinder, but couldn't. "Uh ... OK then."

She continued, "Pastor Zamora let Juanita Perez use the parsonage for the office of our student protest movement since the church didn't use it anymore. Luis Estrada and I are involved with it too. I'm making some flyers to post around the city, adding Juanita and Ruben to the list of the missing. The old flyers keep getting torn down anyway."

"There are others missing?"

"Yes, there are others. No one is sure how many, maybe six or eight. Mostly people who have been complaining about the way things are being run here."

"That's why I'm here," Jake said. "Uh … to find Ruben. Raul is helping me."

Amélia arched her eyebrows, "Raul Salas? How is he involved?"

Now he had done it. Why was he volunteering information to this woman? Deciding to keep his story simple, he said, "Well, I called him when I heard that Ruben and Juanita were missing. I figured he could get his dad to find out something."

"Yeah, I'll bet," Amélia said. "His father's probably the one who had them kidnapped!"

"He's trying to help …really."

"Well, he would say that wouldn't he?" Amélia said. "You don't know what kind of corruption there is in the government here. That's what Juanita, and our whole protest movement has been trying to expose. I think that's why Juanita and Ruben disappeared … the government didn't like what we were uncovering."

Jake felt his temper rising. Why did that always seem to happen when he was around Amélia? They had clashed from the first day he had met her. The mission group had helped repair a church in the village of Los Gatos. Amélia worked as secretary, or bookkeeper, or something like that, and thought she was in charge of everything—a real micromanager.

Jake said, "You may not believe it, but that is what Raul thinks too. But he doesn't think his father has anything to do with it."

"Well, even if he believed that his father was involved, he wouldn't tell you."

"No, that's not true, Jake said. "Raul wants to find out if the government is behind it, even if it showed that his dad was involved. That's what we are going to do."

"You are?" Amélia said. "How do you plan to do that?"

"Well … uh, I'm not sure I should say anymore," Jake said.

"Come on Jake! We're on the same side here. We both want to find Juanita and Ruben."

Amélia just stared at him for a few seconds. Then she asked, "Do you really think he'll be objective?"

"Why wouldn't he?"

"Think about it Jake," Amélia said. "He may say that he wants to know if his father is involved, but if he thinks you are on the track of something that implicates him, Raul may change his mind. He might try to keep you from finding out."

"I could tell you didn't trust Raul ... even when I was here three years ago," Jake shot back. "Remember that night at Ramona's? You were there with Juanita and Luis ... that was the second time Raul brought Ruben and me there."

She hesitated, as if trying to recall. "Yeah, I think so. What are you talking about?"

Jake said, "As soon as Raul left the table to go find Ramona, you all started talking about his politics. The others gave him the benefit of doubt since they were friends, but not you. You just said you weren't staying and flounced off before he came back."

As he spoke, the memory of her walking away from the table, and the sway of her hips under the bright green skirt, flashed in his mind. Where had that come from?

"You're right, things were pretty tense back then," she said. "I really thought he was spying on Juanita and me. We were protesting against President Zelaya's referendum, and Raul's dad worked for Zelaya! But maybe you're right ... he could be OK. Juanita and Luis always trusted him."

"I think he *is* OK," Jake said.

She crossed her arms. "Well, I'll get my things and go," she said.

Chapter 11

After Amélia left the parsonage, Jake set his laptop up on the office desk and plugged it into the DSL modem. While the laptop was booting up he went back to the kitchen, near the rear of the building. Good, there was a coffee maker and some coffee right there on the counter. He started to fill the carafe with water from the sink faucet, but hesitated and looked around the kitchen. Yes, there was a large plastic bottled water jug on the counter—a much better choice. Who knew what might be in the tap water?

As the coffee brewed, he sat at the small kitchen table and thought about Amélia. What a coincidence for her to come here today. He remembered the remark Luis had made three years ago, about Amélia's friends calling her *'El Comandante'* behind her back. Amélia definitely had a commanding personality. He didn't want her help, but she had convinced him to exchange cell phone numbers, saying they should stay in touch. Jake poured himself a cup of coffee. Had he told her too much? Raul might object to having Amélia privy to their efforts. He wouldn't tell Raul about the encounter right now.

Once he was connected to the internet, Jake anonymously navigated to the Honduran Ministry of Intelligence website. He easily moved through the publically available web pages. Then he tried to log into the restricted area, using the user name and passwords Raul had given him. Still no luck! He got the same error message he had obtained when he tried from the States, and got shut out after three incorrect responses. He would have to go to Raul's house and see how things worked using his dad's computer.

Raul picked up Jake a short time later, and they had lunch at "El Fogoncito" in the Cascadas Mall. By early afternoon they had let themselves into Enrique Salas' home office. Jake watched while Raul logged in using the same user name and password that Jake had tried unsuccessfully at the parsonage.

"See?" Raul said. "I can get into the site and find pages for a number of services and departments. The other passwords seem to work on specific pages that have more restricted access. This link is the National Police. Maybe you can help me find out if they have information on Ruben or Juanita."

Jake and Raul navigated through the site, examining logs of arrests, prisoner records, and pages of regulations and inventories. Jake thought it was like looking for the proverbial needle in a haystack.

An hour later Jake said, "This is a waste of time, there is nothing useful." Maybe this whole idea was crazy, to come down here thinking he could find Ruben

"Hey! I just found something," Raul said. "Here's a list with Juanita and Ruben with a bunch of other people …oh, it's from 2009."

"Where?"

"Look, see this page here?" Raul scrolled through the page. "It seems to be a listing of prisoners. Let's see, yeah, from a police substation downtown."

"Yeah?" Jake peered over his shoulder. "Oh wait, that makes sense. Remember the last week of our mission trip down here? The night Ruben snuck off to go with Juanita to some protest rally and they all got arrested."

"That's right!" Raul's shoulders slumped. "This doesn't really help does it?"

They spent another fifteen minutes searching through the police files, to no avail. This seemed to be a dead end. They had paged through every department they could find on the site, but there were hundreds of page links. They would take forever to randomly search them all.

"This is too inefficient," Jake said. "I could write a script to search through the whole site. To automate the whole thing I'd need to use my laptop."

"Great idea, Jake," Raul said. "Oh, before we quit, let me show you something else."

"What?" Jake said.

"See that little logo near the bottom … on the right side? Watch what happens when I click on it." Raul clicked on the logo and a small black window popped up, containing a white text bar with a blinking cursor. There were no instructions or text indicating what the window was for.

"Well that's weird," Jake said. "It doesn't say anything."

"Yeah," Raul said, "Maybe it's some secret sort of thing? Anyway, I tried all the passwords my dad had written down in his little address book, but nothing worked."

Jake had a thought. "It didn't lock you out after three tries?" he asked.

"No, I kept trying the passwords and when I pressed the 'enter' key they disappeared and the little white bar and blinking cursor were still there. Here, I'll show you."

After Raul had demonstrated, Jake said, "That gives me an idea. We may have found a security flaw. I got an error message when I tried to log on to the site, from the States or here in Honduras from the parsonage, and it would cut me off after three tries. I would have to leave the site and come back to even get the user name and password request again."

Raul said, "I'm not sure where you are going with this."

"Well, now that you have logged in securely, it is not restricting the number of tries on this restricted level. The logo and this little window may not be useful ... just some maintenance access ... or something. But it seems odd ... if it is some secret part of the site, something highly classified, and we might have a chance of hacking in. Since we're already logged in as a user on the main site it must not have a lockout feature. But I'll have to use my laptop with a special program to try to hack it. We can do the site searching program too."

It took Jake and Raul about fifteen minutes to find out that they couldn't log in to the site using Jake's laptop.

"It's something to do with your dad's computer," Jake said. "It sends some identifying code when he logs in ... like a security feature."

"What do we do now?"

Jake spent a few minutes examining the Salas computer file structure and settings.

"Well we can't load any of my programs onto your dad's computer. We have to have Administrator privileges, and none of the passwords do that. You don't know how to access that do you?"

"No clue. My dad has some guy named Mauricio that comes from work to do all the set-up on it."

"I thought something like this was a possibility," Jake said, "so I brought a little packet sniffer with me to analyze the code responses your dad's computer sends. It will monitor the incoming and outgoing data packets and send them to a data file using WiFi."

"But aren't they encrypted?" Raul asked.

"Not until your dad or you logs on," Jake said. "Anybody can access the public pages. When your dad's computer sends the user name and password I should be able to decipher the coding on the identifiers on the data packets. Then I should be able to find out what else is being sent to identify that particular computer. But the program will need a number of samples and that's where the WiFi skimmer comes in."

"But you'll have to be here?"

"No," Jake said. "Can we use your laptop? You would have to stay off of it while your dad is home."

"That wouldn't be a problem," Raul said.

"I'll just load the Skimmer program onto your laptop and show you how to start it. When your dad is home, you should start the program and leave it running. It will collect data packets and store them in data files on the hard drive."

"What happens then?" Raul asked.

"We will let it work until your dad uses his computer a few times from home," Jake said. "Maybe a few days. Then you can e-mail me the data files. In the meantime I'll go back to the parsonage and work up an analysis program. Then we can see how to make my laptop mimic your dad's home computer."

"Do you think it will work?" Raul asked.

Jake hesitated, wishing he had more confidence. "I'm not sure, Raul. But I don't know what else to do."

Chapter 12

Amélia listened to the grinding of her rusty 1998 Civic as it tried to start. One day soon it probably wouldn't. Finally it coughed to life, sending puffs of blue smoke floating across the bookstore parking lot. *It's not much, but at least Papá left us something when he died.*

She called Luis on her cellular.

"Are you on your way?" he answered.

"Yes, I'm coming now, Luis. Don't be so impatient. I had to use the computer at the bookstore to print the flyers. I got interrupted at the movement office and couldn't finish there."

"Interrupted? What happened?"

"No te preocupes," Amélia said. "Everything's alright, and I'm on my way. But you won't believe who was there." Amélia pulled out of the parking lot.

Beeep! A truck swerved around her to avoid rear ending the rusty blue vehicle. Amélia dropped the phone and swerved toward the curb in panic. Where did he come from? She felt in the floorboard for the phone, managing to keep the car on a wobbling path down the right hand lane. Two more vehicles went around her, laying on their horns.

She retrieved the phone. "Hello. Luis, still there?"

"What happened?"

"Oh, some stupid truck almost hit me," Amélia said. She pressed the accelerator to match the flow of traffic and got the car under control.

Luis said, "Amélia, someday your driving is going to get you killed. Who was at the office?"

"Jake Grayson. Remember him?"

"No ... oh wait, you mean the mission guy? Ruben's pal ... what was it ... maybe three years ago?"

Amélia said, "Yeah, he came down to help find out what's going on with Juanita and Ruben."

"Huh, good luck with that. He doesn't know his way around here. What can he do?"

"He has help. Raul Salas thinks he can use his father's influence to find things out."

The Honduran Plot

There was her exit. She jammed on the brakes, and shot onto the exit ramp to UNAH with tires squealing. "I'm almost there. I'll tell you about it then. Bye." She rolled through the 4-way stop entering the university campus.

■■■

Hector Arroyo swerved the old Chevy Malibu into the right lane of *Bulevar Suyapa* , trying to make the exit ramp. His rear bumper clipped the front fender of a car in his blind spot, jolting his car, which continued down the road, zigzagging precariously until Hector got it under control. This crazy woman was going to get him killed! Glancing in the rear-view mirror, Hector could see the offending car spinning behind him, other vehicles swerving wildly to avoid it. But he kept rolling, hearing a scraping and rattling sound from his rear bumper, before it tore loose and bounced off the road into the weeds. Well, the car was stolen anyway; what did he care?

He impatiently tapped on the steering wheel as he found an exit, reversed course and made his way back to his missed exit. The woman was unlikely to be going to the *Basilica*, so he would cruise the UNAH campus to locate her car. A moment later he spotted the rusty Civic. The vehicle was as bad as the piece of junk he was driving. Why couldn't he be like James Bond, driving an Aston-Martin, while tailing a beautiful woman driving a Mercedes convertible?

■■■

After delivering half of the flyers to Luis to post around the university, Amélia drove into Tegucigalpa. She punched a number on her cellular phone and listened, waiting for José to answer, as she saw the light at the intersection of *Bulevar Morazán* turn amber, then red. Amélia floored the car, passing the intersection before the side traffic could move.

"*Hola* Amélia, " José said.

"Where are you?"

"The Pizza Hut near the *Parque Central,* downstairs, in the back, behind the stairs."

"See you in a few minutes."

■■■

Hector slammed on the brakes. He thought she was oblivious to being tailed, but her driving made him wonder. He tapped the steering wheel, glancing right and left. At a break in traffic he charged forward running the red light. Where had she gone?

He spotted her turning into the parking lot across from the *Catedral de Tegucigalpa*. He watched as she crossed the street in front of his car, never giving him a glance. Hector parked his car in the parking lot and hurried to follow her. His surveillance of the bookstore had paid off—she was the one working with Juanita Perez. He was determined to follow her and identify the other members of the group. He hurried across the street, through the park in front of cathedral, and past a newsstand. Hector spotted her turning a corner ahead and almost caught up as she entered the Pizza Hut.

■■■

Amélia entered the brightly lit restaurant and spotted the stairs to the left of the receptionist's station. She ignored the receptionist and walked past the stairs, looking for José. There he was, at a table near the back of the room. She ran her hands down her silky black hair and straightened her shoulders. Why hadn't she stopped to put on some lipstick?

As Amélia approached the table, a large man in a dark brown suit rose from the adjacent table, staring her in the eyes and putting a hand inside his coat.

"That's alright, she's a friend," José said, waving the man down.

Amélia stopped, looking from the man to José. "You brought a bodyguard?" There goes a chance for a private moment with José. She sat across from him, a quizzical expression on her face. "What is this all about?"

"I'm sorry Amélia—it can't be helped, my father insists on it."

"Why this all of the sudden?"

He glanced over to the bodyguard and lowered his voice. "You know how it is. Things are getting worse ... Juanita ... rumors of intimidation. Everyone knows my father is trying to clean up things in the military, so they might try to stop him by threatening me."

She frowned. Looking around, she noticed that this corner of the place was sparsely occupied and no one seemed to be paying them any attention. Then a thought came to her—had José told his father what they were doing?

"Does he know about me?" she asked.

"José smiled. "He knows I've been meeting you. He probably thinks we are dating, and guesses that I like you."

She blushed. "You've never told me that before."

Could he really be serious? He had lots of girls he could choose from—rich girls from good families, who went to private schools. Maybe he was just playing with her. Why hadn't she taken time for some makeup?

He said, "I thought you could tell."

"You're not as easy to read as you may think." Amélia forced a smile. She wouldn't let him see her uncertainty. Then her face grew serious. "But … that's not really what I was talking about. I wondered if he knew about your involvement with our political activity group."

"Now I'm embarrassed," he said, blushing.

"Don't be. I'm glad that your first thought was of us,"

"Me too," he said. "Yeah, I leveled with him when Juanita and Ruben went missing. He's on the same side as us. He believes there is a group spanning the military, police, and maybe other government offices, behind most of the corruption and drug dealing."

"Can he help us?"

"Maybe. We should share what we know … all the stuff you and Juanita have found. He might be able to fill in some blanks for you."

"Or maybe our stuff can fill in some blanks for him." Amélia said. She was warming to the idea of having someone they could trust with authority to really investigate.

She looked into José's eyes, but then out of the corner of her eye she saw the bodyguard rise, drawing a pistol from his coat.

Boom! Boom! The deafening noise of gunshots startled her, freezing her, her ears ringing. She stared at a blot of red which appeared on the bodyguard's chest. He grimaced, and fire and smoke erupted from his pistol as he returned fire.

Amélia finally reacted and dropped to the floor, as the dizzying roar of gunshots filled her ears. She saw José duck to the floor behind the table. She reached for him.

"We have to run!" she yelled above the ringing in her ears. "José, come on!"

The banging of gunshots had stopped. She scrambled under the table. José was staring at her, no expression in his eyes—oh! Realization jolted her body like an electric shock as she comprehended his lifeless stare. Her eyes traveled to the red, blood-seeping hole in José's hairline and she watched as it dissolved and blurred through her sudden tears. Ears still ringing, she scrambled up and blindly ran. She sensed movement near the front of the stairs, so she dashed to her left, finding the door to the kitchen and charging through it knocking over a waitress.

She searched for a back door. There had to be one! There! Stumbling toward the exit, with her feet feeling like she was wading through molasses, Amélia reached for the door.

"¡*Alto!* Stop or I'll shoot!"

Amélia turned—a short, dark, muscular man in a rumpled suit pointing a large pistol right at her face. The blood drained from her face. She had never seen a pistol that looked so big. Shaky and weak, she tried to run. What was happening? She couldn't move!

The man approached. He was swarthy, with coarse straight black hair, and strange eyes—watery and inflamed. She could only stand and watch him as he came nearer. Suddenly there was movement behind him, and the waitress Amélia had bowled over brought a large cutting board down on the man's head.

"Run!" she yelled at Amélia as the startled man fell to the floor.

Chapter 13

Mauricio Aguilar imagined himself as a spider sitting at the center of a vast electronic web, feeling the faint vibrations made by his prey. He sat in his small private office in the S&I headquarters data center. He spent most of his Saturdays here, sometimes fantasizing that one day he would get a girlfriend and have something better to do on weekends—but he related to the computers better than girls. Sipping dark, almost black, espresso from a tiny stained cup he peered at the computer monitor in front of him. Cigarette smoke rose lazily from the ashtray beside the monitor, looking like the wispy ghost of a snake, weaving its way toward the screen. A chime had alerted him and, sure enough, there was a new window open on the browser. *Another penetration attempt! Let's see what "Señor Salas" is doing this time.*

Expanding the window to full screen, he set the cursor on a tab marked *"monitor"* and clicked the mouse. Immediately the screen showed the locations on the website that the remote computer accessed and any responses or passwords being typed in. Mauricio smiled as he watched the commands and responses scroll up the screen. His program monitored every move of the computer that had logged in, verifying each step and displaying it on the screen.

Mauricio might be self-taught, but he was certain that few could match his programming skills. He devoured technical manuals, and sometimes even dreamed in programming languages. There was no way Colonel Fuentes could ever replace him, he was too valuable. From his data center "web," Mauricio uncovered the secrets of all the key people in the government, gathering e-mails, sensitive files, and even bank account information. He passed this treasure trove of information to Fuentes, who used it to manipulate people and events.

About two weeks ago he had detected some unusual activity in Director Salas' computer usage. On several attempts it seemed that Salas was in his office on the computer, and logging in on his home computer at the same time. The first attempts were clumsy, whoever was using the computer—he knew it wasn't Salas—had just logged on and jumped

51

around the site. Mauricio concluded that it must be Raul Salas, illegally using his father's computer—he obviously had a copy of the passwords.

Now the boy logged on again and roamed through the site. Then he spent some time searching through the Federal Police records. What was he looking for?

Mauricio was intrigued when the boy went back to the link with special clearance requirements, even though he had been unsuccessful in past attempts at access. Even Enrique Salas was not cleared for access to this obscure link on the site, only Fuentes and a few key associates. The boy again made several attempts to use the passwords. Was he stupid? Why should it work now? There didn't seem to be much to worry about.

It also seemed odd that last week, shortly after the boy had started snooping, a series of penetration attacks had been attempted on his system. Mauricio couldn't identify their source since they used anonymous servers. He didn't see how that could be related to Raul Salas poking around. In any case he had better report both incidents to Colonel Fuentes.

Fuentes answered his cellular, *"¿Mauricio? ¿Que pasa?"*

Chapter 14

Amélia slammed through the door into the deserted alley behind Pizza Hut. She lurched to the right and weaved from side to side as she made her way down the alley, gasping for breath. A movement at the far end of the alley caused her to stop. What was it? She stared through watery, tear filled eyes. She wiped her eyes and could see better. It was a municipal policeman. Amélia stood panting waiting for him. She would tell him what had happened—she would be safe then.

"Don't move! Get down on the ground!" the policeman commanded, drawing his weapon.

Amélia panicked and dove behind a dumpster just to her left. *Boom!* She heard the sound of the gun and simultaneously the slap of a bullet against the metal dumpster. Adrenaline kicked in and she fled down the alley, away from the pursuing policeman. Two more bullets broke the plate glass window of a store across the street as she rounded the corner at the far end of the alley.

"Run! He's got a gun!" she yelled to two girls who had stood gaping in shock as Amélia charged out of the alley and the bullets smashed the window across the street. They didn't need any more encouragement—they turned and ran back the way they had come, and Amélia joined them.

As they ran to the next street corner, two more municipal police appeared at the intersection. What should she do now? Amélia screamed as loud as she could and, in the spreading panic, the other two girls started screaming too.

"He shot at us! He's back there in the alley," Amélia yelled to the policemen who trotted their way.

"He's got a gun! Stop him!" the other two girls wailed.

Amélia kept running past the policemen, who drew their weapons and pointed them down the street as they crouched down and made their way cautiously down the sidewalk to investigate. She had to get out of there before they found out their quarry was another cop.

Amélia made her way back through the park and to the parking lot where she had left her car. She paid the parking fee and looked around.

There didn't seem to be any unusual activity in the parking lot or anyone watching the car. She was in luck, but that wouldn't last long—she was sure of that. She had to get out of Tegucigalpa fast. She would call Luis later, when she was in a safer place.

She started the car without any problem and pulled into the street. This time she went slowly and carefully—she didn't want to do anything to call attention to herself. Driving became more difficult as she left the city, headed for home in Los Gatos, and her view of the road blurred as the tears welled up again. José was dead, she was certain. What had happened? Was it her fault? Probably. And what could she say to his father? He would hate her, and she couldn't blame him. No, she couldn't talk to him.

Amélia drove through the village of Los Gatos and turned onto a small gravel road alongside a stream. She pulled the old car off into the front yard of her home. Her mother sat on the small porch, rocking gently in an old rattan rocking chair and reading her Bible. She seemed to be doing that more often as her strength wasted away from the cancer that was growing inside of her. Now with this new problem, how could Amélia take care of her? They were sure to come looking for her and her car. By now they, whoever they were, probably knew all about her. She would have to talk to her mother about this, but first she needed to decide what she was going to do. Amélia wearily left the vehicle and walked to the house.

"*Mama'*, can I make you something to eat?" Amélia asked, as she stepped onto the porch.

"*No mi hija,*" The frail woman replied. "*No tengo hambre.*"

Amélia frowned, and sighed. It seemed like she ate less and less these days, but she knew arguing would be to no avail. She said, "OK *mamá*, but I will make a sandwich and leave it for you in the refrigerator, in case you get hungry later."

"Are you leaving again?"

"*Si Mama',*" Amélia said giving her a sad smile. I'll talk to you about that in a few minutes.

Maybe she should go to Pastor Lacas to discuss this problem and her mother's worsening condition. She feared it wouldn't be too long before the cancer won the battle it was waging. What could she do about that? Nothing, and now she couldn't even stay to care for her. But Pastor

Lacas would be there to help her deal with things. She would have to ask him for yet another favor.

Amélia was aware that people often thought her to be aloof, but they couldn't imagine the warm place she had in her heart for Pastor Lacas. Despite her lack of faith, he had always looked out for her. He even stretched his church budget to give her a job. She served as a part-time secretary, for a church too small to really need one. He also had her keeping accounts of a small store that sold produce and crafts for the church members. Even if she didn't believe in God, she knew Pastor Lacas was one blessing of her mother's faith.

Amélia went into their tiny kitchen and began to make a couple of sandwiches. She put one in the small refrigerator and ate the other one to calm her jitters. She began to feel a bit of strength returning and by then had decided on her course of action. In her bedroom, she packed a small nylon bag with a few clothes. She wouldn't need much, a couple of pairs of jeans, two or three T-shirts and another pair of practical low-heeled shoes and some undergarments.

Amélia had thought this day might come. Thank goodness for Aunt Yolanda—her advice and warnings over the years had made Amélia keenly aware that drastic steps might be necessary to keep their liberty. She opened a dresser drawer, got out a screwdriver, and pried up a floorboard in the corner of the room. From the opening she lifted out a cloth covered object and laid it on the bed. With a sense of determined regret Amélia carefully unwrapped the cloth, revealing an AK-47 assault rifle with a curved magazine and two extra magazines. She put the extra magazines in the bag and checked over the rifle.

Amélia put the bag and the AK-47, now wrapped in a black plastic garbage bag, into the trunk of her car. She then went to the front porch where her mother was dozing in her chair and gently shook her awake.

"Mamá," she said quietly, "I have to go now. Your sandwich is in the refrigerator, Please be sure to eat it … you need your strength."

"Where are you going?"

"I can't explain right now," Amélia said. "There is some trouble … but there might be someone … maybe police, coming by looking for me …"

"Police? Oh, Amélia!" her mother said, reaching out for her.

"No te preocupes," Amélia said, "I haven't done anything wrong. I am going right now to ask Pastor Lacas to check on you while I'm gone for a few days."

She left her mother and stopped by the nearby church where she found Pastor Lacas. Amélia avoided giving him any details on her reason for leaving. She gave him a hug before she left and wondered when she would see him, or her mother, again.

On the road out of Los Gatos Amélia took out her cellular and called Luis, sideswiping a fencepost near the edge of the narrow gravel lane. Well, another scratch on the old Civic wouldn't make any difference—she would probably never see it again.

"Luis, where are you?" she said when he answered.

"Still at the university. In the library, can you believe it? I'm actually studying."

Despite the situation, Amélia smiled. "Pretty hard to believe ... there must be a girl involved."

"Well ..."

"Listen," she interrupted, "we're in trouble. Watch your back ... they're after me ... uh, probably both of us."

"What happened?"

"I'll explain when I see you. Right now I need you to go to the cellular store and get two phones and SIM cards. Then meet me in the parking lot at the airport entrance. Don't tell anyone ... even the girl ... what you are doing."

"You're scaring me Amélia," Luis said. "What are you talking about? This sounds like a bad movie ..."

"Just do it Luis," she said, "I'm serious. And you should be scared ... I ..." An involuntary sob escaped her lips and her throat tightened up.

"Amélia?"

"I ... I almost got killed this morning!" Amélia blurted out. "They killed José ... oh, Luis ... it was ...I still can't believe it ...horrible!"

"José killed? What happened?"

Amélia struggled to regain her composure. The road was blurry again. "I'll tell you at the airport. Just hurry! Oh, turn off your cellular ... they could try to track us by the phones."

She punched the off button on the phone and careened down the road, weaving in and out of her lane as she pried the battery cover off and disconnected the battery. She had to be sure she couldn't be traced.

Chapter 15

Manuel Fuentes tapped his pen against the corner of the desk as he listened to Mauricio Aguilar describe how the Salas boy, he seemed to be pretty sure of that, was poking around the S&I website. The man seemed to think that giving a blow-by-blow account full of details made him seem smarter. If Mauricio's snooping program was so great, why was he always pestering him for security software upgrades?

"Mauricio, get to the bottom line will you," Fuentes said. "Why are you bothering me at home on a Saturday afternoon for this?"

He listened to another long-winded explanation—something about a cyber-attack—whatever that was.

"And you think the boy did this?"

More of Mauricio's droning. He was getting a headache. Ah ha! Here it came—yet another plea for an upgraded software budget.

"Listen, Mauricio," Fuentes said, trying to keep the sarcasm out of his voice. He did need the man, after all, and Mauricio was loyal and worked hard. "I'll give you some guidelines since you really don't know where these 'attacks' came from, or if the Salas boy is even involved. If he gets into the site again ask Lieutenant Garcia to confiscate the computer and bring him in for questioning." Fuentes hoped Garcia would do just that. He could use the incident to apply additional political pressure on Enrique Salas.

"And if there is another 'cyber-attack,' as you call it," Fuentes continued, "I will give you direct authority to act. You do not have to call me first. If you can trace a location, notify Captain Jimenez who will have the Rapid-Response Strike Team on the move within minutes. I will tell him to respond immediately if you call him."

Fuentes finished his conversation with Mauricio, going over details and deflecting yet another attempt at increasing the software. He had to admit the man was persistent. Despite his annoyance at times, Fuentes was impressed with Mauricio. He congratulated himself on recognizing years ago that this kid from the slums, an army private assigned to his intelligence unit, had a natural talent for computers and anything technical. The decision to mentor him, and exploit his capability, had been a key element allowing Fuentes to rise to power.

Fuentes had just made himself a drink and was contemplating whether he would have his mistress over for the evening, when his secure cell phone beeped. Frowning, he checked the display—it was Arroyo—good. He had the man following up on that rogue newsletter and internet blog that threatened to disrupt his drug trade. Arroyo had neutralized the blogger and her gringo boyfriend, and then Mauricio shut down the blog—but the newsletter activity just increased. This had to be stopped.

"Hector, my friend," Fuentes answered. "Do you have news for me?"

"Yes, but it is not all good," Hector Arroyo said. "I found the woman who had been helping Perez with the blog and newsletter. I followed her, revealing two contacts, when she delivered flyers publicizing the disappearances of Perez, the gringo, and some others."

"That is excellent Hector."

"That is where the good news ends. One of the contacts was José Villanueva, the son of the General. She met him in the Pizza Hut near *Parque Central.*"

Fuentes said, "No, that could work to our advantage. General Villanueva has been a thorn in my side." His mind was already spinning possibilities of how to leverage this knowledge.

"Hector said, "I too thought we could pressure the General and clean up this mess in one bold move. I called Torres, my guy in the MS-13 gang, to help me take both the girl and the Villanueva boy. I had Tamez, the Municipal Police Sergeant, covering the back alley. Unfortunately the plan failed when Villanueva's bodyguard managed to shoot Torres. We killed the bodyguard, but the Villanueva boy and Torres were both killed in the shootout."

"What about the girl?" Fuentes felt a familiar tightness in his head.

"She ran ... tried to go out through the kitchen. I pursued her, almost had her, but someone hit me from behind. When I came to the place was deserted ... everyone had fled. Tamez tried to arrest her in the alley, but she got away."

Fuentes clenched his jaw. Was there any possibility of salvaging some advantage from this disaster? Arroyo had never failed him this badly before. "Hector, this is unacceptable. I expect better of you ...

always before, and we go way back, you have come through for me … but now this!"

"Enrique, I am truly sorry," Arroyo said. "I will make this right. I have already had Sergeant Tamez designate the incident as a drug shooting. MS-13 and the Villanueva boy will both be implicated and there is already an alert out for the girl, Amélia Ramirez. She was a student at UNAH. We have her home address, automobile description and license number. She will be caught soon and publically charged."

Fuentes downed his drink in a large gulp and walked over to the sideboard in the corner of his office. "You had better make that work Hector! Notify me immediately when she is caught. I want to interrogate her myself."

"Yes sir," Hector responded in a more formal tone. "I will make this right. Also, Sergeant Tamez had the Public Relations Department of the Municipal Police schedule a press conference. He will publicize the breakup of a major drug scandal involving the son of General Villanueva and the MS-13 gang. They will ask the public's assistance in the manhunt for the girl, who will be described as a co-conspirator with the General's son. This should reduce the General's influence for a while, so some advantage will come out of this setback."

Fuentes felt some relaxation of the tightness in his head. This could be advantageous after all. He would have his contacts in the military spread doubt about General Villanueva's capability and leadership. After all, if a man can't control his own son, is he capable of effectively leading the army?

"That is very good thinking, Hector" Fuentes said, allowing himself a faint smile. He lifted the bottle of whiskey with one hand and poured the amber liquid over the ice remaining in his glass. "I am somewhat reassured, but you still have much to do to redeem yourself. Start by capturing that girl!"

Chapter 16

Amélia loitered in the doorway of a shop near the front entrance of Toncontin airport. Where was Luis? She had been here nearly an hour, killing time in the shops, sitting on the sidewalk, or walking down to the traffic light at the airport entrance to scan the passing vehicles. So far nobody had paid any attention to her old Civic sitting at one end of the graveled parking lot. She had removed the license plate, fearing that it might alert the police to the vehicle, but wondered if a missing plate might do the same thing.

Finally! She spotted Luis entering the lot in his green pickup truck. Amélia left the doorway, waving for Luis to stop. "Where have you been?" she asked, getting into the truck. "I've been waiting an hour!"

"Tranquilo (calm down)" Luis said. I had to get some money then go buy the cellular phones and have them activated. What is going on anyway? What happened to José?"

"I'll explain," Amélia said, "just drive up to the end of the lot so I can get my stuff out of the car. We need to leave … I've already been here too long!"

She retrieved her bag and the wrapped rifle from the trunk while Luis sat waiting in the truck. Amélia slid the rifle behind the seat of the truck and climbed in.

"Now, what has happened?" Luis turned facing her.

"Not here. Let's go!"

Luis crossed his arms. "We're not going anywhere until you tell me what's going on."

Amélia sighed. Luis could be so stubborn sometimes. "OK, just go across the road to the fast food restaurants where nobody will notice us. Come on, Luis! Really, we can't stay here."

Luis frowned, but put the truck in gear and started moving. "We're going girl, now explain."

Amélia started telling Luis everything that had happened while he drove to the rear of the parking lot between Burger King and Church's Chicken. By the time she finished, they had been sitting in the truck for an hour. She wiped the tears from her eyes and blew her nose on an old napkin she had found in the glove box.

"Man, this is bad, so what do we do?" Luis said.

"I don't know. I'm exhausted." Amélia threw the napkin onto the floor and stared out the windshield. "I can't go home. Can I stay at your house for a while? Just until I figure out what to do.

"We have to find somewhere else to stay," Luis said.

"We?"

"Yeah girl, they probably know about me too. It won't be safe at my place."

"I didn't think of that. They might try to kill you too! The image of José's lifeless eyes popped into her mind. Amélia put her hands over her face. "I hate this! What are we going to do?"

"We will think of something … maybe a friend. Luis reached over and put a hand on her arm.

"And get someone else killed?" Amélia said. "We need to get out of town. Wait, I know! We can go to Aunt Yolanda's farm near Talanga. We would be safe there."

"Talanga?" Luis said. "So, then what? Do we just run and give up on everything?"

"I don't know!" They couldn't give up. She had to expose these creeps—find out why they killed José. "No we don't give up. You're right. We couldn't do much from Talanga."

"Think, Amélia. We knew this day might come," Luis said. "Why do you think Rodrigo and I did all that work … el *túnel secreto*. Our 'safe house' is right here in the city—the office at the old parsonage."

Amélia glanced at him. He was right. In her panic she hadn't been thinking clearly. That was the best place. But Jake Grayson was there. What would they do about that?

"I told you, that Jake guy is there. That's going to be a problem."

"Yeah, you told me, but so what?" Luis grinned at her. "I remember Jake as easy going. What's the gringo going to do, kick us out? Pastor Zamora gave us use of the office."

Amélia raised her eyebrows. "So we just barge in on him?"

"Let me think," Luis said. "You told me he was trying to find out what had happened to Ruben and Juanita, right? Maybe that's how we can fight back. So we tell him that we are trying to find out too, and we can help him."

Amélia pursed her lips. "I don't think he'll like that idea."

"We can convince him, girl. That's the best place for us and the safest. We kept it secret so far, and we already planned in case someone came after us. It's made for something like this."

He had a point. They had to fight back, and that would be the safest place to be.

"Well?" Luis said.

"You're right. I don't know why I didn't think of it. Jake Grayson will just have to deal with it."

Chapter 17

Jake had returned to the parsonage and was putting the finishing touches on a computer program. It would analyze the data he hoped to collect from the Salas computer. He found several useful scripts online and skillfully wove them into his program. He sipped on his cup of coffee and realized it had gone cold, then drank it anyway, not wanting to lose focus on finalizing the program. It was nice to not have to program everything from scratch—the "Python" programming language was ideal for this task. Now he just needed to create some faked data files to test the analysis—a questionable task, since he didn't know just what might be contained in the data Raul's laptop was gathering.

The cup was empty. Jake rubbed his eyes and stretched. Well, he needed a break anyway. He went into the small kitchen and started another pot of the strong coffee he had been enjoying. They had some good stuff down here.

While the coffee was brewing, he tried to call Barbara again—this time she answered.

"Jake, are you alright?"

"Uh ... yeah," Jake said, "I ... you're not still mad?"

"I should be," Barbara said, "but ... like, I can't stay mad at you, Jake. I love you."

He could picture her in his mind—smooth unblemished complexion, except for a few small freckles chasing across the bridge of her nose, strawberry blond hair, and full figure. And that smile! He tried to picture her. Was she was smiling now, or maybe looking worried, with a tear running down her cheek?

"I ... yeah, me too. Listen, I'm sorry I upset you, but I just had to come down."

"You are, like, so stubborn, Jake Grayson! I was scared, and mad too. You just chucked your chances with that Intelibotics thing, and school, and ... like, everything! Are you coming home now? Please say yes—I can't even sleep for worrying about you."

She didn't ask him about finding Ruben. Jake could feel the familiar tightness in his throat that came whenever he knew he was going to say something she would find disagreeable.

"Babe, I just got here ... barely got started. Ruben's still missing."

She hesitated, and then whispered, "I know. I was just ... like, hoping they had found him, or something. I miss you so much!"

"I know, Babe. Miss you too. It won't be long, I promise. I'll call you every day. I've been going crazy not hearing your voice. Please don't shut me out again like you have done the past few days. OK?"

"I won't Honey. It was hard for me too, but I was so upset, and like ... afraid maybe I'd say the wrong thing to you."

They said their goodbyes. Jake poured a cup of coffee and sat thinking about Barbara. There was a sense of wonder that they had become so close. He couldn't imagine how things would be without her. Always awkward around girls, Jake had never "gone steady" in high school. Ruben had been the one to push him into asking Barbara James to the all-night graduation party their senior year. Jake still marveled that she had not only accepted the date, but that they had immediately felt a bond. They had dated each other in the three years since. Barbara fitted neatly into Jake's plans for a successful career, a family, and a happy life.

He wanted to ask her to marry him after they both had graduated. And when would that be? This trip was going to delay that by a semester. Obviously Jason Lee would get the position with the Advances Development group at Intellibotics—there was no way now to get Arvie ready for the final competition. Maybe he could still land some sort of position with Intellibotics. And if he couldn't? He would have to interview with other places. Barbara would have to find a job, and might have to move away. He couldn't ask her to marry him before he had a good job.

He sipped at the coffee. It had gone cold again. Why had he made everything spin off course, dropping school and jeopardizing their relationship, to come down here? It was a futile quest—"tilting at windmills." How could he possibly find Ruben?

Chapter 18

Jake was back in the office working on another program. This one was designed to penetrate the defenses of the Security and Intelligence website, once he was able to log on as Salas. It was a form of a "Rainbow Attack" program. Jake had used an older version, written in the "C++" programming language, when he tried to penetrate the site from the U.S. He hoped this one written in "Python" could be made to work better.

He was startled by a rusty squeak from the front gate, and then a knock on the front door. It was getting dark and he wasn't expecting anyone. It might not be safe to open the door. He was trying to decide what to do when the knock came again, louder this time. Jake rose and peered cautiously out of the window of the office. He couldn't see anyone. Would a criminal knock? Yeah, probably. Now what? He walked into the hallway and approached the front door. Why didn't they have a window in it?—or at least a peep-hole.

"Who is it?" Oh yeah, they probably speak Spanish. *"¿Quién es?"*

"Jake, it's me, Amélia," said a voice through the door. "Luis Estrada is with me. Let us in!"

Amélia? Why would she be here again? Jake wiped his hands on his pants. "Uh ... what do you want?"

"Jake, don't be a dork! Open the door!"

He was being foolish, and rude. He felt his face flush. When he opened the door, Amélia was standing there, a nylon bag in one hand and something wrapped in black plastic in the other. Someone peered over her shoulder—then he recognized Luis.

"I'm sorry ... I just wasn't ... uh, expecting anyone." He pulled the door open wider, "Come in ... uh, of course."

She just stood there. Why wasn't she coming in?

"Thank you, Jake." Amélia rolled her eyes. "If you will move out of the doorway, we will be glad to."

"Oh ... yeah, sorry." They must think he was an idiot. Again heat rose in Jake's cheeks and he shuffled backwards. "Come in the living room." He walked into the small room to the right of the hallway and waved toward a couch.

They all sat down, Amélia and Luis on the couch and Jake in a chair by the front window. Silence reigned for thirty seconds.

"Um, so?" Jake said.

Amélia caught her breath, but hesitated. Luis picked up the conversation. "Jake, it's good to see you again. We are sorry to barge in on you, but we had to, man."

"Had to? What's going on?"

"We're in some trouble, man," Luis said. "Amélia, why don't you tell Jake everything you told me.

Jake became more and more concerned as Amélia related her story. Could all this be true? Why did they come here?

"So, you see Jake," Amélia finished, "we need to stay here for a while."

What? Stay here? He must have misunderstood her. "What did you say?" Jake said.

"We need to stay here! Don't you get what I've been telling you?"

Jake snorted out a breath. "Yeah, I got it. There are some crazy people trying to kill you and for some reason you think I'd want you here so we could all get killed together! No way!"

"Jake," Luis said, "calm down, man. Listen, no one would know, or even suspect that we are here."

Jake raised his eyebrows. "Oh, sure. Your office for the 'protest newspaper,' or whatever you call it, is here. So why wouldn't this be the first place they look?"

Amélia stood up and started pacing the floor. The living room was so small that she almost brushed Jake's knees each time she circled in front of the couch. Jake leaned back in his chair to look up at her without craning his neck.

"It's secret. We've kept the office location very secret, Jake." Amélia waved her hands as she spoke. "Juanita, Ruben, Luis and I are the only ones who come here and we're very careful. Even Pastor Juan who let us use the office here doesn't know what we're doing. He thinks Juanita and Luis are just using it for a Christian student group at the university."

"But you were followed," Jake said. "How do you know they didn't follow you here sometime?"

She stopped and faced Jake, her hands on her hips. "Listen, we were careful, OK?"

"But ..."

Amélia held up her hand, silencing him. She plopped down on the couch again, tears springing to her eyes. "I ... I've thought about it over and over ... José ... it's my fault. I used the bookstore copier to run the flyers. You were here so I couldn't do it here ..."

"Wait!" Jake leapt to his feet. "This isn't my fault! You can't blame me—I didn't even know why you were here."

"Sit down Jake." She motioned her hand in his direction. "I'm not blaming you. It's my fault. Juanita and Ruben told me that someone had been watching Juanita at the bookstore and around the campus. I should have known it wasn't safe. I was at the bookstore to copy the flyers, then delivered them to Luis at the university." She rubbed the tears from her eyes and sniffed. "And then led them right to José ... It's my fault he's dead." She dropped her head into her hands.

Great, they're on the run and their friend is dead. And me?—I'm just thinking of myself. Jake tried to find words to redeem himself in their eyes. "OK, I'm sorry. Maybe I over-reacted."

"It's alright, man," Luis said. "Everyone is a little frazzled right now. Look Jake, we need to just stay a few nights until we decide what to do. What do you say, man?"

"Well ... there is another bed in the bedroom," Jake said. "Uh ... Amélia, you could sleep out here on the couch." He must be crazy getting mixed up in this. *What would Barbara think?*

Chapter 19

Jake lay staring at the ceiling in the dim light from the hallway slanting in through the gap in the bedroom door, left ajar. Luis snored loudly from the bed on the other side of the room. For a little guy he sure did make a lot of noise. It was after midnight and Jake wasn't a bit sleepy. Amélia Ramirez showing up again was going to be a problem. He thought back to their first encounter—back in 2009 on that awful mission trip.

■■■

Pastor Juan had taken the group to the village of Los Gatos to make repairs at the small church of his longtime friend, Pastor Arturo Lacas. For some reason Lacas had asked Amélia to coordinate the work. Jake couldn't imagine why, other than she was some sort of assistant or something. With her overbearing manner, she had not endeared herself to the mission group volunteers. She gave them work assignments, but they quickly switched them around to do things their way. That had not made Amélia happy.

At the time, Jake was attracted to one of the other mission volunteers, Lisa Malone. He managed to partner with her on fixing the footbridge that ran over a small creek. Amélia had caught them goofing off when she came to check on progress. Jake was standing knee deep in the water and was soaking wet when Amélia had arrived.

Lisa stood on the wobbly foot-bridge looking down at him and laughing. "I'm sorry Jake," she said. "I didn't mean to bump you. But at least you're not hot and sweaty anymore."

"What are you doing down here?" Amélia demanded. "I thought you were going to help the other girl paint."

"Oh ... hi," Lisa said. "I came down to help Jake. Cindy wanted Brad to help her paint, so Ruben took his place fixing the roof."

"You, get out of the creek." Amélia said, turning to Jake. "Why can't anyone just do what they're supposed to be doing?"

Scowling, Jake sloshed up out of the creek and approached Amélia. "We are doing what we are supposed to be doing! What do you mean?"

She turned to face him. "Well, she's supposed to be painting, and your friend was supposed to help you. Instead, he's on the roof, doing Brad's job, while Brad is flirting with Cindy. And you're standing here, dripping wet, instead of getting the bridge fixed!"

Jake's face flushed. "We're getting the job done. Just because we aren't doing it just like you think we should doesn't matter. Just leave us alone and the work will go just fine."

"I'm responsible to Pastor Lacas. He told me to supervise this job; to make sure everything was done right."

"Just tell us what needs to be done. You don't have to decide every detail."

"Fine, do it your way. But it had better be done right!" She turned, heading back up the path.

■■■

And now she is out there, sleeping on the couch. This is not what he needed—maybe he could go stay at Raul's house. Jake pulled a pillow over his head in a vain effort to shut out the piercing racket coming from the other bed.

Chapter 20

Sunday morning Jake walked across the street to Pastor Juan's church, which faced the street corner. Beneath its tiled roof was a bright yellow wall, sporting a large white cross above red entrance doors. Raul waited for him at the front gate of the metal fence that surrounded the building. It was also painted a bright red. They love their colors down here, but Jake had to admit it was an attractive building.

"*Buenas días,*" Raul greeted him as he approached. "*¿Que Tal?*"

"Good morning," Jake said. What's up?—how should he answer that? Amélia and Luis were holed up right across the street. They had talked and argued well into the night. Amélia had angered Jake with her strident and insistent manner. Luis was joking and cajoling, all the while trying to play the peacemaker. They had finally convinced Jake that that was the only safe place they had to stay. He wondered what would have happened if he had still refused. They had sworn Jake to secrecy, insisting that he not tell anyone that they were there. That was alright with Jake—he didn't want to explain why he had let himself be manipulated by them.

"Is everything OK?" Raul asked, looking closely at Jake. "You seem sort of quiet this morning."

"Oh, everything's fine," Jake said. He needed to say something positive. "In fact, things are looking up. I finally talked with Barbara and we smoothed everything out."

"Excellent! Raul said. "I have good news too. My dad worked on the computer last night and early this morning, so I have some data for you." He held up a flash drive.

Jake was skeptical. "I'll need him to log-on several times to have a big enough sample to analyze."

"I know. You explained that yesterday morning." Raul chuckled. "Last night I kept interrupting him, telling him my laptop wasn't working, and said I needed to use his computer to check files at the university. He had to log on again each time when I let him have the computer again. About drove him crazy!"

Jake grinned. "Good thinking. Give it to me and I'll try the analysis program later this afternoon."

Raul handed over the flash drive. "Look, Pastor Juan just came out the front entrance. Let's go talk to him before the service starts."

They approached the small, dapper man with salt and pepper hair, wearing blue jeans, and a black sports jacket over a white turtle-neck sweater. A wide smile lit his face as he saw the boys approaching.

"Jake, Raul, good morning!" he said. "Have you heard any news on Ruben and Juanita?"

"Good morning, Pastor Juan," Jake said, shaking the man's hand. "No, nothing yet."

He watched as the man's expression became somber. What would he think if he knew that Amélia and Luis were hiding in his old parsonage? "We are constantly praying for them," the pastor said. He turned to Raul and shook his hand. "I pray for you and Jake to have success in finding out what has become of them. They couldn't have better friends."

"Thank you. We will try," Raul said.

Jake longed to tell Pastor Juan and Raul about his refugee houseguests. Whoever was after them had probably been behind the disappearance of Ruben and Juanita. They tried to kill Amélia—is that what they had done to Ruben and Juanita? What would it accomplish if he brought up all his concerns? It was just wild speculation, and would just complicate things. Jake held his tongue.

"Well, come inside," the small man said, the smile returning to his face. "We are about to start the service. And afterwards, Teresa has a treat for you ... actually, for all of us, a special lunch."

After the service Raul and Jake followed Pastor Juan and his wife, Teresa, to their home in the neighborhood of *Alemán*, a short distance away. Jake rode with Raul in his white Tacoma, and stared out the window without interest at the passing scenery.

When they arrived, Teresa met them at the door and welcomed them inside. Jake's mood brightened as he remembered his first impression of the petite, auburn haired woman from his first encounter three years previously. He had been a little smitten with her. Her warm, vivacious personality, not to mention her beauty, had made him envy Pastor Juan. She was what Jake had always imagined the ideal wife would be like. Of course he had soon been smitten with Lisa on that trip and she was totally different. For that matter what about Barbara?—strawberry blonde, knockout figure, smart and ambitious. She was Jake's idea of a perfect girlfriend or, who knows?—wife.

Amélia—now she was certainly the opposite of Teresa. She was cold and—what?—calculating, logical, driven. True, she was also beautiful, but was tall and haughty as opposed to Teresa's petite friendliness. Why had these thoughts suddenly leapt out? He needed to get back into the present.

"Lunch will be ready in a moment," Teresa was saying. "We're going to eat out back on the patio. Juan's out there now. Why don't you go out there to wait?"

It was a pleasant lunch and Jake enjoyed the Zamora's easy hospitality and also having Raul there as someone closer to his age. Raul was sort of a guide to Jake, filling in on background and customs unique to Honduras as they talked about various things. The only uncomfortable time was when conversation drifted toward Ruben and Juanita. Pastor Juan asked Jake what his plan was to help find out what had happened.

Jake looked away. What *was* his plan? "Well …Uh …Raul and I are hoping to find out if there are any records of them being arrested, or something like that." What else could he say? It all sounded sort of lame.

"Oh," Pastor Juan said, turning to Raul, "is your father helping?"

Now Raul looked uncomfortable. "My father? Oh, yes, my father … he is helping some. You know, government contacts … that sort of thing. But keep this to yourself, please."

Well that was awkward. But at least Pastor Juan seemed satisfied with the vague answers. What would he think if he knew they were trying to hack into the government's computers?

After they left the Zamora's house, Raul wanted to stop to get a few things at a pulpería, a small store selling groceries, candy, various other items, even cell phone SIM cards. When Raul went to the counter to pay for the things he had selected, Jake followed. There was a small stack of newspapers on the counter next to the cashier. Jake's eye was drawn to the paper whose masthead proclaimed "*El Heraldo*" in large red type. There was a picture of Amélia! Involuntarily, Jake sucked in a big breath.

Raul turned to look at him, curiosity showing in his eyes. "What's wrong?"

The Honduran Plot

Uh-oh! Jake thought furiously. What could he say? Finally, "Oh, nothing …uh … I just was clearing my throat."

"Sure, OK," Raul said with a dubious look on his face.

Jake pointed to the papers. "Uh … isn't that what's-her-name, the girl Rubin and I met on our mission trip?"

Raul looked and let out a gasp. "It's Amélia Ramirez! I don't believe it."

Jake picked up one of the papers. The headline read: *"Matan a tres persones en una lucha de drogas."* Jake said, "What … what's it say? I can't read the headline very well."

Raul took the paper and paraphrased the headline and story with Amélia's picture, which looked like a driver's license photo. "The headline says, 'Three persons killed in a drug fight.' Then the story goes on to say that José Villanueva, son of General Jorge Villanueva, and his bodyguard were killed in a shooting at Pizza Hut in *El Centro* yesterday. Eduardo Torres, a member of the MS-13 gang, was also killed. You won't believe this. The police think that Amélia and Torres were the ones that killed the general's son and his bodyguard!"

Jake was trying to wrap his mind around this new development. Had she been lying to him? Maybe she and Luis were members of the gang and made up their story.

"Amélia in a drug shootout? The police are after her?" Jake asked, snatching the paper back. He looked at it, as if he could read it, then shook his head. That was stupid—I'm acting like an idiot. He gave the paper back. "Sorry, wasn't thinking. How well do you know her?"

"Well enough to know this is all bunk," Raul said. "It doesn't make sense … she is no gang member, and I know José Villanueva … he wouldn't be buying drugs. And his bodyguard? That's ridiculous!"

So maybe Amélia and Luis were telling the truth. But this was a big problem. He would be harboring a fugitive from the police. That just wouldn't do. Should he tell Raul what was going on? Maybe he had some ideas on what to do.

"Uh … "Jake said, then closed his mouth. No, he had to think this through. If he told Raul, he would be pressured into some decisions he wasn't ready to make, not yet.

"Uh, what?" Raul asked.

"Oh, I … don't know … what to say. I'm going to buy one of these papers."

"Why? You can't read it."

"Well, I can read a little Spanish ... at least with some help," Jake said. "Besides, it's about someone I know ... uh, used to know. It will be a good souvenir from my trip."

Raul raised his eyebrows, but just said, "Keep the paper. I'll pay for it with my things."

Chapter 21

Amélia stared at the old computer in the parsonage office, as if willing it to come to life and tell her what to do. It was too quiet. Luis had gone to get things from his house, including guns and ammo. Amélia's account of José's death had convinced him that they needed to be ready for anything. She had been anxious, but Luis assured her that he would make sure no one was watching the house, or attempting to follow him when he returned. This forced inactivity was driving her nuts. She had already come close to wearing a circular path in the faded carpet of the living room. Luis should have been back by now. Something must have happened—nothing good.

She should e-mail all the contacts in their group to warn them about what had happened. Once again her fingers rested on the keyboard—then withdrew. Would the e-mail be traced? That might let them find her, or even reveal the identities of everyone in the group, Uggh!

When would Jake come back? He would probably know if e-mailing would be safe—he seemed to be quite a computer geek.

Jake Grayson coming back to Honduras to find Ruben and Juanita was a real surprise. He looked surprisingly older somehow, even though it had been only three years since she had last seen him. Those blue-gray eyes, short cropped hair, and trim build still looked good though. She remembered that day when she had first met Jake.

■■■

Pastor Lacas had asked her to supervise the mission group Pastor Zamora was bringing to fix up the church. She remembered how annoyed she had been at his request—it would mean taking time off from her job at the bookstore. All to babysit some spoiled American rich kids who thought they were saving the world. And Jake—he had been the one to really get under her skin.

She was totally frustrated with the spoiled gringos. They weren't at all serious about things, and were totally disorganized. None of them were doing what she had assigned them to do. When she went down to the foot bridge to check progress, there was Jake, soaking wet in the

75

creek, flirting with that girl. Amélia's temper flamed like a roaring bonfire, and after chewing them out, she stalked back to her office in the church.

A few minutes later Jake came into the church, still soaking wet, and grabbed a towel from the storage shelf in the far corner of the back room. Evidently he thought he was alone, not realizing she could see him through the open office door. He pulled off his shirt and pants, and wrung them dry. Standing with his back to her, wearing only boxer shorts, he then started drying off. She turned her head to look away, but not before his toned muscles caught her eye. Amélia fanned her face which suddenly felt hot. Maybe she had been out in the sun longer than she thought.

■■■

Amélia smiled at the memory. She had been so dismayed by her reaction because Jake was the one who annoyed her the most. The idea that she might be attracted to him had galled her. The smile left her face. Were things so different now? She had really begun to like José, and suddenly he had been killed. She still was trying to come to terms with that, and here she was thinking how good Jake looked. Totally irritated with herself, she returned to pacing of the living room floor.

Soon she heard the front gate creak. Amélia retrieved the AK-47 assault rifle she had stowed under the couch and stood where she could see into the hall to the front entrance. Raising the rifle, she held her breath. There was a scratching sound, a click, and then the knob turned.

Jake bounded through the front door and looked her way before she could lower the AK-47. He let out a gasp and staggered backwards. Newspaper scattered onto the hallway floor.

"Don't!" Jake yelled, raising his hands in front of his face.

She lowered the rifle. "I'm sorry, Jake. Just being careful."

Jake appeared to regain his composure. "Well, thank you for not shooting me! Where did you get that thing?" He stooped and started picking paper off the floor, still eyeing the weapon warily.

"It's a long story," Amélia said. "That's what I had wrapped in the plastic last night."

The gate creaked loudly again, and they both jumped. Jake turned and Amélia raised the rifle again as Luis charged through the front door.

"Man, you gotta see this!" he said, then stopped suddenly when he realized the rifle was pointed at him. "Whoa! Don't shoot me, girl."

"Shut the door!" Amélia said. "You both scared me to death."

Jake grabbed the door handle, but then hesitated. Luis looked at Jake and said, "You better do it, man. She is a drug-crazed, killer gangster."

What did he say? Amélia looked at Luis, trying to read the strange expression on his face. He was grinning, but there was a tension there that told her that something was wrong. Jake just stared at her, but then raised his eyebrows and shot Luis a knowing look.

"What am I missing?" Amélia asked.

■■■

Jake looked down at the newspaper in Luis' hand. He must have seen the story, but here he was, joking about it. Luis obviously didn't believe the allegations. When Jake first saw the story he had doubts about Amélia and was worried about returning to the parsonage. But, by the time Raul had dropped him off, he decided the story was a smoke-screen. Still, he didn't think he could joke about it. They were in serious trouble.

"Let's go in the living room, Amélia," Jake said. "I think Luis has something to show you." Luis gave him an inquiring look and Jake waved his copy of *"El Heraldo"* at him.

"Tell her Luis," Jake said from his position in the chair, facing the others on the couch. "You can read the story better than I can,"

He watched as Amélia's café-latte complexion turned three shades lighter when Luis read the story verbatim. A look of fear came into her eyes.

"This is bad, girl," Luis said after he finished reading. "We have to get out of here."

Yes. That is what Jake wanted to hear. He felt sorry for Amélia, and Luis too. This was certainly some sort of frame job, but he didn't need any part of it. He just wanted to find Ruben and get out of this place.

"Maybe you could leave tonight, after dark, and go someplace out of Tegucigalpa," Jake said. "Wouldn't that be the best thing to do?"

Amélia turned to look at him. The fear had left her face. Her eyes glistened with tears and she was starting to look angry.

"Who do you think is doing this, Jake?" she said.

"What? How would I know?"

"Don't be a dolt, Jake," Amélia said. "I know you don't know the names of the people who are doing this. But think about it. Juanita and Ruben were kidnapped …"

"You can't be sure …"

Her eyes glared. "Yes I can … I know they were! They were part of our group, along with Luis, José and me. Then José was killed and someone is making sure I get the blame."

"Yeah, I get that," Jake said. What was she getting at? That still didn't tell them anything.

"Don't you see?" Amélia said. "You are trying to find Ruben …and Juanita. I don't know how you expect to do it, but it means you are up against the same people that we are."

Jake hadn't really been thinking along those lines. He mentally kicked himself. She hadn't really been asking him who had done it. She was trying to point out that they were up against a common enemy. He always focused on the problem or literal question, part of his technical mindset, rather than grasping what was really the intent or attitude being expressed. He had to work on that.

"OK, I see what you mean," Jake said. "I think you're probably right. So this is all related to the corruption and drug dealing in the government that your group has been trying to expose."

"Yes."

"OK, so we're on the same side," Jake said. "If I can find out anything about Ruben, and Juanita too of course, then I can give you the information. Sure, I can do that."

If this whole thing was coming from somewhere in the government, there might be a better chance of finding Ruben. If he and Raul could penetrate the computers there would be a good chance there would be some clues there. For the first time he began to feel more hopeful.

"How will I be able to get in touch with you?" Jake said. "I could give you my cell number for you to call when you find a safe place."

Amélia shook her head, a look of disgust on her face. Jake looked to Luis who had a frown on his face. What had he missed?

"You still don't understand, do you Jake?" Amélia said. "We can't run and hide. We aren't going anywhere. This is the safe place … at least the safest where we can fight back."

"Not going … fight back?" Jake said. They couldn't stay here.

The Honduran Plot

Amélia looked imploringly at him. "Jake, I know you're a smart guy, even if you are slow to catch on sometimes. You didn't come all this way to find Rubin without some idea you could do it. You have some sort of plan. We need you ... your plan ...to find out who we're fighting. If you can find out what happened to Juanita and Ruben, or even find them alive, that is our only chance."

"I don't know if my idea will really work," Jake said.

"It needs to work," Amélia said. "Jake, think of this. If you start poking around and anger these people they will come after you, just like they came after me. We can help protect you. Luis and I can also help you with your plan. There must be some way we can be useful."

What should he say, or do? Was she right? Jake realized that, right or wrong, Amélia and Luis weren't leaving. He was stuck with them.

Amélia got up and walked to his chair. Laying a hand on his shoulder, she said, "Now tell us what you are planning to do to find Ruben."

Chapter 22

The sun settled behind the mountains to the west, and shadows crept over the cinder block house that had once served as the parsonage for the evangelical church across the street. Jake, his face lit by the glow of his laptop screen, frowned in concentration as he scanned the web page links written in Spanish.

He looked across the room to Amélia Ramirez watching from an old armchair. By her side, leaning against the chair, was the AK-47 assault rifle, looking strangely out of place in the modest room decorated with a picture of Jesus and a wooden crucifix. She had been alternately sitting, standing, and peeking out the front window. Obviously she was nervous. Maybe Luis would come back soon and calm her down.

Why couldn't she go somewhere else? She had been watching him most of the afternoon. Amélia had apparently showered and put on perfume—the faint scent of flowers permeated the room. What was it? Something old fashioned he thought. It reminded him of his aunt, his mother's sister. Yes that was it; she always wore Jasmine. Jake tried to concentrate again, but his awareness of her sitting across the room was a major distraction.

He searched through the pages of website data, looking for anything useful. His Spanish was rusty, and he wondered if maybe he should ask her to help, but he hesitated. The way she watched him, like she didn't trust him to get this right, pricked his ego.

She had no clue what he was doing and couldn't appreciate how much work had gone into this. He had spent much of last night and this morning tweaking his analysis program, and finally it had performed awesomely. The analysis of data from the WiFi skimmer had revealed the secret of the Salas computer. Jake had programmed his laptop to emulate it and easily got into the S&I website. Then he had launched a powerful attack on the secure area. It blew him away how well the Python version of his Rainbow Attack program worked.

He finally decided to quit trying to read, and just download as many files as he could. Raul could go through them later. He stretched as the progress bar on the download crept slowly to the right. As the light dimmed, Jake peered at his notes in the spiral notepad on the desk. It was becoming difficult to see as the twilight rapidly faded. He reached up to turn on a light.

"Stop!" Amélia exclaimed. "What are you doing?"

"Turning on the desk lamp; it's getting dark in here"

"Don't. I don't want to call attention to the fact that we're here."

"Maybe you're right … better to be cautious," Jake agreed, especially since he had penetrated one of the most secure computers of the Honduran Ministry of Security and Intelligence. He mentally pumped his fist and shouted, "Yeah!"

Jake heard a loud squeak from the front gate, and then the sound of the front door being closed and the click of the deadbolt. A moment later the door to the office burst open.

"They're coming!" Luis yelled as he rushed headlong into the room. "Two truckloads of soldiers just crossed the bridge and set up roadblocks at the entrance to the *colonia!*"

Amélia immediately took charge, unplugging Jake's laptop and pulling the connector from the DSL modem. "Go now! Luis, show him the way to the tunnel."

"I haven't got all the files downloaded…" Jake protested as she pulled him up out of his chair.

"It doesn't matter, we can't wait. If the soldiers are here in this neighborhood it can only mean that they know where we are. Follow Luis, don't wait for me," she demanded as she thrust the laptop, cables and power module into Jake's hands.

"Let me get the bag for the laptop," Jake said. Then he heard the squeak from the front gate.

"No time. ¡*Vamos!*" She grabbed up the AK-47 and shoved them out of the room.

In the hallway, Jake followed Luis toward the rear of the house. He looked back for Amélia, but she had turned toward the front door. *Crack!* The door was knocked open, splintering the door jamb where it had been locked and dead bolted. As the first soldier rushed into the opening Amélia fired a long burst from the AK-47. The noise was deafening, making Jakes ears ring. The smell of cordite filled the hallway.

"Oh my God!" she said. "Hurry, I'm right behind you!"

Luis led the way out the back door into a small yard, sprouting weeds and surrounded by a high cinder block wall. Jake looked fearfully at the barred iron gate leading to the alleyway behind the house, half expecting to see more soldiers. He noticed Amélia looking that way too, shakily pointing the AK-47 toward the gate, ready to shoot if necessary.

Luis was moving some old wooden boxes that were piled against the wall next to the house. He pulled a large wooden crate aside revealing a small hole in ground, no more than two feet across.

"Get in!" Amélia yelled at Jake, "There's a tunnel at the bottom, just keep going until you get to the end."

Struggling to keep everything in his hands, and trailing cables behind him, Jake lowered himself into the small hole. He was relieved to find that the space below and the tunnel were quite a bit larger than the hole and he could get on his hands and knees.

"Keep moving!" Amélia said, coming down on top of Jake's back. "We need more room."

"I can't see anything!"

"Just crawl forward, I'll get a flashlight in a minute. We have to get away from the entrance"

Jake struggled ahead on one hand as he clutched the laptop, and everything else with the other. He could feel his knees and pants legs getting wet from the muddy floor of the tunnel. It became pitch black. Luis must have pulled the crate back to cover the hole they had just entered. Jake made slow progress and the cables kept getting caught under his knees as they dragged in the mud. He stopped, trying to pull the cables up into his hand, and Amélia bumped him from the rear.

"¡Andale! Go on! We can't stop. They will find the opening soon."

"I can't see!"

"Just keep crawling…follow the dirt wall with your shoulder…no time for the light."

He heard Luis, behind them, whisper, "It's done … go!"

Jake struggled through the pitch black tunnel. The tunnel must have turned, because Jake's head and shoulder rammed roughly into the dirt. He fell on his face causing Amélia to collide with into him from behind, followed by Luis crawling into both of them. As they tried to get untangled there was a deafening boom and they were peppered from behind with flying bits of mud, dirt and rock.

The Honduran Plot

"They found my little surprise," Luis' voice was faint, as though from a distance. "Wait a minute and let me find a light."

Jake could hardly hear him; his ears were ringing and he was coughing from dust that filled the tunnel. A flashlight switched on and Luis pointed it down the tunnel behind them. It looked like the roof had collapsed about six meters back. Were they trapped?

"What was that?" Jake said.

"I had a ready-made booby trap in place so no one could follow us," Luis said. "Cool huh?"

"Cool? How could you do that?" Jake said. These people were crazy. If he got out of this alive, he was through! He would head for home.

Luis said, "Simple, a tin can nailed in the bottom of the crate with a live hand grenade inside. They pull out the crate to find the tunnel, the grenade pops out of the can, and…Boom!"

Jake shook his head. "I didn't mean like, *really how*. I meant … *that might have killed someone*; how could you do that? And Amélia, you shot that soldier!"

"You don't know these people Jake! They kidnap, torture and kill," she said. Her voice was shaky and shrill.

"Yeah, but …"

"We can't let them catch us! This will buy us some time. As long as they don't find out where the tunnel goes, we should be OK. Give the laptop and the other stuff to Luis. He can put it in the backpack. Let me get in front with the light. We have to keep going. They will be looking around the neighborhood to find where we went."

Jake was still dazed by the sudden turn of events. *We can't get caught, so we just kill them? What has she gotten me into?*

Chapter 23

Amélia took the lead, followed by Luis. Jake crawled behind them through the gloom, following the dim wavering light he could just make out beyond the dark silhouettes of the two in front of him. The air was stale and the smell of the wet earth was strong in Jake's nose. He tried not to panic, but he knew there had been rains which persisted for several weeks and had only recently departed. What if they had collapsed the tunnel? Don't think about it—just follow the flickering light, get as much distance as we can from the soldiers. They must be looking for the exit of the tunnel. Where was it? Jake had no idea. *I just need to stop stressing until we get out of this and I can think.*

The tunnel sloped down and Amélia and Luis stopped ahead of him. Peering past them, Jake could see only dirt ahead, feebly lit by the dim light of Amélia's flashlight. It *had* collapsed! Jake could feel the tunnel closing in on him, and breath came in short pants. They were trapped!

Luis took the flashlight from Amélia and handed it back to Jake. "Here hold the light while I help her."

Help her do what? They were trapped! What could Amélia do? Why were they so calm? The pointed the light forward and could see a piece of plywood covering the floor of the tunnel. Luis helped Amélia move the plywood, revealing concrete humping up from the floor of the tunnel. It was some sort of large concrete drain pipe. A rough hole, about two feet in diameter, was broken into the top of the huge pipe. It had been covered by the piece of plywood. Suddenly Jake was glad he had not said anything. Hopefully they had not noticed how panicked he had been.

He could smell stale air coming from the hole in the pipe. *This must lead to outside.* "What's this?" Jake asked.

"It's the way out," Amélia said. "We can go out through the big drain pipe. This is a main storm drain that was built in this part of town during reconstruction after Hurricane Mitch caused such bad flooding in 1998. It empties into the Choluteca River and we can get out where the drain comes out at the riverbank."

"OK, so this is the tunnel exit, or near it," Jake said, "so why won't the soldiers find it?"

"Luis and I have been planning for this event since we started the newsletter three years ago," Amélia replied. "When the protest movement decided to use the old church parsonage as our office, we knew it might be found out. A tunnel seemed the best way to escape."

"Anyway … the soldiers?" Jake said.

Amélia said, "I think the soldiers will look for an exit to the tunnel in nearby houses. They won't find anything there, and will waste more time looking around the neighborhood."

"But if the area is flooded with soldiers, won't they still see us after we do get out?"

"We're not too near the exit, but almost a half kilometer from it. Maybe the soldiers won't look along the river bank."

Jake's eyes widened. *Maybe?* That didn't really sound like a plan.

"We'll rest here a few minutes," Amélia said. "Luis will check to make sure it's safe to go out."

"And if they're out there, we're in for a long stay," Luis said, pulling a small penlight out of his backpack. He rummaged again in the backpack and pulled out something. Jake shined the light on it and could see that it was a small caliber automatic pistol. What good would that do against armed soldiers?

"I'm going now." Luis tucked the pistol into his belt and lowered himself into the narrow hole until only his head and shoulders showed. Then he ducked, and was gone.

"Does Pastor Juan know about this tunnel?" Jake said. How had they done all this without anyone knowing? It didn't seem likely that the pastor would be mixed up in all this.

"No," Amélia said. "The campus student ministry uses the parsonage office. Luis and Juanita run the ministry and Pastor Zamora thinks that's the only thing going on."

"But you aren't in the ministry, or the church," Jake said. "Won't he wonder about you being there sometimes?"

"He might wonder, if he has seen me, but I don't think so. Besides, he knows I'm a friend of Juanita's." She moved around, sitting in the dirt with her legs crossed. "Make yourself comfortable. We'll go when Luis comes back, and tells us it's all clear."

He followed her lead and felt the damp earth through the seat of his pants. Oh sure, real comfortable. "And if it's not clear?"

"Then we'll wait some more here," Amélia said. "They aren't likely to search the storm drain."

They were trapped like rats, and if the soldiers spotted Luis they would know he had come out from the drainpipe. Then it would all be over. They settled down to wait. Amélia turned off the flashlight to conserve the batteries. Jake sat in the dark and marveled at how little control he had over his life.

Chapter 24

Jake sat in the dark, his thoughts racing. *I swore to never come back here, but I came anyway to find Ruben. Now I'm caught up in some sort of armed revolution and still don't know where he is!*

After they waited for what seemed like hours to Jake, Luis popped his head and shoulders up out of the hole, strangely lit by his penlight from below.

"Boo!" he said with a grin on his face. "I think we can go now. It's dark and they don't seem to be searching the riverbank. There is pretty good cover, with brush and weeds near the edge of the bank. I called Rodrigo with my cell phone. He's going to meet us at the soccer field across, from the Baxter Institute. We can go along the river bank, since that's just a little south of here."

Jake turned on his light to see more clearly. Amélia reached into the backpack and pulled out another pistol. How much stuff was in that backpack anyway? She held out an old, worn revolver to Jake.

"Here, take this," she said.

"I don't want that!"

"You need to take it," She said. "There might be trouble when we get to the river … we can't take chances."

"I don't need it! You have the rifle and Luis has the other pistol. That should be enough."

"Don't be stupid!" she scolded. "If the soldiers see us we are going to need as much firepower as we can get. You have fired a pistol before haven't you?"

"Yes, but not at a live person."

"You had better be able to do it, if they're shooting at us," Luis said. "You don't want to be captured and maybe tortured do you?"

"No," Jake mumbled. "I guess not … OK, if I have to. Give it to me." He slipped the stubby revolver into the pocket of his jeans. It was a tight fit, and felt uncomfortable and heavy. He probably wouldn't be able to pull it out in time if they got into trouble.

Jake and Amélia lowered themselves through the hole in the pipe and followed Luis, slowly crawling through the big concrete pipe. The hard concrete with pieces of debris and small pebbles in the bottom was much worse than the soft mud and dirt of the tunnel they had been in. Jake felt sure his pants would be torn and his knees bloodied, but his pride kept him from complaining to Luis and Amélia. Besides, what good would it do? He crawled on, wincing silently. Finally they neared to the end of the storm drain and Jake could smell the fresh air. Luis switched off his penlight.

"Turn off the flashlight, Jake," Amélia said. "Let's make sure no one is out there."

Oh yeah, good idea. Jake switched off the light and waited for his eyes to adjust to the darkness, he could just make out the forms of the others as they inched to the opening of the concrete pipe. He strained to see something beyond, but could see only a few stars in the night sky. Everything else was pitch-dark, no moon in the sky. They waited, listening for any sound of searching soldiers—nothing. A faint feeling of relief loosened some of the tension in Jake's neck and shoulders. Luis switched on his penlight, revealing a concrete channel sloped steeply down the bank.

"We will just slide down the ditch until we get to the river," Luis whispered. "Keep your light off … we don't want to attract anyone's attention." He switched his light off.

They slid awkwardly down the concrete channel in the darkness. Jake felt the welcome relief of the slight breeze that stirred along the riverbank. By the time they reached the water's edge several meters below where the drain had come out of the riverbank, Jake could begin to make out forms in the faint light of the city scattered by the haze in the sky.

Jake followed Luis and Amélia as they groped their way through the brush along water. To his relief, other than a dog barking in the distance, all was quiet on the bank above them. *Thank God, no soldiers.* Moving south, they passed under a bridge and continued to make their way along the riverbank. Luis led them up the sloped bank through small trees and brush to the soccer field. Jake couldn't see any signs of soldiers or anyone else, including any car to pick them up. *Now what?*

They sat down in the grass and weeds alongside the road and waited, hidden by some bushes. His pants still felt wet and Jake wiggled on the grass trying vainly to dry the seat of his pants. It wasn't that cold but Jake shivered, his mood becoming as dark as the sky above. He had given up so much to come here, and now it was wasted. Would Barbara say, "I told you so?" She had been angry and hurt that he gave up his chance with Intellibotics. Actually, she had termed it "our chance." She had been right—this was foolish.

It was probably another fifteen minutes before headlights appeared at the far end of the road. The vehicle approached, the glare of the lights coming through the branches of the bush, blinding him.

"What if it's the soldiers?" Jake whispered.

"Shh!" Amélia hissed. "They can't see us … just wait."

They remained in between the bushes until the car pulled into a drive across the road and stopped at the closed gate. The headlights switched off, and all was quiet.

"It's Rodrigo," Amélia said, standing up. "Come on."

They trotted across the road to the car and Amélia approached the driver's side window. It rolled down and Amélia asked, "What took so long?"

"Just get in," the darkened figure in the car said. "Luis told me what happened. We have to get out of here—*¡pronto!*"

Surprisingly, Amélia didn't say anything but just got into the back seat and slid to the middle. Jake crawled in behind her, while Luis went around to the other side. The car's dome light illuminated the scene before the doors shut so Jake could see that there was a petite girl in the passenger seat. She stared at him with her mouth partially open. What was so interesting—hadn't she seen an American before?

Rodrigo turned around and said, "I had to pick up Maria before coming out here. What would I say I was doing if I had been stopped coming out to a deserted area like this? This way I could say we were going out parking." Maria giggled as Rodrigo added, "It's not like we haven't done that before."

"OK," Luis said, "we should get going now. The parking story won't work now with the three of us here and, carrying guns."

"Right," Rodrigo said. "Where to?" He started the car, but left it sitting with the headlights still off.

"I didn't think so before," Luis said, "but I think we need to get out of Tegucigalpa."

"I was right the first time," Amélia said. "We should go to Talanga, to Yolanda's."

"OK, but we'll have to take Maria home first," Rodrigo said.

"Talanga? Where is that?" Jake wanted to know. He wanted to get away from these people, to go home and to never come back.

Amélia said, "It's north of Tegucigalpa. My aunt Yolanda has a farm in the country between Talanga and the *Rio Dulce*. Since her husband died, Aunt Yolanda lives there by herself and runs the farm.

"Just drop me off at Pastor Juan's," Jake said. "He'll let me stay until I can get a plane back to the states." He hoped that was true. Pastor Juan wouldn't turn him away, would he? Maybe he could get a flight out tomorrow.

The girl in front said something in a low voice that Jake couldn't understand. "What?" Jake said.

Rodrigo said, "She is worried we'll get caught with you in the car if we try to take you to the pastor's house. Also, they will have your passport flagged at the airport. How can you fly out?"

"Me?" Jake said. "They're not after me!" In the darkened vehicle he could still make out everyone staring at him. What were they thinking? This was all because of Amélia and Luis and their guns.

Amélia said, "Jake, they are after you. Do you think it is a coincidence that after you hacked into the computers, the army just happened to show up?"

"You guys are the revolutionaries running around with guns! They don't even know who I am. Just a tourist for all anyone knows." She couldn't be right. Jake didn't even want to think about that.

Luis said, "No one knew we were there, Jake. You didn't tell anyone, did you?"

"No, but …"

"Listen Jake," Amélia said. "You told me that you and Raul have been trying to get into the government computers. Maybe they picked up on it and somehow traced it."

Well, duh! That was way too logical for Jake to argue. He mentally kicked himself—because he was emulating the Salas computer, he hadn't routed his probes through anonymous routers, but it wasn't really an oversight. He had to get into the site with a normal log-on to get to the layer that would allow him to launch the attack without being locked out.

Luis said, "So man, how long do you think it will take them to find out who was staying at the parsonage. They probably have police over at the Zamora's right now."

"Uh … yeah, maybe you're right." Realization chilled him like Freon circulating in his veins. He shivered, crossed his arms and avoided looking at the girl in the front seat still turned back looking at him. Even in the dimness he could glimpse her wide eyed look of fear. He had become a fugitive.

Rodrigo drove slowly up the deserted street keeping the headlights off for the moment. The road was in darkness but there were street lights a few blocks ahead. As they neared the lit area, an army jeep pulled into the middle of the intersection and stopped. Rodrigo pulled to the weeds at the edge of the road and stopped the car. They watched as two soldiers got out of the jeep and began setting out wooden barriers in the intersection.

"What should we do now?" Rodrigo wondered aloud.

Chapter 25

Manuel Fuentes stepped out of the large black Cadillac Escalade in the parking area across the street from *Iglesia de las Flores*. He ignored his driver who had opened his door of the SUV. There were several army vehicles scattered haphazardly and an ambulance was pulling slowly away. *Not hurrying ...must be fatalities ... what a screwed up mess.* Dark thoughts played through Fuentes mind as he walked down the street and approached the faded blue house across the street from the church, its front gate ajar.

Shattered glass, splinters of wood and blood at the front entrance testified to what had taken place there. Captain Fredrik Jimenez stood smoking, leaning against a porch rail. Jimenez stood up and flicked the cigarette into the yard when he saw Fuentes approaching.

"Captain," Fuentes spoke in a low voice, "has army intelligence screwed up again?"

"No sir ..." Jimenez stammered, "well ... we haven't gotten them yet, but we think they are still underground and we have troops searching for them."

"Underground? Where are they?"

"In a tunnel under the back yard ... they collapsed the entrance with an explosion, but their exit can't be too far away. We have been searching the surrounding properties."

Fuentes looked around and said, "It doesn't look like your plan to surprise them worked too well. I take it you took casualties?"

"Yes sir, one dead and one badly wounded. They were able to get to the tunnel because the soldiers at the rear of the house were late in entering. They managed to shoot the front entry team as they hit the door ... must have had some warning."

Fuentes shook his head. "It would appear so."

Jimenez continued, "Another soldier was killed when he found the tunnel in the back yard. They had booby trapped a wooden packing crate covering the entrance."

"How many were there?"

"I'm not sure … at least two or three. They were young, so it wasn't the pastor of the church. He and his wife don't live here anymore. We think they were students from the university."

"Do you have the pastor or his wife in custody? They should be able to tell us who might be in the tunnel."

"No sir; they weren't at the church or at their house in *Alemán*. We have an alert out for them now. I also set up checkpoints at all streets out of the neighborhood so anyone else coming or going will be questioned."

"Find them! And get the ones in the tunnel out. I want them alive too. No more excuses Captain," Fuentes said. "I will have the whole squad here court marshaled for incompetence if that's what it takes to get some results. Your performance here is inexcusable!"

"Yes sir!" Jimenez gulped.

Fuentes stalked back to the Escalade. Incompetence in the intelligence and security functions was becoming worse each day. He would have to institute a major housecleaning—starting with Captain Jimenez!

A weakling like Captain Jimenez would not have lasted a week in B-316. Jimenez had let a group of students and capitalist sympathizers disrupt his plans, forcing him to use Hector Arroyo to clean up the mess. That just created another mess. Now it appeared that they had penetrated the S&I computer network! He wondered if they had found anything that could expose his operations. He shot a glare at his driver who held the door of the vehicle open, got into the Escalade, and sat staring ahead as the door shut and the driver got behind the wheel.

"Get Major Gonzales on the phone," he barked at his driver. He would have Jimenez demoted and sent for training with one of the more brutal and tough police units. Jimenez would either shape up or it would kill him, Fuentes really didn't care which.

After speaking to Gonzales, and directing his driver to return to S&I headquarters, Fuentes sat back and began planning his next moves—a series of manipulations and deceptions. Since being promoted to Director of S & I, Fuentes had kept a low profile, preferring to remain behind the scenes. He was proud of himself—if only people knew what he had been able to accomplish, they would view him with much more respect. *Maybe someday he should write a book.*

Back in the late 1970s he could have never imagined how far he would rise. In those days he had been a sergeant in Battalion 316, the brutal Honduran intelligence unit, which suppressed any opposition to Honduras' military government.

In the early 1980s right-wing Argentine intelligence units and the United States' CIA began training Nicaraguan freedom fighters, known as "contras" in the Honduran jungles. In neighboring Nicaragua leftist Sandinista guerrillas, supported by Cuba, had defeated the Somoza government in 1979. The United States was determined to halt the spread of communism in Central America. In establishing the contra operation, the CIA collaborated with Argentine instructors who were well versed in torture, kidnapping, and assassination to repress political opposition. They taught the contras, and the Honduran army, these methods. Soon the Honduran police and military used such ways to suppress domestic guerrillas and their sympathizers.

Fuentes became lost in his thoughts back to those days, when he had risen to be a senior non-commissioned officer in Battalion 316. He had been trained by the Argentineans in interrogation techniques, and by the Americans in leadership and war fighting at the School of the Americas in Ft. Benning, Georgia. He would have to give them an acknowledgement in the preface to the autobiography he was imagining. *Maybe someday he really would write it. Wouldn't the world be surprised!*

That had been a heady time. He had the power of life and death over the prisoners he interrogated, and the power was like a drug. He remembered the sexual thrill he felt when he subjected prisoners to brutal interrogation. For female prisoners rape and torture were commonly used techniques. They were never held accountable; the prisoners just disappeared.

The black SUV circled a traffic circle. In the pitch dark night Fuentes could not even see the statue of the Honduran soldier that he knew was on a pedestal in the center of the roundabout. *The night is as black as my heart.* He grinned in the darkness.

In a short time they approached the *Universidad de Defensa de Honduras (UDH),* the University of Defense for the Armed Forces. The S&I headquarters occupied a large building on the campus of UDH in the town of Mateo on the outskirts of Tegucigalpa. The shadowy, illusive organization officially fell under the auspices of UDH. Although it was responsible for teaching techniques for security, communications, cryptology and other related subjects for the military and federal police, in reality it was much more. It could be compared to a Honduran CIA, and had links to the intelligence organizations in all parts of the armed forces and also the federal police. It had an operative arm of its own, known only by rumors as the secret police.

Even Enrique Salas, who as Director of Intelligence for the president, a civilian cabinet position, did not know the full extent of the secretive organization. He had mentored Fuentes in his rise to power, but was unaware that hidden within the organization was a core group which answered only to Fuentes. This group had extended its influence into the military, the civil police forces, and organized crime. They carried out secret and deadly reprisals on anyone Fuentes thought was a threat, always blaming the actions on others.

After Battalion 316 had been made public and disbanded Fuentes had not been able to act on his evil instincts for many years. But after his appointment by Salas, that incompetent weakling, he had risen to power to the point that, once more, he had no real restraints. Fuentes ruled the S&I Directorate and his secret power base with an iron hand and none of his subordinates dared to question him. Indeed, a number of his officers and NCOs seemed to be following in his footsteps in terms of ruthlessness. His superior, Salas, really didn't know what was happening and tended not to question his techniques as long as he got results. Fuentes was amazed at how easily he and General Velasquez could manipulate the weak-willed man.

Chapter 26

Jake looked at the soldiers in the intersection, manning the checkpoint formed by the jeep and the wooden barriers. One of them had an automatic rifle that looked like an AK-47, or maybe it was an M-15—Jake couldn't tell. He kept watch while the other one approached the vehicles. Already, they had stopped and checked a few cars on the cross street.

"I don't think they have noticed us yet," Jake said.

Rodrigo said, "Glad I left the lights off. Even if they look this way, we will just look like a parked car."

"They must be blocking the roads out of the neighborhood," Amélia said. "The only way out of here is through that intersection. We're blocked on both sides by the river and Baxter Institute."

Luis said, "Rodrigo, you got to get by them, man. You can turn right, go past *Boulevar Kuwait*, then go through *La Peña* and *La Cañada* to get to the *Anillo Periférico*."

"If we don't stop, they may shoot at us!"

Amélia said, "Rodrigo, keep the lights off and go right at them. When they look our way, and then turn the lights on … high beams."

Rodrigo turned toward the back. "You think that will work?"

"It has to … what other choice do we have?" Amélia said. "We can't stay here or go on foot."

That's exactly what Jake wanted to do. He could just get out of the car and wander through the properties until he came to a road away from where the police were. Then he would call Raul. He could help. Wait, why not call Raul now?

"Let me call Raul," Jake said. "He can help, or at least maybe his dad can."

"Are you nuts?" Amélia said. "His dad is probably the one who put these guys on to us."

"Yeah man, don't want to do that," Luis said.

Were they right? Jake didn't think so, but he was pretty rattled and really didn't feel confident in arguing the point.

"Jake, give me the pistol!"

He silently squirmed in the seat and dug the revolver out of his jeans. He was glad to get rid of it. There was no way he was going to shoot anybody. He had just taken it to avoid arguing with her.

"You and Luis get down," Amélia said.

She didn't need to say anything to Maria, who by this time, was in the floorboard of the front seat wimpering. Jake looked past Amélia to Luis who had pulled his pistol out. If Luis wasn't getting down then Jake wasn't going to do it either. He wasn't going to show them how afraid he was—besides, he wanted to see what was going on.

As Rodrigo accelerated the car Amélia reached over Jake and lowered the window. She cocked the revolver and pointed it forward. He could smell her Jasmine perfume as she leaned in front of him in the dark. The automobile rushed toward the intersection.

Apparently hearing the noise, the soldiers turned and stared at the darkened car charging toward them. Just as they started bringing their rifles up Rodrigo turned on the headlights, blinding them, and then swerved to the right. Amélia let loose with several shots from the pistol that went wide, but added to the confusion. The sound of the shots was deafening, the flash of exploded gunpowder blinding, and Jake eyes were stung by gunshot residue blasting out from the gap around the cylinder of the revolver going off just a foot from his face.

He instinctively threw himself sideways against Amélia, knocking her into the floor. A second later, safety glass rained over them as a bullet shattered Rodrigo's window just behind his head. He instinctively ducked and car careened wildly through the intersection, missing the right turn and bouncing over the curb on the other side of the road, barely missing a large tree. They screeched through a parking lot and back out on the road heading away from the jeep in the middle of the intersection. The soldiers quickly recovered and fired at the car as it sped away, two bullets thudding into the trunk.

"I think I'm deaf!" Rodrigo shouted as they roared away from the intersection. "You fired that thing right behind me."

"Just be glad it made you jerk forward," Amélia shouted. "Look at that hole in your window ... you could have been killed! Keep going before they get a chase organized. We need to get some distance so they don't know which way we went."

They made their way through several side streets and dropped Maria off at her house in a nearby neighborhood. Continuing through the neighborhoods they made their way down a cobblestone street that connected to the *Anillo Periférico*, or ring road, that went around the city.

"I'm going to stop at that Dippsa gas station," Rodrigo said. "We don't have much gas, and we need something to cover the damage to the car."

Rodrigo bought a roll of duct tape to cover the bullet holes in the trunk. Jake was shocked to find a hole in the seatback just above where he had thrown himself down on. He felt a rush of adrenalin and his legs felt shaky. Amélia *had been sitting there. She might have been killed!*

"Good thing the car is gray," Rodrigo said. "The duct tape hardly shows, and with the rest of the glass removed it just looks like I have the driver's side window down. We should be OK at any police checkpoints."

Amélia said, "They may be alerted. Let's try to avoid them if possible. Instead of going by the airport and the Olancho highway where they are more likely, we can go by way of Valley of Angels. There is a road from there that goes to Talanga. I think there is less chance of checkpoints there."

But when they got to Valley of Angels there was a police checkpoint. Jake was sitting in the front seat with Rodrigo, and could see it was just some policemen standing in the road stopping cars. A pickup truck with police markings was in the grass along the roadside. He watched apprehensively as the car slowed and approached the spot where the officers were talking to the driver ahead of them.

"What do we do?" Jake said. He had visions of them running the checkpoint or, even worse, Amélia shooting the cops. Again he wished he had never come back to Honduras.

"Just sit there," Amélia said. "Don't say anything."

Three officers manned the National Police checkpoint, and one approached the car. His machine gun hung by a strap over his shoulder. Jake was greatly surprised when the officer smiled and shook hands with Rodrigo. What kind of police stop was that?

Rodrigo showed him his license and a registration card that he pulled from a strap on the visor above the windshield. The officer examined the papers under the light of a flashlight and then handed them back.

"Where are you going?" he asked.

Rodrigo pointed with his thumb to Jake sitting in the passenger. "The gringo," he said, "we are taking him back to his hotel, the *Posada del Angel.*"

The officer bent down and shined the flashlight across the front seat, directly into Jake's eyes. Then he shined the light into the back seat, looking intently to see Amélia and Luis. Jake looked back and was again surprised. They were sitting close together and holding hands like two lovebirds. All very innocent looking.

"Very good, have a nice evening," the officer said, then waved them on.

It was only as they rolled away that Jake realized he had been holding his breath the whole time. They traveled on narrow, dark, curvy roads through the mountains. As they wound through the mountains, with nothing to see but trees or brush on either side lit by the peripheral light from the headlamps, Jake could feel his eyelids drooping. Periodic jolts from the many ruts and potholes would cause his eyes to open momentarily, but soon even those faded into nothingness.

In his dream a soldier grabbed his shoulder and was shaking it. Why? A real soldier would have shot him—it didn't make sense. Then the soldier said, "Jake we're here, man. Wake up."

Jake opened his eyes. There wasn't any soldier—only Luis shaking him out of his dream. Where were they? It was pitch black, and Jake couldn't see anything beyond the glow of the car's dome light.

Chapter 27

Fuentes sat in his office at S&I Headquarters, nursing a glass of Kentucky Bourbon. He swirled the amber liquid in the glass. *Why did the gringos he had met always think he drank tequila? That was for Mexicans.* He downed the drink, feeling the warmth of the liquid course down his throat. He immediately poured another two shots into the glass, and opened a jar on his desk with salted mixed nuts. He popped a few in his mouth and relished the crunchy texture and salty, nutty taste.

He should have never told Mauricio to call Jimenez. The man had no finesse when it came to executing an operation. The strike team should have surrounded the building, ascertained how many people were inside and made simultaneous intrusion through the front and rear gates. Then they would have had them!

Maybe the next time he should have Hector Arroyo respond. He could infiltrate quietly and assassinate these people one by one. No, they had lots of firepower. He needed the strike team with an efficient, aggressive leader. The second in command, Lieutenant Garcia, had performed well in field exercises. Fuentes often thought that Jimenez was holding him back, probably afraid the lieutenant would show him up. He would have Major Gonzales make Garcia the interim team leader until he could be promoted to captain and be given official command of the team.

With that decision made, Fuentes wondered if he should see what Greta was doing tonight. The whiskey was kicking in and, just as it made him want something crunchy to snack, the liquor brought out other more basic urges. He could visualize the voluptuous receptionist, his current mistress, and imagined what he could do with her. No, he needed something more to calm the demons that drove him. He knew what he wanted, and that wasn't the kind of thing Greta could fulfill. *Even in fantasy role playing Greta was much too willing.*

Turning to his computer, he paged through the S&I website, entering several passwords until he could access the restricted files which were kept on special political detainees. He found the one which interested him: *Juanita Perez, known also as "Princess Maya" on a subversive internet blog, age 20, single, a student at the University, detained along with a suspected U.S. operative on 05 October 2012.*

Fuentes remembered the woman well. She was petite and attractive. The photo in the file didn't do her justice, but had been scared and shaking. He had treated her well during the interrogation, thinking that there would be time for harsher measures later. Maybe now was that time, although he had no interest in obtaining any answers from her tonight. He descended to the basement level which had the holding cells for prisoners.

He ignored the nervous corporal guarding the cellblock, who leapt to attention as he approached, and went to the prison office. Exiting the office with a set of keys in his hand Fuentes said, "Corporal Delgado, I am going to interrogate a prisoner. I don't want to be disturbed."

"Yes sir!" the guard replied, still at attention, appearing apprehensive.

Fuentes went into cellblock three, a restricted cellblock with limited access, closing the soundproof door behind him. He inserted a key into the door of cell 303 and flung the door open. The woman was startled, and backed against the wall of the windowless cell as he closed the door behind him. He stood motionless for a moment, his eyes moving up and down her body as she gathered the top of the flimsy gray prison dress with one hand. He had remembered her correctly, she was the one he had interrogated about the American boy, and yes, she was quite pretty, even in prison garb.

"Get undressed!" he demanded in a voice made hoarse by his growing desire.

She just looked at him, a shocked and fearful expression her face. Fuentes smiled. He loved the feeling of power and control, and the rush of adrenalin brought on by imagining the thoughts running through the minds of his powerless victims.

When he repeated himself in a louder voice and she still didn't respond, Fuentes backhanded her, knocking her to the floor. He reached down, pulling her to her feet and grabbed her throat in one large hand. As he choked her, bringing tears to her eyes and making it hard for her to breathe, he spoke again, "I said get undressed!"

Fuentes lost all sense of time, as if he were in some sort of a trance, venting his frustrations, rage, and cruelty on the woman. After he was through with her, Fuentes got up and dressed without saying a word and left the cell. When he exited the cell block, and the corporal again leapt to attention, Fuentes put him at ease and handed him the keys.

"Prisoner Perez has admitted to crimes against the state," Fuentes told the guard. "Keep her confined to her cell until I decide on her disposition. Oh … get her cleaned up and tomorrow get the doctor to check on her. She might need some medical attention."

Chapter 28

A shaft of sunlight shining in his face woke Jake, as he lay on top of the covers of a small bed. *Where was he? Oh yes, Talanga ...or close to it ... the farmhouse.* Jake struggled to remember the details of the events from the night before. *What was her aunt's name?*

He looked around the small bedroom, noting the plain, but serviceable, furniture and the no-frills curtains framing a surprisingly clean window, partially open. The air wafting through the gap smelled faintly of wood smoke. The view was of some sort of field, distant hills, blue sky and blazing morning sun. Jake sat on the edge of the bed until he was fully awake.

He was still no closer to finding Ruben. Maybe coming down here wasn't such a hot idea. Now this craziness—how would he explain this to his folks, or Barbara? He had better make some calls. Well, not right away. It would be better to find out what was going to happen and decide how to explain his predicament.

Until now he had thought that Amélia and Luis were exaggerating the sinister nature of Honduran politics. He even was skeptical after seeing that newspaper story naming Amélia as a killer, mixed up in drugs and gangs. Maybe it had all been some sort of mistake. But there is something real about their claims of a serious threat from someone within the government. The reaction to his penetration into the government files had been extreme, certainly not anything he and Raul would have expected. However, Luis and Amélia hadn't seemed surprised. They had been prepared with firearms, the tunnel and escape route.

He had been sucked into this quagmire one naive step at a time, and there didn't seem to be a way to backtrack. Amélia and Luis were probably right—it was the computer hacking that brought out those soldiers. They probably had no idea that Amélia was there, but must have figured it out by now. Amélia and Luis had both left stuff at the parsonage, everything except the backpack and AK-47. Oh yeah, all his stuff, passport, clothes and camera, would have been found too. So he was linked to a wanted fugitive—they probably thought he was part of their little revolutionary band, or whatever it was.

So, where did that leave him? He had no passport and was probably wanted by the police and soldiers, who would shoot first and ask questions later. *Great! I'll just call Mom and Dad, oh, and Barbara, with the good news.*

Jake hadn't prayed much lately. In fact, even while making the decision to come back to Honduras, he had never even prayed about it. Disillusionment, doubt, and discouragement had weakened his faith. Is that what was giving him this feeling of helplessness? But, even though his faith was weakened, maybe it was still there. Maybe it was time to once again put his trust in God. As he bowed his head, Jake prayed: *"Father, God, I know that I haven't prayed to you in a long time ... please forgive me. Lord I don't know what to do ... please let your Holy Spirit guide me. I never even prayed before deciding to come back down here, but I wonder if maybe you are the one who nudged me into returning here. I hope so. Please help me find Ruben and Juanita ...and watch over them, wherever they are. Amélia and Luis are against something evil ... but how can they resist it without fighting and killing, creating more misery and evil. Help me decide what my part is in this ... should I help? Is that your will? Amen."*

Chapter 29

Jake found the others in a small kitchen, seated around a worn, wooden table. Their conversation, in Spanish, stopped when he walked in.

Amélia's aunt stood and broke the silence. "Excuse us, Jake. We were just discussing the situation you are all in. There is some breakfast left. Sit down and I'll get you some. Do you want some coffee too?"

"Uh ... yes, please, that would be great," Jake said. "I guess I slept late ..."

He sat down in the chair the woman had vacated, grateful for her effortless transition to English. Jake leaned over and whispered to Amélia, "I can't remember her name ... what is it?"

"Yolanda Soto ... just call her Yolanda," Amélia whispered back.

"Here you are," Yolanda said, placing a plate of potatoes with scrambled eggs, and a cup of dark black coffee, on the table.

Jake jumped up. "I'm sorry ... I took your chair ..."

"Sit, sit ... I'll just stand here behind Amélia. You sit and eat"

The aroma of the potatoes, evidently grilled with some onions and green peppers, made Jake realize how hungry he was. He took a bite and savored the taste, then tried the eggs. *Wonderful!*

Luis said, "We've been talking about what to do. Amélia and Rodrigo think we need to stay here for a while. But, I'm thinking we need to do something and there is not much we can do hiding out here."

"Everything happened so fast last night," Jake said. "I had just gotten into the secure area when you came in yelling about the soldiers."

"I was surprised when suddenly army trucks stopped and they started setting up roadblocks," Luis said. "But then a squad of soldiers came double-time down the street toward the parsonage. That's when I ran to warn you. They were right behind me, like they knew exactly which house you were in."

"Maybe they were just following you," Rodrigo said.

"No, I don't think they had even seen me at first. I was sort of behind the fence at the church, and the bougainvillea along the fence were shielding me. Then I ran across the street and through the parsonage gate, when I looked back the soldiers were at the corner and headed right toward me. They knew where they were going!

Amélia frowned and spoke quietly, "No one knew we were there. Like I said last night, it had to be the computer thing."

Jake took a sip of coffee and grimaced—pretty strong stuff. "Uh … is there …"

"Here, Jake, put some milk in it," Amélia said, smiling, as she pushed a small pottery picture across the table.

"Thanks. I've been thinking about that, and I think you're right. They somehow traced the location of my laptop, but still, it was so fast … like they were just waiting for me."

"Maybe they were," Amélia said. She frowned, a look of concentration on her face.

"What do you mean?" Jake said.

"I'm thinking that no one knew Luis and I were there, and you had just hacked into the computers, so it's like they were just waiting for you."

"OK, but so what?"

There was only one other person who knew what you were doing, and where you were," Amélia said, arching her eyebrows."

Jake couldn't believe what she was suggesting. "You mean Raul?"

She just looked at him and shrugged.

"He wouldn't say anything about what I was doing!" Jake said.

"I don't trust him."

"You don't trust anybody!" Jake said. She could be so exasperating!

"Calm down you two," Luis said. "We went over this before. Raul told Jake he's not sure he can trust his father anymore. He's pretty sure some element of the secret police is trying to gain control of the government. Besides, it was his idea to get Jake to come down here to help hack into their computers."

Amélia said, "This whole computer thing might have been a ruse to penetrate our group. They're pretty desperate, killing José …" Tears came to her eyes. "… and framing me…"

"Raul wasn't the one behind all that," Luis said.

She wiped the tears away. "I know, but his dad is the Minister of Intelligence. These 'secret police' and army goons probably report to him. Maybe he pressured Raul to get Jake to come down here. He might have thought Jake would lead him to our group."

"Why would they think I would know who your group was?" Jake said. He was trying to follow her logic, but it didn't make much sense. "I don't know what's going on in Honduras. I didn't have a clue about your group until you two came barging in on me at the parsonage."

Amélia said, "Ruben, that's why. He's your best friend and he's right in the middle of it all."

"Ruben?" Jake said. "So, just because I want to find him, they would think I can lead them to your little band of revolutionaries?"

"We're not revolutionaries!"

"I know … sorry. But you know what I mean."

Look at it from their viewpoint, Jake," Amélia said. "They don't know that is all you were trying to do. Maybe they think Ruben came here to help us and, when he went missing, you would come down and contact us or even take his place."

"I don't care what they thought. Raul wouldn't have any part of that. I think he would have warned me or something."

"I agree with Jake," Luis said. "Raul is a devout Christian and does a lot of good, man. He wouldn't be used by his father."

"I hope you're right," Amélia said. "Well, in any case we will have to hide out until we can find a way to get out of this mess."

Jake said, "What about Pastor Juan and Teresa? The secret police, or whoever they are, have a link between your protest movement and the parsonage. They might even think the Zamoras are part of it."

Luis said, "I called Pastor Juan last night and told him about the raid. I had to tell him that Juanita and I had turned the student ministry office into our movement headquarters."

"What did he say? Did he know I was there when it happened?" Jake asked.

"Yeah man, he knows you and Amélia were there. He was pretty upset. He didn't imagine how involved Juanita and I had become, much less that we were using the parsonage for it. He was shocked to hear that the army had raided it. I told him we escaped, but didn't give him any details of the shooting, or the tunnel. I feel really bad about keeping everything from him, but it's better he doesn't know right now."

"What is he going to do?" Amélia asked.

Luis said, "I don't know. I warned him that it wasn't safe to return, but he insisted that he could convince the authorities he wasn't involved, especially since they were out of town at the time."

"Well, he wasn't involved. But I don't think the police or army will buy that," Jake said. Since Jake had actually been there, he was sure that they thought he was their enemy. Pastor Juan had let him and Ruben stay there—they would suspect him too.

"I know man, but he insisted that the worst that would happen is that they would be questioned for a while, then let go. I told him, 'man, you don't know how these people work,' but he doesn't understand how really evil they are."

"Where are they?" Jake asked. "Why can't they just stay put?"

"They are in Los Gatos visiting with Pastor Lacas, but he is worried that if they don't go back it will look more suspicious."

They sat in silence for a while trying to think of what to do. Yolanda finally spoke up.

"I'm sure that the pastor and his wife are good people. We should say a prayer for God to protect them."

"Oh sure! Pray!" Amélia exclaimed. "Like that will do a lot of good. Look where it's gotten the people of Honduras so far."

"Amélia! You shouldn't say things like that. I know your mother has taught you better," Yolanda said. "We have to believe God is good, and he makes things work for the best of those who trust him.

"Aunt Yolanda, I just have trouble believing that. Look at the evil and injustice in this place. Look at the poverty everywhere. I think people pray for God to fix things out of desperation."

Jake could understand her point. He had struggled with the same issues after his mission trip three years before. It had opened his eyes to the condition of much of the world. Before that he had a comfortable, secure life. It had been easy to assume God was in control and gave blessings to those that believed in him. But that assumption had been shattered by the reality he saw on that trip.

Jake was glad to be home with familiar surroundings and activities after the trip. He won a scholarship from Intelibotics Corporation to Texas A&M University and enrolled as a freshman in electrical engineering. His life was back on track. The discouragement and anxiety that he had experienced in Honduras were fading memories—most of the time. Then one Sunday morning he went to a small church near the campus.

▪▪▪

The minister, as part of the sermon, read from the book of Matthew, Chapter 6, verse 26, saying:

"Look at the birds of the air; they do not sow or reap or store away in barns, and yet your heavenly Father feeds them. Are you not much more valuable than they?"

Jake felt tears well up in his eyes. A vision of children picking through the trash at the garbage dump of Tegucigalpa flashed in his mind—emerging from his memory, almost as real as the day he had witnessed it. Anger welled up inside and he wanted to stand up and shout at the preacher, "Aren't the little children in the dump more valuable than birds, but how is God taking care of *them*?" After that, Jake only attended church one more time during his freshman year, and he knew his faith had been shaken.

▪▪▪

The memory of that morning lingered. *That was the last time I sincerely prayed, until this morning.* Was Amélia right? Was he just praying out of desperation?

His musing was interrupted by Amélia. She said, "We need to do something about this besides pray. I'll call Pastor Lacas. Maybe he will be able to convince them to stay a while longer. They can work up a good story … something convincing."

"They can tell the truth, man," Luis said. "They didn't know about anything we were doing there."

Yolanda had walked around behind Amélia's chair. Amélia turned in her chair and looked up, a defiant glare in her eyes. Yolanda knelt down so her face was even with Amélia's.

"You know I love you," Yolanda said softly. "You are my sister's only child and I loved you from the day you were born.

Amélia's expression softened. "I know Aunt Yolanda, and I love you too. I meant no disrespect. I just don't believe the way you and Mama do. Please don't be mad at me."

"I am not mad at you. That is why I told you I love you … so you would know I will try to never get mad, or lose my patience …because I just want what is the very best for you.

Now there were tears in Amélia's eyes. "Thank you. I know you do."

Yolanda gently put her hand on Amélia's arm. "What I want you to understand something. No matter what you do, God loves you as much, maybe even more, as I do. He wants what is best for you, and that is for you to believe in him and trust him."

Jake was moved by Yolanda's words as he watched the two women. Could he be assured that God loved him, and wanted the best for him, with all that was happening?

Luis said, "Yolanda is right, girl. But let me add something. We can pray for God to help us. But that doesn't mean we sit back and do nothing, waiting on some miracle. God works through people. He expects us to use our brains and energy to do the right thing."

Amélia's mood brightened. She said, "Thank you, Luis. Alright, let's do something. As I said, I'll call Pastor Lacas and see if he can get Pastor Juan to stay over until we find out just what the situation is back in Tegucigalpa."

"How can we find out?" Rodrigo said.

Jake said, "I'll call Raul. Maybe he can find out through his father without arousing any suspicion. He needs to know what's happened anyway."

"Don't tell him where we are!" Amélia warned.

Luis shot her a glare. "Don't start that again!"

She countered, "It's safer. He doesn't have any need to know anyway."

Jake held up his hand. "OK! OK, you two, cut it out. I won't tell him where we are. But I need to tell him everything that happened, since he was helping me. He can also put a good word in with his father for Pastor Juan and Teresa since he has worked with them for years.

"That sounds like a plan, man," Luis said. "You can use one of the burner phones."

Raul didn't answer; instead a Spanish voice-mail message said something and a tone beeped. Jake hesitated a moment before realizing he should leave a message, then said, "Raul … uh, there's a problem … call me back."

Chapter 30

Jake spent the rest of the morning trying to make some sense of the files he had downloaded before being so rudely interrupted. Most were in Spanish and he was having difficulty understanding all of the text. What little he could decipher told him that they appeared to be intelligence assessments, orders for operations, or administrative documents. They didn't seem to be of much use in finding Ruben. Maybe Luis could go through them later to see if he were missing anything. The few documents he found in English seemed to be business correspondence or technical documents—totally useless.

Yolanda interrupted him. "Jake, it looks like you all will have to stay here for a while. We are going into Talanga to get some clothes and anything else any of you need."

That was welcome news. Jake's clothes were dirty and smelly. He had showered in the small shower stall of the farmhouse, but then had to put his dirty clothes on again. He guessed that Amélia and Luis had done the same thing. Only Rodrigo still had clean clothes, but he didn't have any extras.

The town of Talanga was larger than Jake had expected. Yolanda parked her old station wagon in front of a small food market. Next door was a meat market and Jake walked over to the open front window above a tile counter top. Large pieces of meat and a rolled chain of some sort of sausages hung from hooks above the tile surface. The proprietor waved a few flies away from the meat, smiled, and said something in Spanish. Jake interpreted it as asking if he wanted to buy some meat. He shook his head, no, and retreated back to the others standing by the station wagon.

Yolanda said, "Luis, you come with me to get some groceries. Rodrigo can buy some clothes for both of you, since you are about the same size."

"I can buy my own clothes," Luis replied, indignantly.

111

"Oh?" she said, "How much cash do you have? Besides, I don't want all of you in there buying clothes at once. It might attract too much attention."

"I have a credit card," Luis said. "It has enough limit to let me buy a few clothes."

"I'm not sure there are any stores here that will take credit cards. Besides, you had better not use one," Yolanda told him. "If they know who they are looking for they will monitor your card transactions. The same goes for you, Jake. I think you all had better use cash."

"Not a problem," Jake said. He had gotten plenty of cash before leaving the airport.

Yolanda pawed through her purse and pulled out a small wallet. "Rodrigo and I have enough for groceries and clothes for him and Luis. Amélia, do you have enough?"

She dug into the pocket of her jeans and pulled out a few bills. "I'm a little short Aunt Yolanda."

"Oh dear, we may have a problem getting everything," Yolanda said.

Everyone looked to Jake. He imagined that he could read their thoughts. *The rich Americano has plenty of money.* A guilty thought prodded him—he probably had more cash on him than the others combined.

"I can help," Jake said. He pulled out his billfold and handed some bills to Luis. "Here. Can you buy me some deodorant, razor blades and shaving cream while you are in the store? I'll pay for the clothes for Amélia too."

"Thank you Jake," Amélia said in a sweet voice. He looked at her sharply, trying to detect any trace of sarcasm.

Jake and Amélia found a store that sold clothes, and entered together. Rodrigo waited a few minutes before entering, and then ignored them. Jake imagined they looked innocent enough to not cause anyone to take particular notice of them. They were just two friends shopping, acting normal—nothing wrong with that. Jake felt the tension that had been his constant companion retreating, leaving a brief reprieve from the reality of his situation. Jake managed to quickly find a couple of pairs of jeans and four T-shirts that would do. Amélia though, seemed to be taking a long time deciding on everything. Jake sat in a chair waiting. She was looking at herself in a mirror, after coming out of the back room where she had changed for the third time.

"Come on," Jake urged. "Let's get out of here. It's not a fashion show."

"No?" she replied, twirling around and leaning over toward him in a low cut peasant blouse, "I thought you were enjoying the view."

Jake blushed, and was suddenly very aware of her slim figure, dark hair, and catlike grace. What was she doing? This wasn't a date. He wondered what Barbara would think if she knew he was on the run with this woman.

At the register, Amélia told the cashier, "He will pay for mine too … he's my boyfriend." Jake blushed again, looking down and shuffling his feet. He could hardly wait to leave the store.

After a quick stop to get some gas, Yolanda drove them back to the farm. Amélia sat in front with her aunt as she had going into town. Jake, sitting in the back seat behind her, watched her silky black hair and thought about how she had looked in the store with that mischievous smile. *I have to admit, she's an intriguing person.*

Back at the farmhouse, reality returned. Raul still hadn't answered Jake's message, so Jake sent him a text: *"Call me. Big problems"*

Jake still hoped that Raul could get his father to clear things up, at least for him. Even Luis thought that was improbable. Jake felt sure that as far as Amélia and Luis were concerned, the situation seemed hopeless. They both were tightly linked to a group that included Juanita, Ruben and José Villanueva. Now Juanita and Ruben had disappeared, and José was dead. What hope was there of finding anyone who could clear this up for them? They both seemed skeptical that Raul and his father would help, even if they could.

They explained to Jake that in 2009, before President Zelaya was forcibly removed from Honduras, their student protest group was vocal in its criticism of the government. Raul, whose father was in the administration, had taken the other side and defended Zelaya. Jake remembered, from his encounters with all of them on his mission trip, that there seemed to be some tension when Raul was around the others.

"I thought that we had improved our friendship with Raul after Zelaya was thrown out and his father stayed with the new government," Luis said.

"I thought so too," Amélia said. "Especially when Zelaya snuck back into Honduras and holed up in the Brazilian embassy, Raul seemed to change. His father did nothing to support Zelaya's actions. I think that influenced Raul."

"That's right, man," Luis said. "We were still protesting Zelaya's return using the newsletter and Juanita's 'Princess Maya' blog. But even though he had backed off, we still avoided talking about politics with him."

"Well, we still can't be sure where Raul stands," Amélia said.

"I still don't think Raul is a problem," Jake said. "I don't understand why Ruben and Juanita were taken away by the secret police, if that's what happened to them."

"It was the 'Princess Maya blog for sure, man," Luis said. "She was trying to expose government corruption."

Amélia said, "But we were anti-Zelaya back in 2009, and then supported the new government under President Lobo. Juanita wasn't criticizing the government in her blog. If they were targeted because of the blog, then it has to be just someone corrupt … not really the government."

"Maybe it wasn't anyone in the government," Rodrigo said.

"Who else could it have been?" Jake asked.

"Maybe some gang or something; some sort of criminals," Rodrigo said.

"I hate to think of that possibility," Jake said. "It would mean, more than likely, that they were dead, murdered. At least, if the government has them, there is some possibility they are being held somewhere, still alive."

"There are lots of candidates for who might be the bad guys," Amélia said. "Juanita's blog started pointing out the problems that the government still had not resolved; street gangs, police corruption, housing for the poor, the protest suppression and all kind of other social injustices."

"I thought things had gotten better," Jake said.

"They have, man … some," Luis told him. There are still problems though. I don't know if we will ever get rid of corrupt police and politicians."

"And the drug smuggling problem has gotten worse, or at least more visible," Amélia added. "It seems like almost every month or so there is news that another drug smuggling plane is found in *Mosquitia.* Juanita has been blogging about that and trying to find out about rumors of government officials being involved in the drug trade."

"That's bad," Jake said. "Maybe the drug smugglers took them." He hated to think what that might mean.

"That is what I was saying," Rodrigo said.

"Wouldn't there be someone in the government trying to find out who the corrupt people are, and doing something about it?" Luis said.

"José's father, the General, was trying to root out corruption in the military, Amélia said. "The corruption is undermining President Lobo's government."

"Maybe that is the problem bothering Raul's father," Jake said. "Maybe he doesn't know who is corrupt in the government, or if he does, he can't prove it."

"We don't even know which side he is on," Amélia said. "Maybe he is one of those undermining the new government; he used to be one of Zelaya's key people."

"But the new government kept him on," Luis said.

"Maybe Raul isn't sure which side his father is on," Jake said. "He wanted me to hack into the computers to find out what is going on."

"Or maybe Raul and his father are on the same side, and are just using you as a way to penetrate our movement," Amélia said, raising her voice.

"OK … I don't know for sure …we have been over that!" Jake replied. "But I have to keep trying; then maybe we can find out. And I hope there's something in that secure database that will help us find out what happened to Ruben and Juanita."

"So, now what?" Luis asked.

Amélia stood up and started pacing the floor. "That's the answer Jake. It's our only chance to get out of this mess."

"I'm not following you," Jake said.

"Don't you see? If you can find out enough to know who took them, and why, then we will know who the enemy is. We can get the evidence we need to convince someone that I didn't kill José. I'm willing to bet the same people who did the kidnapping are behind the attempt on José and me."

Jake said, "I need to talk to Raul. Let him know what happened."

"Don't …"

"I know, I know. I won't tell him where we are," Jake said. "And I think you are right ... the S&I computer, it's our best chance. Tomorrow we need to go back to town and find a place to get an internet connection."

Chapter 31

Pastor Juan Zamora could see that his old friend, Arturo Lacas, was worried. The older man was pacing the floor of his modest living room, his hands locked behind his back. Juan glanced over to his wife Teresa. She cocked her head and shrugged. Juan knew that meant she would go along with whatever he wanted to do. Estrella Lacas sat beside Teresa on a small couch.

"I think that Luis had a good point last night," Arturo said. "If you just return to the city you will probably be arrested."

"I'm sure that I can explain to them that Teresa and I had nothing to do with the incident," Juan said. He wanted to reassure his friend. "Whatever had gone on, it must be some sort of misunderstanding, out of their control. As far as I knew the office was being used for a student ministry. I had no idea Luis was publishing an underground newspaper. And what is a 'blog?' I don't keep up with all these computer fads of the young people."

Arturo was not convinced. "Amélia Ramirez also called this morning. She urged me to convince you to stay here."

Estrella said, "You are welcome to stay here as long as you like."

Juan winced at the mention of Amélia's name. He hadn't had the heart to tell them all of what Luis had shared with him the night before. He just couldn't do it—he didn't even know how to start."

"We can't stay here forever. What do you think we should do?" Teresa asked.

"Let me think," the older man replied. After a moment he asked, "Do you know anyone in the government?"

"Well, not directly," Juan said, "but I know Raul Salas pretty well; his father is highly placed in the government, Chief of Intelligence, or something like that. Raul is a Christian, and volunteers with some of the ministries helping the street children and those living in the dump. He has helped us with some of the mission volunteers from the U.S."

"That's perfect. Would he vouch for you with his father?"

"I would think so."

"Alright," Arturo suggested, "how about this? Have him contact his father, and he can arrange a meeting with the right people. You can explain that you had nothing to do with the event at the parsonage."

"Well, as I said, the student Christian ministry used it, but I didn't know that Luis and Juanita were using it for their underground newsletter. Maybe I should have known, and probably would have if I had really given it much thought."

"The army wouldn't raid the place for a student protest newsletter, would they? What else was going on? Maybe there is more to it that you don't know."

"Obviously so! Jake Grayson, Ruben Avila's friend, was with them. He came back a few days ago to help find Ruben who, along with Juanita Perez, seems to have disappeared. Ruben had been staying in the old parsonage, so we let Jake stay there too. Luis said that he and Amélia Ramirez had come to the parsonage because the police are looking for her."

Teresa said, "You didn't tell me that!"

Lacas sat down in a chair across from Juan. "Amélia didn't say anything to me about the police looking for her."

Juan debated how much to say. He had avoided this last night—a sin of omission. The story Luis had told him was pretty incredible. He wouldn't have believed it if it was anyone else but Luis. He did trust the boy.

"Well, it is a bit confusing," Juan said. "According to Luis, there was a shooting Saturday in which General Villanueva's son, José was killed."

"Oh, dear!" Teresa said.

"Well it gets worse," Juan said. "Amélia was with José when it happened and barely escaped with her life. Since we came here right after Raul and Jake left our house, we haven't seen the paper, but it carried the story of the shooting."

"There is so much crime here," Arturo said. "So the police think Amélia is a witness to the shooting? Is that why they are looking for her?"

Alright, here came the difficult part. Juan knew that Arturo had known Amélia, ever since her mother started bringing the girl his church. Amélia had been just a child in those days and, after her father died, Arturo had done all he could to help them. This was going to shake the old man.

"No Arturo, I am sorry to say that José and his bodyguard were killed in a drug shootout. A gangster from MS-13 was also killed. The police are saying that Amélia was in the gang with him, and they are accusing *her* of murder!"

There was a collective gasp from the others, and Juan could see that Arturo was visibly shaken. Suddenly his friend seemed gray and old. Everyone seemed shocked beyond speech. Juan decided to wrap up this sad tale.

"Anyway, Luis accompanied Amélia to the parsonage, thinking that would be a safe place to hide. Jake Grayson was there with them yesterday when soldiers raided the place. Apparently they somehow escaped from the soldiers that came after them. I wish we knew more about what is going on, but that is the extent of it."

Estrella said, "I will not believe that Amélia had any part in drugs, or gangs, or … murder!"

"I don't either. I believe Luis, and he insists that she is being framed because they are making someone uncomfortable with their newsletter. He says the Villanueva boy was working with them."

Arturo said, "Well, maybe you are right about talking to the authorities. They can't think you were part of some drug gang. Particularly if you willingly go to the federal police to explain."

"I think that I must," Juan said. "This situation isn't going to go away, so the sooner I straighten it out the better."

Arturo nodded his head. "Set things up through Raul and arrange to see the police tomorrow afternoon. You can stay here until tomorrow morning. That would be best."

After some discussion between Juan and Teresa, it was settled, and Juan stepped out of the room to make a call to Raul Salas. Surely they could resolve this situation if Enrique Salas made the arrangement with the police.

Juan wasn't able to connect with Raul until late in the afternoon. When Raul called him back he had already talked to Jake and had inquired about the events at the parsonage.

"I also found out from my father that there is a bulletin for the federal police and army intelligence to pick up both you and Teresa for questioning," Raul said.

"But we weren't there!" Juan protested. "We can't tell them what happened."

Raul said, "This is very serious. Soldiers were killed, and they know that you must have a connection to the people who were there."

"Killed? ...Luis didn't tell me that!" Juan said, raising his voice. He felt like everything was spinning out of control. "How could that happen? Who would ...?"

"I don't know exactly," Raul said. "Jake told me it happened so fast that they hardly had time to react, but the soldiers broke in, Amélia shot at them. Look, it's very serious, but if my father can recommend that you come in and give a statement, then you have a better chance of being believed."

"Being believed?"

"Yeah, that you and Teresa didn't know what was going on ... that you didn't have anything to do with what happened."

"We didn't!" Juan was feeling dizzy. This was much worse than he could have imagined.

"I know," Raul said in a soothing voice. "Calm down and let me see what I can do. Don't call Luis or Amélia, the less contact you have, the less you know, the better."

A few hours later Raul called back.

"I talked to my father and told him you were worried about what to do. I assured him you weren't involved in any of this, He made the arrangements for you to be interviewed in the morning. I'm praying that you will be able to convince them."

"So are we supposed to go to the Federal Police headquarters on *Paseo el Picacho*?" Juan asked. *And what if I couldn't convince them?* He was just the pastor of a small church. They wouldn't think he was part of anything criminal, would they?

"No, no," Raul said. "The Federal Police aren't handling this. It comes under the Ministry of Defense. You should report to the Ministry of Security and Intelligence in Mateo, on the grounds of UDH, the Armed Forces University there, tomorrow morning at ten o'clock. You should ask to speak to Colonel Fuentes; he will take a personal interest in your situation."

Chapter 32

Raul closed his cell phone and sat back to think. He was surprised to find out that Pastor Juan didn't know many details of what had happened. It seems that Luis or Amélia would have confided in him, especially since all this had happened in Juan's parsonage.

Well, they weren't confiding in him either, were they? When Jake had called earlier that day the conversation had been strange. In his mind he played back the conversation with Jake after he had called back, responding to Jake's cryptic voice mail message.

■■■

"Hey man, we're in trouble!" Jake had answered immediately.

"What are you talking about?"

"The rainbow attack worked … I got into the S & I restricted site and downloaded some files, but then they came and I had to pull the plug … Amélia shot some of them!" Jake said.

Raul hadn't understood. "Amélia? What are you talking about? Who came?"

"The soldiers! She just shot them!"

"Wait a minute; slow down!" Raul said. "Start from the first and tell me what happened, step by step."

Jake related all of the events that had happened at the parsonage, including the fact that Rodrigo had helped them escape. Raul was amazed by the turn of events. Now Jake was caught up in the problems of Amélia and Luis. He hadn't seen that coming. Things were getting complicated.

"Where are you?" he asked.

"Never mind," Jake said. "Can you find out what's going on?"

"I don't know; maybe I can find out through my dad," Raul told him. "I don't see how they found you in the first place."

Jake said, "I don't know if they came after me because of the computer stuff, or they somehow knew that Amélia was there."

Well, if they were there because of the computer hacking, they will tie you to it," Raul said. "All your stuff is there in the parsonage, isn't it?"

"Yeah, I figured that out already. But how they got there so fast, that's really the question isn't it?"

"What?"

"If it was the computer penetration, how did they find me so quickly?"

"I don't know. How much time were you on?" Raul said. "Where are you now? Are you all OK?"

There was a hesitation, and then Jake said, "Uh … We're all fine. I'm going to try again. It did take a little while to crack the password, but I didn't expect they could find me. Can you find out if they had a way of tracing back to our location?"

"My dad indicated that they didn't do those kinds of things, that time I talked to him about their computer systems," Raul replied. "Besides, since you had his password, they would just think it was him logging on. Why would they try to trace it?"

"Hmm … I don't know; something happened."

■ ■ ■

As Raul thought back over the conversation, he realized that Jake had twice avoided saying where they had gone. *He doesn't trust me.* Well maybe that was just as well. He didn't really need to know. Maybe this whole computer idea was a wild goose chase. And now Jake was in trouble, and he might be too. If the computer hack really had been discovered, it would eventually be traced back to his father's account, and to him.

What if the whole thing had been about Amélia and Luis being there? She was being sought for murder. That was more likely. Maybe someone saw her, or maybe she had used her cellular phone and they tracked it using triangulation from cell towers; they had that capability.

If this was all about the trouble Amélia and Luis were in, maybe the computer issue wouldn't even come up. Then he would be in the clear. His father's influence with Colonel Fuentes might help him believe that Pastor Juan had nothing to do with these horrible events.

Raul began to feel a little more hopeful, until he had the thought: *But Jake was part of the shootout. Computers or no computers, Jake was in serious trouble!*

Chapter 33

Pastor Juan steered his old white van around the traffic circle in Mateo. He eyed the statue of a Honduran soldier in full camouflage battle dress, holding a rifle, dominating the center, as if guarding against intruders. An actual soldier dressed in drab, olive-green fatigues, observed from a small guard shack on the right hand side of the road. Teresa waved to the guard who remained impassive.

Juan caught her gesture out of the corner of his eye. "Are you nervous, dear?"

She laughed. "Me? No, of course not, everything will be fine. Sure, nothing to worry about …at all." She gripped her small purse tightly.

Juan slowed the van and looked over to her. "Teresa, dear, I know this is serious. I am not naive, but we can explain things. I am a respected pastor, and I think the authorities will take our word that we are not involved."

She cleared her throat, and said, "Do you really think we can?" She didn't look his way, just stared out the windshield.

He nodded his head. "I pray that we can, and that God will watch over us. This meeting with Colonel Fuentes was set up by his boss, Enrique Salas, so we should have an impartial official to listen to our claims. We will convince him that we are innocent. Maybe even persuade him that the others were acting out of fear, and used poor judgment in resisting the soldiers."

The old van chugged by several entrances to various military properties in Mateo. When they came to a blue and white sign that designated the entrance to UDH, Juan turned into a drive. As they wound their way on the entrance road, Juan felt sweat beginning to dampen his shirt. Soon they came to a gatehouse and barrier, forcing them to stop. A military guard in camouflage fatigues, carrying an automatic weapon of some sort, eyed them from the gatehouse. Beyond the pipe barrier blocking the road, Juan could see the large building that Raul had described. Another guard approached the van and asked what they wanted. A few moments later, Juan was relieved to find out that their appointment with Colonel Fuentes was on record, and they were directed to the headquarters building.

Morning sun filtered through the wall of windows that fronted the lobby of the Ministry of Security & Intelligence Headquarters, throwing shadows across the floor. Dust motes floated in the air, made visible by the low sun streaming through the windows. After hesitating to get their bearings, Juan and Teresa approached the reception desk where a woman was talking on the phone. Juan straightened his sports jacket, and caught the attention of the attractive woman with striking blue eyes and short cut, dark blond hair.

"Ahem, we are here for an appointment with Colonel Fuentes."

"One moment please," she replied coolly, while looking them over with interest. "Please sit over there to wait."

As they sat in the uncomfortable chairs of the lobby, Juan looked around at the armed soldiers standing at every entrance to the room, even the elevator.

"Apparently they take the 'security' part of 'security and intelligence' very seriously," he whispered to Teresa.

She frowned at him. "Shhh!"

He reached out and patted her on the arm. "We'll be alright."

Soon a soldier came out of the elevator, spoke briefly to the receptionist and walked over to them. "Come with me please," he said. "I'll take you to Colonel Fuentes."

They followed him to the elevator, which still stood open. The soldier entered behind them, pushed a button to close the door, and then pushed another button marked "B." Juan supposed that meant a basement level. Sure enough, the elevator started to descend.

Juan gave Teresa a concerned look. *Surely a Colonel would have an office on one of the main floors.*

Juan and Teresa followed the soldier—he thought of him as more of a guard now—into a narrow dingy hall. What a change from the immaculate lobby above. They approached a door, guarded by another armed soldier. A sign on the door read: "Interrogation Room 3."

"In here please," said the guard, opening the door.

Teresa took a step back. Evidently his wife had picked up on the sign's nomenclature. Juan caught her arm. "It's alright; this is to be an interview after all." He wished he felt as confident as he imagined he sounded, but the word "interrogation" had thrown him too.

As they entered the room a man, dressed in an officer's uniform, rose from a chair beside a small table and said, "Ah, Pastor Zamora and Mrs. Zamora ... welcome! I am Colonel Fuentes. Please excuse the décor, but there will be fewer interruptions here, rather than in my office." He waved the guard out and closed the door.

Juan cleared his throat. "Uh ... yes, that is understandable ... uh, fine."

"Please take a seat," he said, motioning to a pair of chairs on the far side of the table.

Juan pulled out a chair for Teresa and the two of them sat. The dark complexioned man seated himself across from them, rested his elbows on the table and formed a steeple with his fingers.

"Now tell me what sort of revolutionary cell you are running out of your church."

"Rev ... what? Revolutionary cell?" Juan sputtered. "No ... the parsonage is used for a student ministry ... from the university. They may ... well, they do ... take part in some student protests, but they are not revolutionaries. Is that why you raided it?"

"A student ministry? It's a long way from the university—half way across town."

"Well ... ah, yes," Juan said. "Some of the members of our church go to the university and they didn't have a place near the campus to use. We had plenty of room and office equipment in the old parsonage ... so we let them use it."

Fuentes raised his eyebrows skeptically and went on to spend several minutes explaining that they had found evidence of an anti-government resistance movement in the parsonage. That didn't make sense. Juan knew Luis and Juanita were concerned with social issues—but they weren't anti-government!

"Not only that, but your 'ministry students' have tried to gain illegal access to our computers," he said.

"Computers ... you mean hacking them? Why would they do that?"

"You tell me. When we sent soldiers to arrest them we were met with armed resistance."

"I don't understand that," Juan said. He was truly at a loss to explain that, but he tried. "She must have been in fear for her life. And evidently she had a gun,"

"She?" the Colonel said. "Who is she?" He looked pointedly at Juan.

Now he had done it. He had to watch his words more carefully. This man had him saying things before he had thought them through. His shirt felt thoroughly damp now. He would have no choice but to give them Amélia's name. Mentally berating himself, he tried to distance himself and Teresa from Amélia. Well, in truth, they really didn't know her all that well. She was close to Pastor Lacas, and friendly with Luis, Juanita and Ruben, but maybe that didn't have to come out. He wondered if he was doing the right thing.

"Well ... and I really don't know for sure ..." *Slow down, choose your words carefully.* "We heard that the person that fired at the soldiers was ... uh ... a young woman named Amélia."

Teresa turned to him, her eyebrows raised. What must she think of his selling out the young woman? What choice did he have now, since he had slipped up already?

"Amélia?" Fuentes said. "Do you mean Amélia Ramirez?"

"Uh ... I think so. I mean, yes that is her name."

Teresa chimed in. "Really Colonel, I'm sure the young woman was just panicked."

"And you said she had a gun. What kind of gun?"

"I don't know!" Juan said. "We hardly know her. We were just told she shot at some soldiers that raided the old parsonage for some reason. We don't even know what this is all about!"

He was relieved to see Teresa shaking her head in agreement. Fuentes scowled and slammed his palm down on the table, causing both Juan and Teresa to jump.

"That 'gun,' as you call it was a full automatic weapon that fired over a dozen rounds in a couple of seconds! An illegal weapon, something only a revolutionary or a terrorist would use. You knew that, didn't you?"

Juan and Teresa exchanged glances.

"No! I swear!" Juan said. He couldn't catch his breath, and couldn't think of what to say. How could they distance themselves from this? Minister Salas was supposed to arrange a polite interview where they could tell what they knew, not this! He glanced again at Teresa and saw that her face had gone pale. *God, help me. Give me the words to say.*

Colonel Fuentes continued. "They not only shot and killed one of the soldiers and wounded another, they also killed another soldier with a hand grenade!" He pulled several photographs out of a folder and threw them on the table. "Look at the evidence for yourselves!"

Juan and Teresa stared at the gruesome photos, showing blood, bodies and destruction at the parsonage. They were both speechless. A hand grenade? Could it be true? This was much worse than Juan had ever imagined. *Why hadn't Luis or Raul really prepared him?*

It seemed to Juan that a lot of time had passed, and they were still talking. Despite their best efforts Juan and Teresa could not make the Colonel understand that they were not part of some armed resistance movement. As the questioning progressed, they had been led to admit that a young man from the U.S. had been staying at the parsonage.

"His name is Jake Grayson," Juan said. "He was here three years ago on a mission trip, and returned last month because a friend of his has gone missing."

"Oh?" Fuentes said. "Who is his friend?"

"Another student from the U.S. named Ruben Avila," Juan said. "He and his girlfriend are missing." There, he did it again, giving more information than the question required. Juan was not used to speaking with—what?—cunning and maybe deviousness. *Well, the Lord said 'Therefore be as shrewd as snakes and as innocent as doves,' didn't he?*

Fuentes raised his eyebrows, staring at Juan. "And the girlfriend?" Fuentes prompted.

"Oh ..." Juan said. "She ... she is a student named Juanita Perez."

Fuentes nodded, as if agreeing to Juan's statement. "I see," he said quietly. Then he smiled.

Juan watched the man carefully. He had picked up on something odd in Fuentes countenance when he mentioned Juanita, maybe a knowing glimmer in his eyes. And that smile—never reaching the eyes, the mouth pulled back in a tight imitation of a real smile.

The questions continued, varying in pace, sometimes easier and innocuous, and then suddenly shifting to accusations that caught Juan off guard. An hour later Juan slumped in his chair, ran his hand through his hair and tried to focus. He blinked his eyes and said, "Uh ... what was the question?"

"You know what the question is! You have been skirting it every time. If you don't give me a straight answer this time you, and your pretty wife here, will pay dearly. Now, was it Luis Estrada who was the third person at your parsonage?"

Juan shifted his eyes away from the evil man across the table. Teresa was hunched in her chair, her elbows pulled in to her sides. Her eyes were squeezed shut. He had to stop this. Juan crossed his arms and stared down at the table, without focus, not really seeing anything. *He wasn't going to say another word!*

"So we know Juanita Perez, Amélia Ramirez, and probably Luis Estrada are the Honduran students who were working with two foreign agitators, Ruben Avila and Jake Grayson," Fuentes said, smiling, evidently very pleased with himself. Juan waited for what was to come next.

"And what about Raul Salas? Fuentes said softly.

"Raul?" Juan said. Another twist in this ordeal—why was he asking about Raul?

"Yes Raul! The Raul who got his father to set up this meeting— the Raul who helped your Jake Grayson hack into government computers—the Raul who has been manipulated by *your* subversive American contacts. That Raul!" Fuentes' eyes blazed, his dark complexion turned even darker and reddish.

His contacts? The wall of defense that Juan had tried to maintain in his mind, crumbled. Resistance fled, and the only thing remaining was the faint hope that Teresa would be freed and could get him a lawyer.

"I ... I... Look, maybe you don't believe me. I can see that. But ... my wife, Teresa, here ...she's just a pastor's wife. She hardly knows these people. Blame me if you want, but she is innocent. Let her go."

Suddenly Fuentes got up and opened the door. Motioning the two guards into the room he told them, "Put them in adjoining cells in cellblock three. Issue them standard prison garb for now. I will be back tomorrow to interrogate them further. No registration in the computer for now. They are high security prisoners, mention them to no one."

"*¡Si Commandante!*" both guards replied in unison.

Teresa let out a high pitched wail and collapsed to the floor when the guard pulled her out of her chair. He pulled her up, causing an agonizing scream, and then shoved her into the hallway.

The Honduran Plot

Juan tried to intervene but his legs felt heavy and lifeless. "Stop! She doesn't have anything to do with this!" he yelled. He barely got out of his chair before the other guard grabbed his arm and twisted it behind him. Agonizing pain shot through his shoulder as he was manhandled out the door.

Chapter 34

Back in his office Fuentes sat thinking about the situation. Smiling, he picked up the phone and dialed the front reception desk.

"Yes sir?" Greta Rojas purred in her sexiest voice, "What can I do for the Colonel today?"

"Greta darling, you can always find something exciting to do for me. Did you register Pastor and Mrs. Zamora when they came in?"

"Yes, I was on duty then … why?"

"They were never here. Make sure that the records show no trace of them. Also, personally notify the guard shack to delete the entry from their logs."

"*Si, mi Coronel… ¿circunstancias especiales, si?*"

"That's right."

She feigned a pouting voice. "But I am *so* disappointed. I hoped you wanted more, as you said something exciting."

"I might, if you can wait until tonight," he said. "One other thing. Have one of your trusted assistants deliver the pastor's car back to the church he runs in *La Vega*. A soldier from the strike force can show him where it is and bring him back here. Sergeant Pinero has the car keys in the basement office. Understand?"

"*Si, mi Amor*, I understand perfectly. Perhaps you will need my help with these people. I can have the little man with the salt and pepper hair talking in no time."

Fuentes knew she could. Greta was his mistress, and her sexual and sadistic appetites matched his very well. He thought it must be that combination of German and Argentinean bloodline. Publically she was just a receptionist, but her real job was one of his secret operatives. She was perhaps his best resource in gaining information and blackmail leverage on politicians, police officials, and drug smugglers. But in interrogation, she was unequaled. He remembered learning of her background, back in the early nineteen eighties when they had first met.

■■■

The Honduran Plot

Greta's father, a young Nazi S.S. Lieutenant, had assisted in the escape of Adolph Eichmann from an American internment after World War II. Together, they fled to Argentina where they were welcomed by Juan Peron's government. He, and others like him, had been instrumental in passing on the brutal tactics used by the Nazis to the Argentinean secret police. Greta's mother was the last, and favorite, of a series of mistresses her father had kept. He adored the little girl and told her many stories of the glory of the Third Reich. He died when Greta was fourteen, and her mother married Captain Rojas of the Argentinean secret police. Two years later the new family had been sent to Honduras to help in the training of General Alvarez's infamous Battalion 316. That is where Fuentes first met her. He was captivated by the beautiful blue-eyed girl. But she was unapproachable.

Captain Rojas was notorious for his amorality, and Fuentes heard rumors of an incestuous relationship with his stepdaughter. By the time she was eighteen she became an informal member of B-316, and her stepfather's personal interrogator. Fuentes was both horrified and fascinated at her use of the sharp knives that had belonged to her father. She could get anyone to admit to anything, though they seldom lived for more than a few hours afterwards. She seemed to revel in the pain of the prisoners she interrogated. The years had passed, and their paths crossed again. This time he was in a position to get her a position in S&I and win her favors.

■■■

With that background, no wonder she is bloodthirsty. Fuentes' thoughts returned to the present, and he considered her offer. "If you are very good to me tonight, I might think about letting you interrogate one of them, but only if extreme measures become necessary."

"And if you're good to me, I might let you watch me do it," she purred and hung up.

Fuentes suppressed an involuntary shudder. He couldn't imagine wanting to view one of her bloody interrogations. He had only used Greta on the toughest cases. The closest he had come to watching her was to see her threaten prisoners with the knives—they had usually spilled their secrets to prevent her from having her way with them. A few had resisted her threats, and Fuentes wisely left the interrogation cell before she could start on them. He remembered hearing the screams

131

start as he hurried away down the hallway. She often had gotten the information he needed, and she always got them to admit something.

He might use her again if he couldn't get Zamora to talk. Juan Zamora knew much more than he was letting on, and was tougher than he looked. He didn't buy his innocent pastor act. He had too many connections to his enemies. Was it possible that he was cooperating with the American CIA? Were these students, or missionaries, or whatever they were, possibly agents? Someone had given information to the Perez woman. Her "Princess Maya" blog had posted a rumor about secret drug flights from Venezuela going through Toncontin. If Rodriguez, or even worse, General Velasquez knew about that they might cut him out of his lucrative deal.

His interrogations of Perez and her boyfriend had been unsuccessful in finding any real connections. They both had claimed that the information had been sent to them by way of an anonymous e-mail. The American had admitted to going to the airport and seeing the Venezuelan aircraft land and leave again. That didn't prove anything because, after all, there was the Oilfield equipment cover story. But the fact that someone had linked that plane to the drug shipments told Fuentes that the source knew too much. Despite rigorous interrogation the young American insisted that he had no idea of who had given them the information. The interrogation had been pretty rough and drawn out, so Fuentes was convinced that he was telling everything he knew. The woman had the same story, so that was a dead end also. *Well, she did have other uses—he would keep her around.* There was no sense in having Greta interrogate either of them. She would get them to say anything to stop the pain, but none of it would be real. He would just continue to hold them until this situation was resolved.

Pastor Zamora had connections to both of these people, and now there was a penetration of the defense computers and a shootout at the parsonage at his church. Enemies kept popping up, and the pastor seemed to be the common element. *The wife—she is the key to unlock the stubborn pastor. He would tell everything to not have to watch her be tortured.*

Chapter 35

Ruben Avila woke up shivering and hungry. No, not hungry—starving! He guessed that he must have lost twenty pounds since being thrown in here. What had woken him up? *Oh, there is a food tray near the opening at the bottom of the door.*

His appetite had returned—an encouraging sign. After being punched repeatedly in the stomach by his sadistic guards, Ruben had feared that there were serious internal injuries. Pain, every time he had taken a few bites, had killed his appetite.

They left him alone most of the time now. During the first few days there had been interrogations almost daily that seemed endless. As he was unable to give his captors any information, the intensity of the sessions became more brutal. Ruben had read of "water boarding" in news articles about accused terrorists being held by the U.S. at Guantanamo prison, in Cuba. He had never believed that was really torture—*now he did!* He still had nightmares that he was drowning. Even now, just thinking about it, his hands began to tremble.

■■■

He couldn't breathe! He knew he was going to die, to drown. His lungs burned and he struggled to get loose, but his arms and legs were held. Finally, after agonizing minutes, he could hold his breath no more, he tried to suck in air, but got only water instead, His body convulsed. He was drowning! And then he blacked out.

When he came to he lay naked on the cold, wet concrete floor, his chest throbbing, vomit drooling from his mouth. All he saw was a pair of combat boots and the wet, slimy concrete floor. Ruben turned his head upward, revealing the guard standing over him. The interrogator, a small man in a rumpled gray suit, and another guard stood at his side.

"We almost didn't get you back that time," the interrogator said. "I think next time you might really die."

The guards knelt down and Ruben tried to scramble away, but he was so weak that they easily overpowered him. They pinned his arms and legs.

The interrogator squatted beside Ruben's head, the dreaded bucket of water scraped across the concrete as the man pulled it nearer. He pulled a dripping wet towel out of the bucket and said. "Now, tell me what I need to know, or this time I'll really have to drown you."

Ruben clenched his jaw, and could hear the sound of his heartbeat pounding in his ears. Black spots swam before his eyes and he became dizzy. *He didn't know the answers!* ▪▪▪

Ruben found himself hyperventilating—this happened every time he woke up and started thinking back over his ordeal. He sat on the edge of his cot and probed his stomach with his fingers, pushing gently. Only a little soreness, and now his appetite was back, so he must be healing. Did he dare try to eat? He shuffled to the door and retrieved the battered aluminum tray. *What delicacies were there today?*

He sat picking at his breakfast; a small glob of stale tasting beans, a few vegetables, and an aluminum cup of cloudy water. So far so good, maybe this slop wouldn't make him sick.

He chewed the beans slowly, as well as he could with two teeth missing. He swallowed, and his tongue probed the place where a tooth was missing. What was happening to Juanita? The thought of her being tortured invaded his mind. He tried to shut it out, but terrifying and sickening images of her being mistreated flashed through his imagination. Each time this happened, tears flooded his vision.

Ruben heard the clattering of trays being put in a cart in the hall. Lunch time was over; they would be coming in to pick up the tray and cup. Could he possibly overpower the guard picking up the trays? He was feeling stronger, but no, that wouldn't work. He'd just get beat up again.

The door opened and a guard came in, but didn't pick up the tray. Instead he shut the cell door behind him. He put his fingers to his lips, indicating for Ruben to be quiet.

"You are Ruben Avila," he said in a low voice. It was a statement, rather than a question.

Ruben just stared at him. *What now?*

The Honduran Plot

When Ruben didn't say anything, the guard continued, "I am Corporal Delgado, Josué Delgado, and I need to tell you something."

Something was wrong here. Was this some sort of new interrogation trick?

"José, why are you talking to me? What do you need to tell me?"

"Not José. Josué ... pronounced 'Ho-sway' ... Joshua in English." Delgado stepped closer. In a low voice he said, "You know Pastor Zamora?"

"Yes ... uh, Josué," Ruben said. Was this was some kind of trick? Deception rather than torture maybe?

"I know you do," Delgado said quickly, apparently sensing Ruben's wariness. "What I mean is to tell you that I started going to his church, so I heard about you and Juanita Perez disappearing. Later I got assigned to this cellblock, and I found out that you were in here. I didn't know what to do. How could I tell anyone about you being here, and what you have been going through? And who would I tell? I didn't know what to do so I waited ... now it's even worse. I can't be part of this anymore."

Ruben was trying to sort through this rapid dump of information. This guy knew a lot about what had happened. About Juanita! More than anything he wanted to know about her, but also he was afraid of what he might find out.

"Juanita ... is Juanita ... did they hurt her?" Ruben blurted out.

The guard looked away and appeared to be considering whether to answer. He looked back at Ruben. "Listen," he said, "I know some of what you have been going through. They worked you over pretty good."

Pretty good? What an understatement.   Ruben tried again. "Juanita. What about Juanita?"

"I know a guard who has heard some things," Delgado said.

"I don't care about that! Tell me about Juanita! What are you hiding?" Ruben rubbed his hand over his face. Would this guy ever give him a straight answer? He no longer worried that Delgado might be trying to trick him. He didn't worry about anything except what had happened to Juanita.

Delgado held out his hands and looked around as if fearful that someone might be listening to them. "Shhh! Not so loud. Calm down and I'll tell you. They think you are some agent, the main one running things, and that she was just writing the blog. That is why they tried to break you, but only questioned her a few times. She was not put through the kind of things you were."

Ruben exhaled. *Thank God!* He needed to find out more, He couldn't process all the stuff Delgado had already told him. He needed to concentrate. "Is she here? What did you ask about Pastor Zamora for? Why ..."

"Hold on. One thing at a time," Delgado said. "Yes she is here, a prisoner. Let me get this out, no interruptions. I told you I have been going to Pastor Zamora's church. That is why I am talking to you. My conscience has been bothering me and I can't work in this place anymore. I didn't know what to do. I was going to Pastor Zamora for advice, and about helping you and Juanita. But now it's too late. He and his wife were arrested and put in here yesterday."

What was going on? Ruben struggled to make sense of all this. "Why, what happened to make them arrest Pastor Juan and Teresa?"

"A lot has happened," Delgado said. "On Monday the Army Rapid Strike Team raided Pastor Zamora's old parsonage, the one across from the church."

"Was it because of me?" Ruben asked. "That's where I was staying."

"No, it wasn't that. I'm not sure what caused the raid, but there were a couple of the soldiers killed and a manhunt for the people who got away. They arrested the Zamoras because they believe he is part of this revolutionary group."

Ruben could hardly believe what he was hearing. He lowered his head and chewed on his lip. Things were getting worse. "They wouldn't believe me. Are they going to interrogate Pastor Juan like they did me?"

"I don't know what they will do," Delgado said. "But I need to tell you everything. I didn't tell you everything about Juanita. She wasn't interrogated badly, but ... well, Monday night ..."

"What?" Ruben almost shouted. "Tell me! Is she OK?"

"Shh! be quiet, someone might hear us," Delgado said. "She is better now ... she ..." He looked away, appearing to decide on the words he wanted to say. "She just got roughed up a little. I don't have any details, but is feeling better now I think."

Roughed up—what did that mean? This man seemed reassuring, and wanted to help. He no longer felt suspicious of his motives. Like a sprout of a plant emerging from the ground, a feeling of hope rose up within Ruben. With imploring eyes Ruben asked, "Are you going to get us out?"

"I don't know what to do," Delgado said. "We *all* have to get out of here. I can't continue working here. These people are evil, especially Colonel Fuentes."

"You have got to help us..." Ruben pleaded.

Delgado's forehead wrinkled. "I will try to do something." He wrung his hands. "But I don't know how, and who else can I trust to help on the outside?"

Chapter 36

Mauricio Aguilar hung up the phone. That was a surprise—Lieutenant Garcia had been put in charge of the Rapid-Response Strike Team. More importantly, Mauricio still had full authority to send the team out if he detected another attempt to penetrate the S&I website. After hearing that Captain Jimenez had been demoted and reassigned, Mauricio feared that he would share in the blame for the failed raid. Evidently Colonel Fuentes felt that he had alerted Jimenez in plenty of time. Mauricio knew he had taken too long, but he wasn't going to tell anyone.

He stubbed out his cigarette, and went to make an espresso at the small machine in the corner of the computer room. While he waited for the hissing espresso maker he thought about that incident.

■■■

He hadn't thought that the attempts to penetrate the website had been a serious threat. He had mainly brought the problem to Fuentes to get his budget increased. But two days ago there had been a major change. Raul Salas, or whoever was helping him, had launched a fairly sophisticated attack on the site, generating thousands of passwords per second in an attempt to enter the restricted area. Since the intruder had already successfully logged into the website, there was no lockout after a certain number of failed passwords. Mauricio mentally kicked himself for failing to learn how to configure the old security software to provide multiple lockout layers. He had been lobbying for months to get the security software replaced with something more effective.

Mauricio still wasn't too worried. He initiated his counterintelligence program to record details of the intrusion attempt, and the tracking function finally spit out the location. It wasn't the Salas residence—the computer had moved!

The sophisticated attack and evidence that it wasn't coming from the Salas residence finally got him in high gear. Mauricio alerted Jimenez to send out the strike team from army intelligence. Only then did he think to manually break the connection. To Mauricio's dismay, his review of the incident logs showed that the rogue computer had succeeded in breaking into Fuentes' most secure area and started downloading files. Several highly classified documents had been downloaded before the tracing program had completed its work and Mauricio had broken the connection. He didn't put that in his report; Fuentes didn't handle bad news very well. Especially since the culprits had killed two soldiers in their escape.

■■■

Mauricio took his espresso in the little stained cup and sat at his desk. He really should wash that cup someday. He lit another cigarette and watched the three flat screen monitors on his desk as they displayed status and traffic on the S&I website and also from the personal computers of the people Fuentes considered important. He went back to imagining that he was the spider in the web of data.

He had just taken the last sip of espresso, feeling a few powdery grounds in the bottom of the cup, when a red-bordered window popped up in the central monitor. Another penetration attempt! Mauricio's heart rate sped up and he quickly stubbed out the cigarette.

The alert window was replaced by the tracking program. This time Mauricio thought to alert Lieutenant Garcia to have the team standby before the trace was completed.

Mauricio tapped his pen against the keyboard. The trace was taking too long! Finally a welcoming ping, and the window of the tracking program showed that the rogue computer had moved again, to the little town of Talanga. Mauricio was surprised that they had internet there. He manually broke the connection and immediately gave the location to Garcia, who said he could have a helicopter to the location within thirty minutes.

Chapter 37

Jake liked the internet café in Talanga, an unpretentious place; no soy-decaf-caramel lattes here. The coffee was strong and good. He breathed in the aromas coming from the small kitchen and knew the food would be delicious. Maybe they would order lunch later.

According to Yolanda, the place had just opened, bringing high speed internet and WiFi to Talanga for the first time. The soothing earth-tones and sturdy wood furniture appealed to Jake. He chose a table in the rear corner of the room with his back to the wall to prevent glare from the front window. Luis and Amélia joined him, bringing him a small cup of the strong Honduran coffee. They sat at the table, watching quietly. Jake repeated the steps that he had written in a small notebook. He successfully logged in to the S&I secure website, moved through layers of web pages, and found the obscure logo and cryptic log-in window. But when he entered the password that his program had broken, nothing happened. Jake tried again carefully copying the long string of alphanumeric characters from his notebook. Nothing—the blinking cursor in the white entry bar mocked him.

"The password must have been changed," Jake said. "I'll need to break in again."

"Think you can get in again, man?"

"I should, if they haven't completely changed the software," Jake said. "But it will take time, just like it did Monday."

Luis leaned over to see the laptop screen. "Man, I'm always amazed when I read stories about hackers breaking into computer systems. It just seems impossible ... so many password combinations. When I forget my password or mistype it, I get shut out after a few incorrect attempts. I don't see how the program can find one password in thousands, or millions.

Jake thought for a few seconds before answering. "Well, it's all pretty amazing. The security programs keep getting more sophisticated and the hackers keep catching up and using computer power to overcome the security measures. The more sophisticated programs using public and private keys would be impossible for me to penetrate, but this one is older and uses a single key that can be broken."

Luis smiled. "No idea what you just said, man. Anyway, how could you know that?"

"It's not easy," Jake said. "It takes a lot of patience and time, and use of software tools to 'footprint' the website. We find out file and directory structures, hidden directories, software versions used, and lots of stuff. Some sites have remote access flaws that allow hackers to access to the computer mainframes. Anyway, we can find out a lot."

"Too complicated for me, man." Luis sat back.

Jake glanced at the laptop, chugging away on the password problem. "I don't understand a lot of it myself, but I try to keep up with it. The best way to understand it is to become a hacker too. There are whole communities of hackers sharing programs and data. When I couldn't penetrate the website, I asked for help. My contact and her hacker buddies were able to figure out the kind of old security program these guys are using. They gave me a program to use as a starting point. I translated it to 'Python,' another high level language, added some modules already developed and available on the internet. I was surprised as anyone when the thing worked."

As if on cue there was a "ping" from the laptop and the webpage of the secure part of the site appeared on the screen. The program had penetrated the site again.

Jake stopped talking and began examining the various descriptions and links on the page.

"Help me out here," Jake said. "Monday night, I just highlighted some documents and downloaded them. None of that was too useful."

Amélia came around to the side of the table where Luis and Jake were sitting. They all watched the screen as Jake explored the web pages in the secure area of the site.

"Wait," Amélia said, pointing to an underlined link on the screen. "That one says 'Strategic Plans - Zopilote.' That's kind of strange."

"Why," Jake said.

"Well, 'zopilote' is a kind of bird, a type of buzzard. Strategic plans and buzzards?"

"Man, it has to be some kind of codename," Luis said.

Jake clicked on the link revealing a list of documents. Selecting one of those opened to a listing of hexadecimal characters.

"Well, this isn't too useful," Jake said. "I don't know what to make of this. The filename extension shows this to be a .txt ... a text document. But all it is a bunch of hexadecimal numbers. Maybe it's some kind of data ... or another layer of encryption."

"What are you going to do then?" Amélia asked.

Moving back to the listing, Jake highlighted the list of documents and clicked the mouse over a menu tab. "I'm just going to download all these files. I can look at them offline."

A window popped up showing the progress on the documents being copied. Jake tapped his fingers on the table. The progress bar at the bottom of the window seemed to be moving at an agonizingly slow pace. Suddenly the download window disappeared and another small window popped up saying, "Connection Terminated."

"Rats!" Jake said. The barista behind the counter turned and looked their way.

"What?" Amélia asked.

"I got knocked offline, Jake said. "Now I have to start all over again."

Amélia said, "You don't need me for that. I'm going back out to the station wagon, I forgot something."

Jake idly waved his hand as she left the table, his eyes focused on the laptop screen. He closed the window on the screen and redirected the browser to the S&I website again.

"Do you think you can get in again?" asked Luis.

"Well, the program worked twice now, so I think it's worth trying again," Jake said. "I'm hoping it was some sort of automatic timeout in the system, and not that someone has detected that we penetrated the site."

Thirty minutes later Jake ran his fingers through his hair and let out a heavy sigh. He had repeated all the previous steps, but nothing worked. Luis and Amélia had gone to another table to give him some space. He had tried several times, and wracked his mind to figure out what was going wrong. *Maybe I need another coffee.* He became aware of a low noise that got his attention. It came and went, but was getting progressively louder. *A motor maybe?*

The Honduran Plot

Soon it had everyone's attention and the walls and windows vibrated with a horrendous "*Whup-whup-whup.*" Jake ran to the front window, as did everyone else. They gawked at a monstrous, dark green helicopter blowing up dust and trash as it settled onto a vacant lot across the street. *Here we go again!*

Chapter 38

Corporal Delgado walked slowly along the sidewalk, his head down and his mind questioning. The prisoner had been suspicious of his motives and afraid to give him any information. He had tried to convince the man of his sincerity, describing his conversion to Christianity, and how he knew Pastor Zamora. The delay made him late returning from the tray collection duty, and had angered his supervisor. An unauthorized cigarette break made a good excuse, but had gotten him two weeks of KP duty. He wasn't worried about that. If he went ahead with his plans he would be a deserter within a few days.

Ruben had finally given him two names with cell phone numbers. Luis Estrada meant nothing to him, but the other, Raul Salas, was a surprise. He knew Raul Salas was the son of the Minister of Intelligence. What did that mean? Why was a friend of the minister's son in prison? He would avoid that complication. He would try to call this Luis Estrada guy.

It was evening before Josué could bring himself to make the call. His hand shook as he keyed in the cell phone number he had been given for Luis. He tried three different times, but it always went directly to voice mail. Ruben had said these guys could be trusted, but he wasn't going to leave a message. It was bad enough that his number would show on the caller ID. He didn't want anything traced back to him.

That left Raul Salas as the only other choice. He hesitated—did he really want to do this? He had to, but he would be cautious. The phone was answered on the second ring.

"*Hola. ¿Quien habla?*"

Delgado hesitated, then managed to find his voice. "Hello, are you a friend of Ruben Avila?"

"Yes," Raul immediately answered. "Who is this? Do you know where he is?"

"I am a friend," Delgado said. "I know … he needs your help. We need to meet."

"Why can't you tell me where he is?"

"Better to meet ... then I'll tell you." There was silence on the phone. Had Raul hung up? "Are you there? I'm a friend, but I have to be careful."

Raul finally replied, "OK, we can meet. How about the *Parque Central* tonight? By the statue."

"That would be good ... no, wait; how about the Pizza Hut that is near there? That might be less obvious than two guys talking in the park. OK?"

"Sure, no one should pay attention to two guys eating pizza on a Friday night."

"Nine o'clock?"

"OK. How will I know you?"

"I'll be wearing an Atlanta Braves baseball cap. My name is Josué. Take the stairs up to the second level. I'll be up there."

"See you then."

Chapter 39

Fuentes paced his office. His stomach rumbled. He should have had dinner brought in, but it was urgent that he come up with a plan of action. What damage had been done? Mauricio had not been able to tell him what had been revealed. All he could do was whine about security software again. Evidently what they had was about as effective as a strainer trying to hold water. Two penetrations of their secure site, and both times the culprits had escaped!

The strike team that had been dispatched by helicopter to Talanga had arrived at the internet café only thirty minutes after Garcia had issued the order. They had stormed out of the helicopter and charged into the café, only to find it empty except for a terrified barista and two other customers. The barista said there were three people, two male, one female, using a laptop. They escaped out the back door as soon as they saw the helicopter touching down. A search of the area yielded no results

He had planned to interrogate Zamora that afternoon, but cancelled those plans when all this computer nonsense began. There was much to do on his secret plan, and very little time to get everything lined up. Fuentes had been on the phone, alternating between encouraging and coercing that sniveling weasel, Enrique Salas, to change his provincial and timid mindset before he could reveal the whole extent of the plan to him.

He had been dealing with Salas for over four years. They had conspired to move the country into a close alliance with Venezuela, working with Hugo Chavez, the President of Venezuela and Manuel Zelaya, who at that time had been the President of Honduras. But their plans were stalled when the Honduran Congress used military force to remove Zelaya from office in 2009. Chavez made several public statements to the world community supporting Zelaya's return, but beyond that he really made little effort to support the ousted president. Fuentes and Salas also distanced themselves from Zelaya, so they were able to stay on with the new government.

The Honduran Plot

It had been a frustrating few years since then. Salas had been generally ineffective, and Chavez had been preoccupied with his fight against cancer. When General Velasquez started running things in Venezuela, Fuentes saw his chance and bypassed Salas. With Chavez out of the picture, Fuentes positioned himself to become closely allied with Velasquez. The powerful General controlled the political future of Venezuela and also a lucrative drug trade. Fuentes would soon be his right-hand man.

Over the years, Fuentes had built up a loyal following in the federal police, corrupting key officers with the drug money that had begun to flow. He even provided drugs to a number of police personnel, addicting them, to expand his control. Fuentes used his federal police contacts to intimidate anyone threatening his political cronies. His control of the Army Intelligence group gave him both legitimate power, and included a clandestine core loyal only to Fuentes. When the case could be made, such as with the strike team raids to capture the computer hacker and a murder suspect, the official, legitimate side of the operation could be publically used. This allowed media publicity and Federal Police cooperation. The clandestine side, operating secretly, and wearing balaclavas to disguise their identity, terrorized anyone who was a threat to Fuentes.

However, Fuentes could not influence or control the military generals and the more level headed leaders in the Honduran government. He had to come up with a bold plan—something far beyond the manipulation of protests and politics that they had been trying unsuccessfully for the past few years. He had done just that, and had convinced General Velasquez that Venezuela's support would put them both in positions of unimagined power. Now it was time—everything was in place—and he couldn't let a possible revelation of secret plans deter him. He had to strike now, and he had to explain to Enrique what his part in the plan would be.

■■■

Fuentes knocked on the door of Enrique Salas' office in the *Casa Presidencial*, the presidential office building.

"Enter," Salas responded through the partially open door. Then he waved to a chair across from his desk when Fuentes entered.

"Good evening Enrique," Fuentes said, as he sat. "It was good of you to see me on short notice tonight. I'm sorry if I upset you on the phone this afternoon."

"That is alright Manuel. I understand that you are frustrated by our lack of progress. I can understand if General Velasquez has been pressuring you. You said you had something urgent to discuss?"

"Two things, actually," Fuentes said. He put a serious look on his face. He intended to use the computer breach to get Salas on the defensive. "The first issue is an uncomfortable one."

"Uncomfortable? Go on, what is it?" Salas said, with raised eyebrows.

"Well ... I have issued a detention warrant for your son, Raul."

"What! What are you talking about?" Salas rose out of his chair.

That got his attention. He had never seen the pudgy man move so fast before. Fuentes waved his hand for Salas to sit back down.

"Sit down; ... don't get excited. He's not under arrest, just being sought for questioning as a material witness for a breach of government security."

Salas was red in the face. "What breach of security? What does Raul have to do with it?"

"Calm down, Enrique," Fuentes said. "You have received word about the computer penetration last Monday, and the failed raid on the old parsonage where the hackers were."

"Yes, of course," Salas said. "That is why I set up the appointment for Pastor Zamora to come see you. Raul explained that they had nothing to do with it."

Fuentes shook his head, a sad look on his face. "What you may not know, Enrique, is that the computer breach was done using your passwords."

"My passwords? What are you talking about?"

"The first few times were from your home computer, then later from the parsonage. It seems logical that Raul is somehow involved."

Salas refused to believe Raul was involved. Fuentes explained about another computer which was a clone of Salas' home computer. Then Fuentes told him about the failed raid in Talanga that afternoon.

"These people are a danger to the government," Fuentes said. "I need to question Raul to get any information he has on this Jake

Grayson, who may have been using him. We also think Pastor Zamora may be involved. He never showed up for that appointment."

Salas slumped over, holding his head in his hands.

"Enrique, don't look so desperate," Fuentes walked around the desk and put a hand on his shoulder. He had the man softened up now. Time to make him feel a little gratitude and get his cooperation.

"I don't think Raul knew his computer mischief would lead to such a serious situation. I believe he was misled by that Jake Grayson that is a friend of his. Why don't you call him and tell him to come see me tomorrow morning we can get this cleared up."

"But if he is arrested ..."

"Don't worry my friend. I'll put a hold on that detention order if he agrees to come in," Fuentes said, patting him on the shoulder. "Why don't you contact him right now and get him to agree?

Salas got off the phone moments later, having gotten agreement from Raul. Things were going well. Salas was feeling vulnerable and somewhat indebted to him, making it easier to manipulate the situation. It was time to introduce the plan that he and Velasquez had conceived. Salas had to play a key role. He would object, but Fuentes would give him little choice.

"Enrique, you know that the country has turned from the principles we supported since Zelaya was removed from power. The working people and the labor unions are unhappy. The international community has applied pressure for reform, but that hasn't been enough to allow us to take power. We have to take charge of the situation now."

Salas said, "I have done everything I can to gain power in the cabinet. The president trusts me, but I can't control things. And there was no way I could get him to accept closer relations with Venezuela. He is dead set against that."

Fuentes smiled, and said, "Yes, 'dead set' is the right expression. I have worked a plan with General Velasquez that will bring us into alignment with Venezuela. You are the key to that plan, and will be the future president of Honduras. We will change history."

Salas looked stunned. "What?" he said. "Have you gone *loco*?"

"No my friend; I know exactly what I am doing. I will tell you what you have to do. There are risks, but I think everything can be accomplished. The next cabinet meeting is next week; isn't that right?"

"Yes, that's right, a week from today," Salas said.

Fuentes took his seat in front of the desk. "Hugo Chavez was very smart to have chosen General Velasquez as his chief political adviser. The man is brilliant and you and I should continue to follow his advice. He is more cunning than the both of us together. He has proposed a strategy that can indeed elevate you into the highest position in the country."

Salas asked, "How in God's name could such a thing happen?"

Fuentes said, "I'll go over the details with you next week. Let's get this misunderstanding with Raul out of the way first. Make sure he comes to see me tomorrow. And keep an open mind about the future. Velasquez is brilliant about these things. He understands political power and world politics. He will make us both powerful men."

Chapter 40

It was late in the afternoon before Jake, Amélia and Luis made it back to the farmhouse. Jake knew that they were lucky to have escaped capture. Well, it wasn't all luck—he had to admit he was impressed. Amélia, quick to react, had led them out the back entrance of the café.

Jake vaguely remembered that she had gone to the car while he was busy on the laptop. She had scouted out the alley behind the building, and then moved the car to the street behind the café. When the helicopter set down, Amélia led them out back, across the narrow alley, and through the rear door of a shop behind the cafe to the car on the other street. They had driven out of the range of the strike team's search, and made their way out of town without incident.

They were sitting at the kitchen table and Jake was looking at some of the data files he had managed to download.

"I don't think we should try the computer again," Amélia said. "They always seem to know where we are."

"Duh!" Luis countered.

Jake was spooked by the rapid response to his penetrations each time he had broken in. There was no way he was going to try that again. What else did they know?

"Do you think we're safe here?" he asked.

"We should be OK," Amélia said. "There is not much to connect me to my aunt. Who would even know that we are related? And the farm is still in her husband's name too."

Luis asked, "Can you figure out the stuff you downloaded?"

"I don't know yet," Jake said. "They are evidently just text files with columns of hexadecimal numbers."

"You said that before, that Hexa-whatever thing," Luis said.

"OK, let me explain," Jake said. "You know that computers use 1's and 0's to compute and store data; right?"

"Yeah man, I know that part. It's because the voltage is either on or off, so it can represent only a 1 or 0."

"That's right, Jake said. "Each 1 or 0 is called a bit, and they are put together to make higher value numbers; these are binary numbers. I won't try to explain how the binary numbers relate to regular decimal numbers. That's not important to understand now."

"That's good," Amélia said, "because I really don't care. This is all over my head. I'm going to take a shower." She got up and left the room.

"No, keep going," Luis said. "I want to understand."

"Well anyway ..." Jake said. Amélia *in the shower*—he had trouble concentrating on what he was saying. "Uh ... anyway, maybe we shouldn't go into all the detail; that would be a math lesson in itself. Let's just say hexadecimal numbers are base-16 numbers that are a simple way of representing binary numbers used in computers."

"I have no idea what you mean, but that's good enough for me," Luis said. "So what do you do now?"

"Well, I know these represent sets of numbers, and that they probably would represent readable documents if they could be decoded. I'm going to write a program to try various ways to unscramble them and see if I can come up with something. The fact that the numbers are arranged in groups of eight gives me some idea of where to start, at least if it's a simple coding method."

"Better you than me," Luis said. "I'll leave you to it. I'm going to see what Rodrigo is doing."

Jake sat at the table and began writing a program to run some decoding trials on the documents. He thought what he was doing was a long shot, but he didn't know what else to do. Occasionally he caught himself daydreaming, his fingers motionless on the keyboard, wondering if Amélia was out of the shower, and what she might be doing, or wearing, or not wearing. He shook his head and thought to himself *I've got to stop this.*

After dinner Jake went back to his laptop to work on his programs. Guilt ate into Jake's mind and body. The recently eaten dinner roiled in his stomach. He had to call his parents to let them know what had happened. Maybe they had some leverage, through a congressman or something, which they could use to get him out of this jam. He needed to call Barbara too. She must be worried from not hearing from him. What was he doing down here having thoughts about a Honduran girl? How could he explain it, even to himself? No, he wasn't going to try to explain it—he was never going to admit it. Barbara was his future. They had made plans. Why then, did those seem so far away—like something he remembered from a past life? This place was making him crazy!

Jake was still ineffectively poking around with his program when he was interrupted by "The Aggie Fight Song" on his cell phone. He hesitated to answer it. His doubts and indecision had kept him from calling his parents or Barbara. What if it was one of them? What would he say now?

He looked at the caller ID—it was Raul. He answered.

"Jake! I've got something on Ruben!"

Jake felt a surge of excitement at hearing the name. "What? Do you know where he is? Is he OK?"

"Slow down. I don't know much of anything," Raul said. "I got a call from a guy who said he had talked to him ... that Ruben gave him my name and cellular number."

Ruben is alive! But relief turned to worry—maybe this was a false alarm. "Didn't he tell you anything?"

"Not much," Raul said. "He was very mysterious, or maybe just very cautious. He said he had to meet me in person. I'm going to meet him tonight."

"Call me afterward," Jake said.

"I will. But listen, we have other problems. You have stirred up a hornet's nest with the computer hacking. My father called me and said I'm wanted for questioning, and that Pastor Juan never showed up to explain that he had nothing to do with this. They are looking for him too."

"Where are they?" Jake said.

"I don't know. They don't answer their cellular, and Pastor Lacas hasn't heard from them since they left his house early this morning."

"What are we going to do?" Jake asked.

"I don't know," Raul said. "My dad made an agreement that I would come in for questioning tomorrow, so I should be OK for tonight. I think all of you have to stay out of sight until we find out what is going on. Are you safe where you are? By the way, where are you?"

Jake thought about what to say. Amélia didn't trust Raul, but he did. Raul hadn't known where they were and the soldiers still showed up in Talanga. They must have had a way of finding the computer. Jake realized now that he should have tried to use an anonymous web site to hide his URL, but he had thought that might invalidate the response code emulating the Salas computer. Besides, the extra delay time might lessen the chance of his rainbow attack program working.

"We're at Amélia's aunt's farm near Talanga," he said, deciding it was best if Raul knew what was going on. "I think it's safe here. They almost got us in town, but no one should find us here."

"Stay there. I'll meet this guy tonight and call you back."

Jake had a sudden thought. "Do you think they can trace our cell calls?"

"I hadn't thought of that," Raul said. "But, I don't think they're that sophisticated …I hope not."

Chapter 41

Raul pulled into a gravel parking lot about a block south of the *Parque Central* in the old downtown section of Tegucigalpa. He paid the attendant working there and mounted the iron stairs to a paved parking lot on a higher level. It had become dark, and between the buildings he could see a crescent moon hanging in the west. He paused, looking around, there were few people around, but no one seemed to be paying any attention to him. It wasn't cold but he shivered and jammed his hands in his pockets. Raul entered the park in front of the Cathedral of Tegucigalpa, paused the globe of the Earth on a pedestal in front of the cathedral. He pretended to study it, again looking to see if anyone was following. Walking through the park to the statue of Francisco Morazán on horseback, he circled around it and back to the pedestrian walkways west of the park. He chided himself for being so jittery. A short walk west and then north brought him to the Pizza Hut.

The hostess greeted him when he entered, and offered to seat him, but he told her that he was meeting someone on the upper dining level. Before she could reply he bounded up the stairs which led to the second floor. There were a few customers there and it took a moment before he spotted someone with a red ball cap sitting in a corner table. It was an Atlanta Braves cap. The big guy wearing it was dressed in jeans and a black tee shirt.

"Josué?" Raul asked as he approached the table.

The man stood and offered his hand for a handshake. "Yes, Josué Delgado. You are Raul?"

Raul nodded and shook his hand. "What's going on? Where is Ruben?"

"Let's sit down. I'll explain everything," Josué said. "Here comes the waiter. Let's order something first."

After the waiter had left the table, Josué spoke in a low voice. "I am a corporal in Army Intelligence, part of the Security and Intelligence Ministry."

Raul said, "My father is the Director of Intelligence for the president; he has oversight over them."

"Yes, well anyway, my job is to be a guard at the S&I headquarters. That is where your friend is ... he is a prisoner there."

"A prisoner? Why?" Raul said. "What about Juanita Perez; is she there too?"

Josué nodded his head. "Yes, both. But the situation has grown worse ... Pastor Zamora and his wife ... they are both being held there too."

Raul could hardly believe what he was hearing. Could he trust this man? "I was told the Zamoras didn't show up for their appointment."

"Don't believe that. They were taken prisoner, then the pastor's car was taken back to his church. There will be no record of them being there, so it looks like they never came. That is how they make someone disappear, like your other friends."

"Why are you telling me this ...why should I believe you?"

"I know, I know," Josué said, holding out his hands as if motioning Raul to stop. "Let me explain everything to you. Then you will see I am sincere."

Raul sat back, staring at Josué. "OK, I guess ... How did you get my number?"

"I told Ruben Avila that I would help him. He told me to call you or a guy named Luis."

Josué told about his visit to Ruben in his cell and his decision to help. Raul listened for any hint of insincerity in his voice, and could not find any. The waiter brought their pizza, and Josué continued while they ate.

"Ruben Avila has been beaten, and tortured."

Raul dropped his slice of pizza. "What?"

"I told you; Fuentes is an evil person. There is no accountability for the prisoners in cellblock three. It is like a secret organization inside the S&I Ministry."

"But my father ..."

"Your father doesn't know what's going on!" Juan said.

Could that be true? Maybe that was what his dad seemed so worried about. He and Jake had speculated that someone in the government could be behind the disappearances. Suddenly Josué seemed more credible to Raul. A sense of relief came when he realized it also meant that his suspicions about his father were unfounded.

"Maybe I believe you," Raul said. "But how could they cover something like this up?"

"Fuentes can do anything he wants, and get away with it," Josué said. He gestured with a slice of pizza. "His whole department is filled with people who are either ignorant or corrupt. I didn't even know until my boss assigned me to block three. He offered me more pay, a cut of the illegal money, and warned me that anyone who goes against Fuentes is a dead man."

"But you are here now. What changed?" Raul asked.

"A girl I like asked me to go to Pastor Juan's church with her. After a while I started believing, and finally I became a Christian and was baptized." Josué hung his head and wiped a tear from his eye with his knuckle. "Pastor Juan is the one who baptized me. I began to feel really bad about what I knew was going on at S&I headquarters. I can't be a part of that anymore. I am worried sick about what might happen to Pastor Juan and Teresa. Ruben and Juanita have already suffered from what Fuentes has done, but we need to act quickly to keep him from hurting the Zamoras!"

"OK, let's say I believe you," Raul said. "What can we do?"

"I don't know... I'm scared," Josué said. "But we have to do something ... find a way to get them out,"

Raul stared across the table at Josué Delgado. If what he said was true, he had to take some action. He tried to come up with some explanation of why this man would contact him and spin this story if it wasn't so. "Why should I believe you? Maybe you're just telling me all this to trick me into admitting to something incriminating,"

"I'm not! You have to believe me," Josué pleaded. "Look, here is my military I.D. card and pass for S&I headquarters. That shows you that I am who I say I am."

Raul examined the card and badge the man had shoved across the table. His rank showed as a corporal; not likely someone with that rank would be an S&I investigator. Besides, he was supposed to go in tomorrow for questioning, why would they go to all this trouble, instead of just picking him up early? Juan seemed to be telling the truth, or was an excellent actor.

Raul said, "OK, that makes sense. I guess I believe you. Will you help me get them out?"

"Yes, yes …. That is what I was trying to tell you," Josué said. "I am deserting. I won't be part of that, and there is no other way out. I'm leaving tomorrow … for somewhere."

Raul needed to come up with a plan. He needed the others – if he knew where they were. He asked, "Josué, are you on duty tomorrow?"

"I'm supposed to be, but I told you, I'm not going back!"

"I need to call some people who can help us. They need to hear your story."

"What people?"

"Friends. Who else do we have?" Raul said. "Then we have to go to Talanga!"

Chapter 42

It was near midnight when Josué finished telling his story and answering everyone's questions. They all sat around the table in the farmhouse. Yolanda had put out some snacks, but no one seemed to feel like eating. Jake was stunned; he didn't know what to think. The mystery of Ruben and Juanita disappearing had been cleared up, but the situation seemed impossible to fix.

"We need to tell someone what is going on," Raul said.

"Who could help?" Jake asked.

"Maybe if we talked to my father ... Josué could tell him what Fuentes ..."

"No, we can't take that chance!" Amélia said, cutting him off. "No offense Raul, but the man works for your dad. We don't know where he really stands in all this."

"Bull!" Raul spat back at her. "He wouldn't condone that kind of stuff."

"Yeah man, but would he take our word over that of the guy he works with?" Luis asked. "Would anybody believe us for that matter? We got no proof *amigos*!"

Jake thought for a moment before saying, "Anyone in the government could be working with Fuentes. Whoever we confided in might rat on us."

"What about the newspapers? Maybe make all this stuff public ... someone would start an investigation," Raul said.

"Again, no proof," Luis said. "They wouldn't take the risk if they couldn't verify any of it. Besides man, there may not be much time. What if they do something to Pastor Juan or Teresa? We are pretty much on our own to fix this, now!"

Amélia spoke up: "Well, we need to come up with a plan. We can use Josué as our 'inside man' at S&I headquarters."

"And do what?" Luis asked?

"That's what we need to figure out," Amélia replied, "even if it takes all night. Aunt Yolanda, do you have some paper and pencils? We need to put down ideas and plans."

Jake listened to this with growing concern. Things were getting out of hand. No, they had gotten out of hand days ago. It was like he was trapped in some horrible nightmare.

Amélia gathered everyone around the table, including Yolanda. "We have to have a plan worked out tonight. Raul is supposed to see Colonel Fuentes in the morning. Maybe he can be a distraction somehow." She paused. "Josué, you said you are scheduled to work tomorrow. Is that right?"

"*Si*, my shift starts at noon." The big man put his hands in his pockets and shuffled his feet. "But ... I wasn't going back. I told Raul that I can't be a part of that anymore."

Amelia gave him an intense look. "You are going back. We need you!"

Jake thought to himself: *That is just like* Amélia, *to be the one to take charge. No wonder Luis calls her "El Comandante."*

They worked furiously through the night, throwing out ideas, rejecting ideas, arguing and agreeing. Yolanda kept them filled with strong Costa Rican coffee that Jake thought was the best he had tasted. As the night wore on and the balled scraps of notebook paper littered the floor around the table, Jake began to think maybe the plan had a chance.

Finally, at about two in the morning, Amélia said, "That's it. I think this will work. Everyone make notes on the times and your duties, and then try to get a little sleep. We have to get this right or ... well, I don't want to think of what could happen"

As Jake got up from the table he was startled to hear Amélia add, "Oh, one more thing. Everyone gets up at six in the morning. We have to have time for some firearms training before we leave for Mateo!"

Chapter 43

Jake wanted to tell Amélia something, but they were on a narrow trail through the trees which wound up the side of a mountain. Each time he almost caught up with her, the trail turned and she seemed further away when he rounded the twist in the trail. Finally, he caught up, just steps behind her, but her hair looked red, not black—that wasn't right. As he reached for her shoulder she turned around—but it wasn't Amélia—it was Barbara James! Before he could draw his hand back someone grabbed his shoulder and shook it …. Jake came groggily awake and looked up at Luis.

"You need to get up *amigo,*" Luis said. "Everyone is in the kitchen."

Jake sat up, rubbing his eyes and thinking about the dream.

"Come on *hombre,*" Luis said. "We got to get moving. Are you OK?"

"Yeah … weird dream," Jake mumbled as he got up. "Go on. I'll be there as soon as I get my pants on."

The scene in the kitchen took Jake by surprise. Instead of the smell of Yolanda cooking breakfast, the smell of gun oil hung in the air. Amélia, Luis, Rodrigo and Yolanda sat around the table drinking coffee. Raul and Josué had left earlier in the morning. On the table lay three rifles; the same kind Amélia had used to shoot the soldiers. Jake stopped in the doorway, unsure what to do.

Amélia looked up and smiled. "Good morning Jake. There are some tortillas and beans over there by the stove and some coffee too. Grab a quick bite; then we're going out back for you and Rodrigo to learn how to shoot the AK."

Jake stared at the weapons on the table; despite her comment the night before he hadn't expected this. "Where did those come from?"

Yolanda spoke up. "They are mine. My husband fought with the Contras against the Sandinistas in Nicaragua when he was in his early twenties. He kept these, taken from each man he killed."

"I thought you were just a kid when all that happened," Jake said, trying to figure the timeline in his head.

"*Si* ...I was probably only about fourteen when all that happened. Francisco was about ten years older than me. That all happened years before I met and married him. But he told me the stories and taught me to shoot many kinds of weapons. I kept them after he died."

Jake had just bitten into a tortilla filled with beans, and mumbled with his mouth full, "Why?"

"Because I am a 'Los Gatos cat' I guess," she said, laughing. "Do you know that story?"

Jake thought back to what Pastor Juan had told them on the mission trip the past year. He remembered it was when they went to Los Gatos to fix the church. He tried to recall the story.

■■■

It had been an early Monday morning in 2009 when Pastor Zamora picked up the mission group in his white van. As they rode to the village of Los Gatos, one of the other missionary kids, Davy, asked, "Doesn't *los gatos* mean 'the cats' in Spanish?"

"Yes, it does."

"Seems like a weird name for a town," Davy mused.

"Well, it's just a small village and the name wasn't official for many years," Pastor Juan answered. "No one knows for sure who first called it that, but there is a local story of where the name came from."

"Tell us the story," Davy said. They all listened, seemingly interested in the story.

"OK, it seems that an old woman who lived in the village found three kittens in her yard one day. She thought one of them was pretty and decided to keep it as a pet inside the house. She thought it might be good to have cats outside to keep mice away so she left the other two under the front porch. Soon one of those ran away into the woods.

"The old woman loved the inside cat and pampered it in every way. The cat would sit in her lap and be petted for hours. When she ate her meals, the cat got the best scraps.

"The outside cat occasionally got food scraps, but mostly existed on mice and birds he could catch in the yard. It slept under her front porch, but would let the woman pet it.

"The cat which ran away became wild and untrusting. It would not let anyone near it. Eventually the wild animals killed it.

"When the old woman died, the pampered inside cat didn't know what to do. It would not let anyone take care of it or feed it. It had become dependent on the old woman and didn't know how to take care of itself. Without the old woman to pamper it, it felt rejected and alone. So it soon wasted away and died.

"The outside cat, on the other hand, kept right on living his independent life as it had always done. It had enough human contact to keep from going wild, but remained independent and was capable of taking care of itself."

"I'm not sure I get it," Davy said. Jake wasn't too sure either.

Pastor Juan explained: "That is the one that the people of Los Gatos identify with. They are proud and independent, but accepting of other people, and of a just government to organize things. They don't want to be dependent on others or on the government, like the pampered cat. They also don't want to rebel and go their own way like the wild cat. This story explains their conservative values and they are proud to be 'outside cats.' I think you will like them."

■■■

Jake hadn't thought of that story since the days he had been on the mission trip. He tried to answer Yolanda. "Uh … I think so. I remember it but I'm not sure what you mean."

Amélia spoke up. "It's about being independent," she said. "We in Honduras have been threatened by both right wing dictators and communist guerillas. After the congress got rid of Zelaya, we thought that finally Honduras had gained some dignity. The military acted on principle and wasn't bought off by the corrupt elements of government – or so it seemed. Now I'm not so sure…"

"But with machine guns …" Jake said.

"That is why I kept them," Yolanda interrupted him. "To remain independent we have to have the means to protect ourselves. It's hard for you to understand because the United States has had a stable government and freedom for so many years. But we remember what it is like to be abused by those in power."

Luis spoke up. "Listen man, do you think we could get Juanita and the others out of prison any other way?"

Jake had to admit he had a point. He was surprised by his own reaction. He didn't feel particularly fearful; he just didn't have confidence they could pull it off. "Well, I guess we had better learn how to use these machine guns in case we need to use them."

Amélia said, "I hope we won't have to use them. If we do this right we can just use them to disarm the soldiers and force them to obey our orders. Like we discussed last night, Josué can make sure the cellblocks are secure and help us get the prisoners out. We should be able to do this without firing a shot; but just in case, you have to know how to use the weapons effectively."

"First lesson," Yolanda said, picking up one of the weapons. "This is not a 'machine gun'. It is an AK-47 assault rifle. These were made in Russia and supplied by Cuba to the Sandinistas, like I told you before. Because of its low cost, durability and ease of use it is one of the most widely used and popular assault rifles in the world.

"I will teach you and Rodrigo how to use them. Amélia and Luis have already been trained so they can help you as we go through the lesson. Amélia, you can help Jake. Let's go out behind the house to the hillside which will act as a backstop."

Outside the lesson began in earnest. Yolanda, Luis and Amélia each demonstrated how to fill the curved magazines with the bullets, and then insert and remove the magazines from the rifle. Then Amélia handed her unloaded rifle to Jake.

"Wow, that's pretty heavy!" Jake exclaimed.

Yolanda laughed, and said, "*Si,* you have already learned something! This is the older design with a solid milled receiver. It weighs about four point two kilograms without the magazine and bullets; that's over nine pounds. These two newer ones manufactured after 1959, called AKM, have stamped sheet metal receivers and weigh about a third less. You and Rodrigo take them."

She then demonstrated to them how to fire the weapons. "To fire, you insert a loaded magazine, move the selector lever off of safety, pull back and release the charging handle to load the first round, aim and then pull the trigger." The bullet pinged off one of the rocks she had placed on the hillside as targets. "In this setting the AK only fires once. You have to release the trigger and press it again for the next shot; what you would call semiautomatic. This is the setting I want you to use."

"But it does fire a lot of bullets at once?" Jake asked, looking at the safety lever.

"Yes," Yolanda said, "If you set the selector to the middle position, full-automatic, the rifle continues to fire until the magazine is emptied or you release the trigger. But I don't want you to use that. That thing can fire roughly six hundred rounds a minute. If you held the trigger down for just three seconds, you would fire all thirty of the rounds in your magazine. You would have no accuracy. They would go all over the place and then you would be out of bullets."

They spent the next hour practicing all aspects of the weapon and shooting at rocks placed on the hillside. Amélia and Luis also practiced a little. Jake was impressed with the ease and expertise Amélia demonstrated as she handled the weapon and pinged small rock after rock up the hillside. Jake wondered about Yolanda's late husband; he must have anticipated a revolution because he evidently had bought (or stolen?) several magazines and many boxes of bullets for the three AK-47s he had confiscated from the Sandinista soldiers.

After this introduction Jake felt familiar with the rifle and was confident he could handle it—if it came to that. Yolanda had even let them try the full-automatic setting one time with about twenty bullets in the magazine. Jake's shots climbed up the hillside away from the large target rock he was aiming for; Amélia's stayed on target, chipping chunks off the rock.

A short time later they left the farm in Rodrigo's car. Luis sat in the passenger seat, Jake and Amélia in the rear. As they headed for Mateo, Jake wondered if he could do his part. Maybe they could pull this plan off without having to get in a firefight. That was the plan at least, and it might have a good chance of working.

No matter what happened in the next few hours, his life had changed forever. There was no thought of turning back now. The odd thing was that it didn't seem to be unbelievable, or crazy. He had awakened this morning to a new Jake Grayson. Somehow his mind had processed the situation. Some mental switch had been thrown, bringing an unlikely combination of emotions: fear, determination, and even adventure. The old goals and dreams from his life in the United States seemed to recede into a corner of his mind—something for later, perhaps.

There was something else too. When Amélia reached over and squeezed his hand, Jake felt … confidence.

Chapter 44

Raul had only gotten a few of hours of sleep before driving Josué back to the parking lot to pick up his car. Josué would just have enough time to go home and change into his uniform before reporting for his guard shift. Raul went home and showered, then brewed a pot of strong coffee. Two cups later, he felt like his batteries had been recharged. He drove down the winding road into the old center of Tegucigalpa, on his way to Mateo. He mentally rehearsed his story regarding the computer hacking. He would admit to some of the things they had done, in hopes of skirting around Jake's more serious attempt.

He arrived late for the appointment, earning him a penetrating look from the icy blue eyes of the receptionist at the headquarters building. He was quickly escorted to Colonel Fuentes' office on the second floor.

"I'm sorry to be late, sir," Raul said when he was shown in to the office. "There was much more traffic delay than I had anticipated."

Fuentes didn't rise from his chair—he just sat behind his desk and glared at Raul. An uncomfortable silence gnawed at Raul's nerves. Finally the Colonel pointed to a chair in front of the desk. "Sit!"

"Yes sir," Raul sat in the hard bottomed chair and squirmed uncomfortably in the seat.

"Your father explained to you why I wanted you to come in for this interview, didn't he?" Before Raul could answer Fuentes continued. "I suppose because he is Minister of Intelligence you think you can just wander in any time you please. Because he has oversight over my organization you think you won't be subject to penalties like any other person who endangers national security!"

Raul caught his breath and felt the heat rising to his face. "No! ... Uh ... no sir! I'm sorry I was late ...meant no disrespect." He had to turn this around. It wasn't starting like he thought it would.

Fuentes made no pretense of politeness out of respect of Raul's father and his position. He called in Lieutenant Garcia, one of his army intelligence officers. The interview degraded into an intense interrogation, starting in Fuentes' office and later moving down to an interview room in the basement level. Raul tried to be evasive and stall for time.

Raul's anger flared and he could feel waves of heat course through his body. Evasion was futile. Why was he stalling for time? That wouldn't work. He wouldn't give them anything—he would just shut up. He made their voices fade into the distance, a sort of self-hypnosis.

Suddenly Garcia grabbed his arm and strapped some sort of leather belt or cuff to it. Raul tried to jerk away, but the man's wiry strength overpowered him. He was strapped to the arm of the metal chair. Then, despite his best efforts to resist, Garcia attached restraints to his other arm and both ankles. As Raul tried to resist he could smell the sweat and feel the wetness of the other man as he held him and strapped the leather, binding him tightly to the chair. Raul panted raggedly and tried to catch his breath.

Leaning in close to Raul's face, Fuentes spoke in a menacing whisper: "I have had enough of this nonsense Raul."

Then Fuentes gave him an injection with some kind of drug using a small hypodermic with a fine needle. Raul felt lethargy wash through his body. He was tired, exhausted, and the fight went out of him, replaced by dread.

He watched helplessly as Garcia brought some sort of box, an electrical device obviously since he plugged it into the wall. Raul felt so tired, his arms and legs were leaden, and it was an effort to breathe. But that didn't lessen his fear as Garcia strapped electrodes around his ankles and attached wires running from the box.

"Each time you fail to provide an acceptable answer to my questions I will push this button. You won't like the result. No one will believe you if you try to tell them we tortured you. Even your father would not believe that I would treat you with anything but the most respect. The restraints and electrical contacts are designed to not leave visible marks. Besides, the drug you were given will make your memory of all this seem like a fuzzy nightmare, if you remember it at all." Fuentes chuckled. "But, it won't dull the pain."

Raul was in a foggy dreamlike state. *I won't ... won't what? Oh yeah, Jake and the computers ... the plan ... where was* Amélia? *Were they supposed to be here? Can't tell.*

Then the first jolt of electricity hit him and it felt like his legs and groin were on fire. He screamed and pulled against the restraints, trying to get away from the pain even though his rational mind told him it was useless. But he wasn't too rational by now.

■■■

For Josué the morning seemed to creep by. He had arrived for his shift on time, but felt fatigued from lack of sleep and worry. He kept imagining that his shift supervisor and Celestino Anaya, the other guard in the basement, were covertly watching him. Did they know something?

Then, just before eleven o'clock, Colonel Fuentes and Lieutenant Garcia brought Raul Salas down and went into an interrogation room. Raul was supposed to be meeting Colonel Fuentes in his office. He was supposed to come up with a diversion—something to delay and distract. They weren't supposed to be down here.

Josué felt like he might throw up. Could he do this? What was happening to Raul? Had he told Fuentes about their plans? They had been in the interrogation room for a long time, and he and Celestino heard shouts and screams through the walls. Raul was going to give the whole thing away!

Things were getting out of control. It was almost time for the kitchen worker to bring the food trays for the prisoners on cellblock three. The plan had been to wait until after the trays were delivered, and his supervisor left for lunch, then he would disable Celestino and call for an ambulance because of the "accident."

How could the plan work with Fuentes and the army officer interrogating Raul in there? His sergeant wouldn't leave for lunch with Fuentes around. He had to think of some way to make the plan work, but right now his mind was blank. Think!

■■■

They were running late, and Amélia had been urging Rodrigo to hurry all the way on the drive from Talanga. They encountered a police checkpoint on the way into Tegucigalpa, and Jake held his breath as the officer looked in the driver's side window. Luckily, the stop had been routine. Rodrigo had shown his registration and told the officer they were going to the university. They were waved on with no further questions.

The Honduran Plot

They made a detour to La Vega and, sure enough, there was Pastor Juan's white van sitting in front of the church, where Josué said it would be. He had been told it was returned to the parking lot after the Zamoras had been secretly detained. They planned to move it to a more secluded place and use it as their get-away vehicle. Luis was able to break into it and find the keys, and Rodrigo followed him to the planned rendezvous site. It only took a few minutes to conceal the vehicle in some trees and bushes. Jake could see Amélia impatiently checking the time on her cellphone.

It was almost noon when they passed the drive that led to *Hospital Militar*, the military hospital in Mateo. Rodrigo made a U-turn a short distance beyond the gate and pulled to the side of the road. There were no cars in sight, so they all got out and gathered at the rear of the vehicle.

Rodrigo opened the trunk and retrieved a backpack, three AK-47s and loaded clips hidden under a piece of carpet. Jake scanned the road both ways as Luis and Rodrigo pulled balaclavas over their faces. What if someone came down the road? Amélia sent a text message to Josué on her cellular, then put on her own mask. The three of them hurried away from the road to the trees where they were less likely to be seen by passing vehicles.

Jake hurried to get into the driver's seat and then put on sunglasses and a ball cap. By this time he was sweating profusely. He patted the reassuring bulge of the old revolver in his jean's pocket. He slowly drove back the short distance to the hospital entrance. He turned into the drive, and let the car coast to a stop beside the yellow gatehouse at the white, wrought-iron gate which blocked the drive. Feeling foolish, Jake unfolded a large map and held it up on the steering wheel. He sat looking at the map, hoping he looked like a lost tourist. He waited with a knot forming in his stomach. Nothing was happening—couldn't they see him? *Come on, do something!*

Finally a guard emerged from the gatehouse and approached the car. As he did so, Jake could see three masked figures appear from behind the gatehouse brandishing AK-47s. Amélia and Rodrigo entered the guardhouse door which had been left ajar, while Luis shouted for the startled guard to raise his hands. Within minutes they had both guards subdued without firing a shot. So far, so good.

Jake drove through the gate and pulled off the drive onto the grass. Continuing, he pulled the vehicle into a stand of trees and bushes which would hide it from sight. By the time he got back to the gatehouse the others had stripped one of the guards of his uniform, leaving him in his underwear, bound and gagged with duct tape. Rodrigo put on the uniform, ready to wave on any vehicles entering or exiting the hospital drive. They were ready.

■■■

The vibrating cellular phone startled Josué just as the food trays arrived. Distracted, and still trying to decide what to do, Josué took the cart holding the trays without speaking a word to the kitchen worker. This earned him a suspicious scowl and he realized something was wrong. "What?" he asked the man.

"What is wrong?" the man asked. "You are acting strange!"

"Uh ... no," Josué responded. "Well ... yes ... The Colonel is down here. Some sort of interrogation. Sorry ... go on, it's OK. I've got to get these distributed."

After the man had left, Josué fished out his cellular and read the text. "Ready," it said. He needed to put the plan into action before someone noticed the others near the hospital. He opened the door to cellblock three and shoved the cart inside. Returning to the outside hall he went to Sergeant Pinero's office. He pulled out his service pistol, a heavy 45 caliber semi-automatic, grabbed it by the barrel and held it like a hammer, keeping it beside his leg, out of sight.

"Yes?" Pinero said, looking up as Josué entered his office. "Is something wrong?"

"I think so," Josué said. Then he struck the sergeant on the side of the head with the pistol.

Sergeant Pinero fell out of his chair, onto the floor. But it wasn't like the movies Josué had seen. The man was just stunned, not knocked unconscious. Quickly looking to see if Celestino had noticed anything, he closed the door. Josué turned to find the sergeant rising to his feet and pulling his weapon. Josué hit him again with the pistol and this time the man stayed down.

Josué was perspiring and breathing heavily. His hands shook as he picked up the phone and dialed the medical emergency number.

"Send an ambulance immediately to S&I headquarters!" he shouted into the phone. "Colonel Fuentes has been attacked by the guard sergeant and is badly hurt."

The Honduran Plot

He slammed the phone down and pulled out the cellular. Pressing the speed dial for Amélia, he waited for her to answer. For this to work, the others would have to help him disable Celestino, the lieutenant and Fuentes. He couldn't do all that on his own. He wondered what he would do if someone found him in the sergeant's office before the others arrived to help. *What if the hospital called to verify his report before sending the ambulance?*

Chapter 45

Jake, Amélia and Luis waited nervously in the brush along the gravel drive to the military hospital. Amélia answered the incoming call from Josué and the color drained from her face as she listened to what he had to say.

"I don't know if we can," she said into the phone. "They are trained soldiers; we can't get into a gun battle with them! What? OK, maybe that is right … do what you can." She snapped the cellular closed and pocketed it.

"What's going on?" Jake asked. He was getting a bad feeling about this.

"Josué just called for the ambulance, but there has been a change of plans," Amélia said. "Instead of having to only take care of one disabled guard, now we have to somehow take on two soldiers and Colonel Fuentes - and also rescue Raul."

Jake felt a chill run down his back, and was at a loss for words. He was getting in too deep, but they had little choice but to continue.

"We can't do all that!" Luis exclaimed.

"We have to, things are already set in motion" Amélia replied. "Come on, get ready. The ambulance will be coming any second."

Jake retrieved his AK-47 and a balaclava from the trunk of the car. Amélia had already readied her rifle, and took her position in the brush to the side of the gravel drive. Luis took the other side of the road and charged his weapon.

"Come on Jake," Amélia shouted. "They will be coming any time now"

Jake awkwardly pulled the balaclava over his head, trying to decide whether the opening for his eyes should be pulled down below his nose or not. Why hadn't they shown him how this ski mask thing was to be worn? He took his position with Luis on the other side of the drive from Amélia. Rodrigo stood in the middle of the drive, in front of the closed gate facing the road from the hospital. Jake's mouth felt dry, like it was filled with cotton, and he heard the sound of a vehicle approaching.

An ambulance came barreling around the curve and came to a screeching halt as Rodrigo, in uniform and holding his rifle in the air, motioned for it to stop. It finally stopped about six feet from him, and he yelled, "Out of the vehicle! Put up your hands!" while gesturing with the assault rifle. From the sides of the drive Luis, Amélia and Jake ran to the vehicle pointing their AK-47s at the rear door, the driver and the other medic. Slowly the medics complied, looking scared and confused.

"On the ground! Now!" Luis screamed at them.

Jake shakily held his rifle on the two men lying prone in the drive. *I never pulled back the charging handle!* He couldn't do anything if they tried to get up, except maybe hit them.

Amélia opened the rear door to make sure no one else was in the ambulance. Luis made the medics strip off their uniform shirts, and Rodrigo secured them with duct tape. Amélia stood guard while Jake helped Luis and Rodrigo drag the men into the guardhouse. Rodrigo stood in the doorway to keep a watch over the bound medics and guards, while giving the illusion that all was normal to hospital traffic.

Jake and Luis put on the medic's uniform shirts and got into the cab of the ambulance. Amélia got into the rear and hid the AK-47s and the backpack containing spare magazines of ammunition and more duct tape under a collapsible gurney. As they drove out the drive and turned toward the S&I headquarters another ambulance turned into the hospital drive with its siren screaming. Their luck had held and no one had come into the drive while they were hijacking the ambulance.

Amélia sent a text to Josué: "Coming now. Still OK?"

"OK. Will notify front gate," came the reply.

"We're all set," Amélia said.

Jake said, "What if they find out what Josué is up to before we get there?" His mind was racing through all the things he thought could go wrong. There seemed to be countless possibilities.

"We'll know when we get there, man," Luis replied.

That thought didn't make Jake feel any better. A short time later, Jake saw the sign reading *Universidad de Defensa de Honduras* on the right side of the road.

Luis turned the ambulance into the drive and flipped on the siren and emergency flashers. As they roared past the first buildings the drive split and he took the right hand fork. Jake saw a large three-story modern building surrounded by a high chain-link fence topped with razor wire.

The front gate was rolled open but the drive was still blocked by a metal pipe barrier at the guard shack. Jake tensed up as they neared the gate. This is where they would encounter problems if Josué had been discovered.

By the time they reached the gate the guard had raised the barrier arm and waved them through. Jake breathed a sigh of relief and turned around to see Amélia crouched down behind their seats with her AK-47 at the ready, the safety selector in the off position. "It's OK," Jake said. "Evidently the guard at the gate didn't question Josué's call that an ambulance would be coming."

"I'm keeping the safety off just in case," Amélia said. "Luis, cut the siren; we don't need it now. Go around to that drive to the left of the building after you get through the parking lot. The basement entrance is in the rear."

The rear entrance was a large overhead door set behind a low concrete loading dock with a smaller door to one side. Luis backed the ambulance up to the loading dock and cut the engine. Through the side mirror Jake saw the smaller door open. A guard came out, holding his rifle at the ready position. *Now what?*

Luis said, "I'll get out and distract the guard."

Jake just nodded and kept watching through the rear view mirror. Luis had just stepped out of the ambulance when there was a movement from the door behind the guard. From the shadows of the open doorway Josué struck the guard in the head with the butt of a rifle, and the man dropped to the concrete and stayed down.

"Help me get him inside," Josué said as both Jake and Amélia emerged from the ambulance. "Then put on your masks and come in quickly. Keep quiet. Fuentes and an intelligence officer are still in the interrogation room with Raul."

Luis helped Josué drag the guard into the supervisor's office and they laid him next to the unconscious sergeant. Jake and Amélia brought in the weapons, spare magazines and tape from the ambulance. While Josué was taping up the unconscious men, a scream rang out from the room down the hall.

"What was that?" Jake asked.

"It's Raul. They are hurting him I'm afraid," Josué said.

Amélia and Luis started for the door. "Let's go!" Amélia cried.

Josué dropped the tape and grabbed her arm. "Wait," he said in a loud whisper. "We need to get the others out to the ambulance first. If shooting starts the place will be swarming with guards in no time. We won't have time to rescue them then."

"But Raul ..." Jake protested.

"We'll get him in just a minute," Josué said. "I'll open the cellblock for you, and the three of you can go get them and take them to the ambulance. The cell numbers are 303, 309, 321 and 322. I'll keep watch in the hall." He finished taping up the guard saying, "Sorry Celestino, my friend." Then turning to the others he said, "Come on, and keep quiet."

He led them to the cellblock and unlocked the entry door. "Here, take these keys," he said, handing them to Luis. The big silver one unlocks the cells. Hurry!"

Josué kept watch in the hallway while Jake went with the others to get the prisoners. It didn't take long, but Ruben was weak and couldn't walk fast. Juanita seemed like a zombie. Jake couldn't understand what was wrong. Ruben hugged and kissed her, tears rolling down his cheeks, but Juanita just stood there with her eyes tightly closed. Pastor Juan and Teresa were crying too. Jake's eyes filled with tears and he had a lump in his throat.

"Hurry, we have to go," Amélia said as she and Luis pulled them toward the entrance of the cellblock.

Chapter 46

Raul was in a fog of confusion. The pain in his legs throbbed and he wondered if he would be able to even walk again. What? Someone was talking to him …oh yeah; Fuentes was still screaming questions at him. He couldn't remember what he had been asked, but he could remember the pain when he gave an answer that Fuentes didn't like. He vaguely remembered the army guy laughing at something he said, and Fuentes saying, "Pay attention!" before he pressed that button unleashing another wave of pain. He hated Fuentes. You weren't supposed to hate—you were supposed to forgive. He couldn't do that. Maybe he couldn't live up to what God demanded of … Another wave of pain hit him! He had lost track of the questions again.

∎∎∎

Fuentes had gotten all he could out of Raul. The boy was drifting in and out of consciousness. "Go get one of the prison guards and have him locked up in cellblock three," he told Lieutenant Garcia.

The man started out the door, then stopped, drew his pistol and shouted, "Halt! What is going on out there?"

Fuentes quickly drew his pistol and joined Garcia at the doorway. The officer raised his weapon and fired. Two shots in response cut him down. Fuentes pulled back into the room, trying to figure out what was going on. Dropping to his knees he peered around the door frame. A bullet splintered the edge of the door facing not six inches above his head! He again pulled back, but not before he was able to see who was shooting at him. It was one of his guards, Corporal Delgado! More disturbing was the fact that behind the corporal he had seen several masked persons and some of the prisoners. What was going on? *An escape, obviously!*

He grabbed the phone on the wall, holding his pistol on the door in case anyone tried to enter. No dial tone; the phone had been disabled.

∎∎∎

Jake was startled by the first shot. They had just exited the cellblock, urging the rescued prisoners to hurry, when someone shot

Josué in the arm. Before Jake could decide where the shot had come from, Josué cursed and returned fire down the hallway hitting his assailant, and driving another man back into the open door of the interrogation room.

Josué shouted, "Get them out now!" and fired another shot at the face that appeared around the door facing near the floor.

Jake steered Ruben and Juanita through the door. Amélia and Luis followed with Pastor Juan and Teresa. Jake opened the rear door of the ambulance, and the freed prisoners were hustled inside.

"We have to go!" Amélia shouted. "The gunfire will bring all the guards!"

"Raul's in there; we can't leave him!" Jake yelled, starting back toward the door.

"I'll come with you," Luis said.

Jake hesitated. "No, you and Amélia get in the ambulance and be ready to go. I'll help Josué find Raul."

He charged through the doorway before either of them could argue. Inside everything was quiet. Josué still had his pistol trained on the open door of the interrogation room. Blood was flowing down his other arm. "It's Fuentes, alone in there with Raul," he told Jake. "I disabled his phone, but we have to do something before someone responds to the gunshots. Follow me!"

Jake checked his AK-47 to make sure the safety lever was off, charged the weapon and followed Josué as he slowly ventured down the hallway toward the open door.

Before they could get very far the elevator door across from the interrogation room opened and two soldiers came out, their weapons raised. Luckily the first person they saw was Josué, who was in uniform. Their slight hesitation was all Josué needed, and he fired, dropping one of the men. Jake immediately fired at the other soldier, hitting him in the leg and forcing him to retreat into the open elevator. Another shot rang out and Josué crumpled to the floor. Jake fired at the doorway without thinking, driving Fuentes back, and then fired again at the soldier attempting to come out of the elevator. The man groaned and fell back into the open elevator as its door tried to close and then opened again when it encountered the man's body.

Jake's mouth dried up, feeling like it was full of cotton. He felt shaky and his heart was pounding. Nothing seemed real and he shook his head to clear it. *Did he just kill a man?* He wasn't sure the soldier was dead, but his thoughts were interrupted when Fuentes fired again at Jake.

Boom! Boom! He felt a sharp sting in his right leg, and the shakiness caused by the rush of adrenalin turned to aggression. Jake charged directly toward the door, acting on instinct, firing his rifle again and again at the figure in the doorway until the man was down and all went quiet again. The man, Fuentes he presumed, was lying unconscious on the floor, bleeding from the chest, leg and arm. *Is he dead? Where's Raul?*

Jake found Raul in the interrogation room, staring wide eyed at the masked figure which had appeared in the doorway. He appeared somewhat dazed and was bound into his chair with leather straps. Wires ran out from his pants legs to a device on the table.

"Raul, it's me … Jake. We have to hurry!" he said as he moved to unbuckle the bindings restraining Raul.

When his hands were free, Raul pulled up his pants legs and ripped the electrodes from his legs while Jake undid the straps holding his ankles to the chair legs. Jake helped him up and steadied him as they made their way out of the room.

The elevator door was still bumping over and over against the body of the soldier who lay half in the elevator. He left Raul leaning against a wall and went to check on Josué, but it appeared to Jake that he was dead. Jake felt a pang of regret, but there was nothing they could do. They had to get out of there and they couldn't take Josué with them.

Together they made their way out the door. Raul seemed to be gaining more awareness and strength. Jake helped him into the rear of the ambulance and climbed in after him. It was crowded but at least they had everyone together now—except Josué.

"We're in. Go! Go!" Jake yelled. He turned to pull the rear door shut when he saw a soldier run out of the rear door of the building and raise his rifle. Jake heard the noise of the rifle firing, felt a massive wave of pain in his chest, and then everything went black.

Chapter 47

In the driver's seat Luis heard, *"We're in. Go! Go!"... BAM!*

He jammed his foot on the gas pedal and the ambulance leaped forward. More gunfire erupted and there was a sound like someone was banging on the side of the vehicle with a hammer as bullets punched through the metal. Screams erupted from the passengers in the back. The rear doors banged open and shut when the ambulance swerved.

The vehicle careened around the side of the building, spraying gravel from its rear wheels. Luis could see soldiers on the lawn aiming their rifles toward him. He left the gravel drive, bouncing over the bumpy grass, and hugged the side of the building, protecting his side of the vehicle and giving Amélia a clear field of view to the soldiers. "No need to conserve ammo now!" he yelled to Amélia. "Keep them from shooting us!"

Amélia pushed her AK-47 out the window, the selector lever set to the full automatic position. Luis prayed her firepower would intimidate the soldiers. She swung the rifle from front to back as she held the trigger down. *BRRUPT!* Casings flew out banging against the doorpost as the thirty round magazine emptied in just a few seconds. The shots probably went wild, but all the soldiers threw themselves to the ground to escape the deadly hail of bullets.

Luis bounced back on the drive and roared across the parking lot, toward the front gate. Amélia removed the spent magazine and slammed another one in place. She charged the weapon and leaned out the window. Again on automatic fire she pulled the trigger for a short burst, breaking two of the guardhouse windows and chipping the walls with bullets. The pipe barrier across the drive was down. Luis aimed the ambulance toward the tip end, which he thought would be the weakest point, and yelled to Amélia to get down. *BANG! SCREECH!* The front of the ambulance hit the barrier, bending it backwards, and ripping the tip of the pipe down the side of the vehicle.

"Man that was intense!" Luis flipped on the siren and emergency lights, roaring out of the drive and fishtailing onto the main road leading out from Mateo. His senses felt wide awake and a sense of elation filled him. He imagined the damage to the ambulance wouldn't be noticed and no one would attempt to stop them before they could get far away.

Luis came down off of his high as he became aware of screams and crying coming from the rear of the vehicle. Amélia left her seat and crawled in the back with the others.

"Jake! Oh my God!" he heard her cry.

■ ■ ■

Amélia had finally reacted to the sounds of distress coming from the rear of the ambulance. She crawled between the seats into the rear of the crowded ambulance. Everyone was jostling against one another as Luis roared down the road and around curves. Amélia became oblivious to all that when she saw Jake. He laid face up, unconscious, the front of his shirt soaked with blood. Pastor Juan had his hand pressed on Jake's upper chest, near his right shoulder. Blood seeped out from under his hand, pooling on the ambulance floor. Teresa was frantically pulling open compartments and drawers in the ambulance.

Jake looked pale and Amélia couldn't tell if he was breathing. Tears welled up in her eyes and she felt her throat tighten. "We've got to do something!"

Except for Pastor and Mrs. Zamora, the others seemed immobilized by shock at the sight of Jake's body on the floor. Raul still looked dazed, and Ruben held Juanita who had her eyes closed and was trembling.

Amélia's heart pounded. "He's not breathing!"

Pastor Juan grabbed her arm as she leaned down to give Jake mouth-to-mouth resuscitation. "He's breathing; I already checked. Teresa's trying to find something to apply to the wound to stop the bleeding."

About that time Teresa turned back around with a handful of square gauze pads, scissors and a roll of tape. "Here, open these!" she told Amélia, thrusting the pads into her hands. "I'll do the tape," she added.

Amélia frantically tore open the packages of gauze. *He was breathing!* She tried to keep her balance on her knees as Luis wove back and forth in the traffic on the road leading out of Mateo toward Comayagüela. Teresa cut the front of Jake's bloody shirt and pulled it back as Juan released the pressure he had been applying. Blood oozed out of a hole on Jake's upper right chest, just below his collarbone.

Juan said, "Put a bunch of those pads over the hole and press down while Teresa tapes them."

Teresa tried to apply the tape, but it wasn't sticking. "There's too much wet blood; the tape won't stick!"

Amélia was thinking more clearly now. She took some of the gauze pads and wiped around the edge of the ones she was pressing upon. "Try it now."

"OK. That's good, but I think he's still bleeding from his back." Teresa said. "Let's turn him over, quickly!"

Jake's back looked much worse than his chest. The bullet had torn a ragged hole just below his shoulder blade. Amélia's throat ached and she was sobbing as Juan packed some gauze in the hole and she applied more pads on top. Teresa taped them tightly and found a sheet to wrap around Jake.

"We have ... to get him ...to a hospital now," Amélia said between sobs.

Luis yelled back to them: "We're coming up to *Hospital San Jorge* in just a minute. I can pull in there!"

"Wait, there has to be an alert out," Juan said, looking intently at Amélia. "I don't think it's safe."

"We have to stop! Jake's hurt bad," Amélia said, raising her voice. "Luis, get him to the emergency room now!"

Luis yelled back, "It's coming up now. Get back up here with me ... we'll make up some kind of story." He swerved sharply, earning them a sharp horn blast. Amélia was thrown off her knees, but scrambled up and went to the front. As she plopped into the passenger seat Luis whipped into the hospital's drive. Following the sign with large letters saying *"EMERGENCIA"* took them around to the side of the hospital.

Two police officers were standing on the loading dock in front of the emergency room doors, smoking cigarettes. Their eyes opened wide at the sight of the ambulance roaring toward them. One officer raised his hands in a gesture to halt them while the other dropped his cigarette and fumbled with the safety strap on his holster, trying to draw his pistol.

Luis slammed on the brakes as the officer with his hands up yelled for him to stop. The other guard finally got his pistol out, flipped off the safety and pointed it right at them. Suddenly a hole appeared in the windshield, accompanied by the sharp pop of the gunshot and flying chunks of glass.

"Oh my God!" Amélia screamed. "Go! Get out of here; they're shooting!"

Luis threw the ambulance into reverse and jammed his foot on the gas pedal. The ambulance screeched backwards, careened as Luis performed a skillful three point turn, and roared up the drive. The mirror on the door beside Amélia exploded sending glass shrapnel flying. Two bullets punched through the rear doors, only missing the frightened passengers because they were all lying flat on the bloody floor, screaming.

Chapter 48

Enrique Salas was working in his office at home, but had difficulty concentrating. He hadn't heard from Raul and was worried about the outcome of his meeting with Colonel Fuentes. *Surely they must be through by now!*

The phone rang and Salas picked it up and spoke: *"Saludo ... ¿qué? ... ¿en cuando? Si, por supuesto."* His face was pale as he slammed the phone down and hurried to his bedroom to change.

Mrs. Salas looked up from her magazine as Enrique entered, dressed in suit and tie. "Where are you going?" she asked. "I thought you were working in your home office today."

"Someone took Raul! He's in trouble. I'm going to S&I headquarters. They are sending a driver ... he should be here any minute." This was terrible—he didn't know how to explain it.

"What?" Confusion showed in her expression. "Who took him? What are you talking about?"

He came to her and said, "There was an attack at S&I Headquarters. Armed gunmen broke out some prisoners, killed some guards and badly wounded Colonel Fuentes."

She threw the magazine to the floor. "But what about Raul? I don't understand what that has to do with him."

"He was ... uh, meeting with Fuentes there when it happened. Now he's gone ... they must have kidnapped him." He couldn't understand any of this.

"Why? I mean, why he was meeting with Fuentes?" she said, frowning. "Who would kidnap him? And ..." Tears started running down her cheeks, dripping, staining her blouse.

"I'll explain later; when I know something. I have to go now," he said, holding her shoulders. "I'll find out more when I get there. You wait here."

∎∎∎

Mass confusion reigned when Enrique Salas arrived at the S&I headquarters building. Armed patrols were roaming the streets around

Mateo and Comayagüela, and the battered entrance barrier at the headquarters building was heavily guarded. Major Rivas, who was Fuentes' second-in-command, filled Salas in on the startling, and embarrassing events of the day. As Enrique sought more information on what had exactly happened, things seemed more confusing.

"It is very serious, sir," Rivas told him. "There was an attack on the prison in the lower level of the building. Colonel Fuentes has been taken to the military hospital in serious condition and is currently in surgery. Four ..."

Salas interrupted him. "What about my son, Raul? You told me on the phone that he had been kidnapped. That doesn't make any sense!"

Rivas held up his hands in a placating gesture and said, "Yes sir, I know. Please calm down and we can work this thing out together."

"Alright, just explain what happened," Salas said in a quieter voice.

"As I was saying, Colonel Fuentes was badly injured and four others were killed in the basement level of the building. Lieutenant Garcia and Colonel Fuentes were interviewing your son in a room on that level. Something concerning a computer breach. When everything was over there was no sign of your son, so we can only conclude he was taken."

"You said four were killed. Do you think Raul was hurt?"

"We can't be sure sir. There is a fair amount of blood down there, including some going out the back door. Someone was wounded, but we can't tell who."

In the basement level, Salas was introduced to Sergeant Pinero, the sergeant in charge of the guard detail, and Corporal Anaya, a guard. Both had been knocked unconscious and tied up with duct tape. They had appeared to be coming around when they were found, so they were not taken to the hospital until they could answer questions about what had happened.

As Salas questioned the sergeant, he gained little of value.

"I already told Major Rivas that I don't know what happened. All I remember is the guard coming in the office ... I think he hit me with something, knocked me out."

"One of your guards? Who?" Salas asked.

"Corporal Delgado. I remember him coming in the office and then everything is weird, like a dream, but I remember trying to get up and him swinging at me," the sergeant replied. "When I came to, I was taped up, and then I heard all the gunshots."

"Delgado was one of the ones killed, wasn't he?" Salas asked.

"Yes," Major Rivas said, "We think he was part of the escape plot. Fuentes or Garcia must have exchanged fire with him first. The two privates who were killed were responding to gunshots heard on the first floor and took the elevator down to see what was going on."

"What about you?" Salas said, turning to Corporal Anaya. "What did you see?"

"Uh …. Well …I think it maybe was Josué …uh, Corporal Delgado. He was acting all uptight this morning," the young guard replied.

"Well, tell him what happened, Corporal!" Rivas prompted.

"Oh, yes sir!" Anaya said, sitting up straighter. "Well, I heard a siren outside; then it cut off. I went out the back door beside the loading bay, and there was an ambulance backing up and parking. The driver got out and I was just about to ask him what was going on when … well, uh, that is all I remember. Someone hit me in the back of my head."

"OK. I agree with you," Salas said, talking to Major Rivas. "It does appear to be an inside job. Delgado must have been the one to call for the ambulance. So who escaped?"

Major Rivas and the sergeant exchanged glances. "Well sir, I don't think I can tell you that," Rivas said.

"What?" Salas was dumbfounded.

Finally, under pressure from Salas, Major Rivas revealed that the records for cellblock three were in a *black* classification, with *need to know* restrictions.

Salas exploded: "I am President Lobo's Chief of Intelligence! As such, I have oversight over all matters concerning the security of Honduras. Don't you think I have the need to know?"

After more argument, and threats from Salas to involve the president if necessary, Rivas relented. "Come upstairs to my office and I will *read you in* to the program. Then we will review the prisoner records."

Salas was amazed to find that the prisoners in cellblock three were unknown to any other persons in the government, except for a select few that reported to Fuentes. A check of the cellblock records revealed that two prisoners were missing; an American male named Ruben Avila, and a Honduran female named Juanita Perez. Salas didn't recognize either name. He noticed Rivas frown when scanning the records. *There is something he's not telling me.*

Rivas received a call from one of his patrols, and passed on the information. "They reported finding two ambulance attendants, and two guards. They were in the gatehouse of *Hospital Militar*, bound and gagged with duct tape." Rivas shook his head. "Evidently the gate at the entrance to the hospital grounds was left open and people passed in and out most of the afternoon without questioning why there were no guards on the gate."

The patrol brought the men to the S&I headquarters for Salas and Major Rivas to interview. The ambulance attendants told a story of being hijacked by masked gunmen, and they thought one of them might have been a girl. A few minutes later they received a report that an ambulance matching the description of the hijacked vehicle, and showing visible damage, had pulled into the emergency entrance of *Hospital San Jorge*. The guards there had panicked and fired on the vehicle which had once again escaped. Salas pieced together the events of the audacious breakout, but still didn't understand why they would kidnap Raul. *Would they demand ransom?*

Salas was on his way out when Greta Rojas rushed to intercept him at the door. He couldn't keep himself from staring at her trim figure and bright blue eyes as she approached. *Fuentes has excellent taste in receptionists.* As she got closer, he could see the redness around her eyes. So she has shed a few tears—she doesn't have ice in her veins after all.

"Director Salas," she said, "I received a call from the hospital. Good news, the doctors say that Colonel Fuentes made it through the surgery and has been taken to intensive care. They say he should fully recover in time. He can have limited visitors in a day or two."

"Thank you Greta," Salas replied. "I'll go see him as soon as possible." He watched her as she walked back to the reception desk, wondering if she knew more about what was going on. Knowing Fuentes, he couldn't imagine that they didn't have some kind of personal relationship. *With Fuentes in the hospital, this might be a good time to get closer to Ms. Rojas ... see what she can tell me; there is a lot going on here that I don't understand.*

Chapter 49

Luis wove through traffic, wishing he could go faster. "We have got to ditch this ambulance"

Amélia still sat in the passenger seat with her AK-47 between her legs. "How is Jake? I'm coming back there," she said, with her head turned toward the rear.

Juan said, "I think he is stable. Teresa and I are taking care of him. Stay up front and help Luis."

Luis said, "What about Josué?" No one answered. "Where is Josué? Isn't he back there?"

Raul coughed and said in a strained voice, "Jake helped me out. I was pretty much out of it, but I'm pretty sure he got shot. I remember Jake bending down over him."

Luis exhaled loudly. "Man, this wasn't supposed to happen." He said a quick prayer for Josué. Maybe he would be alright. Possibly no one knew he was part of their attack.

Luis imagined that there was an alert out for the ambulance. In his mind he could visualize police swarming the roads, and the damaged vehicle being as obvious as if it were glowing in fluorescent red paint. "I knew we should have parked the van closer. Can you tell if anyone is following us?"

Amélia shot him a scowl. "Duh …I don't have a mirror on this side."

"Huh? Oh yeah, girl … I knew that," Luis said. He shot her a smile.

"I need to go back and check on Jake."

Luis glanced her way. "No you don't. Pastor Juan said he was OK. I need you up here with the AK in case someone tries to stop us." If no one was following them, it would be safe to go get the van. Maybe he could even slow down a little too. He stared intently into his side mirror, causing the ambulance to wander from side to side due to his inattention.

"Watch out! You're going to get us into a wreck," Amélia yelled.

"OK! OK! Take it easy. I can't see anyone back there," Luis said. "I'm going to go back across the river and get to the van."

"What are we going to do about Jake?" she asked.

Juan spoke up from the back. "He is still unconscious, but I think most of the bleeding has stopped. How far do we have to go?"

"A long way," Amélia said. "But first we have to change to the van we left near the peace memorial. Will he be OK?"

"I hope so," Juan said. "I don't know for sure. Only God knows."

"Well *God's* not telling us, is he?" Amélia snapped.

Luis looked over and saw that tears welled up in her eyes again. "He will make it, girl." Luis hoped it was true. He said another prayer as he drove.

They crossed to the Tegucigalpa side of the river and looped around the National Stadium. He turned onto the road leading to *El Monumento a la Paz,* the peace memorial sitting on top of an isolated hill overlooking the stadium. The pavement gave way to gravel, with bumps and ruts, as they wound their way up the hill.

Luis was satisfied to see that a faint indication of tire tracks in the grass, and some mashed down weeds near the side of the road, were the only evidence of the place where they had hidden Pastor Juan's van. He turned off the road through grass, brush and trees of the park area surrounding the monument. Nosing through heavier brush, he pulled the ambulance alongside the old white van.

Luis and Amélia got out of the ambulance, their assault rifles held at the ready. All seemed quiet. He had been worried about homeless people who often lived in the park, but the area seemed clear. Amélia opened the rear of the ambulance, revealing the fear filled faces of their passengers.

"Come on out," Amélia told them. "There's no one around. Jake's still unconscious?"

"Hey, that's my van!" Juan exclaimed when he got out.

Luis smiled at him and said, "My apologies Pastor Juan, but we had to borrow it. We didn't think you would mind."

Juan looked confused and asked, "How did you find it? We were in it when we went to S&I headquarters ... I thought it was still there."

"No, it was in front of the church. Josué knew you had been imprisoned and asked around. He found out that they put your van back there. I think you were supposed to be one of the 'disappeared ones.'"

"Josué Delgado?" Juan frowned. "He's a member of my church. Is that the Josué you were talking about?"

"That's right, he is one of the guards where you were held. He told us that you had been locked up... and about Juanita and Ruben too."

"Thank God for him. And also that you have the van," Teresa said.

Luis said, "Hurry, let's put Jake in the floor of the van and get going."

Amélia pulled the pad from the gurney that was in the rear of the ambulance. "We can put him on this to be more comfortable, but he's going to be hurting if he comes to."

Teresa said, "I have morphine and antibiotics. I found the key to the locked medicine cabinet on the key ring you took from the *medicos.*"

Within a few minutes they were ready to go. Luis said, "Pastor Juan, maybe you should drive. The van is registered to you; we might be able to get by a police checkpoint if they aren't too suspicious."

Juan looked at him, raising his eyebrows. "With this bunch of refugees in prison garb?"

"I'll sit up front with you wearing the attendant's shirt; maybe they won't notice if we distract them," Luis said. "We can say that Jake had an accident and we have to get him to a hospital. They might not look too closely if we urge them to hurry."

Amélia said, "Quick, we have to get going."

A moment later they were on their way to Talanga. Pastor Juan drove slowly and carefully, turned onto *Bulevar Suyapa* and blended in with the traffic.

Chapter 50

Charlie Hedges sat in the captain's chair of the thirty-eight foot sports fishing boat, drink in hand, and watched his bikini-clad wife scrubbing down the front deck. His boat, Caribbean Mist, was tied up at a leased dock in Roatan, an island off the northern coast of Honduras. Life was good, he thought, watching the petite shapely figure of the raven haired Brazilian as she bent over to wring out a sponge into the bucket of suds-filled water. He thought back to the night he had met her in Rio five years earlier.

■■■

"My name is spelled Lygya," she had said, then laughed at the quizzical expression on his face. "Think of saying *leisure* with a southern accent ... sort of like *Leezhia*, honey."

He had been captivated by the bouncy, energetic charm of this woman who was teaching a group of tourists how to do the Brazilian Samba in the hotel bar. In little less than a month they had been married, and he had never regretted it for a moment.

■■■

His reverie was interrupted by his cell phone vibrating in the pocket of his shorts. He pulled it out and held it at arm's length. *I really should get some reading glasses.* He squinted at the text on the screen. It was Ramon.

"Tell me you're making progress," he said into the phone. His eyebrows rose, when he heard the reply from his contact in Tegus.

"Right now *señor* I am making progress down *Bulevar Suyapa.*"

What did that mean? It was just like Ramon to make him have to ask. "Alright Ramon, I'll ask. Why are you calling to tell me that? "

"Watching the old parsonage and the church paid off. There was a white van there ... I think it is the pastor's. Anyway *señor*, guess who showed up?

"Ramon, get to it! Stop playing twenty questions." This man drove him nuts.

"Okay *señor*, sure. Amélia Ramirez and three others showed up and one of them took the van. I followed them and then you will not believe what happened."

Charlie waited, and then it became obvious that the man was waiting for him to ask what happened. "Ramon, just tell me!"

Ramon finally proceeded to relate the story all the way through. He had been right—Charlie could hardly believe the audacity of the raid to free the prisoners. Ramon had followed them every step of the way. The man was good at that. No one had spotted him, and he was following the old white van as it left Tegucigalpa.

When Ramon finished, Charlie said, "Follow them to where ever they are going, then call me. I'll come down tomorrow morning to meet you. Maybe we can use this."

He hung up the phone and grinned. He needed someone like Amélia Ramirez and her gang. Anyone that could pull off such a stunt was invaluable. How had she known that Fuentes was holding her friend in that secret little prison he ran? Charlie was aware of the news article in *El Heraldo* naming her as a murder suspect, and now this. That meant they needed him too—they could help each other. Suddenly life was exciting again.

"You got that look on your face," Lygya said, joining him on the rear deck.

"Well, watching you scrub down the deck in your bikini will give a man ideas," he said, leering at her.

"Not *that* look *gringo!*" she said, laughing and punching him in the arm. "You know what I mean; you're thinking about going into the field again."

"Well ...yeah," Charlie said. "That was Ramon. We might have a chance to do something about Fuentes now."

"Fuentes? I thought the agency told you not to take any action on him."

"Politicians!" he said. "They don't want to be accused of interfering, so they would just let a country go to hell."

"Well?" she said arching her eyebrows. "You're not going to go against them are you?"

He hesitated. Did he dare going against agency orders? "You know we had the goods on Fuentes and that Venezuelan, the one who works for General Velasquez ... uh, I think he's using the name Rodriguez now."

"Yes, you told me. But the agency told you to stand down."

"Well, I did ... mostly. I had Ramon leak some news to that student protest newspaper, and their 'Princess Maya' blog, to shine a little light on his activities. Thought maybe somebody in the Honduran government would pick up on it and investigate."

"And did someone do anything?"

"Well, nothing happened for a while, but then Friday night Juanita Perez, the student who ran the blog, disappeared along with her boyfriend."

"You think Fuentes took her?"

"We can only suppose," Charlie said, finishing his cocktail. "Anyway, I've had Ramon keeping track of Perez's friend Amélia, to see what she might do. A few days ago she apparently stirred up a hornet's nest. Fuentes sent a strike team out to capture her and her companions at the office they had in the old church parsonage. She eluded them ... even killed a couple of soldiers doing it."

"Wow! My kind of girl," Lygya said.

"Yeah, but get this," Charlie said, "today they busted her friend, and some others, out of Fuentes secret prison in S&I headquarters."

Lygya's mouth opened and her eyes widened. "No! How could they do that?"

"I don't know how, but they did."

"Wait a minute, how did you even know that?" she asked, cocking her head to one side and putting her hands on her hips.

He laughed, saying, "That's why they pay me the big bucks."

"Well, that must be why you're such a rich *gringo*," she purred, putting her arms around his waist. "Really ...how do you know?"

Charlie felt her warmth through the tropical shirt he wore. *My smart and sexy wife.* "Let's go below, to the cabin," he whispered.

"Stop that," she said, pushing away. "Tell me!"

"It's no big secret," he said. "I heard about the shoot out and escape from the parsonage and had Ramon keep an eye on the place, in case some of the group showed up back there."

He paused, reaching out for her, but she backed away.

"Anyway," he continued, "Ramon saw a guy get out of a car that had three other people in it. He took the pastor's white van from in front of the church. So Ramon followed the car and van. They hid the van in the trees below the peace monument. He got a good look at them. It was the Ramirez woman and three guys. He followed them and saw the whole rescue."

Charlie told her the whole story as Ramon had relayed it to him. Lygya listened with rapt attention, and was wide eyed at times.

"That is amazing," she said when he had finished. "I'd like to meet that woman. So they escaped like a bat out of you-know-where—how is Ramon tracking them?"

"When they escaped, Ramon went back to where they had hidden the van. Sure enough, they showed up later and transferred to the van. They apparently rescued four people, but it looks like one of the rescuers got shot doing it."

"So what are you going to do?" she said, tilting her head again.

"I've decided that Ramon and I have to help them. This may be what we have been waiting for ... to push someone into taking on Fuentes."

"They won't let you interfere," Lygya said. "You told me how cautious and indecisive the politicians in the agency have gotten."

"I didn't say I'm telling them," Charlie replied. "Better to ask for forgiveness than permission. I'm leaving to meet up with Ramon in the morning."

"Then I'm going with you," she said, staring him in the eyes.

Charlie knew better than to try to argue with her. Oh, how he loved this woman!

Chapter 51

Amélia sat in the floor of the van, cradling Jake's head in her lap. Her stomach churned and she felt nauseous at times. Maybe it was the smell of blood, sweat, and fear—all of them were pretty ripe—or maybe it was worry. What if Jake died? She didn't want to think of that. The others rode in silence. Ruben had his arm around Juanita's shoulders, but she seemed not to notice. Juanita hadn't spoken since being rescued. She just stared straight ahead, as if lost in her own thoughts—another worry for Amélia.

The trip had taken several hours. It was dark now and, to Amélia, it felt like it was taking all night. They took the back road they used before, instead of taking the Olancho highway, where they would be more likely to be stopped. Their luck held, and there was no checkpoint at *Valle de Angeles* this time. Shortly afterwards, Jake stirred and started moaning. It was only then that they noticed he was still seeping blood and found a leg wound. Teresa gave Jake a shot of morphine, and bandaged the leg which had only been grazed. Finally Jake settled down and went back to sleep.

"What are we going to do? We have to get him to a hospital," Amélia whispered.

"I know," Teresa said, placing her hand on Amélia's shoulder. "Why don't you call your aunt … see if she can arrange something when we get there?"

"Of course," Amélia said, wiping her eyes. "Why didn't I think of that?" She took the tissue that Teresa was holding out to her and blew her nose. *Why did I let myself fall apart like this? I've got to figure out how we get ourselves out of this mess instead of crying and blubbering.*

She pulled her cellular out of her pocket and looked at the screen – no bars. Finally, as they got nearer to Talanga, the cellular showed that service was available and she called Yolanda. Amélia gave her a short version of the day's events and told her about Jake's condition.

"Go to the hospital that is behind the *llantería* on the main street. I'll meet you there," Yolanda told her. "I know a doctor there who we can trust; we are old friends."

Amélia moved up front, kneeling between the seats. She scanned the road, searching for the *llantería*, or tire shop, and soon spotted a building with several lights on. In the light of the bare bulbs she could see tires stacked in front and a tin-roofed awning at the side. A man was removing a tire from its rim while a skinny teenage boy was checking a mounted tire for leaks in a half-barrel of dirty water.

"There ... left up here," Amélia said.

Juan turned into the short street beside the store, and drove a half-block where the street ended at a brick wall with a solid wooden gate. A guard at the gate stopped the van, but let them in when they told him that they had an accident victim and a doctor had already been called. They found a sign reading *"EMERGENCIA"* above a large red arrow pointing to a double door in the brick building. Amélia felt a surge of joy at the sight of her aunt waiting in the doorway.

"Thank God you are here," Yolanda said, as she opened the sliding door of the van, and saw Amélia cradling Jake on the floor. "Bring him inside; there is a gurney just inside the door. Dr. Salinas is already here getting ready."

■■■

They waited for several hours in the small waiting room before Dr. Salinas came out to tell them about Jake's condition.

"Everything went well," he said. "Very lucky ... the bullet went in just below his collarbone ... passed through without hitting any major arteries or organs. It exited just below the shoulder blade. Considerable tissue damage and the exit wound was pretty nasty. Required a lot of stitches."

"But he will be alright?" Amélia asked.

"Yes ... thankfully he is young and healthy," the doctor told her gently. "He should heal without any major problems. May have lost some use of the muscles near the right shoulder. Going to need some physical therapy to restore strength in that arm."

"How long will he have to stay in the hospital?" she asked.

The doctor glanced over to Yolanda, hesitated, and then said, "He can't stay. Your aunt told me that the situation is, as you might say, sensitive. The federal police or someone else will probably check all the hospitals. My story is that he was never officially here. My nurse, the front gate guard and I are the only ones who are aware of what has

195

happened here tonight. And don't worry, they can be trusted. He can recover at your aunt's farm just fine."

■■■

It was almost midnight before they got to the farm. Amélia was relieved to find that Rodrigo had gotten there earlier in the afternoon. She felt a little ashamed that, in all the excitement, she had not even thought to worry about him. While the others were getting Jake into the house she ran to her brother and embraced him with a big hug. "I'm so glad you are here. Did you have any problems?"

"No," he said, "as soon as I saw the ambulance blast past the hospital gatehouse, I got out of there. Is Jake going to be OK?"

"I hope so ..." she said. His face blurred, as tears welled up in her eyes again.

A short time later, Amélia sat in a chair that she had pulled up beside Jake's bed and watched him as he slept. She didn't care what the others thought about this. She openly displayed the feeling she had for Jake, one that she had only just discovered for herself. Maybe she was being foolish. She was a poor Honduran girl—certainly not someone an affluent American would want. Well, she couldn't help it and wasn't going to worry about that now. Amélia closed her eyes and fell asleep.

Chapter 52

Jake became aware of a throbbing ache in his chest—shoulder?—no, both. What was wrong? Where was he? Everything was black—maybe he should open his eyes, but it seemed like a great effort. There, a crack of light widened to what? A ceiling that gave him few clues to where he was, or what had happened. He was in a bed and the pain in his chest was intensifying.

Then he remembered the impact of the bullet and the wave of pain that accompanied it. *That's it, I was shot. What happened after that? Where am I? Not a hospital.*

Turning his head, he saw Amélia sprawled in the armchair beside the bed. Her head was back against the chair, and silky black hair draped down on one shoulder. She breathed slowly through her partially opened mouth, sound asleep. For a while he just watched her, as if he had never really seen her before, his eyes taking in her beauty.

The pain interrupted his contemplation. He tried to speak: "Ughh …Am … Amélia," was all he could get out. His mouth was dry and his vocal chords didn't seem to be working right.

She was startled awake, her eyes opening wide. She ran her hands through her hair and wiped her eyes. "Oh, you're awake!" She looked at him closely. "Are you hurting?"

"Yeah … hurts some. Water … I'm thirsty," he croaked.

"I'll get you some water, and Teresa has something for your pain." She stood, and then hesitated, leaning over toward him.

Jake lay still as her face approached his. *What was she doing?* She kissed him on the cheek!

"Be right back," she said, and then hurried out of the room.

Jake was wide awake now, as he watched her leave the room. *Wow!*

Within a minute the room was crowded as everyone pushed in to see how he was. All Jake could really focus on was that his mouth felt like it was filled with cotton and the pulsing wave of pain was building and pushing out thoughts of anything else.

Amélia finally appeared with a glass of water. "Not too much, just a sip or two, you don't want to get sick." She reclaimed the chair at his bedside and put the glass to his mouth. The water was cool and wonderful.

Teresa was on the other side of the bed, and she gave him a shot of morphine. Jake waited, but it still hurt. "It isn't working."

"Give it some time," Teresa said gently, and patted his hand. "Here, take these pills, you still have a fever."

Why would he have a fever? He didn't argue though. He let Teresa put the pills in his mouth and Amélia gave him another sip of water. Finally, and not any too soon, the pain began to recede. And Jake felt a pleasant drowsiness. But he wanted some answers. "What happened? Is everyone ..." His eyes began to droop. He jerked them open. *What was he asking? Oh, yeah ...* Then he was aware of Amélia grabbing his hand. *Her hand is warm ....*

"Just get some sleep, Jake. You need to rest." Her face hovering over his dissolved into warm blackness as he shut his eyes. He could smell a faint scent of Jasmine.

Chapter 53

Amélia shooed everyone out of the bedroom. They all went back to the main room and kitchen of the farmhouse. She felt some need to take charge of the situation, but wasn't sure what to do. Everyone had apparently felt exhausted. It was late Saturday morning and they still had not discussed everything that had happened. It appeared to Amélia that emotions were raw and nobody felt like talking.

"I'm glad that Jake woke up," she said. "He's getting better." Nobody said anything.

Ruben and Juanita sat on the couch in the living room. They had been quiet all morning. Amélia had tried to talk to Juanita earlier, but couldn't keep a conversation going. Even Ruben seemed to be getting shut out. Juanita was going through something bad, but Amélia couldn't get her to say what it was. Maybe Pastor Zamora could talk to her.

Pastor Zamora and his wife were in the kitchen helping Aunt Yolanda prepare some lunch. At least those three were alright, so it seemed to Amélia. She joined them.

"Let me help with lunch, Aunt Yolanda. What can I do?"

"The house is pretty crowded. We are going to eat under the covered patio behind the house. You can set out some paper plates, plastic utensils, and napkins on the tables out there."

Amélia made herself useful, and when the pastor came out to set a salad on the table she approached him. "Pastor Zamora, I'm worried about Juanita. She just isn't herself. Could you talk to her … maybe find out what is bothering her?"

He gave her a smile. "I already did that this morning, Amélia. I can tell you that she had some very traumatic experiences while she was being held captive. She won't talk to me or Ruben about them. I think Teresa might be able to help her, get her to open up, but it will take some time."

"It hurts me to see her like that," Amélia said.

"Yes, it hurts all of us who are close to her. We just have to wait and pray."

There he goes again with the God talk. She had been hearing that from Aunt Yolanda, Luis and now the pastor. It didn't seem like God was helping them much. They were all afraid to go anywhere but the farmhouse. No one was helping them. She had to do something, but what?

After lunch they were sitting around the two tables. Amelia could see the rolling hills and gentle mountains to the east. It seemed so peaceful here. She wished she could just stay here and forget about her problems. But she was always the practical one—she couldn't allow herself that luxury.

"Listen everyone," she said, "I think we need to talk about what we have been through. We have been avoiding it all morning, and that is not particularly healthy."

Pastor Zamora backed her up. "I think Amélia is right. We need to assess what everyone saw and heard. This will help us know what to do next. God knows, right now I'm not too sure what to do."

There were a few murmurs of assent around the tables. Amélia looked over to Juanita, but she didn't look back, just stared at her plate and picked at her food.

Raul volunteered to go first. He told them of his interrogation by Fuentes and Garcia, and the torture that they inflicted on him. When he mentioned that he had been drugged and couldn't remember everything that had happened, Amélia became alarmed.

"You don't know what you told them?" she asked in a tight voice.

"I don't remember much about what they asked me," Raul said. "I mean everything is hazy … sort of runs together. They kept asking about the computer break-in …"

"But you were here at the farmhouse with Josué!" she interrupted. "Did you tell them where we were?"

"Uh … no, I don't think so," Raul said, frowning. "I … well … no, I don't think so. I was pretty out of it, so I'm not sure. But I was having trouble even following their questions; I was so confused and hurting every time he pressed that button. I don't think I was very coherent at all."

"We can't take a chance," Amélia said. "We need to go somewhere else."

"Wait a minute," Yolanda said. "Don't panic yet. If they knew where you were don't you think they would have already come here? It took hours coming to Talanga, waiting at the hospital, then coming here and staying the night. If they knew about this place we would all be in jail by now."

"Or dead, man," Luis said. Everyone looked at him. "Hey man, it's true."

Amélia could sense some of the tensions subside. "Ruben, you and Juanita have been awfully quiet. Can you tell us about what happened?"

Ruben looked at Juanita, who had closed her eyes and put her head down. Ruben looked at the people gathered around the tables and shook his head. "We both had a pretty rough time in there. I really don't want to talk about it yet, and I don't think she does either."

Amélia could see that Juanita's fists were closed tightly, her knuckles white. "Alright, we can understand that. Can you at least tell us how they got you, or what the people looked like?"

Ruben had a look of anguish on his face. "OK, we had just left *Carnitas* when a couple of guys jumped us. I don't remember much about it, but I think one of the guys was the one Juanita told us was following her. The other was a tall man she had seen with him once." Juanita, eyes still closed, nodded her head.

"Go on," Pastor Zamora gently urged.

Ruben shook his head. "No, nothing else would be useful. Besides, it's painful to talk about it right now."

Amélia said, "He's right. We don't need to know all the details. Raul and Josué already told us before we got you out that Colonel Fuentes was the man responsible for all this." She saw Juanita flinch at the mention of the man's name.

Pastor Zamora said, "I wish we had known that before Teresa and I agreed to go see him."

Raul said, 'I'm sorry Pastor Juan. When my father said for you to meet with him, I had no idea what he was doing. It was only later that night, when I met with Josué that I found out about Fuentes. Didn't think to call you back."

Suddenly Juanita stood up and looked around angrily. "Stop! Stop talking about that man. He is evil. I can't listen to you talk about him anymore!" She stormed back into the house. Ruben followed right behind her.

Everyone was agape at the reaction. Amélia had been concerned about Juanita's moodiness and reluctance to talk since the rescue. Now she realized the seriousness of Juanita's trauma, and the ugly possibilities of what lay behind it finally dawned on her. Her heart ached for Juanita.

"We all need to be careful what we say around Juanita," Amélia said. "We need to be gentle with her and shouldn't try to cheer her up."

"I think that is right," Teresa said. "There isn't anything we can say now that won't hurt ... just make her remember ... well, whatever has happened to her."

Pastor Zamora said, "Teresa, we should go in and call Arturo and Estrella. They must be worried sick. Maybe he can arrange for someone to take my place at tomorrow's church service. I think we need to stay out of sight for a while."

■■■

Raul remained outside and agonized about whether or not to call his father. What would his father say when he told him what Colonel Fuentes had done? As Director of Intelligence, his father worked closely with Fuentes. Would he believe it? What if Fuentes had been killed? Even if not, would his father be legally obligated to help capture all of them? Maybe he shouldn't call.

His thoughts were interrupted when Pastor Juan came back outside. "You look to be in deep thought. I hope I'm not bothering you."

"No, you aren't bothering me. I'm trying to decide whether or not to call my father." Raul explained all his concerns to the pastor, glad to have a sounding board. At the end of Raul's explanation, Pastor Juan said, "Raul, I understand your concerns. It occurs to me that your father is in a situation where he will be torn between his duty and feelings of loyalty to Colonel Fuentes, or supporting you as his son."

"I don't even know if he will believe me," Raul said.

"If you don't tell him what you know, he will be more inclined to believe whatever he hears from Fuentes or any of the others. Maybe he doesn't know what kind of man Fuentes is. If you don't tell him, you are leaving your father exposed."

"Let me think about it," Raul said. "Maybe I'll call him tonight."

Chapter 54

Enrique Salas decided to wait until Saturday afternoon before going to visit Colonel Fuentes. During the morning he had read every police and military intelligence report available concerning the incident at S&I headquarters. Some things still didn't make sense to him. Interviews of personnel at the facility left some discrepancies. No one could account for the fact that while there were supposedly five prisoners in cellblock three, the number of meals ordered had been for seven prisoners. Three prisoners were left in the cells. No one could imagine why Corporal Delgado had apparently helped the other prisoners escape. Salas only got confused stares when he asked if two or four prisoners had escaped. Something didn't add up. The corporal apparently even killed Lieutenant Garza and one or maybe both soldiers who had responded by way of the elevator.

Salas was deep in thought as his driver took him to the military hospital. *What had happened to Raul?* There had been no demands for ransom. *Has he really been kidnapped? Could he have had some part in the events that had taken place?*

Fuentes must know why all this happened, and maybe he was the reason that things didn't add up. He could never fully trust the man. *And what about all that crazy talk about me becoming the president the last meeting we had? Is the man crazy?*

As Salas entered the room in the ICU he was surprised to find Greta Rojas already at the colonel's bedside. "Excuse me," he said. "They didn't tell me that anyone else was in here."

She turned, gazing at him with those penetrating azure eyes, and smiled. "That is alright Director Salas," she said. "I was just checking on the colonel. He was awake earlier, but I'm afraid he has drifted off to sleep now."

"I see," he said, unsure of what to say to her. "Well ..."

"I'm glad you are here," she interrupted. "Maybe we can talk about how things can get done while he is incapacitated."

"Well ... there are procedures ... um..."

"Oh, I know ... I know," she murmured, placing her hand on his arm. "I didn't mean, uh, official chain of command and all that. You see, I'm worried about some of the things Colonel Fuentes is trying to accomplish, and I know you and he have had some discussions ..."

He wondered where this conversation was going. At the same time he was intensely aware of her personal magnetism and beauty. He could smell a hint of intoxicating perfume. Struggling to find what to say he muttered, "Well, we have discussed a number of things ... I'm not sure ..."

She put her finger on his lips, stopping him. The intimate gesture startled him and quickened his pulse.

"Shhh," she whispered. "I know you aren't sure how much you can say to me. This isn't the place to discuss such things. We need privacy. Can you come to my home tonight?"

Come to her home? His brain seemed to have stalled, but then shifted into a fantasy which played in his mind, and accelerated as he gazed into her eyes. He realized she was waiting for a reply. "Well, yes, if you think that would be best," he said, trying to keep his voice neutral, thinking that any moment the spell would be broken. *Could she be attracted to him? What about her and Fuentes?*

"That would be good ... would be the best thing for us," she said quietly. "I think we will both benefit from having a friendship, Enrique. It is alright if I call you by your first name, isn't it?" Without waiting for an answer, she extracted a card from the small purse she was carrying and handed it to him. "Eight o'clock," she murmured, and slipped out of the room.

With her out of his sight rational thought returned. What had he been thinking? He was a married man. Still, he needed to find out what she knew, and what this unexpected turn of events was all about. The thought of seeing her in a private setting still had a certain appeal.

■■■

It was early evening and Salas sat in his study, recalling his conversation with Greta Rojas. She said that she was worried about some of the things Fuentes was trying to do. What could she mean by that? Maybe she knew about their ongoing connections with General Velasquez. He would try to get some answers later in the evening. One thing Salas knew about political power was that having more information than the other guy gave you an advantage. Something about Fuentes and this whole situation wasn't right.

The phone rang and Salas answered. It was Raul! At the sound of his voice he was elated, then shocked as the words sank in.

"He tortured me, Dad ... he tortured me," Raul said, breaking into a sob.

"Who? Who kidnapped you?"

"I wasn't kidnapped. Fuentes tortured me ... they rescued me ...Josué ...Corporal Delgado ...helped. I don't know what would have happened if they hadn't."

Salas talked with Raul for the next several minutes, asking questions and finally getting it clear in his mind what had taken place the day before at S&I Headquarters. His bitterness grew at the thought of the reassurances Fuentes had given him about interviewing his son. *Fuentes had planned from the start to torture his son!*

Raul was vague on details of the breakout, but was able to tell him that in addition to the American and Juanita Perez, the pastor and his wife had been held prisoner. They had all gotten away, except Josué Delgado. Salas broke the news to his son that Delgado had been killed in the shootout and that Fuentes had been wounded.

"I am so glad that you are alright," Salas said. "I couldn't imagine what had happened when they said you were kidnapped. I was afraid you would be held for ransom, or even killed. Are you sure about these people? They won't hurt you?"

"They are my friends, Dad," Raul said. It's Fuentes and his men who are the enemy! You have to do something about him. Tell me you didn't know what he was doing."

"No! Well, he runs a pretty secret group, so I don't know all the details of his operation. But, I swear, I had no idea he was holding people in secret or resorting to torture." This was much worse than he had imagined. He could never admit to his son that he was connected tightly to Fuentes. What about their plans with General Velasquez—could he ever explain away that?

"You have to do something about him Dad."

"I am going to find out everything that is going on, Raul. I'll go to the hospital tomorrow and interview Colonel Fuentes. Maybe I can even have him arrested and court-martialed. In the meantime, until your legal status gets cleared up, stay where you are. Let me get your mother, she is worried sick about you. Don't tell her a lot of distressing details, alright? Just reassure her that you are alright."

■■■

Later, he sat in his chair by the fireplace, nursing a snifter of brandy. His wife had reacted predictably to Raul's call, with weeping and hysteria. Afterward, she had gone to bed with another of her migraine headaches. He turned the problem of Fuentes over in his mind, examining it from various aspects, but nothing seemed clear. The nerve of the man! He would get payback for what he had done. In the meantime he would find out what Greta knew, and what she wanted to talk to him about. Maybe he could somehow use her against Fuentes.

Thinking about going to see her stirred feelings in him again, the kind he hadn't had in a long time. She was a beautiful and exciting woman, and her apparent interest in him fueled his self-esteem which had been waning lately. His wife did little to make him feel manly in recent years. He still loved her, but they had drifted apart; the marriage had become stale. He had his career; she had her friends, clubs and charity events.

Making up his mind, he showered, shaved and dressed in a pair of slacks, casual shirt, a blazer and brush-shined loafers. Entering the darkened bedroom, he told his wife: "I'm going to meet with Major Rivas to try to find some answers to this situation with Colonel Fuentes. I'll be late coming back; I'll try not to disturb you." He gave her a dry kiss on the forehead and left.

■■■

A short time later his car turned into Greta's drive and stopped before the closed gate. Rolling down the window, he pushed the button on the post beside the drive, and heard her voice, sounding metallic through the small speaker; "Yes, who is it?"

"It's, uh ... Enrique," he said, feeling awkward talking to a speaker post.

"Of course; I was hoping you would come," came the reply, and the gate opened.

She had opened the front door by the time he walked up the steps to her porch. She stood, leaning against the door-facing, her hair backlit by the light from the living room. Standing there, barefooted and wearing a simple but elegant flowing dress, her beauty took his breath away. Somehow it was as if he was seeing her in a dream, that none of this was real, and the impression made his heart race.

"Come in," she said, motioning him into the room and shutting the door behind them. "Would you like a glass of wine? I'm having some, a nice Malbec."

"Yes, uh … Greta, that will be nice." He sat down at one end of the couch while she poured the wine. He looked around the tastefully decorated living room with approval. Earth tones, tasteful framed art, and low lighting somehow seemed to affirm her taste. She sat down beside him on the couch, offered him his glass and raised hers.

"To new friendships," she said softly, clicking the edge of her wine glass against his.

After a bit of small talk, the conversation turned to the dramatic raid on the headquarters, and to Fuentes. "I'm worried about Colonel Fuentes," she said. "That's what I wanted to talk to you about."

"The doctors said he would fully recover," Salas responded. He hoped it would be a slow painful recovery. That would serve the man right.

"Oh, I know. That's not what I mean," she said, sipping the last of her wine and putting the glass on the coffee table.

"What do you mean?"

"Well, it's the way he has been acting lately," she said. "He has been moody, erratic in his behavior. Most people don't see it, but I do."

"You do … in your capacity as receptionist at headquarters?" He tilted his head and watched her closely.

She blushed. "No, not that … of course not. You're very perceptive. I should have expected that." She placed her hand on his and continued, "Yes, we were romantically involved, but that is over, has been over for a while."

Her hand over his felt warm and soft. He gazed at her face and neckline, his pulse quickening. What was it about this woman that could send his emotions into overdrive so quickly? It nettled him to have it confirmed that she and Fuentes had been romantically involved, but at least that was over. So what? He wouldn't let that deter him. He put down the wine-glass he had been holding and turned to her. "What is it that you think I can do?"

"I think you …we can do a lot. You are a wise man Enrique," she said, smiling at him. "You have political connections. I think you already know a lot of things about Colonel Fuentes ... uh, Manuel. If others knew about those things ... well, you both might have problems."

"So you want me to help keep Manuel out of difficulties? Why would I want to help him? You don't know what he did to my son!"

She placed her other hand on his knee. "Enrique, no. I'm thinking of both of you. If Fuentes calls trouble on himself, you will be hurt too. I'm trying to warn you, and I can help you ... would like to be the one helping you."

Could this be true? Or was she just trying to manipulate him? Her touch made him want to believe she was sincere. He was still curious as to how much she knew. "What kind of confidential things do you think I know about Manuel?"

"Some things ..." She hesitated, and looked away. She squeezed his hand tightly. "For instance, I am aware of the trip the two of you took to Venezuela to meet with General Velasquez."

So there it is, she knows! He stared into her eyes and asked, "What else?"

"I don't know," she said, grabbing his other hand. "Don't be mad Enrique. I'm on your side. I'm not a threat to you, quite the opposite. I want to help you."

"You want to help me?"

"Yes!" she said. "I look up to you and Manuel. You both are smart and ambitious, and want to do what you think is best for the country. But you are more ... mature ... wiser. I think you are the one who can get the proper things done. You can keep Manuel from messing things up."

He wanted to believe her. But, somewhere in the back of his mind, he wondered if this could be what he hoped. "Maybe, but you still haven't told me what Manuel is doing that might endanger the both of us."

"Let's not discuss those things right now," she said. "I want you to know that I can be a help to you. That other stuff is business, and we can go over them later. But tonight you should know ... since breaking off with Manuel, I have been more aware of you. You have a quiet strength and wisdom. And ... I'm very attracted to you."

With that, she leaned forward and kissed him gently on the lips. He pressed his mouth into hers and felt her respond more urgently.

"We could ... we will, be a good team together," she said when they finally separated.

She stood and pulled him to his feet. Without another word she led him by the hand into her bedroom. Any restraint he might have had fell away. In a delirious fog of desire he undressed her and pushed her toward the bed.

"Leave the light on," she said. "I want to see us together."

Salas beheld at her lying on the bed. That was the best idea he had heard in a long time.

Chapter 55

Jake was half awake, trying to ignore the throbbing pain in his shoulder. He tried to get back into the dream he had been having—he hazily drifted back—he was in the swimming pool with Barbara James, at the graduation party. By that time they were the only ones left in the pool and the warm water made an intimate setting. Jake gazed into Barbara's sapphire eyes and then down to the paleness of her breasts showing above her swim top. As they stood close Barbara put her arms around Jake's neck and gave him a kiss. "I'm glad you asked me to be your date tonight," she whispered.

He felt her hand on his forehead. No, it wasn't Barbara' hand—where was he? The throbbing shoulder brought him awake and he opened his eyes. In the dim light he could make out Amélia standing over him with her hand on his forehead.

"Good, your fever has broken," she said.

Jake was at a loss for words. The sudden switch in his mind from Barbara to Amélia brought on a budding of guilt, like a small seedling emerging from the ground. What was he doing down here, feeling emotions for this woman when he and Barbara were practically engaged?

"How is your shoulder?" Amélia asked.

Relieved by the distraction from his thoughts and the growing seedling of guilt, Jake answered truthfully. "Hurts like a bear. Just woke me up."

Amélia patted his cheek lightly and the gesture made Jake uncomfortable. He turned his face away slightly and she pulled her hand back. She looked at him for a moment, and then said, "I'll go get Teresa. She can give you something."

When she left the room Jake wondered how much she had read into his reflexive action to her touch. Well, maybe it would be good if she had picked up on the vibe. They were getting too close. Everything about this whole situation was bad. Now that he had found Ruben, he had no more need to be down here. He had already sunk his chances of getting the internship at Intellibotics. Maybe he would get a thank-you note from Jason Lee. Maybe he could recover somewhat by still getting on with them, even if it wasn't in the Advanced Development Group.

The little sprout of guilt continued to grow and blossom in Jake's mind. He had avoided calling Barbara. She must be frantic by now—or furious. They had made so many plans and dreamed of a future together. Then he had jeopardized their future by coming down here. A shiver ran down Jake's back as he thought of Josué being felled by a bullet. It could have been him. He remembered the hazy details of his irrational charge against the soldiers in his attempt to free Raul. What had gotten into him? What had given him the courage, or was it just stupidity?

Teresa came into the room, followed by Amélia. Teresa said, "Jake, I have one last shot of the morphine to give you, then we are out."

"Out?" What would he do? His wound was better, but the pain was still pretty severe.

"Don't worry. Tomorrow we will switch you to some pain pills. It is just as well, we wouldn't want to keep you on the morphine too long. Do you understand?"

Jake nodded his head, "Yeah … OK …Maybe that's better. The morphine is making me sleep all the time anyway."

She gave him the shot, and Jake felt the smooth wave of relief course through him.

Amélia had stayed behind after Teresa left the room. "Would you like me to sit with you for a while?"

She appeared to be a bit unsure of herself. It wasn't her usual demeanor, and he regretted that he had turned away from her touch earlier. They had been through so much together—it was only natural that they had become close. It didn't mean he loved Barbara any less, did it?

"Sure, that would be nice," he said. "But don't be surprised if I go to sleep on you."

Chapter 56

Luis struggled to stay awake while on guard duty. It was late—he had watched the fat crescent moon set in the west, made coffee in a vain effort to fight off drowsiness, and kept his watch from the front step of the farmhouse. He suddenly became aware that a pickup truck had turned into the long gravel drive which led to the farmhouse. *Man, this can't be good.*

He slipped through the front door, fairly certain that he couldn't be seen from the distant truck. He woke Rodrigo and Amélia, and then returned through the darkened front room to look out the window. The vehicle had approached to within a hundred feet of the house and just sat there, headlights on, engine idling. Amélia and Rodrigo came behind him armed with their AK-47 assault rifles. Yolanda, who had also wakened when he disturbed Amélia, came behind them, yawning.

Amélia said, "Luis, go out back and work yourself around to cover the front. Be careful to not be seen."

"Give me a few minutes to get in position," Luis said. "I'll have to move slowly."

"That's fine. We aren't going to do anything. Who knows what this is about? They seem to be just waiting for us to make a move."

Amélia and Rodrigo took up positions at the front windows, and Luis slipped out the back door. He slowly made his way around to some bushes on the right side of the house where he could see both the truck and the front door. He didn't think he would be seen since the moonless night cloaked everything in darkness and he was outside the main beams of the headlights.

■■■

Amélia, peering carefully around the windowsill, saw someone get out of the pickup. *It's a woman!* She watched the petite woman made her way onto the front porch. A few seconds later, a bold knock sounded on the front door.

Amélia hadn't seen anyone else exit the truck. The lady didn't seem to be a threat, or appear to be armed, so Amélia whispered to her aunt, "It's a woman. She's probably not dangerous. Get the door. We will be ready with the rifles just in case."

Yolanda approached the front door and switched on the porch light. Amélia appreciated her aunt's thinking. The woman would be in the glare of the light and unable to see into the darkened room.

Opening the door, Yolanda said, "Hello, may I help you? Why are you here?"

From her position behind the wall, Amélia could hear the reply.

"I need to talk to Amélia Ramirez. We know she is here."

Immediately, her senses were on full alert, and she flipped the safety selector of her rifle to the semi-automatic position. Holding the weapon in front of her, she came slowly around the door behind her aunt until she could see the woman. "Who are you?"

"Be calm, I'm not a threat," the woman said, retreating a step. "My name is Lygya Hedges, and my husband and a friend are in the truck. We were trying not to alarm you, to give you time to see that we weren't trying to surprise you, but I can see that didn't work. We mean no harm and are here to see if we can help you."

"Tell the others to come out of the truck," demanded Amélia. Something was weird here.

"I will. As soon as you put the AK on safety," the woman replied.

Amélia complied and the woman turned around and waved her hand in the air. The lights and the motor were turned off in the truck. Two men got out and walked to the house, their hands held open and out from their sides to show that they were unarmed. They joined the woman at the front door and for a moment, everyone just stood there.

"Well, you might as well come in," Yolanda said. "We can't all just stand on the porch."

They all moved into the darkened living room and Yolanda turned on the overhead light.

"Aunt Yolanda, would you check them to make sure they aren't armed?" Amélia asked politely.

Yolanda checked the three of them, doing a fairly expert pat-down. The woman had bronze skin and black hair, very striking. Amélia didn't think she was Honduran. The two men both looked Hispanic, possibly locals. Yolanda nodded to Amélia, and directed the visitors to sit on the couch.

Once they were seated the woman continued her explanation. "As I said, we are here to help you. We are aware of the trouble you are in, and might be useful to you."

"But who are you?" Amélia asked. "How did you know we were here, and why would you want to help?"

One of the men answered, "It will take some time to explain. Why don't you call in your friend, with the other rifle, who is still outside? Then we can talk."

Amélia pursed her lips and stood staring at the visitors. They must have been pretty sharp to have spotted Luis in the darkness. She gave a reluctant sigh and told Rodrigo, "Go get Luis. Let's see what these people have to say."

The man said, "You should wake the others. Everyone probably needs to hear what we have to say."

Did these people know everything? Amélia couldn't see how that was possible. Well, at least they hadn't brought the army or police, so maybe they wanted to help. What choice did she have except to hear them out?

Everyone, except for Jake, had gathered in the crowded living room anxiously waiting to see what their mysterious visitors had to say. The man seemed to recognize that Amélia was the one in charge, so he looked inquisitively at her. She just nodded her head to him.

"My name is Charlie Hedges, this is my wife Lygya and he is my friend Ramon. Ramon has been watching your activities …"

There was a babble of overlapping questions. "You're watching us? Who are you? Why?"

He held up his hands to silence the outbursts. "… and so we know the problem you are in."

"Why were you watching us?" Amélia asked, demanding to be heard, and assuming the role of spokesperson for the group.

"The simplest answer is Colonel Fuentes," Hedges said. "He is the source of all the problems, and the reason some of you were arrested. Or maybe it should be termed, illegally detained. By the way, he is still alive. Whoever shot him didn't kill him."

"You're right. Fuentes is the main problem," Amélia said. "But why are you interested, and how do you know about us?"

"I have been watching Fuentes for some time. I work for a government that is friendly to Honduras. We have an interest in seeing that there are no covert actions that would threaten your government, or ours. We are the ones who e-mailed the tip about illegal drug smuggling. The tip you used in your newsletter, and Ms. Perez featured in her blog."

Amélia looked over to Juanita who was standing in a doorway, partially hidden by Ruben. She didn't make eye contact, but just stared at the strangers. Amélia ached to have her best friend back to normal, to be a sounding board as she sorted through ideas and plans.

"That was you?" Amélia said. "Why didn't you tell us Fuentes was involved?"

"I had to be careful to stay under the radar, so to speak," Hedges said. "We hoped that if you publicized rumors of government involvement in drug smuggling, someone in your government would chase down the lead."

"Why didn't you just tell our government?" Raul asked.

"It's like I said, we can't actively interfere in your government. It's better if no one knows we are here, just watching, gathering intelligence. My superiors don't even know I am talking to you. In fact, I went out of my authority to leak the rumors, and I'm definitely violating our policy by telling you any of this."

"Who are you, CIA?" Amélia asked. The name, Charlie Hedges, sounded American, even if the man did look Hispanic, maybe Mexican. Maybe it was a cover name?

"I can't say," Hedges said, smiling at her. "But I think that, by working together, maybe we can bring down Colonel Fuentes and maybe even get you all out of the mess you are in."

Amélia hesitated. She had no reason to trust this man, but they seemed to be out of any other options. So far, she hadn't detected any insincerity in his or the woman's voice.

"OK, let's say I believe you." She looked around at the others for confirmation, and upon receiving several nods to the affirmative, put her put her AK-47 down. "How do you think you can help us?"

Chapter 57

Enrique Salas arrived at *Hospital Militar* early Sunday morning and demanded that he be allowed to see Colonel Fuentes, even though visiting hours weren't until ten o'clock. His mind alternated between memories of the previous night with Greta and his anger over what Raul had endured. He strode into the room as Fuentes was just starting to examine contents of his breakfast tray.

"Manuel, I'm going to have you court marshaled!"

Fuentes looked up, startled, but quickly regained his composure. "Enrique, calm down. You are going to do no such thing. Let's talk about this problem."

"You tortured my son!" Salas shouted. His face felt warm and his hand shook as he pointed his finger at Fuentes. "I should kick you out of that bed and stomp on you ..."

He noticed a movement at the door. Two nurses accompanied by a guard had responded to the uproar. They came charging into the room, one of the nurses going to the bed in a protective position to keep Salas from approaching. The other nurse grabbed his arm while the guard stood back, but put his hand on his pistol grip and unsnapped the strap holding it in the holster.

"Sir, be quiet! This is an ICU unit; you must calm down or you will be removed," she said, getting in his face.

"OK, I'm being quiet," Salas said. "I am Director Salas and I report directly to the president. I'm having this man placed under arrest." He pointed to the guard, an army corporal. "You, stay in this room to guard the prisoner until the arrest warrant is processed!"

The corporal looked uncomfortable, then stood a little straighter and said, "Sir! This is a military facility and Colonel Fuentes is in our care. You are not authorized to give orders here, and you will be removed if you continue to create a disturbance."

Salas felt himself losing control of his emotions, and he sputtered, trying to get the words out. "Don't ... don't tell me what I can do. I'll have the general in charge come down here if you don't follow my orders. Go get your commanding officer, soldier!"

The corporal stood his ground, just staring at Salas, his hand still on the pistol. The nurse said, "Please sir, stay calm. I'll go get someone in charge to talk to you. Let's all be reasonable." Then she left the room.

Fuentes spoke, peering from behind the nurse who was still standing protectively in front of the bed. "Enrique, please stop. Let us discuss this like civilized people. You have much to lose if you persist in this manner."

Salas was incredulous. "You want to talk about it? After what you did to Raul?"

"Yes, I do. You do too, if you will only stop and think rationally. I am sorry that I had to hurt Raul a little, but there is no permanent effect. He has gotten mixed up with some people who can destroy everything we have worked for."

"I can't forgive what you have done." Salas responded, calmer now.

Fuentes said, "I don't expect forgiveness, but we must work together. Just hear me out, in private."

Everyone stood still for a few moments. Then Salas nodded his head to the nurse and guard. They both looked toward the bed and Fuentes nodded also, giving them permission to leave.

When they were alone Fuentes said, "It is obvious that you have talked to your son. Where is he?"

Salas fought to control his emotions. "I won't tell you that."

"I guess I should have expected that," Fuentes murmured. "We can discuss how to handle Raul later. Right now we need to find agreement to achieve the goals we have been pursuing."

Salas pulled over a chair and sat stiffly, facing the bed, but not too close. He asked, "What do you mean by 'goals we have been pursuing?'"

"You remember our meetings with General Velasquez. He was frustrated that we have accomplished so little in our efforts to gain power."

Salas said, "Yes, I know all that. We tried to push sentiment toward Venezuela, and away from the U.S., but so far we ... well, we failed."

"Did you think Velasquez would give up so easily? Fuentes asked in a scornful voice.

Salas found himself speechless, and could only glare at him with hate filled eyes.

Fuentes continued, "We, Velasquez and I, have continued to plan and take actions to eventually make things go our way."

"Oh, I believe that!" Salas said, again raising his voice. "You have been kidnapping and torturing people, secretly imprisoning them … and what good has come of it?"

"Yes I have," Fuentes said, "You don't know the half of it. While you were trying to be the good, obedient bureaucrat in the new government, I have been preparing the way to achieve our goals.'

"You have achieved nothing!" Salas retorted.

"That is not true Enrique. I have put together an organization that penetrates the military and the national police. I have supporters in key parts of those organizations who will come to our support in a crisis. I can help you achieve the success you want. But now, you must help me."

"I won't help you do anything!" Salas said, again pointing his finger at Fuentes.

"Calm down Enrique! Yes you will. You must, or you will be ruined."

Salas squinted his eyes. "Me, ruined? I don't think so. You are the one who will fall!"

Although Fuentes was seriously wounded and bedridden, his voice gave no indication of weakness. "Enrique, there is evidence of your trip to Venezuela, of your meeting in secret with General Velasquez. What do you think that will do to your career?"

"You were there too! You will go down with me." Salas wasn't going to let the man get the upper hand.

Fuentes gave a wry grin, and said, "Sadly for you, the evidence I have doesn't show me as being involved, only you. If it is released, you will be considered a traitor by many. Oh, and there is one other thing … your little tryst with Greta Rojas last night. How do you think that will enhance your reputation?"

Tryst? What did he know? Maybe he had someone watching her place. "What are you talking about?"

"You know what I'm talking about Enrique. Don't act innocent with me!"

Fuentes must have had her house under surveillance. The man was obviously still infatuated with her. Salas said, "There is no evidence, just your assertion. I don't think Greta will say anything,"

The Honduran Plot

Fuentes smiled again, as he reached with his good hand into the drawer of the hospital tray which was pulled across his bed, the breakfast on it getting cold. "Have you seen my new smart-phone?" he asked. "It can receive internet, videos, and all kinds of things ... truly amazing. Here look at the quality of this video," he said, swishing and tapping his finger on the touch-screen, then handing the device to Salas.

Salas took the smart-phone and looked at the screen. There was the image of Greta lying naked on the bed, her face turned away from the camera. No one would be able to recognize her. As he watched he saw the image of himself disrobing and climbing onto the bed over her supine body. He felt his heart pounding and the pulse throbbing in his head. He hated the man!

"What do you think your political supporters would think of that video, if it were released?" Fuentes asked in a reasonable tone of voice.

Salas was speechless, and still couldn't tear his eyes from the actions taking place on the tiny screen. Greta never turned her face toward the screen. He had been set up!

"Don't take this personally Enrique," Fuentes continued. "This is just politics, the application of power and influence to achieve the desired results. None of this has to come out. You can achieve your ambitions, but only if you cooperate to assure our success. You need me, and I need you. I can survive without you, but Enrique, you cannot survive without me!"

Chapter 58

Jake awoke Sunday morning in a normal manner. He looked over to the chair—no one there—he was alone. The shoulder pain was there, but not too bad. He felt clear headed, the fuzziness that had plagued him, no doubt due to the morphine, was gone. And he was hungry!

He tried to get up. Pain throbbed in his shoulder—not a good idea. Maybe he should call for help. "Hello, can anyone hear me?"

"Yeah man, we can hear you." Luis walked into the room. "About time you woke up, dude. You missed all the excitement last night."

"Excitement?"

"Yeah man, the spooks were here."

"Spooks?" Jake furrowed his eyebrows. What was Luis talking about?

"I'll get Amélia and Raul. They can explain better than me." He left the room.

In a few seconds Luis came back with Amélia and Raul, and Teresa followed close behind. They spent a few minutes telling him a brief version of the previous night's strange encounter. Then Teresa checked his temperature—no fever. She gave Jake one of the pain pills.

"Could eat something," Jake said after swallowing the pill.

Teresa said, "We will help you up and walk you to the kitchen. You need to start walking some to get your strength back."

She nodded to Luis who grabbed Jake's good arm and helped him sit up on the edge of the bed. Jake felt slightly dizzy, but otherwise not too bad.

"I'll go get Aunt Yolanda to fix you something," Amélia said in an upbeat voice.

At the kitchen table Jake thoroughly woke up, aided by drinking Yolanda's strong coffee. Some potatoes and a fried egg cured the grumbling in his stomach. While he ate, Amélia related details of her discussion with Charlie Hedges.

"So what did the two of you decide he can do to help us?" Jake asked.

"Your files. He can help with those."

That wasn't what Jake had been thinking. He was imagining some sort of help running interference with the police, or enlisting help from other parts of the Honduran government. He thought maybe even the man could get the American Embassy involved.

"I don't understand," Jake said. Maybe his thinking was still a little sluggish.

Amélia sat forward looking at him from across the table. "Remember at the café in Talanga ... before the helicopter came? You said that the files you found in that Strategic plan folder were all encrypted. Maybe you could decode them, but maybe not."

Jake understood now—it made perfect sense. Who better to decrypt files than some spy, or whatever this Hedges guy was? A part of him resisted the idea though. Jake recognized that it was his ego talking, but he could probably write a program to break the code if it wasn't anything too sophisticated. So far, these guys seemed to be pretty amateurish at their security efforts.

"I was going to work on a program to try to break the encryption."

She smiled and reached across the table, placing her hand on his. "I know, Jake. You probably could, but this guy has some professional resources behind him. We talked about your files, and he thought he could help. Besides you're still not a hundred percent yet."

"You're probably right. I could still work on them, though. I'll give Hedges a copy on a flash drive. We can both be working on them. It will give me something to help take my mind off my shoulder."

Amélia squeezed his hand. "Perfect ... makes sense. They will be here shortly. Do you want me to get your laptop?"

A half-hour later Jake and Amélia sat at the kitchen table with Charlie Hedges, who was scrolling through files on Jake's laptop. Hedges had come alone. Raul and Luis hovered in the background, watching. After eating Jake felt much better; the pain in his chest and back had subsided to a dull ache, and his mind seemed clearer.

"Tell me again, how did you obtain these files?" Hedges asked.

"How isn't too important. Where I got them is the key thing," Jake said.

"OK, where?" Hedges said, rolling his eyes.

"They were in a classified section of the Honduran Ministry of Security and Intelligence web site. We are pretty sure that not even the president's Director of Intelligence has access to that area, so it must be something important," Jake said.

"And how would you know that?"

Jake could hear the skeptical tone in his voice. Breaking in to the conversation, Raul said, "Because my father is the Director of Intelligence, and I had his list of passwords."

"Your father is Enrique Salas?" Hedges said in surprise. "Well, he may have access and just didn't write the password down. He shouldn't have written any of them down, bad security practice." Raul looked a little put out at that reply, but didn't respond.

"Maybe so," Jake said, jumping back into the conversation. "Anyway, the point is that all I found was some text files with groups of hex numbers. There were also a few binary files, which aren't in any file format that I was able to identify. I thought they might even be some sort of compiled executable program."

"They might be most anything," Hedges said, scanning Jake's list of files which had unintelligible names and which, according to the directory listing, were either .txt or "unknown file type."

"Yeah," Jake agreed. "But notice many of them are large, and of the exact same length. That seemed strange to me. It gave me the idea that maybe they were encrypted in some special way and that might be a clue."

"I have no idea," Hedges said. "But I know some people who could tell us. How about letting me send a copy of these files to them? If anyone can figure it out, they can."

Jake held up a flash drive. "We thought that's what you would say."

Hedges took the stick. "I'll need to transmit this to the people who might decrypt the files, if indeed they are encrypted. Might take a while... maybe a few days."

"I thought you guys had supercomputers that could break codes in just minutes, or at least hours," Jake said.

"Us guys?"

"Yeah, Amélia told me you said you were with a government agency."

"I am, but I might be in someone's agricultural department for all you know. I'm not some super spy. Besides, I told her I'm doing this in an unofficial capacity. I'll have to get someone to do me a favor to get any computer time. It's not like I have a supercomputer at my disposal."

"Sorry." Jake felt like he had been handed a pretty good brush off.

Amélia said, "Charlie, we do appreciate your help. Please try to help us as soon as you can. We're in a quandary here."

Hedges smiled at them. "I know. In your position, I'd be going out of my mind. Just lay low here. I think you're pretty safe. I'm having Ramon and Lygya call in some sighting tips on you, Amélia ... from other places. You're the only one publicly wanted. The raid on the S&I Headquarters is being called a terrorist attack. No mention of any prisoners escaping."

"That's odd," she said.

"I agree," Hedges said. "Shows they're hiding things. I'll get back as soon as I can."

They watched Hedges drive away down the long gravel driveway. Small dust clouds blew in the breeze behind the departing pickup.

"He has to be CIA," Jake said.

"I don't care who he is if he can really help us," Amélia said. "I think we can trust him."

"I sure hope he's on the level," Jake said. "Do you think we are safe staying here?"

"I think so, at least for a while. Raul must not have given Fuentes any hint of the farm or they would have been here by now."

"It's odd that they are calling our raid a terrorist attack," Jake said.

Amélia said, "Maybe not too odd. I think Fuentes did an illegal kidnapping of Ruben and Juanita and probably of Pastor Zamora and Teresa too. They can't admit to having them as prisoners. But that doesn't mean that some of his secret hit squads aren't out there looking for all of us. We have to be careful and stay out of sight. This is a good of place to do that."

Chapter 59

Enrique Salas was enraged. He thought about just approaching the hospital bed and strangling Fuentes. He could do it—the man was incapacitated. How had he ever thought this man could be his key to power with the Venezuelans? He had been swayed by his personal association with Hugo Chavez and, later, General Velasquez. But he saw clearly now—Manuel Fuentes had never been his friend or colleague.

"If you don't cooperate you will be humiliated, both professionally and personally," Fuentes said, coldly. "The choice is yours Enrique, you can be universally scorned, or you can be the man who saved Honduras from ruin. It's your only choice now."

Salas sat there, feeling a mixture of outrage, betrayal, fear and humiliation. He couldn't believe the depth of manipulation Fuentes and Greta Rojas had used to ensnare him. *I can't believe how naive I have been.* He felt like a trapped animal, searching for a way out of a trap. His position seemed hopeless.

As his mind cleared, he suddenly focused on the last part of Fuentes' statement. "You said 'the man who saved Honduras from ruin.' What do you mean?"

Fuentes smiled that cold smile of his and said, "If the country were in a serious crisis you could be the man to step up and take charge. You could be a hero to the people."

"Crisis? What are you talking about? There is no crisis."

"Listen to me Enrique. There will be a serious crisis. I'll explain it to you. When this happens you will need my help and I will guide you through it. Together we can accomplish all the things in this country that we have discussed."

"Have your wounds made you delirious?" Salas asked, giving him an incredulous look.

"No, I'm very aware, and I know what needs to be done. I have been in contact with Velasquez, and you need to listen to what ..."

"But I think ..."

"I said listen! Don't interrupt! There will be a joint military training exercise about a week from now between Venezuela and

Guatemala. There will be land, air and sea war-games going on right next to Honduras."

"That isn't a crisis," Salas responded.

"No, but during that time you will be attending the president's cabinet meeting. During the cabinet meeting there will be a terrorist bomb attack, killing the key heads of the Honduran government ..."

Salas couldn't stop himself. "What? How could you know ...?"

"I said listen!" Fuentes said. "When this happens you will be the highest ranking cabinet member to survive. You will take charge, declaring emergency powers, but the situation will be volatile. There will be a power vacuum unless you can maintain order. To do that you will call on Venezuela to provide assistance, since they will have forces which can help immediately."

"But if that happened the military would be sure to object!"

"Of course," Fuentes said. "But we are prepared for that. I have a few highly placed officers whose loyalty is to me. They can slow responses and provide inside information. The Venezuelan armed forces already have a strike plan to neutralize the Honduran forces. Within twenty four hours you will be the acting president of Honduras, operating under military law. Because of the terrorist strike you will have support of much of the international community."

"That's preposterous," Salas said. "There is security to keep such a thing from happening. Terrorists can't place a bomb in the cabinet meeting."

Fuentes gave him an intense look and slowly said, "They won't have to, Enrique; because, you are going to bring the bomb!"

Chapter 60

Jake and Amélia sat in rattan chairs beneath the terra cotta tiled roof of the front porch of the farmhouse. Jake was silent for a few seconds, staring into space. For the moment they were safe. It was the first time since this ordeal had started that he really had time to reflect on anything other than the trouble he was in.

"I need to call my parents. Last they heard, I was staying in the parsonage, and still looking for Ruben. That was … gee, a week ago! They must be worried … must have been trying to call me."

"Ruben already called his parents to tell them he was safe," Amélia said. "He didn't tell them what had happened to him and Juanita, only that they had been arrested on false charges but now were free."

"Oh … they will have called my folks. They must be wondering why I haven't called," Jake said. "I had better call right away."

"You can to go to the kitchen to use Yolanda's phone. We haven't been using the burner phones Luis bought on the off chance that Fuentes' men might be monitoring, trying to find us."

Jake stood and felt woozy. He had been up too long for his first day out of bed. He reached out toward a column of the porch.

"Are you alright?" Amélia said, grabbing his good arm.

"I just felt a little light headed for a moment." He reached for Amélia to steady himself. She put her arms around him, holding him steady, looking him in the face.

"Are you OK?" she said. "Do you want to sit back down?"

"No … I'm just a little weak," he said. "Let's just stand here a moment."

They stood, holding each other, swaying slightly. Jake could feel her warmth and smell her delicious scent. He looked at her, then lowered his head and kissed her gently on the lips. She responded and the kiss became stronger, more urgent. Finally Jake pulled back and looked at her. Both of them were breathing heavily.

"Wow!" he exclaimed. "That's what I needed to make me stronger." They kissed again and Jake could feel her responding to him.

"Maybe we need to get you to the phone," she said, blushing, as she pulled back and looked him in the eyes.

He walked slowly into the house. *Why did I just do that? I just lost control. I feel like I'm cheating on Barbara. I've got to get back some focus—my perspective has been distorted by all this drama! But, wow, did that feel good!*

Jake placed his call using the old yellow wall phone in the farmhouse kitchen. He sat at the table, with the long spiral cord stretched loosely to his chair. He waited while the operator put through his collect call to the States.

"Hello? Jake, are you alright?" His mother's voice, tense and excited came through the speaker.

"I'm OK Mom. Sorry I couldn't call sooner." How much had Ruben told his parents? Jake mentally kicked himself for not having checked with Ruben before making the call.

"That's fine honey, I'm just glad you are safe, and that you found Ruben. Let me get your father on the other extension, then you can tell us all about it." He could hear a muffled sound of her calling his father's name.

She's glad I'm safe, so Ruben must not have told his parents too much. He wanted to tell them everything that happened—to hear their comforting words. He wanted to go home, and get his life back on track. But right now Jake couldn't do that. He had to shield them from knowing everything that was happening, until he could extract himself from the mess he had gotten himself into.

His father came on the line and Jake gave his parents a highly edited, and partially true, account of events that had taken place. He blamed Ruben's *mistaken arrest* and *legal troubles* for the delay in calling and the inability to return home at the moment.

"I still don't see why you can't come home now," his mom said. "The whole reason you went down there was to find Ruben. He can work out his legal problems without you, can't he?"

How he wished he could *just come home.* He wanted to do it, but knew he couldn't. It was time to grow up, to take responsibility. He had to make it clear that he was making the decision to stay, not asking their permission. "I know Mom, but there is a lot going on here and I don't think I can come home for a while."

The conversation went in circles, with Jake trying to say as little about the circumstances they were in, and both his parents pressing to know why he couldn't come home immediately. He finally ended the call by reassuring them that he loved them and would return as soon as he could.

Next he called Barbara. But he didn't want to make it a collect international call. He got one of the cellular phones from Luis. Despite Amélia's concerns, he and Luis decided there was little chance of the call being tracked. He sure hoped so! As he listened to the ring tone, Jake tried to think of how to start the conversation.

"Hello?" came her tentative response. Of course, he realized, there wasn't any caller ID to tell her who it was.

"Babe, it's me," Jake said. *Great opening dipwad! So romantic.*

"Jake! Oh my God, are you alright?"

"I'm OK. Sorry I haven't been able to call. Things have been a bit crazy down here."

"I'm glad you're OK. I've been worried sick. I called your mom and she said, like, no I haven't heard from Jake either. Why did you do that Jake Grayson?" He could hear her start to sniffle.

"Honey, I couldn't call. There ..."

"What do you mean you couldn't call? You knew I was worried sick about you going down to that third-world Hell-hole. But you went anyway ... didn't call ... didn't matter about me!" The sniffling increased to all out crying and deep breaths.

Jake held the phone out from his ear. He had to calm her down. He spoke loudly into the mouthpiece. "I couldn't call! I've been shot ... laid up for a couple of days ...out of touch."

Silence on the other end, then, "Shot? Jake that's crazy, what are you talking about? Oh my God, I knew something like this would happen. You are just throwing away our future with this reckless ... Wait ... really, were you really shot?"

Jake felt his spirit falling, like a bird with a broken wing. This wasn't right. It wasn't what his almost fiancée should say, was it? Where was her compassion, love, and gentleness? Somehow his mental picture of her shifted.

"Honey ..."

"Oh Jake, I'm sorry, forgive me. I just got so rattled by not being to get hold of you. Then you, like, tell me you got shot? Of course I went off the deep end. Are you sure you are OK? Can you come home?

"Maybe soon. When I get everything here cleared up," Jake said. "Listen I have to go now. I'll call you again when I can, OK?"

"OK, Jake. I love you. Come home soon." He could hear the sniffling again.

He put the phone down. *She still never asked about Ruben.*

Chapter 61

Charlie and Lygya were back aboard the yacht docked in Roatan. Charlie wanted to get down to business right away, but he had to keep up his cover—an aimless expatriate enjoying the good life. They had taken a charter flight from Tegucigalpa, and a taxi to the boat. He played the part, what would be expected, just in case anyone was watching. He and Lygya changed into swim suits, mixed up a blender full of frozen margaritas, and played footsie on the rear deck.

After a brief time, Charlie thought enough time had passed for anyone to lose interest. Keeping up his cover was a pleasurable job—he kissed Lygya deeply and embraced her.

"Why don't we go below?" she said giving him a coy smile.

Inside the cabin, he closed the entry hatch and pulled the curtains over the windows. Then they were all business. Lygya inserted a small key into an unobtrusive hole in the rear of the TV satellite receiver. Turning the key switched antennas and activated hidden transceiver functions. A small dish antenna, unseen under the white dome on the mast of the ship, aimed to a point in space where, 22,000 miles above, a U.S. Milstar satellite rode in geosynchronous orbit. Charlie removed a ruggedized laptop computer from a hidden compartment in the forward bulkhead. Connecting the units with a small cable and booting up the computer took only a minute. Charlie logged in with a long alphanumeric password he had memorized.

"Everything working OK?" Lygya asked.

"Yes, downlink beacon signal strength looks good and we have phase-lock," Charlie said. "Here goes; I hope they will listen to me."

He started a program which securely encrypted all data and formatted it for transmission through the EHF (Extremely High Frequency) transmitter hidden in the antenna dome. What transpired after that was a series of real-time encrypted text messages to his contact at the National Security Agency, located at Fort Meade in Maryland. He also contacted his superiors at CIA Headquarters in Langley, Virginia.

Charlie argued his case: his actions were in the category of oversight, he had not violated the national sovereignty of Honduras; the information had been obtained by others; the information had a high possibility of uncovering illegal activities that could jeopardize a friendly nation; and only by decrypting the data could they decide whether or not to take action.

Finally he convinced his superiors, and got permission to submit the data files. He plugged the USB flash drive into the laptop and transferred the files Jake had provided. Selecting a unique burst FTP (file transfer protocol) function in the program, he highlighted Jake's files and clicked a screen button marked XMIT. A high data rate burst transmission, spread over several frequencies in the EHF band was completed in a few hundredths of a second. This would be virtually undetectable, even if someone were searching for it.

They disassembled the equipment and stowed it away. Then Charlie said, "It's been a long day. Let's go to sleep. We probably won't have any results for a few days. We can go snorkeling tomorrow, afterwards I'll check in, just to see what the crypto geeks think."

Chapter 62

Jake's mood drifted downward, like a drowning swimmer, sinking into a pool of dark dissatisfaction. He went to the bedroom and got one of the pain pills, returned to the kitchen, and washed it down with a glass of water.

He returned to the front porch chair and sat, staring blindly into the distance. He had always planned his life, his career, and his dream of finding just the right girlfriend. He had visualized an exciting career at Intellibotics. He had dreamed that eventually he and Barbara would get married, maybe have children.

What had he done? Things were so off track now. This emotional, unplanned fool's errand had ruined everything! Well no, he couldn't really believe that. After all, what would have happened to Ruben if they hadn't rescued him? But still, what was he going to do now? Jake smiled wryly. He had heard the expression: "Life is what happens to you while you're busy making other plans."

He heard the front door open and looked around. Amélia came out and sat beside him.

"So did you get everything straightened out with your folks?" Amélia asked.

Jake swallowed. "Well, not really. They can't understand why I just don't come home."

"Didn't you explain why?"

"I told them I needed to stay for a while," Jake said. "I didn't think I should tell them about everything that has happened. They would freak out if they knew what we did, and the situation we are in."

"So what are you going to do?" Amélia asked.

Jake didn't have an answer. He needed to get his life back on track. How could he do that until he got home and started undoing the damage this quest had done?

"I don't know, now that we have found Ruben and Juanita ... well, I guess ... uh ...I don't know, maybe my folks are right," Jake said. "Maybe, when it's safe to go, I should leave. I'm not sure what I can do here."

"You're not sure?" Amélia said, crossing her arms, her voice raised.

"Well, uh ... not really. I mean, we really don't have a plan right now, any of us."

"*My* plan is to somehow defeat Fuentes," Amélia said, her dark eyes glittering. "Don't you see that? We have to show everyone how evil he is." He has to be stopped!"

"I know; you're right," Jake said. "But we can't start an armed revolution. I don't see how I fit in to all this. Maybe Charlie Hedges is going to bring some help, or maybe Raul's father can do something about Fuentes. But I don't see how all of us can take him on."

"You're not sure ... so you'll just leave?" her voice had risen even more.

"No, not right now ... but, do you know how to take him on?"

She scowled at him. "Maybe not yet, but I'll think of something ... I won't just give up!"

Jake could see that she was getting upset. "I'm not saying you should give up. I'm not giving up ... I just don't see how I can help you in this."

"Then maybe you *should* go!" she shouted, tears starting to glisten in her eyes. Go back to your ... Barbie ... or Barbara, whatever her name is!

"Wait, I really ..."

"Just go Jake! I don't need your help!"

She rose from the chair and stormed back inside the house, slamming the door behind her. Jake stared at the closed door. He thought he was being reasonable, but her reaction surprised him. What did she expect? He had to go home sometime didn't he? This wasn't his country—he couldn't just live here. And really, what more could he do about Fuentes now? He had already shot the man while rescuing Raul. The front door opened again.

"What's the matter *amigo*? You look like you just stepped in a pile of stink and can't get it off your boot."

Jake looked up and saw Ruben. His friend came out and sat down in the chair that Amélia had recently vacated.

"Maybe I did," Jake said. "I think maybe I made Amélia mad at me."

"You think?" Ruben said, arching his eyebrows. "I could hear her yelling from inside. What is it with you and your lack of skill at reading girls?"

"She got mad because I said that I would have to go back home sometime soon. There's no way I can just stay here."

"And you don't have a clue why that set her off, do you?"

"Well, I know she would like me to help with this situation," Jake said. "I just don't really know what I can do."

Juanita appeared at the front door, but Ruben waved her away. Looking at Jake, he said, "I was right, not a clue."

Jake was starting to get annoyed now. "Maybe not; tell me!"

Ruben shook his head. "Nope, not a clue. She loves you, you dumb clod!"

"But ... wait ... no, that can't be right," Jake mumbled, trying to pull his thoughts into coherent order.

Ruben was staring in his eyes and nodding his head. "*Si amigo*; that is the problem. You have to decide what to do now."

"Decide? I have no idea what to do," Jake lamented. "I don't know how I feel. I mean so much has happened."

Ruben nodded his head, a grim look on his face. "Yes, so much has happened. My life has changed, *amigo*. Juanita and I are ... sort of lost."

Jake furrowed his brows. Something in Ruben's tone of voice seemed ominous.

"Lost? What do you mean?"

Ruben inhaled sharply. "We were both damaged, Jake. Things can't go back where they were. I can only hope that God will lead us through this wilderness. We don't know the way."

Jake was trying to put this all together. "Damaged ... wilderness? Ruben, I don't understand."

"I was tortured and still have trouble thinking of anything else. Juanita was ... raped," Ruben said quietly. "We haven't told anyone else, Jake. It took over a day to get her to tell me. It's like she is in limbo. Don't know how long it will take to for her to cope with what was done to her."

Jake ached for his friend and Juanita too. The impact of how they had been hurt made Jake feel ashamed that he had been wallowing in misery over his plans gone awry.

The Honduran Plot

"I didn't realize … don't know what to say."

"Don't say anything. I'm not telling you this for you to say anything. I'm telling you because you're my friend. I need your support and friendship, Jake. And I think you need mine too. Your life has changed too, buddy, whether you realize it or not."

Jake struggled for words. "Now that I finally found you, Ruben. I just naturally thought we would go back home. Yeah, I like Amélia … I think … we only kissed a few times. You can't just decide you're in love, just like that."

"I think maybe that sometimes that is just the way it happens."

"What? You mean like 'love at first sight?' That's a cliché," Jake said.

"Cliché or not, I think that is the way it happens. Maybe not 'at first sight,'" Ruben said, making air quotes with his fingers. "But for some it happens pretty fast. Look at me and Juanita. We are bonded now, not just by love, but by the suffering we have endured together."

Jake couldn't believe what he was hearing from his friend. "So … what? You just throw out all your plans and run off with some Honduran girl?"

Ruben scowled and shot back, "Juanita's not just some Honduran girl!"

"OK! I'm sorry, I didn't mean it like that," Jake backpedaled. "But what I mean is we were both in college, had plans for our lives. So how does Juanita fit into that life … your life?"

Ruben hesitated. "That life … that life I had planned wasn't real, not something that had to happen. That is all changed now. Because of Juanita the course of my life has changed. Everything is different now."

Jake's eyes widened and his jaw dropped as the words of his best friend sank in. "So everything? …" Jake fumbled for the right words. "Home, college, us … all changed? Are you doing that?"

"Jake, I'm not just abandoning everything. My parents and friends, you especially, are still part of my life. But it's changed. I have to make a life that has Juanita as a major focus. So the other things are still there, but the structure changes."

"Structure …" Jake said, still trying to adsorb all this.

Ruben continued, "I don't have it all planned out. I think God puts people and situations into your life to give you the opportunity to change and grow. You can't know in advance what your life will be like. You can only take one step at a time, go with the flow."

"There you go with the clichés again," Jake said smiling. "So what are you going to do?"

"I don't know yet, but I do know one thing …"

""What's that?" Jake asked.

"I can't go back home now, at least not for a while," Ruben said. "And when I do go back, I'm taking Juanita with me."

Jake sat looking at his friend, glad for the reprieve from having to explain his feelings. It was easier when the attention was on Ruben's plans. That, however, didn't last long.

"So?" Ruben said.

"What?" Jake asked, pulling his thoughts back to the issue at hand. "You mean me? I haven't thought any of this through, this stuff with Amélia."

"Is there anything more important to figure out right now?" Ruben asked.

"I guess I see what you mean. I've been worrying about how my life has gotten so off track … how to get it back on track. I guess I'm sort of lost too."

Ruben said, "Maybe you don't need to get it back on. Maybe God has put you on a new path. Find out what he has in store for you."

"That is … scary," Jake said.

Chapter 63

Sunday evening Enrique Salas sat, once again, on the couch in Greta Rojas' apartment. He could not imagine that he would ever set foot in that place again after her betrayal. But she had been convincing when she called.

∎∎∎

"Wait Enrique," she said, crying. "Manuel forced me to do it; I didn't want to. He threatened to have me killed, and he would have done it. I had no choice. I hate him!"

"You don't hate him. You are still his lover!" Salas said savagely. "You betrayed me! I'm the one who should have you killed."

"No, don't say that," Greta wailed. "My affair with Manuel ended and I'll never go back to him in that way. I told you that he had become erratic. Please Enrique, believe me. Come to my place tonight, let me convince you. The two of us together can oppose him if we work together instead of against each other."

∎∎∎

And so he had come, his suspicion warring with desire. His craving for her was still there, even after everything that had happened. How long ago had it been since he had felt the rush of emotions that he had experienced in her arms. It was like he was eighteen again, and the euphoria suppressed any guilt he felt about betraying his wife.

As she had the night before, Greta brought him a glass of wine and joined him on the couch. This time she sat farther away, keeping her distance, her demeanor more professional.

"Enrique, I am so glad that you agreed to talk to me," she said. "This situation with Manuel, Colonel Fuentes, is complicated. It could be dangerous for both of us, but by working together I think we can see our way through it, maybe even take advantage of it."

"I'm willing to listen to what you have to say," Salas said, sitting upright and stiff on his end of the couch. He still didn't trust her, but a chance that she was sincere kept hope alive.

"Well, I think we need to talk openly and honestly," she said. "I know that he is blackmailing you for something. He said as much when he demanded that I seduce you and video record it. Really Enrique, I had no choice … he could have ruined me, or even had me killed as he threatened to do."

"It was the most humiliating thing that ever happened to me," Salas said.

"I'm so sorry," she said, reaching toward him but then, pulling her hand back. "Do you think it wasn't humiliating to me too? Just the thought of him watching that video makes my skin crawl. I couldn't have gone through with it if I didn't …uh, if I didn't really like you. I wasn't lying when I told you that I admire and like you, Enrique. Please believe me."

Could this really be true? Fuentes had coerced him with a carrot-and-stick approach. Greta was the carrot, and political blackmail was the stick. He realized now how devious Fuentes was, and her story of threats against her didn't seem as preposterous as he once would have thought. He still didn't see how he could get out of this crazy scheme Fuentes and General Velasquez had cooked up. Maybe it did make sense to develop an alliance with Greta. Possibly they could extract themselves from this situation. And there were other advantages.

"If we would agree to some sort of cooperation, what would our relationship be?" he asked, watching intently for her reaction.

"Well," she said, looking at the wine glass she twirled in her hands, "we could have a close relationship. You are still an influential and powerful man, despite Manuel's threats. I can assist you in many ways."

"So a political relationship then?"

"More than that," she said after sipping some of the wine. "I want to be a companion to you in many ways, political and personal. We need to get over our mistrust and help each other."

He wanted to believe her. Somewhere in the back of his mind he recognized that his position, and ability to help Greta succeed, is what attracted her. But he clung to her words about looking up to him and respecting him. He was only about ten years older he estimated, refusing to acknowledge there might be little physical attraction for an overweight, older man.

"Mistrust, that's our problem you think. Do you mistrust me?"

"No, not really," she said. "I was worried that you might try to get back at me for setting you up with that video. I'm not so worried now. I think you understand the pressure I was under."

"I want to believe you."

"Then do believe me. I want you to trust me." She put her glass down and reached out, taking his hand. This time she didn't pull back. "Now tell me what is it that Fuentes is trying to blackmail you into doing? Maybe there is a way I can help if you confide in me."

He wanted to tell her. He had not been able to confide in anyone, and felt lonely and isolated. Now his infatuation with her beauty allowed him to imagine a portrait of them together as partners and intimate friends. So with that picture crystallizing in his mind, he began to tell her of the scheme Fuentes and Velasquez were coercing him into.

When he had finished she sat quietly, thinking about all that he had said. He watched her, becoming anxious, wondering if he should have spilled his guts the way he had. Still, he felt better just having told someone of his dilemma. "Well?" he said when he could wait no longer.

"Do you think it could work?"

"Do I? ... No! It's crazy ... terrorism." He found himself breathing hard at the thought.

She placed her hands on his again. "Calm down Enrique. We don't want you having a heart attack."

"I'm calm ... well maybe not so calm."

"We have to think this thing through," she said, looking in his eyes. "If General Velasquez has the power of the Venezuelan military behind him, then maybe it's not so crazy. And I don't think it is really terrorism."

"How could it not be?"

"Look, many of us in this country would like to see it aligned with Venezuela. You and Manuel even agreed on this didn't you?"

Salas thought about what she was saying. "It would bring prosperity in trade with other ALBA countries and plentiful, low cost oil from Venezuela."

She squeezed his hands. "So this would be more like a political coup. With most of the opposition leadership gone there wouldn't be a lot of bloodshed that a revolution would cause. Only a few people would be killed. So it is not terrorism against the people of Honduras."

"Maybe so," he said. "But I don't want to be the one doing the killing. Besides, if all that happened, what is to keep Fuentes from killing me too?"

"From what you have told me, he needs you. You would be acceptable to the people of Honduras as their president. Fuentes doesn't have the credentials or stature."

"You could be right," he said. Her statement pleased him, fed his ego and lessened the feeling of humiliation and outrage he had been feeling. "You know, you have a way of making me feel better. Maybe we would be good partners."

Her face lit up. "Thank you Enrique," she murmured. "I am pleased that you think so. I think we have to take this situation one step at a time to see what develops. We can work closely together to avoid any pitfalls. There doesn't seem to be a good way out of the situation. So maybe we can use the situation to our advantage. Do you agree?"

"I haven't found a way out that doesn't ruin me. Maybe you're right."

She rose from the couch and told him, "Wait here one minute. I'll be right back."

She walked into the bedroom. He watched, remembering the last time when he had accompanied her. He waited, standing by the coffee table, until she returned. "Here, a peace offering," she said, handing him a tiny digital video recorder. "This will never enter my bedroom again … unless you decide to bring it someday. The memory chip is still in it. I thought you might want it for a souvenir of the beginning of our relationship."

Chapter 64

Monday morning Jake avoided interaction with anyone, as much as possible without seeming rude. He had tossed and turned most of the night, plagued by the thoughts running through his head. Ruben's words the previous afternoon had their intended effect. Jake was rethinking everything—what his goals were, how he felt about Barbara, or Amélia, what obligation did he have to stay, or how could he possibly leave. Only one thing seemed clear—that he had no answers.

He retreated to the front porch and sat in the familiar rattan chair. He seemed to be spending a lot of time there, avoiding people. Like before, it didn't seem to be working.

"You look like you are much better."

Startled, he looked up and saw Teresa standing in the doorway. "Yeah ... it still hurts a little, but the pain pills seem to keep it under control. You were a good nurse. Thank you."

She sat down beside him. "Thank you, I was glad I could help a little."

"I'm just thankful it is not worse than this," Jake said.

"Yes, we all are. I think God has answered our prayers,"

"Prayers?" Jake questioned. "I know we always say that, but they didn't keep me from getting shot in the first place."

"Yes that is true," Teresa said. "But you could have been hurt much more severely, or even killed. If the bullet had hit a bone and broken up, or deflected, or torn an artery, the damage probably would have been fatal. We all prayed for you in the ambulance. I'd say God has answered our prayers."

"I'll bet Amélia didn't pray for me."

Teresa chuckled. "Well, maybe not. That is not for me to judge, so I don't know."

"And what about Josué? He's dead ... his prayers weren't answered." Jake wondered if you could know any prayer was really answered, or whether it was only random chance at work.

Teresa appeared to reflect on his words for a moment. "I remember Josué from when he was baptized and joined our church about a month ago. He has accepted Jesus Christ as his savior, so no matter what happened he is fine—he is with God. That is what I truly believe."

"Well, yeah, I guess that is right," Jake said. "But then why pray for someone to be healed if they are just as well off dying and going to Heaven?"

Teresa smiled that kind smile of hers again and said, "That's a good question. I'm no religious philosopher but I think I might know the answer to that, at least for my own mind. We pray for things we want, and we pray that things will be done as God wills. So it's like this; God has a purpose for everyone on this earth, so I pray for people, and that they can fulfill God's purpose. And, if that means they have a better life here on earth, then that is good. If they survive and that makes those who love them happy, then that's good too. We can't know what God's will is, but we can let him know what we want and then ask that 'God's will be done' and mean it."

Jake managed a smile, saying, "I think maybe you *are* a religious philosopher."

Teresa laughed, and then her face took on a more serious look. She said, "Just remember to pray and God will guide you."

"But if God is going to do what is best ... things we can't always know ... uh, and wait, he knows what is in our heart, right? So, why do we need to ask him for the things we want if he already knows?"

Teresa said, "I think we are told to pray to God for our own good, not because he doesn't already know what we want. Prayer is a form of worship, a thing that fosters dependence upon God. We can pray for what we want, but not expect a yes-or-no answer, or even any answer in the time we think appropriate. But if we pray and then just wait patiently on God, I think he will guide us. We just have to listen to that internal guide, the Holy Spirit within us. And Jake, don't be hesitant to pray about Amélia too. I know things seem a little rocky now, but prayer can help."

"So you know about her being mad at me?"

"Jake, everyone in the house knows! We could all hear the two of you," Teresa said with another kind smile.

Later, Jake sat there thinking about the things both Ruben and Teresa had said to him. He realized that he had a lot of maturing to do in his faith as a Christian. He had always gone to church, ever since he could remember. And so, he had just accepted it without question and hadn't ever really dug deeply into why he believed what he did.

As with many people, church and faith were part of Jake's life. But, for the most part, that didn't play much part in guiding his decisions. He had made plans for his life—things he imagined would make his life better. He had made friends, played sports, planned for college and a career and dreamed of finding that perfect girl. He even thought he had found her in Barbara.

In all of this planning and dreaming he had not relied on God, or even really thought about it. Sure, he considered himself a Christian, he believed, even went to church, but in most ways he was like everyone else. Christianity hadn't made much of a difference in his life. Then as he had grown up and encountered the problems of the world, especially on that first trip to Honduras, he had felt all his beliefs crumbling. In his uncertainty, he had stopped praying regularly.

So maybe it's time to really make a change. I've gone back to my old ways in the last few days. He remembered his heartfelt prayer he had prayed almost a week before. After that prayer he had decided on actions, some dangerous, with a sense of purpose and calm. Was that God's guidance? He didn't know. *How could you ever really know?* Then an unexpected thought popped into his head. *You pray and listen, and then you have a feeling of certainty when the Spirit guides you.*

Jake thought about Ruben's decision to stay in Honduras and his devotion to Juanita. That must be a sign of true love. He didn't exactly understand how his feelings toward Barbara had changed, but he knew they had. So many things seemed to have changed. Maybe he could never go back to the way things were.

What was he going to do about Amélia? He had hurt her, just when they had started showing a degree of intimacy. They faced challenges in just a week that many people don't encounter in their whole lives. They started to know and depend on each other, and then he started talking about going home. He could see it now. Had he led her on? If so, it wasn't intentional.

Answers eluded him. Ruben made it sound so easy with his clichés—one step at a time, go with the flow. Jake didn't know what to do, how to take the next step. Then it occurred to him that Teresa had been saying something similar when she said he should pray and wait for God to guide him. Would God show him the next step? He would follow her advice and seek God's guidance. He closed his eyes and began to pray:

Lord God, please help me; I don't know what to do. I am torn between going home and staying here. Please give my parents a sense of comfort and patience while I am delaying, when they want me to come home. I know that I have hurt Amélia, *but I didn't mean to. I'm not sure what my feelings are, but I am attracted to her.*

I realize now that she must have deeper feelings for me than I had ever imagined. Maybe I am just waking up to our relationship, but it is still difficult for me to believe things can work for us in the long run. How can they when her life is here in Honduras and mine is back at home? Lord, please guide me; help me know what to do, not just about this but for all the other things in my life.

I know I haven't relied on you and I'm sorry—please forgive me. Lord, please forgive my sins. Forgive me for the taking of lives when we tried to rescue Ruben and the others. Thank you for putting all these people in my life. I suppose this is your way of growing me. And ... uh, I guess that's all.

In Jesus' name, Amen.

Well, maybe that is what God wanted, Jake couldn't be sure. As he sat there, waiting to see if he felt any different, he realized most of his anxiety had disappeared. *Amazing!*

Chapter 65

Enrique Salas walked down the hallway looking for Fuentes' room. He had been moved out of ICU and reportedly was making good progress. Salas felt better this morning and was actually looking forward to hearing more about the audacious plot. *Greta was right, the more information I have, the better we can judge what action to take.*

When he got to the room he rapped twice on the closed door and entered. Fuentes was sitting up in bed talking to a man in the chair at his bedside. As the man rose Salas appraised him. He was in civilian clothes, but his bearing suggested that he was military, or ex-military. He had short-cut hair, a medium complexion and was relatively handsome.

"Enrique," Fuentes greeted him, "I am glad you came. Meet Mr. Rodriguez, my friend from Venezuela. Benito, this is Enrique Salas."

"I am pleased to meet you sir," the man said as he shook hands with a firm hard grip.

Salas was a little surprised by the apparent cordial reception he received. Perhaps Fuentes was putting on a show for the Venezuelan's benefit. After shaking hands Salas pulled up another chair and both men sat. He looked from Rodriguez to Fuentes and said, "You asked me to be here Manuel. I hope you are feeling better."

"Yes, thank you," Fuentes said. "I asked Benito to join us since he is deeply involved in the plans."

"The plans ..." Salas repeated, looking curiously around the room.

"Don't worry, the room is clean. I had one of my techs sweep it for any listening devices just an hour ago. We can discuss things freely here as long as the door is closed."

"Alright, that is good," Salas said. "I am in the dark about 'the plans' so why don't you tell me about them, since apparently I am deeply involved."

"Enrique, loosen up ... stop being so resentful," Fuentes said.

No, evidently Fuentes wasn't trying to make things appear cordial in front of the visitor. Salas steeled himself for what he was about to hear, and vowed to himself that he would not show any emotion.

"You are the key to the plans. I am sorry that I carried the planning forward without your involvement, really I am. I felt it was prudent, but then when you balked upon hearing of the idea, I felt the need to apply a little coercion. I had to, this is too important. You will thank me in the end, when we are successful."

"I will reserve judgment for now," Salas replied, relaxing his stiff posture a bit. "And how does Mr. Rodriguez fit in?"

"He is the representative for General Velasquez in this operation. He will coordinate our activities with those of the Venezuelan military during exercises with Guatemala. He knew you would be coming here this morning and has brought you something. It's another surprise for you, so don't be offended."

What now? He watched as Rodriguez got up and opened one of the cabinets in the hospital room. He pulled out a scarred briefcase and presented it to Salas.

"That's my briefcase!" Salas exclaimed. "What is this about? Where did you get it?

"I had some of my men 'liberate' it from your office before all the excitement happened. With everything that has gone on, I guess you haven't missed it." Fuentes continued, "You and the briefcase are the two elements which can make our plan successful. Will you just listen as I explain without objecting and getting upset?"

Salas considered this a moment, and put the briefcase on the floor. "I am curious. And since I have little choice but to be involved in this crazy plot, yes, I will listen closely."

He thought about the miniature digital recorder Greta had given him. It was tucked in his pocket, and he hoped it would pick up Fuentes' voice. Even though there would be no video, he would have some sort of tangible evidence to use against Fuentes.

Fuentes began his explanation: "I have already explained the basic idea to you. The president and his cabinet are killed in a 'terrorist bomb attack' and you, through some chance of fate, have survived. As the senior cabinet member, you will be in a position to declare yourself acting president on a temporary basis. We know that the Supreme Court will try to weigh-in on whether or not that is a legal act, but there will be confusion and delay. I have made preparations to take advantage of the situation.

The Honduran Plot

"I have at my command a number of key people in the national police and the armed forces who will support your call for emergency powers and imposition of martial law. The military leaders will probably agree to the imposition of martial law, but will argue that they should be in charge, and will dispute your authority. My people will immediately start a campaign of disinformation and propaganda which calls into question their motives. There will be much unrest, some attacks on military and police personnel, and civil protests in your support. We will provide 'evidence' that some of those openly opposing you were linked to the bomb attack."

Salas could envision such a bold plan working. Political unrest and disputes were not unknown in Central and South America. After all, hadn't President Zelaya been stripped of his power in 2009 and expelled from Honduras.

Fuentes continued, "Because of the crisis you will ask our ally, Venezuela, for military support to prevent the Honduran military from initiating a government coup. General Velasquez, speaking for the Venezuelan government, will immediately respond. He will publically offer the use of his military forces, on exercises in Guatemala. Within hours the Venezuelan forces will apply tactical surprise and overwhelming force to take over key Honduran bases.

"You will claim that the resulting resistance by the Honduran military was actually a military coup attempt that the Venezuelan forces helped you defeat. With those forces under our command we will be able to crush any resistance and establish a new socialist government. It will be as I said Enrique. You will be the next president of Honduras. And of course, I will be your right-hand man!"

Salas sat looking from Fuentes to Rodriguez, his mind grappling with the audacious concept. How could he stop this crazy plan without sacrificing his reputation and career? Even if he were willing to give up everything, would he be able to succeed, or would Fuentes and Velasquez find another way? What if it did succeed? He would be president, an important head of state known the world over. That did have a certain appeal.

"And how does this event take place?" he asked. "You want *me* to take part in a bombing?" That idea was the most frightening thing about this whole plan. Salas wasn't normally one to get his hands dirty while trying to achieve his goals.

"Ah, that is where your briefcase comes in. Explain it to him Rodriguez."

Rodriguez, who had been silent until now, picked up the briefcase and said, "As you can see, your briefcase looks like it always did, at least at a casual glance. It easily passed through the security screening here at the hospital. Our technicians in Venezuela have made a few key modifications. Actually the sides and bottom are slightly thicker and it weighs a bit more than it did. The sides and bottom contain sheets of powerful plastic explosives which can be triggered by a cell phone and detonator that is built into the back side, right between the hinges."

"Are you serious?" Salas asked, his face blanching.

"Deadly serious," Fuentes broke in. "Even disguised as it is, the briefcase would probably not pass the screening at the *Casa Presidencial* except for one thing—that thing is you. As a cabinet member, if you were to arrive by helicopter with a military escort, you would likely not be subjected to the screening devices which are used at the public entrance on the north side of the building."

Salas had difficulty following the plan. "That doesn't make sense. Why would I be arriving at the cabinet meeting by helicopter?"

"We will arrange a trip for you to inspect security capabilities for the ARCOS-1 submarine cable facility on the north coast in Trujillo. It is where fiber-optic communication cables arrive on-shore and are routed to various locations in the country. You will be flown back just in time for the cabinet meeting, accompanied by Major Rivas. I believe you have met him."

Salas considered this and stared at his briefcase, which Rodriguez had placed back on the floor. "So I am supposed to carry a bomb around for five days?'

Fuentes and Rodriguez both smiled. "No Enrique, your briefcase will be given back to you on the helicopter ride. You can bring materials for the cabinet meeting in a folder and transfer them to the briefcase so everything appears normal. The helicopter will land at the helipad by the parking lot on the west side of *Casa Presidencial*. From there you can directly enter through the security office at the front of the building with Major Rivas and avoid any screening."

"I am amazed," Salas said. "Do you really think this can work?"

"It will work ... it must work," Fuentes said.

The Honduran Plot

"But why do I have to do it? How can I be sure I won't be blown up along with the others?"

"Enrique, we need you. There is no other way to get the explosives into the cabinet room. It is thoroughly checked before the meeting. But no one would expect the cabinet members themselves of bringing in explosives. The briefcase is safe. It won't go off accidently. The number of the cellular inside is a special one, not even valid, so no one will call it, even accidently."

"So after I arrive at the meeting?" Salas said.

Fuentes explained further. "At some time during the cabinet meeting you will receive a call on your cellular, and must excuse yourself saying that there is a family emergency. You will forget to take your briefcase, which you will leave on the floor by your chair. Then go to the lower floor, down by the dining room or on the patio down there where receptions are held. You will be safe there. After the explosives have detonated, you can take charge as the only one surviving the blast. Then we will stay in constant communications to coordinate everything. Major Rivas will be there to assist you and provide secure communications ability."

"You have thought of everything apparently," Salas said.

"Let us hope so," Fuentes said. "And Enrique, be assured that you have no choice in this matter. You will be watched, and you must do as instructed. To try to betray us would be very foolish!"

Chapter 66

Charlie Hedges was furious. He had never felt so frustrated and angered by the political decisions he was forced to live with. If he was going to prevent disaster, he would be forced to find a way to circumvent his orders. So on Monday afternoon he returned to the farm on the *Rio Dulce* north of Talanga.

Charlie cleared his throat and addressed the group. They were all there, crowded into the living room. Jake sat on the couch with a loose shirt covering his bandaged wounds. Charlie noticed that the girl, Amélia, who had protectively hovered over him a few days before, was now standing on the other side of the room.

"I came back to tell you what we have found out, and to ask for your help. We were able to decrypt the files that Jake gave us. They were mostly secure e-mails between Colonel Fuentes and several other people. The information is explosive, literally!" Charlie could see the confusion on their faces. "If this whole thing is not a hoax, it reveals a plot that affects the security of Honduras."

"Why did you come back here?" Amélia asked. "Isn't that the kind of secret things that diplomats or high level officials discuss?"

"That's a good question," Charlie said. "The conclusions we have drawn from the messages are very alarming. Normally there would be urgent calls between our government and yours to discuss the threat, but there are several problems."

"What kind of problems?" Yolanda asked.

"I can't say ... unless you can convince me that I can trust each one of you. I want to talk about your situation so I can make a decision on how much to reveal."

"You're the one who came to us. Now you can't trust us?" Amélia protested, stirring some mutterings of agreement from some of the others.

Charlie had to know more before he could share his information. He held his ground. "Yes, I came to you. I want to help, but please understand that I have to protect myself. There are things I need to know to assure that I'm not going to embarrass my government."

Finally the group agreed to tell him anything he needed to know to gain his trust. He covered names and background of each of them and some more details about how they had become involved in their present dilemma. Finally he focused his attention on Raul.

"Your father is Director of Intelligence on the president's staff, and prior to that he held a similar position reporting to the previous president, before Zelaya was removed. Isn't that true?"

"Yes sir," Raul said.

"Where is all this going?" Amélia interrupted. "Just tell us what the problem is and stop dragging this out like a legal deposition!"

"OK, I'll cut to the chase," Hedges said. "We think that there is a plot to overthrow the government. Colonel Fuentes seems to be the central person involved. Raul's father is identified as one of the people involved. He is apparently working with Fuentes."

"He is not working with Fuentes!" Raul protested, jumping to his feet. "Fuentes tortured me! I told my father ... he was furious. I called him, so he probably has the phone number on caller I.D. ... didn't ask where we are hiding ... hasn't told Fuentes. If he had, they would have found us by now."

Amélia turned toward Raul, looking at him in wide eyed disbelief. "You told your father where we are?"

"No! I said he didn't ask. It's OK, he won't try to find out ... made him promise."

"Oh, sure ... then we're perfectly safe," Amélia replied in a sarcastic tone.

It took another fifteen minutes for Charlie to get everyone calmed down. During the exchanges between the members of the group, he became convinced that they were sincere. He believed Raul was not a threat, and could be counted on not to inform his father of their discussions. Besides, he had little choice but to trust these people if there was any hope of preventing disaster.

"Let's get back to our discussion of the problems," Charlie said. "I'll have to trust all of you if there is any chance of stopping this plot. Before I get into the plot, let me tell you why I have to depend on your little group of counter-revolutionaries," he said with a wry grin.

"The first reason is that my identity cannot come to light, so I can't take any direct action. No one is supposed to know that I am keeping an eye on things here."

"But we know who you are," Jake said.

"Do you?" Charlie countered. "I'm just a name to you. I never have showed you any form of official identification. Anything you think you know is just speculation."

"He has a point," Yolanda said. "We really don't even know what country he is from, or where he lives."

"Let me continue," Charlie said. "One of the things my government does not want to do is reveal any information that would give others information on our intelligence capabilities. Another thing is that we legally can't interfere in the affairs of a sovereign country. I have been skirting around this issue, pushing the envelope so to speak, because of the things I have learned about Fuentes. The only reason they agreed to decrypt the messages was because I hadn't actually been involved in stealing the files. So we're just sort of unofficially helping you out. For those same reasons we can't go to your government and tell them what we know. Another issue is that if we did, we might be revealing what we know to some of the people involved in the plot. We got a list of Fuentes' undercover operatives in the military, but who knows if there are others elsewhere in the government."

"What can we do?" Amélia asked.

"I don't know," Charlie said. "If your past actions are any indication, I'd bet you can come up with something. Reading the e-mails and doing some guess work, we think that the major parts of the plot are figured out. Their operation is code named '*Zopilotes*', like the buzzards like you see circling the dump in Tegucigalpa. An appropriate name I'd say."

"Are you going to give us the decrypted files?" Jake asked.

"Yes, and I'll help you as much as I can, unofficially. My bosses don't even know I'm here or that I have the decrypted files."

"I thought you said they agreed to decrypt them," Jake said. He looked confused.

"They did agree, and then when they found out how serious this was, they refused to tell me what they had revealed." Charlie fumed again with frustration and anger just telling them this. "Only because I have a friend at the puzz ... well, never mind. We have worked a lot of operations together and both get fed up with the bureaucracy and indecision. He sent me the files, and analyst's conclusions, without proper authorization. Like I said, I'm going out on a limb here; don't let me down. Here …" He tossed a USB flash drive to Jake.

They gathered around the kitchen table, crowded around Jake's laptop, while Charlie showed them the e-mails. The vague outline of the plot began to emerge.

"As you can see," Charlie said, "it appears that they are discussing plans to ask Venezuela for assistance after some sort of attack on senior members of the government. But it's not clear what that is, or when it will occur. What is clear is that it is anticipated that Enrique Salas will emerge as the spokesman for the government, or perhaps as the only surviving member of the cabinet, and be the one to appeal to Venezuela. We think that the attack must be a bombing."

All eyes turned toward Raul.

"Look, none of these messages are to, or from, my father. They just talk about the role he has to play, but he doesn't seem to be involved in all this planning," Raul said. "I told you he isn't working with Fuentes."

"But it appears that they are planning to get him involved as the central guy in this plot," Charlie countered.

"Maybe that's their weak point," Raul said. "He wouldn't take part in anything like this unless Fuentes forced him somehow."

Charlie said, "These messages seem to be between Fuentes and a number of people that were identified as being in the Honduran military or the national police. Also there is a list of military bases and unit designations. It could be a list of embedded supporters within the armed forces that Fuentes can count on to cooperate with the Venezuelan forces."

"I still don't understand why you can't directly warn the president about this plot," Jake said.

"I wanted to," Charlie said. "We went over that. I've been ordered not to do anything. They won't even tell me about the information. It's only because of my buddy that I have this information. They can't find out what he did or we would both be in trouble … probably go to prison."

Amélia said, "Even with the seriousness of this plot they shut you out and told you not to do anything? How can they just sit back and let this happen?"

Charlie could understand their indignation. He shared it. But in fairness he told them another reason his superiors had taken their timid position. "They aren't here, haven't talked to you like I have. They aren't trusting people. For one thing; I can't verify the source of the information directly. And I couldn't verify how you came to receive it. I told them about your group, but they said that, for all we know, you could have faked these e-mails yourself."

"That's crazy, man!" Luis said. "Why would we do such a thing? Just make up something like ... uh, you know, like ... it's just crazy!"

"Calm down," Charlie said, holding up his hands. "I said that I believe you. It's the people I report to. They won't risk the embarrassment of revealing this to your government if they aren't absolutely sure. They have even speculated that someone leaked this information to me, so we would do just that, and cause an international incident."

"But I can swear to the fact that we got this from the Ministry of Defense computer," Jake put in. "We all can."

"I know, but they don't know who you are and there is no time for a lengthy investigation. We think the most likely time for something like this to be carried out is when your president has his regular cabinet meeting at *Casa Presidencial*. That's just four days from now! Believe me; all I can do is to depend on you to find a way to stop it."

"I can understand your reasoning," Amélia said. "I still don't like the idea of us having to do something about this mess, but I believe you now. It's really up to us. I don't know how, but we will try to do something. I just hope it's not too late."

Chapter 67

Friday morning Enrique Salas watched as the helicopter lowered itself gently onto the surface of the ARCOS-1 Submarine Cable Facility parking lot. This was to be a fateful day in his life and his mind was racing. He had not found a way to avoid going through this ordeal. *This is crazy, but I have to make myself do it. I just have to go through with the plan. There is no time left to find any alternative. When this is over, if I can come out unscathed, I have to decide what to do about Greta. Maybe she is a mistake, but I don't want to give her up.*

Fifteen minutes later, as he viewed the mountains and hills passing below the helicopter on its flight to Tegucigalpa, he became queasy. The briefcase in his lap seemed like a ticking time bomb. Major Rivas rode in the seat beside him and was almost bouncing up and down with excitement. Salas just felt dread, like a condemned man on his way to the gallows.

What if Fuentes had a hidden agenda and planned to blow him up along with the rest of the cabinet? Would there be someone else conveniently absent from the meeting, just waiting to take over? Maybe the whole plan had been lies and this was some sort of double cross.

"Everything is in place and ready." Rivas' voice came through the intercom headset he wore to allow communications over the noise of the helicopter. "I've been talking to the Colonel over a secure radio link. All key military and police personnel, the ones we will rely on, are poised to do their part when disaster strikes."

"I don't know if I can do this ..."

"You can sir!" Rivas said. "I'll be right downstairs on the other side of the courtyard. I'll be in touch with the others by encrypted digital radio to make sure all the timing is right. After the meeting is underway, I'll call you to create the emergency call that requires you to leave for a few minutes. You can come down to where I am and we will go into a safe area."

"And if you call the other number I'll be dead!"

"Sir, please ..." Rivas pleaded. "I have taken precautions. There will be no mistake."

It's not a mistake I am worried about!

Rivas continued, "Remember, as soon as the detonation occurs we will go up onto the balcony near the damage from the cabinet room. I'll use some debris to dirty your clothes and face to make it look like you were just outside and barely missed being caught in the blast. I'll be there to help you take command and to assure that the security troops who respond follow our directions. We will establish emergency communications through the security office and you can issue the public announcement. I have some notes for you to refer to. If you say something wrong people will understand that you are in shock, so we can correct it easily. You will do fine."

The helicopter slowed over the city and settled to the circular helipad. Two military policemen awaited them as Salas and Rivas emerged from the helicopter. *"Señores, bienvenidos a Casa Presidencial,"* said one of them as they both saluted. Salas followed the escorts across the car-filled lot toward the building. Salas had always admired the view of bright red bougainvillea, and behind them, the large columned building which housed the executive branch of the Honduran government, but today it seemed foreboding.

As he walked, the briefcase seemed to get heavier with each step. Pessimistic thoughts kept running through his mind. *What if Fuentes lied about the cell phone calls? Does he really need me after this is over? Maybe this thing was just on a timer, set to go off when the cabinet meeting convened. I must be crazy for trying this.* He felt sweat soaking his shirt collar and trickling down his back. *Can I do this without my nervousness giving me away?*

Despite his insecurities, Salas followed through as planned and soon entered the darkly paneled cabinet meeting room. Gazing at the portraits of past presidents lining the walls, he wondered if indeed someday his portrait would hang there. Soon other members of the president's cabinet arrived. Salas did his best to engage in small talk, but he hardly heard what people were saying. Several times he found someone staring at him, waiting for him to respond, and he had to apologize for his wandering attention. Finally he took his seat, saying that he wasn't feeling well. He opened his briefcase, took out his cell phone and a small notepad, and then placed the briefcase on the floor beside his chair. He stared at it momentarily and shuddered.

The Honduran Plot

The president arrived and the meeting began. As it proceeded, it seemed to Salas that each second stretched into minutes. Finally, just when he thought something had surely gone wrong, his ring tone sounded from his cell phone on the table in front of him. He knocked his water bottle over trying to reach it to silence the offending ring. Everyone gave him reproving stares as he answered, saying, "*Un Momento ...*"

"Please excuse me ... my wife ... she's been ill ... upset ... some sort of emergency. I'll take the call outside and not further disturb the meeting," Salas said, in apology for having the cellular on, and the even greater sin of answering it during the meeting. He placed his notepad on the table, pocketed his pack of cigarettes, and left the room.

Outside on the balcony he looked down, past the fountain in the courtyard below, and focused on Major Rivas under an arch beneath the balcony on the other side. By now he was sweating profusely and he wiped his forehead with his handkerchief. Rivas noticed the movement and motioned for him to come down to the ground floor. He followed Rivas through the building to another courtyard, near the entrance to the magnificent state dining room. Long tables, covered with white and blue tablecloths, were set up under a canvas awning in preparation for an outdoor reception.

They paused beside the fountain and pool at the center of the courtyard. It was only then that Rivas spoke. "Did everything go as planned?"

"Yes, I think so," Salas replied. "They accepted the reason for my taking a call during the meeting, and I left the briefcase sitting beside the chair."

"Excellent. Are you ready? Remember what to do?"

Salas nodded to the affirmative. Rivas opened his cellular and punched in the number for the detonator in the briefcase. Smiling an evil smile and looking Salas in the eye, he pressed the key to initiate the call. Salas could see Rivas tense, anticipating the blast.

Chapter 68

Four days before the critical cabinet meeting, Raul had called his father at his home. He had been concerned about calling his father's office from any of the phones they had, so Raul anxiously waited until his father would have come home from work. After Charlie Hedges had made known his father's involvement in the plot, Raul, Amélia and the others had spent hours discussing the situation. They finally decided that Raul had to personally meet with his father to understand how deeply the man was involved.

"I have to talk to you," Raul said. "It's important, urgent."

"Are you still safe there?"

"Yes, I'm good, don't worry about that," Raul told him. "But we have to meet.

"You can't come here, there are people watching."

"People watching? Who? Are they looking for me?" Raul questioned.

His father hesitated, and then said, "Maybe that too, but I think they are keeping an eye on me."

Raul said, "Well, if they are following you, I'll have to come to the house. Otherwise they would see us meet. I can get in undetected."

Enrique Salas hesitated, then said, "You didn't sound surprised when I said I was being watched."

"No, I would put nothing past Fuentes."

"We have both learned that. We have to be very careful. How can you come here without being seen?"

"Remember how I used to sneak out and explore the hillside when I was a kid? That old place in back of the house where the chain link fence is just held by twisted wire at the bottom. I can get in that way and nobody will see me come in."

His father said, "You're probably right. I doubt anyone is watching the back of the house."

"I'll see you tonight, after dark. We have to talk."

■■■

The Honduran Plot

Amélia accompanied Raul to meet his father. He drove Rodrigo's car up the winding road to Picacho, the small mountain overlooking the city of Tegucigalpa. They passed his house and then the American ambassador's house. Raul couldn't see any sign of someone watching.

"I don't see anyone," Raul said. "Maybe we should just go back to the house."

"They could be watching from anywhere," Amélia said. "Just stick to the original plan ... it's safer."

Raul's jaw tightened, but he didn't say anything. She always had to be the one in charge, but this time she was probably right. He continued up the hill, and parked in front of the Copantl "Hotel el Picacho." They went through the front entrance, walked casually through the lobby and exited through a rear entrance. The grounds were lit by subdued lights placed strategically along the walkways and shrubs. Raul led her to a gate at the rear of the property and they stepped into the dark.

The landscape on the hill behind the hotel property was dimly lit by a first quarter moon, looking like a shining silver coin cut in half and tossed into the sky. The upscale houses that lined the winding road could be seen down the hill on their left.

"See the lights from the house down the hill about 50 meters?" Raul said. "That's the ambassador's house. We'll work our way down the hill behind it then through the trees to our place."

"It looks dark down there. I can't see any more house lights."

"I told my father to leave all the outside lights off and to disable the alarm. We should be able to sneak in without anyone seeing, even if they are watching the place."

Twenty minutes later they had crawled under the loose section of fence, crept through the yard and entered the house through a rear door. They found Enrique Salas in the den.

"Where's Mom?" were the first words out of Raul's mouth.

"She is out at some event with some of her friends. We're alone. Who is this?"

"This is Amélia Ramirez," Raul answered. He saw his father nod his head slightly and decided he already suspected who she was.

A half-hour later they were still sitting in the den. Raul told his father about all of the experiences they had gone through. He asked a few questions but, for the most part, had remained silent. However, when Raul revealed the content of the e-mails regarding the plot, and the fact that he knew that his father was somehow involved, that changed. His father grimaced and moisture brimmed in his eyes. He looked from Raul to Amélia, and cleared his throat.

"It is true," he said, dropping his head and wiping the tears that had suddenly rolled down his cheek. "I have sunk to a deep, dark place … I don't know how to get out. At first I thought that cooperating with Fuentes and working with General Velasquez would help us take the country in the right direction. Three years ago I thought Zelaya had the right answers and maybe I could rise to power with his help. But Zelaya's bid for more power failed."

"As it should have!" Amélia said.

"Not now Amélia!" Raul said. "Let him talk … go on Dad."

But Enrique just sat there, mute, his head in his hands.

Finally Raul said, "Dad, you have to talk to us. What about this plot? How are you involved? I can't believe you are in league with Fuentes. He's … evil!"

Enrique raised his head, again looking from Raul to Amélia, his eyes rimmed with red and his face flushed. "I'm so ashamed …"

"Tell me what's going on," Raul said. "You know Mom and I will love you, no matter what. We have to fix this."

At the mention of Raul's mother, the color drained from his father's face. "I … I'll tell you. I've failed you both, but now there is no way out … no way."

With Raul's constant encouragement he spent the next hour relating his spiral into the orbit of Fuentes and the Venezuelans, first Hugo Chavez, and later General Velasquez.

Raul was both repulsed and fascinated by his father's revelations. Amélia surprised him by sitting quietly and letting him take the lead in the painful process of pulling the painful details from his father. He appreciated her discretion.

Enrique Salas revealed that he was central to the bomb plot. He insisted that there was no way to get out of it. He would be ruined politically if he backed out, possibly even killed.

"Fuentes has years of evidence on our meetings with the Venezuelans," the elder Salas said. "He controls the evidence and can make it appear that I acted alone or at least that he had minimal involvement. There is no way for me to be credible against him."

The Honduran Plot

"We have to tell someone. You have to stand up to Fuentes and stop this thing," Raul pleaded.

"I can't! Don't you see? No evidence on him ... I tried to record him in the hospital when he talked about the plot ... just garbled, indistinct voices."

"Well then, it's your word against his. But you're on the President's cabinet. They would believe you over Fuentes."

"It wouldn't work, Raul. They have my briefcase with the bomb so I can't even touch it until right before the meeting. They have evidence implicating me. I'd take the fall for the whole thing. No one would believe me. I'm totally isolated ... no way out. At one point I had even decided that I would be smart to go along with it," he said. "I could become the next president and an important world figure."

"You couldn't," Raul said. "You're not a murderer!"

"Do I have a choice? They would find a way to do it without me, but I'd be ruined ... jailed and disgraced."

Amélia had been silent as she listened to the exchanges between Raul and his father. Raul looked to her for help.

Finally she spoke up. "If we can find a way, a way to stop the bomb, and a way to get someone to listen, will you help us?"

Enrique stared at her. "It's impossible," he mumbled.

"No, nothing is impossible, or at least we shouldn't believe so, until we have tried everything we can think of. We have to find a way!"

Raul could see the fire in her eyes, and he jumped to her support. "Just give us a day or two to come up with something before you give up hope. Don't do anything until then."

Enrique exhaled, and appeared to deflate. Raul thought his father had aged ten years in the few days since he had last seen him. "I won't do anything. I don't know what to do anyway. It's only a few days until the cabinet meeting. I can't see a way out ... maybe I should just kill myself ... save the family from disgrace."

Chapter 69

Back at the farmhouse Raul and Amélia filled the others in on the dire situation. Jake looked around the table at the shocked expressions on everyone's face. He had readily accepted the idea of a plot to seize power from the government with the help of Venezuela. Nothing could have prepared Jake for the news of an attempt to take out the president and his entire cabinet, with the exception of Director Salas of course. Already Jake's brain was going into overdrive as he began sorting through possibilities of action they could take.

"Your father must refuse to take any part in this, and we must go to the authorities with what we know," Pastor Zamora insisted. "We cannot allow them to put lives at risk!"

"But he will be blamed for everything!" Raul protested.

"Better that than risking the life of so many people!" Zamora retorted.

"Everybody, wait a minute," Jake said. He could envision several problems with that approach. "Pastor Juan, I understand your argument, but I don't think that will work. If Raul's dad refused to go along, or just hid, there would be no proof there was even a bomb—Fuentes or one of his men has it."

"We have to do something, Jake."

"Yes sir, I know," Jake said. "But here's the problem … we, I mean Amélia, Luis and I, are subjects of a manhunt already. By now Fuentes has probably cooked up a story to explain why the rest of you were in his prison. If we come forward we would be arrested. If we give the information to someone else we still won't be credible."

"But you have the secret documents," Teresa said.

Jake looked around the room. Was he the only one who could see the problem? Why was he the only one arguing?

Amélia met his eyes and nodded. "Go on, Jake. You're doing a good job of thinking it through."

Well, at least she's speaking to me now. He could see Raul and Luis nod in agreement. Jake continued. "No one would believe the documents are real. You heard that Hedges guy … his bosses thought we might have forged them. Besides, we killed guards during the breakout and wounded Fuentes. Who's going to believe what we have to say?"

"That's the trouble," Raul said dejectedly, "there is no way out."

"I think there could be," Jake said. He paused, still sorting through options and possibilities. He talked his way through the process. Telling others his plans had always helped Jake refine them on the fly.

Pastor Juan said, "You made some good points. We're listening … please continue."

"Alright, we need to find someone who will believe us, or at least give us a chance. I have an idea about the bomb, but one of you has to find someone who will listen to us."

"Tell us your idea about the bomb first," Amélia said.

"If we could de-fuse it, so it didn't go off, then Mister Salas would have it for evidence that the plot was real."

"But then we're back to his being framed," Raul said. "Fuentes would say it was my father's plot!"

"That is why the first step is getting someone in power to hear us out. Then the bomb gives additional proof. But to be believed, we have to let the plot be played out so that it becomes clear who is involved."

There were frowns and wrinkled foreheads around the room as the others considered his words. Amélia gave him a long look, curiosity etched on her face. "How would that work?"

"OK, here it is," Jake said. "Raul's dad said the bomb is triggered by a cell phone. Are you certain of that?"

Raul answered, "Almost certain. We talked to Dad about that quite a bit. A timer wouldn't work. He was told the timing could change— some delay, someone late, who knows? The plan is that they call my father, so then if everything is right, he excuses himself from the meeting. If the timing is off, he says he will call back later, and then leaves later when the time is right."

"That makes sense," Jake said. "My idea is that we could jam the cell phone signal so the bomb can't be triggered. The bomb will be safe for some bomb squad guys to disarm it and gather evidence on who might have built it. That should clear your father, Raul."

"Jamming the cell phone system sounds impossible," Amélia said.

"I think that I can do it," Jake said. "We wouldn't have to jam the whole system. Besides, we need for Raul's father to be able to get his call. I can make a short range jammer that he can put in the briefcase when they give it to him … maybe hidden in his papers or something. It would be only inches from the receiver of the bomb, but far enough away from his dad's phone to not affect it."

"But still," Amélia said, "what about Major Rivas? He'll be right there to blame Raul's dad. Then there's all the people Fuentes has hidden in the military and police. They will try to oppose any attempt to make this work."

Jake thought about her point. That is why he liked to talk through the process—it helped refine his ideas. The answer clicked in his head and he smiled. "Somebody has to call your dad, then they will try to call the phone triggering the bomb. The cell phone records will prove who did this. Your father can reveal the plot, and the people who help us will have the proof."

Amélia said, "We still have that problem … who would listen to us? When you first mentioned that, I thought of General Villanueva, José's father. But that won't work. After José was killed, I tried to call him and he wouldn't talk to me. I guess he believed that stuff the papers said about me."

Pastor Juan spoke up. "When you said something earlier, about finding someone who would listen to us it got me to thinking. My brother has a close friend who is in the navy special forces … like your Navy Seals. Anyway, I know him too, and I think he would believe what I tell him. I guarantee those guys aren't about to be influenced by someone like Fuentes. They would help us if I can convince him that the country is in real danger. We have to get my brother to go with us to help convince him."

"So do we have a plan?" Amélia said. "Can we do this in time? Jake, what do you need to build this jammer thing."

Jake looked around. Everyone was gazing at him expectantly. He felt a lump in his throat as the burden of responsibility landed squarely on his shoulders. "Tools … parts, that's a problem. Wish I had my shop down here."

Luis said, "I know a guy, man. Has a radio and TV repair shop, plus he is an amateur radio operator. Maybe we could see if he can help."

"But we will be taking a huge risk with other people's lives," Pastor Juan said. "If this jammer doesn't work all the cabinet members could be killed. I'm having second thoughts."

Yolanda spoke up for the first time. "Not to mention what would happen to the country!"

"I know you're right," Jake said. The thought of many lives being in his hands terrified him. "I don't want to be responsible for a disaster. Can anyone think of some other way? I can't."

He looked around the room. Silence reigned. Finally Pastor Juan said, "I think we should all pray about this tonight. It is a momentous decision. We can discuss it more tomorrow."

"Juan is right. We should pray for the Holy Spirit to guide us," Teresa Zamora said.

"I agree," Yolanda said.

Jake saw Amélia roll her eyes at those statements, but others nodded their heads.

"Amen!" Jake said, earning him a scowl from Amélia.

Chapter 70

Jake returned to the rattan chair on the front porch. He was beginning to think of it as his chair now. He watched the moon, a shining half circle, setting in the west, and a thought came to him. He remembered when they had frantically escaped through the tunnel, the pitch black night matching the darkness of his mood. Then there was the crescent moon that night when they found out where Ruben was. Later, by the night before the prison rescue, the moon had grown larger, as had his hope and confidence. Still larger as they got help from Hedges and uncovered the bomb plot. It was halfway to full now, and he had big decisions to make. What would the full moon bring?

His musings were interrupted by the sound of the front door. Someone always seemed to seek him out when he retreated to this spot. Jake turned and was surprised to see that it was Amélia. An uncomfortable silence ensued as she walked to the small wall enclosing the front porch. Her arms were folded across her chest, and she ignored Jake while watching the moon, almost hidden by the hills now.

Finally Jake broke the silence. "Come have a seat."

She turned and looked at him, a cold expression on her face. Arms still hugging herself, she hesitated, and then took the chair next to his. "You seemed to have decided to stay for a while. Or is it just that you can't get out of the country right now?

Off to a good start—she just stuck the knife right in. On the other hand, she was here wasn't she? Why would she come out here if she didn't want to listen? Jake hoped his words conveyed more confidence than he felt.

"I ... I'm not running away. I thought about the things you said, and things Ruben said. I'm going to help ... need to help."

"That is good, I suppose. Do you think you can do that thing of jamming the bomb?"

"I've been thinking about it, but haven't got things all planned out. In theory, it should work though."

"Humph, maybe you should get Pastor Juan to ask God to tell you how to make it work."

The Honduran Plot

"I take it you don't like his idea of praying about it?" Jake still had mixed feelings about prayer too, but thought it was probably a good thing to do now.

"I don't believe all that mumbo jumbo," she said in a low voice. "I guess I am in the minority here."

That triggered something in Jake's mind that he had been wondering about. "I don't understand your connection with the others. You don't seem to be a believer, but when I met you three years ago you were working at the church for Pastor Lacas, and you knew Pastor Juan. You're close with Luis, Juanita and to some extent with Ruben. They are all devout Christians."

"So you think I'm an atheist and shouldn't hang out with Christians. Is that it?"

"No! I'm sorry I'm not trying to judge you." Jake reached over and touched her arm. "I'm just trying to understand where you're coming from."

Her quick flash of anger seemed to subside. "Alright Jake, that's fair. I shouldn't be so touchy. It's just that I'm always the different one with this bunch. I'm not an atheist—I guess you could put me down as an agnostic."

Jake really wanted to understand this girl. No, not girl, she was a woman. They were both adults now. If there was going to be anything between them, and Jake wasn't sure there could be, it wasn't going to be a teenage romance. A guilty thought of Barbara flickered through his mind.

Jake squeezed her forearm. "Tell me about why you think that way and how you got to be so close to the others. I really want to know."

"Alright," Amélia said. I'll start from the beginning. My mother was raised in the Catholic Church, like most of the people in our village. A neighbor lady persuaded her to come to the small Protestant church run by Pastor Lacas. She told my mother there were things in the Bible that the priest never talks about, and other things that he claims God commands that aren't in the Bible."

"So she joined Pastor Lacas' church," Jake prompted.

"Yeah, I was eleven, and my mother dragged me there almost every Sunday. My Papa didn't go very much either. He always claimed to be too tired after working the week cutting timber for the lumber company. What about you ... did you always go to church?"

Jake thought back. "I must have. I can't remember any time when we didn't."

"And did you believe all those Bible stories?" Amélia shifted in her seat to face Jake.

"Well, I always wondered why two armadillos would have left the Ark after the flood and wandered to Texas before settling down." He grinned, but didn't know if she could see it in the darkness.

"No, really Jake, did you?" She said, sounding serious. "I used to argue with Luis all the time about that. Church was where we got to be friends. He believed everything, but I told him it was just a bunch of old stories. I guess we still have arguments about belief, even today."

There was a touch of sadness in her voice. Jake felt that she was trying to make him understand, and at the same time feeling him out. There were a lot of things he wasn't sure of. He had never tried to put his thoughts on faith in words.

"Sometimes I'm not sure just what I believe, Amélia. There are stories, poems and songs that tell about God. I don't know if a lot of them are literally true. Maybe they weren't even meant to be … maybe they are to just explain the … relationship."

"Relationship?"

"Yeah, between man and God." Jake was having trouble describing how he felt, maybe he wasn't really sure. He plowed on. "There are stories that teach faith, and reliance on God." Others show how God is faithful and true to His word. Are they actual historical events? I don't know. Maybe it doesn't matter."

Amélia chuckled, and then said, "You sound a lot like Luis when we used to argue. Of course when we were little it was more like he would say, 'is too,' and I'd say, 'is not!' Of course Mama and Pastor Lacas always agreed with Luis. When I got into my teens I just stopped going to church. My mother tried to convince me, but my father told her that if I didn't want to, then she shouldn't make me."

What could he say to that? Jake didn't think there was much he could say that Luis and the others hadn't already said. Besides, he wasn't too sure about a lot of things himself.

"I'm sorry," he said.

"Don't be sorry! I'm not someone to be pitied just because I don't believe like the rest of you," Amélia said. "I'm going to bed … it's late." She got up and disappeared through the front door.

The Honduran Plot

Jake could smell the lingering scent of her perfume. *Way to go Jake!—Mister Eloquence.*

Chapter 71

Tuesday morning everyone was gathered in the kitchen and living room. Amélia paid no particular attention to Jake, but addressed everyone in general. "Listen everybody; we have to make a decision. Are we going to try to stop this plot by ourselves? Should we risk it?"

Everyone crowded into the kitchen. Jake adjusted the sling on his arm and sat down at the table. Amélia sat across from him. He waited for her to look directly at him, but she never looked in his eyes.

"Jake, it depends on you, man," Luis said. "Can you do it?"

Jake had an answer, but he wanted to find out how the others felt before going too far. "I think so, Luis. But, what about the rest of you? You had overnight to think about all the things we discussed yesterday."

"And time to pray!" Amélia said.

"Alright Amélia, enough of that," Yolanda said. "Pastor Juan, what are your thoughts?"

The little man stood up and ran his hands through his salt-and-pepper hair. "Well I did pray … most of the night, in fact. I don't see how anyone is going to believe us, but my mind kept returning to thoughts of my brother's friend. Maybe it is God leading me in that direction."

Teresa said, "He might know of another way… something that will keep us from risking the lives of the President and his entire cabinet."

"Or my father's life," Raul added.

Pastor Juan sat down. "I prayed for that too, but I don't have a lot of confidence that will happen. We still need for your father to gain possession of the bomb as proof."

A good point," Raul said. "And we need some evidence of Fuentes and his men being involved to prove my father isn't the one doing this."

Jake hoped there was some way out that didn't rely on him, but he doubted that was possible. He too had prayed, and had felt a sense of calmness and certainty. He had spent the next hour before going to sleep running options through his mind. He had considered and rejected design options, selected the best and visualized how he could build the jammer. He knew he could do it. "I think we have to keep going with the plan for now," Jake said. "If we wait to see if this Navy guy offers other solutions, it may be too late for me to get the jammer built and tested."

Amélia looked him in the eyes. "You haven't answered Luis' question. Are you sure you can make this jammer thing work."

He smiled at her, but received a cold stare in return. Silence descended over the room. All eyes were focused on Jake. "Yes, I am sure that the thing can be made to work. I thought about the design last night ... even got my calculator out to check some assumptions about the r.f. field strengths and ... well, never mind."

Amélia looked around the room. "Certainly that is good news. Is everyone agreeable with taking Jake at his word that he can do this?"

There were nods and mumbles of assent around the room. Jake watched in admiration as Amélia suggested assignments to carry out their plans. She was definitely a leader.

"*¡Si, comandante!*" Luis said when she finished, and gave her an impish grin.

■■■

Rodrigo drove his car to take Jake and Luis wherever they needed to go. Their first stop was to the electronics repair shop. Everything depended on Jake finding the right parts and tools to make the device. If they didn't get any cooperation, Jake was out of options.

"This guy, Mr. Flores, should be able to help," Luis said. "He has all the test equipment and tools to fix things. Like I told you he is a radio ham. His call sign, I think, is HR1 FZ ..."

"Luis," Rodrigo interrupted, "please stop babbling. You must be nervous."

"Well ... uh, yeah, a little, man."

Jake said, "How do you know this Mr. Flores?"

"Friends in high school ... they liked all this electronics stuff. Mr. Flores used to show them how to build things and help them with finding parts for projects. I went in there with them sometimes, just for fun. But me? Never too interested in that kind of thing. I don't know if he will remember me. What if he won't help?"

"Let's cross that bridge when we come to it," Jake said, sounding more calm than he felt.

Luis smiled. "Ok, cliché boy. Let's go inside and talk to him."

When they entered the shop a small, thin man greeted them. "How can I help you?" He peered over his thin reading glasses, focusing on Luis. "Wait, I know you. You used to come in here with Benito and Jorge ... uh, you're Lugo ... no, that's not it ...Luis ... *¿Si?*"

"Yes sir, I am. I'm surprised you remembered me," Luis said. "Well, we need your help, *Señor Flores.* I can't explain everything, but my friend here, Jake, needs to build a circuit and I thought maybe you could let him use your shop. We can pay for parts and things."

"That is unusual. What kind of circuit?" Flores said.

"Well sir, it is an urgent situation," Jake answered. "We need to build a short range cell phone jammer."

"A cell phone jammer!" Flores exclaimed. "I don't think that's a good idea."

Luis said, "Wait sir, we're not just trying to make mischief. This is really important. You know Pastor Juan Zamora don't you?"

"Yes, of course," Flores said. "His church, *Iglesia de las Flores,* and I share the same name. I've known Juan for several years. What does he have to do with this?"

Luis gave Jake a glance, then turned his attention to the small man. "Pastor Juan has another very important meeting right now and couldn't come with us. Can you talk to him on my cellular? He will tell you how important this is. You have to help us. Please?"

Flores frowned at Luis, but accepted the cell phone that Luis held out to him. "Well, I guess I can take some time to talk to him. He is a good man. Besides, business is slow and you have aroused my curiosity."

"The number is already in, just press the call button," Luis told him.

Flores talked to Pastor Juan for several minutes, questioning, arguing, and finally agreeing to help. Terminating the call, he said to Luis, "OK, I still don't know what this is about but Juan has convinced me that it is important that I help you. He says he can tell me the whole story when everything gets resolved."

Jake was pleasantly surprised when he saw the repair shop in the rear of the building. It had everything he could have asked for in the way of test equipment, soldering stations, lighted magnifying viewers and parts. Flores showed Jake where the parts he requested were located and helped him get everything he needed including a small printed circuit board used for prototyping.

"How are you going to be able to make this thing?" Luis wanted to know.

"Well," Jake said, pulling a cell phone out of his pocket, "Yolanda gave me this to sacrifice. I'm going to take the circuit board and antenna out of it. Then I'm going to build a 555 IC square wave circuit to modulate the cell phone's oscillator ..."

"Wait man, I don't understand anything you just said," Luis protested. "Just tell me in layman's language what you are going to do. I don't need all those details."

"I get that a lot," Jake said, feeling chagrined. "I guess it's the nerd coming out in me again."

"I think I see what you are doing," Flores said.

Luis said, "Yes sir, I'm sure you do ... you speak the language. But I don't."

Flores smiled and said, "I understand. Sometimes we technical types, nerds if you will, forget that many very smart people just haven't studied the things we have. We get too wrapped up in the things that fascinate us to think about the fact that many aren't that interested in all the technicalities."

Jake said, "That's right. Let me reword what I was saying. I am going to use my circuit and the guts of this cell phone to transmit a wideband signal that will interfere with the other cell phone's receiver. If it can't receive the signals from the cell tower, because they are jammed, then it won't work at all. So, the command to ... uh, well ..." Jake stopped talking and glanced toward Flores, who was following the conversation closely.

"OK, got it," Luis said. "Go ahead ... don't let me get in the way."

Jake worked for about three hours with Flores helping him. When he was finished he had a circuit board filled with parts, watch batteries and the PC board from the old cell phone held on with double sided tape and secured with black electrical tape. The whole thing was only about a quarter of an inch thick, and the size of a business card. He held it up for Luis to see.

"Well man, it's ugly," Luis said. "Will it work?"

"It's a work of art; a thing of beauty," Jake said with a grin. "When I pull out this little tab of thin plastic it should turn on. Call Pastor Juan again and let's see what happens."

Luis placed the call and told Pastor Juan they were doing tests. Jake pulled the plastic tab out from the metal clip holding it to the circuit board, and put the jammer down on the workbench.

"I lost him," Luis said. "It must have worked. I'm trying to call him back but nothing is happening."

"Step back a few feet," Jake said. "We will see at what kind of distance this thing is effective."

"Alright man, I have service again," Luis said after he had backed away from the device.

Jake said, "Now come slowly toward the workbench. Stop when you lose the connection."

"Give me a test count Pastor Juan," Luis said and walked slowly forward. When his phone got within two feet of Jakes device he stopped. "That's it man. He's gone."

Jake was elated and gave Luis a high five. "Since it will be in the briefcase, just inches away from the detonator cell phone, we should have no problem, even if the batteries weaken."

"Detonator? ... Wha ... what detonator?" Flores looked at them with alarm.

Jake looked to the little man, his eyes wide. He hadn't meant to say that. He shoved some bills, a few thousand Lempiras, into Flores' hand. "Here sir, please take this for the parts and letting us use your shop. We really appreciate your help."

Luis came to the rescue. "Like Pastor Juan said, we can tell you the story when it's all over. Don't worry, sir. You have done a good thing by helping us."

They left the man staring, open mouthed, with a hand full of bills.

Chapter 72

Amélia and Pastor Juan sat in a small café in Comayagüela, the sister city to Tegucigalpa, west of the Choluteca River which separates the two cities. Juan's brother, Guillermo, and his Navy contact, Captain Alvarez, sat across the table. Alvarez had suggested the café as their meeting place because it wasn't too far from the Navy facility south of the city, but far enough that it was unlikely he would encounter anyone he knew.

Amélia listened as the man talked to Pastor Juan. She had expected him to be large and muscular, her idea of a Special Forces officer. Instead, Alvarez was of average height, but trim, and obviously physically fit. On closer inspection, Amélia thought he had a way of carrying himself, and of talking, which hinted at hardness and determination.

Juan, as spokesman, had carefully explained the situation to Guillermo and Alvarez, starting from the disappearance of Ruben and Juanita. Amélia added to the story, telling about the investigation into drug smuggling and their eventual knowledge that Colonel Fuentes was behind the kidnapping and the drugs.

"I know about Fuentes being corrupt," Alvarez said. "My commander, Admiral Zuniga, has been trying to determine who else he has corrupted. We think they are mostly in the Army. He doesn't have many friends in the Navy, and we think there are just a few in the Air Force. We have identified some of his people, but not too many. I would love to take the bas ..." He stopped, and glanced at Amélia. "Uh ... him down, but we don't really have any proof."

"I think we have the information you need," Amélia said, taking the messages that Hedges had provided and pushing them across the table. She watched while he examined the papers and smiled at his reaction. While Alvarez scanned the documents his eyes occasionally widened and several times he nodded his head when he apparently found information which confirmed some of his suspicions.

Juan's ring tone sounded and he excused himself from the table before answering his cellular. He walked to the back of the mostly empty café. A few minutes later he returned to the table. He told Amélia, "Jake's creation seems to work. He disrupted our calls several times while he and Luis were testing it."

Alvarez looked up quizzically. "What is that about?"

"We'll tell you in a minute," Juan said. "What did you think about the information we showed you?"

"I can believe it is authentic," Alvarez said. "It confirms some of the things I had already learned from my commander. We need to get this to him as soon as possible. From what I read, we also need to neutralize this Salas guy. He seems to be central to whatever they are planning."

"That 'Salas guy' is Director Enrique Salas, the president's chief of intelligence," Amélia said. She wondered if *neutralize* meant what she thought it did.

Alvarez took a deep breath and looked from Amélia to Juan. "That Salas? That could be a real problem."

"No, he may be the solution," Amélia said. "He has come over to our side. I won't go into details about that. But he has told us some key parts of the plot, and that is why we need your help ... urgently!"

Alvarez listened as Amélia and Juan told him the details of the plot and their plan to thwart it. Amélia could see him fidgeting in his seat, and running his hand across his close cropped hair.

When they finished he looked to Juan's brother. "Guillermo, you told me your brother was a pastor of a small church?"

When Guillermo nodded in the affirmative, Alvarez pointed at Juan. "This man comes in here, accompanied by a beautiful woman, tells me he wants to take down the head of the secret police, and risk the lives of the President and his entire cabinet, and you expect me to believe he is a preacher!"

Juan said, "I assure you ..."

Alvarez held up his hand, cutting him off. "No offense, pastor. I believe you. It just sounds a little ... no very, crazy ... *¡mucho loco!*"

Alvarez suddenly stood up. Amélia and the others took the hint that the meeting was about over, and did likewise. He grabbed Pastor Juan by the hand and shook it vigorously. "You are my kind of man, preacher! We will help you. I have to take this to Admiral Zuniga immediately, and you have to go with me!"

The Honduran Plot

Amélia let out a huge breath, and felt a little shaky. They had their ally. This thing could work! Another thought came to her. "Captain, do you think you, or maybe your commander, could convince General Villanueva to help us? He blames me for his son's death, and won't talk to me."

Alvarez lost his smile, and regarded her curiously. "I heard about his son. You were somehow involved?"

"I was there, and almost killed too." Amélia couldn't stop tears from filling her eyes. The Captain's face became a blur. "José was my friend, and I never wanted him to be hurt. I'm sure Fuentes was behind what happened. Tell that to General Villanueva." She grabbed a napkin off the table and blotted her eyes."

Alvarez reached out and touched her shoulder. "General Villanueva is a good man, and Admiral Zuniga knows him well. You can tell the Admiral about what happened, and I am sure he will get the General to listen."

Amélia hoped that he could make that happen, and managed a small smile. "I appreciate your help sir."

Alvarez smiled and looked from one to the other. "Now let's go see the Admiral and start working to shore up your plans. We will get that bas ... uh, Colonel Fuentes."

Chapter 73

Friday morning, the President of Honduras and members of his cabinet met upstairs at the *Casa Presidencial*, blissfully unaware of the deadly bomb in their midst. Enrique Salas stood under the canvas canopy in the reception courtyard finally daring to breathe. Beautiful tranquility filled his senses. Dapples of sunlight thrown by the foliage painted the pavestones, and the sound of the fountain caressed his ears.

Major Rivas frowned at his cell phone and punched desperately at its keys. "Something's wrong!" A full thirty seconds had passed since he had tried to detonate the bomb.

Salas turned and was startled to see three commandos, in full battle gear, had magically appeared behind Rivas. Their stealthy approach had escaped Salas, even though he had known that they would be coming. They grabbed Rivas, disarmed him, and snatched the cell phone away.

"We will keep this for evidence," one of the commandos said. "Director Salas, I am Captain Alvarez. I will now accompany you to the cabinet room where you can explain the situation to the president. The bomb technicians will be right behind us, as will be my commander, Admiral Zuniga."

■■■

Salas hesitated at the door to the cabinet room. The guard at the door looked at him curiously. Ignoring the guard, Salas steeled himself for the ordeal which was to follow. He hoped he could come out of this with a shred of dignity. Taking a deep breath, he rapped sharply on the door and walked in with Captain Alvarez by his side. All heads turned in his direction.

"What is the meaning of this?" the president demanded. "We are in a private meeting! Salas, who is this? What is going on?"

"My greatest apologies Mister President," Salas replied. "This is Captain Alvarez of Navy Special Forces. We are here to inform you of an attempt on your life."

Before the president could respond, the door behind Salas burst open and Admiral Zuniga strode in, followed by a half dozen commandos and two men in heavy bomb disarmament gear. Admiral Zuniga ignored any military or political niceties. "Mister President, for your safety you and your cabinet members will please allow my men to accompany you to the small conference room in the presidential office. It will be crowded, but it is a safe place where you can be briefed on what has happened."

Salas stood mutely as the commandos led the dazed and confused president and his cabinet members out the door. Admiral Zuniga turned to Salas and Alvarez. "Captain, you and Director Salas are to stay here to brief the bomb technicians on the device. In fifteen minutes, report to me in the President's Conference Room."

...

Later, Salas stood before the President, Admiral Zuniga, and General Villanueva. A few select cabinet members also remained in the small conference room.

Admiral Zuniga said, "The rest of the cabinet members have been taken back to the cabinet room, which has been cleared of the bomb. They will be given a summary of events which leaves out details of your involvement, Director Salas. How the Navy discovered the plot will also not be disclosed. Following that, they will be sworn to secrecy and required to sign formal non-disclosure statements."

The Admiral turned to the President. "Now sir, Director Salas will tell you how this plot evolved and how he was forced to be involved. Captain Alvarez can also provide details on how the plot was discovered and defeated."

Salas gulped as the Admiral waved him forward. Sweat broke out and he felt like he was burning up. Hesitantly at first he began to reveal his years of deception. As he unburdened himself, he felt as if he has shed a great weight he had been carrying. He told of Fuentes coercion and blackmail to force his participation. But he kept Greta Rojas out of his confession—he just hoped Fuentes would too, when he was arrested. When he finally finished telling his story to those assembled, Salas stood, his head down, dripping with sweat.

"You risked our lives on a piece of amateur, home-made electronics?" the President yelled, becoming red in the face and spraying spittle across the table. "And you Admiral Zuniga, you went along with this! I will have you demoted and thrown into the brig. This whole debacle is unthinkable!"

Salas listened as the tumultuous meeting continued in an effort to reassure the President. Captain Alvarez verified that a Navy electronics expert had examined Jake's jamming device, and pronounced it reliable. He explained that the jammer had been put inside the case of a gutted calculator to avoid detection. Salas had transferred that along with his papers into the briefcase when he was picked up by the helicopter. The President was assured that the experts thought there was no chance that the device could be detonated.

When asked about arming the device, Salas said, "Sir, I pulled the plastic tab, activating the jammer, when I removed my cell phone and notepad, before placing the briefcase on the floor. We had tested the arming method before. This was done well before you entered the meeting, so you were always safe."

The rationale of letting the plot continue was also a hard-sell to the shaken President. Salas sat defeated, hardly listening as the Captain and the Admiral walked the President through the strategy.

"We had to assure full secrecy so no one could be told there was a threat," Admiral Zuniga explained. "Until the plot was allowed to play out, we couldn't be sure that there wasn't some other cabinet level official under Fuentes' control. We also needed time for the Navy Commandos, and two Air Force Special Forces units, to be put into place to interdict the military units loyal to Fuentes. If we had warned you, and someone loyal to Fuentes found out, there might have been serious bloodshed."

Thanks to the decrypted documents, a detailed list identifying these traitors was known. A low point in the meeting was when the President was told that Colonel Fuentes had escaped. Apparently, upon the delay in hearing from Major Rivas, he had correctly surmised that the plot had gone awry and had put into effect his escape plans.

While listening to this, a shamed Enrique Salas sat quietly, and his thought returned to Greta Rojas. He realized now that his lust for her had been a major factor in his failure to find a solution to the problem which Fuentes had become. In all of his revelations, to Raul and Amélia, and later to Pastor Zamora, Jake Grayson and the navy personnel, he had never told them about his affair with her, or of the blackmail video that Fuentes had forced her to make. A part of him still wondered if, after all this was over, he might resume a relationship with her someday. He still continued to daydream, remembering their times together.

The Honduran Plot

"Director Salas! Enrique, I'm speaking to you!"

The president's voice interrupted his reverie. Salas jerked his head up in sudden awareness and said, "Yes sir! Of course Mister President, what is it?"

Sternly the president spoke: "Your behavior during this affair has been despicable. However, because it would cause great embarrassment to the lawfully elected government of Honduras, and because you finally came to your senses, your part in this plot will remain secret, and you will not be charged with a crime. Tomorrow you will submit your resignation for 'personal reasons' and I will accept it without public comment. Is that understood?"

"Yes sir," Salas replied, hanging his head.

"To the rest of you," the president continued, looking around the room, "secrecy is absolutely required. The other cabinet members have already been required to sign non-disclosures and you will be required to do the same. The other cabinet members were given a sanitized account of events, and they will naturally be curious to learn other details that have been revealed in this meeting. I demand you to never disclose anything to them, or anyone else; do not confirm or deny any speculation, no matter what the source. Your non-disclosures will be quite restrictive and prevent you from doing so.

"Admiral Zuniga, you and Captain Alvarez are to be commended for your actions. General Villanueva, your cooperation and the action taken by the Air Force is also appreciated. I will issue a presidential order, back-dated, commanding your forces to take military action necessary to detain all personnel unlawfully acting at Colonel Fuentes' direction. They, and Fuentes when you apprehend him, will be court-martialed for treason. Evidence obtained will be classified as 'top secret' in order to protect our intelligence resources. This ignores the fact that we actually don't know, but only have suspicions, of where most of the intelligence originated. There will be no further attempt to discover that source, since it is undoubtedly friendly to our nation. Are there any questions on all that?"

Admiral Zuniga stood and said, "Thank you sir. Everything you have ordered is understood and will be carried out. There is one other issue that I would appreciate your guidance on."

"Yes, go on," the president urged.

"There are several Honduran citizens, and two American citizens, who are privy to the intelligence we have. They are our source of it, and they have met the person responsible for obtaining the decryption of the information. Some of them participated in an armed breakout of prisoners that were being detained illegally by Colonel Fuentes and his men. Some members of Fuentes' army intelligence unit were killed. How do you recommend these persons be handled?"

The president appeared to think for a moment and replied, "What would be your recommendation Admiral?"

"Sir, I believe these people are the real heroes of this entire affair. Without their diligence and perseverance in exposing Fuentes and freeing their friends we might not have even known about this plot. My recommendation is that they be commended for their actions and granted immunity from prosecution for any laws they have broken in doing so. Of course they should be briefed on the requirements for secrecy and made to sign non-disclosure documents also. I would have Captain Alvarez take care of that personally since he was their original contact."

The President hesitated, stroking his beard. "It will be done; please see to it."

Enrique Salas breathed a sigh of relief. At least Raul and his friends would be in the clear. This whole affair would not taint them at all. He rehearsed, in his mind, what he would say to his wife.

Chapter 74

Jake didn't know how much longer he could wait to find out what had happened. Something was wrong. The cabinet meeting should have started hours ago. He looked around the living room and adjacent kitchen of the crowded farmhouse. They were all still here, most sitting around nervously, waiting. It seemed that everyone was hoping, praying or just lost in their thoughts. Amélia had retreated into silence, occasionally glancing his way. His life had been put on hold.

Finally the phone in the kitchen rang, and all eyes turned that way as Yolanda answered. She listened, and then held her hand over the mouthpiece. "Raul, it is Captain Alvarez. He wants to talk to you."

Jake tensed up. Something must have gone wrong. He watched as Raul talked, nodding his head, his face serious. The conversation took a while, but finally Raul hung up. Immediately everyone gathered in the kitchen.

"Captain Alvarez said my father was safe. Jake, your jammer worked perfectly. Everyone is alright. They arrested Major Rivas, the guy who took Dad to the meeting. He was the one who tried to trigger the bomb."

"Praise God!" Pastor Juan said.

Raul said, "Yes, he has answered our prayers I think. But there is one problem."

"What is the problem?" Amélia asked.

Raul looked around the room, shook his head and let out a breath. "Fuentes escaped, and some of his men are missing too. They can't find him anywhere. Alvarez says we should stay here until he comes out to give us a full debriefing later today. He is hoping that they can capture Fuentes. He wants to make sure he doesn't try to retaliate against any of us."

They all agreed that it would be best to stay until Alvarez gave them more details. Jake, once more put off calling home. His thoughts and emotions raced from one thing to the other. He was elated that the plan had worked, and felt like calling his parents to tell them what he had done. Could he tell them? Or was this going to be some sort of secret he couldn't reveal? He longed for home, but didn't long to be back with Barbara. When had that changed? He was being unfair to her. They had planned so much together. Maybe it was because he had been here so long, in this place that seemed like an alternate universe.

Jake got up and went into the kitchen to pour himself another cup of coffee. Amélia, Luis and Yolanda were there, cleaning the rifles and pistol, preparing them to be wrapped in plastic and hidden away.

"Anyone want more coffee?" he asked. "There is a little left."

"Not me," Luis said.

"I don't want any," Yolanda said, "but why don't you pour that out and make a fresh pot. It's been sitting there for a while now."

Amélia ignored him completely. *Still getting the silent treatment.* Jake felt uneasy as he rinsed out the pot and refilled the basket with a filter and fresh coffee. He retreated back into the living room, wondering why her silence made him feel so bad. He alternated between being angry with her for being mad at him, and wanting to go to her and say anything he could to make her happy.

Yolanda and Luis had just returned from hiding the weapons in an outbuilding behind the farmhouse when a helicopter appeared and touched down on the bare field of grass in front of the house. For a moment Jake felt panicky, remembering that day in Talanga when Fuentes' soldiers had come pouring out of the big green helicopter. But this machine was smaller and only one person emerged, Captain Alvarez.

He gathered everyone in the main room of the farmhouse, and gave them a detailed account of the events that had taken place. Everyone listened in rapt attention. Jake couldn't help but feel a sense of pride when Alvarez described how impressed the bomb squad had been by the idea of the jammer. Alvarez thanked them for their efforts and informed them that they had received presidential pardons for any laws they had broken.

"So, as of now, you are free to return to your normal life," Alvarez concluded. "You will need to sign these statements regarding the secrecy of your involvement with this affair."

"And we aren't required to do anything more?" Yolanda asked skeptically.

Alvarez smiled, saying, "I know what you're probably thinking about. You're worried because we know you have guns, and they are illegal weapons."

"Well ..."

"Listen, I have done some investigation into your backgrounds as a result of all this," Alvarez said. "I know that you, your niece, and Luis all grew up in Los Gatos. And of course I know the story about the old lady and her cats. It is my personal opinion that an outside cat must have some claws to remain truly independent and safe. There are no public reports of any illegal weapons. I have made sure everything is wrapped up as far as the military and the police are concerned. The files are closed."

"Just like that?" Amélia said. "Everything is over, like it never happened? We don't have to worry about the police or those army security guys?"

"That is correct," Alvarez said. "We believe that it is better for the country to let these things remain out of the public eye."

"So we can leave now?" Jake said. "It's safe to make flight reservations back to the United States?"

Alvarez rubbed his chin. "Yes go ahead and make plans, all of you. But before you actually leave wait until I can give you an update later tonight. Most, if not all, of the men that Fuentes corrupted have been identified and arrested. Several others under suspicion are being watched. As for Fuentes, I imagine he is trying to find a way out of the country."

Amélia turned from shooting daggers at Jake and said, "Maybe we can help you with that." She looked to Juanita who nodded in agreement. "Ruben, tell him about the airplane you saw after we got that anonymous tip about the drug smuggling."

"I thought you already told him about Fuentes receiving drugs," Ruben said.

"I did," Amélia said, "but I didn't provide details about what you saw. I think he might be interested in that airplane."

Chapter 75

Jake was back in his customary rattan chair. He watched Pastor Juan's old white van leaving a trail of dust that glowed in the light of the setting sun. It disappeared down the long drive in front of the farmhouse, leaving Jake alone with his thoughts.

Pastor Juan and Teresa had said their goodbyes, a tearful parting, and were going back home. Before they left, Jake had asked Pastor Juan for some advice.

"I just don't know what to do," Jake had said. "Amélia won't even talk to me, since I told her that I was planning to go home."

"And why do you think that is?" Juan asked. "You must have some understanding of that."

"Yes, of course," Jake said. His face grew hot. "I'm not completely dense. We have developed feelings for each other. But what can I do?"

Juan, speaking softly, asked, "What is God telling you to do?"

"I don't know if He is telling me anything!"

"Are you sure? You have to trust and listen. Didn't you tell me once that you had come to believe that it was God who caused you to come back to Honduras?"

"Well, I came back to find Ruben ... but, yeah, I do remember telling you that I felt this 'nudge' ... uh, a sense of conviction that I thought *might* have been from God." He felt ridiculous admitting it. Wouldn't he be sure if God had really told him to do something?

Juan said, "And what do you think God might be telling you now? About Amélia I mean."

Jake sighed. "That's just it ... I don't know. When I look at her she looks different to me now. Like everything I notice about her is just ... she looks beautiful ... I admire her strength, her intelligence ... just the way she is." He could feel the blood rising in his face. He must seem like an idiot to the older man. "But I can't just throw everything away, my school, my plans ..."

"Do your plans seem as promising now, if you consider not having Amélia in them?" Juan asked.

The Honduran Plot

"I haven't thought of them in that light ... but no, I guess they don't. Right now having her not be angry with me is the only thing I have been thinking about, but I still don't know what to do."

"Maybe you just need to take things a step at a time and let God guide you. He may not give you a roadmap, but if you listen to him, he will give you guidance at each turn in the road. That's all I can tell you."

Jake remembered the many times Ruben had tried to get him to open up to new experiences. He had told Jake that he was trying to fit the world into his idea of what he had planned for his life. Maybe that was what Pastor Juan was trying to tell him too.

Jake wished he could talk to Ruben again, but he and Juanita had gone earlier, soon after Captain Alvarez had briefed them and departed with their sworn statements of secrecy. Ruben was going back to Texas to see his family, but planned to return to Honduras on a work visa. He confided to Jake that he and Juanita had unofficially become engaged.

Jake had called his parents. They had agreed that he would return home the next day, on the same flight as Ruben. That's when Amélia had left the house in tears. Somehow he felt like he had betrayed her. Did she really expect him to stay here?

He sat there, watching the sun disappear behind the mountains. His mind churned with conflicting feelings, and amazement at the changes Honduras had made in him. His old life and ambitions seemed like a story he had read, or a remembered dream. He became aware of time passing only when he realized it had gotten dark. Then it dawned on him, a sudden self-realization, that he no longer had that feeling of uncertainty. The disquiet that had been plaguing him had just vanished! He hadn't been consciously praying, just thinking and letting his feelings pour out. *And now it seems like I have an answer... know what to do ...maybe it was praying after all.*

■■■

Stepping out onto the patio behind the farmhouse, Jake halted—where was she? He almost turned to go back inside when he saw her in the yard. She was watching the moon, almost full now, ascending silently above the distant hills to the east. Her silhouette took his breath away. Yes, this was real—he was doing the right thing.

He came up behind her and savored the Jasmine scent he had come to associate with Amélia. "I didn't mean it ... didn't think," he said.

She remained staring into the silvery light, a fragrant statue. Jake reached out and touched her neck, warm, pulse pounding. She flinched at his touch, but made no other move. He placed both hands on her shoulders.

"I'm staying for you ... for ... us."

She turned and he could see tears on her cheeks, glistening in the moonlight—diamonds on mocha. "Us?" she whispered. "Is there ... can there be, *us?*"

Reaching toward her, Jake said, "I want there to be."

Amélia let out a sound, something between a sigh and a sob. "I don't see how, not now."

Jake pulled her into her arms and felt her slim body, somehow softer than he had imagined.

"We can make it happen," he whispered. "This is where God has led us ... you just have to believe."

She closed her eyes and leaned into him. His pulse quickened, his hope rising in step with his heartbeat.

"I'd like to believe ... about us ... about God. I'm just not there yet, Jake."

He struggled to find the right words. "This is just the beginning for us. I don't know where it will go."

"Can it go on?" she murmured, nuzzling his cheek.

A sense of assurance coursed through his body. "We can make it work. But first I want you to come back to the States with me."

She pulled away, a questioning look on her face.

"You are *loco!*" she said, looking at him in amazement. "I'm not running off with you!"

"I don't expect you to run off with me. We can come back in a week. I just want you to go with me to meet my parents. Then we can come back here."

"Here? Honduras? Are you really staying?" Amélia said. Moonlight glistened in her eyes, still brimming with tears.

"I think you know," Jake said. "We need to see where this is going. My parents need to meet the woman who is pulling me here ... changing my life."

By now she was smiling through her tears.

"Yes, you crazy *gringo*, I'll go with you!" She pulled him toward her and he was lost in a long passionate kiss. He closed his eyes, feeling warmth flooding his senses. Then suddenly, she pulled away. "But what will you do here?"

Jake opened his eyes. Had he ever seen a woman so beautiful as this one before him, with tears drying on her cheeks? "I can continue my studies here, at UNAH, for a year, or even two. We can take it step-by-step and see where God leads us," He smiled at her. "Oh, I forgot; you're not sure there even is a God, are you?"

She smiled and took his hand with both of hers. "I'm becoming more comfortable with the idea. Let's go tell Aunt Yolanda."

Chapter 76

Greta Rojas looked out the flyspecked, grimy window of the small customs office. Night had fallen and lights struggled to illuminate the dark recesses of Toncontin International airport. She was dressed sensibly in jeans and a blouse, a lightweight jacket, and walking shoes. She eyed her small travel bag on the floor, sitting next to a larger bag belonging to Manuel Fuentes.

Manuel had talked her into this. Why had she listened to him? Just because he had to flee, giving up everything, why should she? Who knew she was involved, and what if they did? She could disappear on her own if necessary. It wasn't too late.

The door creaked open and Manuel came in. "I paid the customs officer well. He won't tell anyone we were here."

"Why don't we just kill him? Then we can be sure, and save the money," she said. "The plane is late. Are you sure that they aren't abandoning us here."

"It's not late. Don't worry, it will come. I talked to General Velasquez personally. He assured me that Rodriguez would bring us to Venezuela. He values me ... even though things didn't work out here. I can be of use to him elsewhere, maybe Mexico."

"I don't want to live in Mexico!"

"We have to make ourselves valuable to Velasquez. You do want to be with me, don't you?"

Did she have a choice, now that Salas had ruined her plans? "If that pig, Enrique Salas, hadn't betrayed us we wouldn't be running. I should stay here and show him how sharp my knives are while I slowly kill him."

It was there in her mind, a growing knot of red rage. She could always feel it coming on. Men were always ruining her plans—her stepfather—now Salas had failed her—and Fuentes too. Yes Manuel—as bad as the rest—after she had given him everything, done whatever he said!

The door to the little office opened and the customs officer came in. "*Jefe,* the plane has landed. It is coming down the taxiway."

The Honduran Plot

Through the grimy window Greta could see the Gulfstream G200 taxi to the front of the customs area. The whine of the engines reduced to a murmur coming through the walls as they were cut to idle power. A door in the side of the fuselage opened, lowering stairs. Her magic carpet of escape—or a flight to banishment? Did really she want a life tied to Manuel?

The customs officer sat at the desk, ignoring them. Fuentes picked up his bag. "Come on, we have to go. They won't wait."

It was the moment of decision. She would be giving up everything. Greta's face felt hot. Hatred for Fuentes and his stupid plans flooded her brain. The knot of rage expanded, tinting her vision with angry streaks of red, as she picked up her bag and followed him out the door. She would make all of them pay for ruining everything she had worked for!

"Come on!" Fuentes yelled over the whine of the waiting aircraft. He stood on the tarmac, waving her forward, moonlight lighting his face.

Greta approached and set down her bag. She glared at him and reached inside her jacket. She could see Fuentes' eyes widen in surprise as she pulled out a stiletto and thrust it into his throat. "I'm not going to Mexico!"

Greta turned and went back into the customs office. The man inside looked up from his papers on the desk, an expression of curiosity on his face. It would be the last thing he saw, as she thrust the stiletto with deadly accuracy. Feeling inside his coat pocket, she found a large wad of bills. Going outside again, she wiped the stiletto clean on Fuentes fallen body and returned it to her jacket. She undid Fuentes' belt and unbuttoned his pants. Yes, there was his money belt! Greta pulled it loose and stuffed it, with the wad of bills, inside her travel bag, adding to the other cash she had brought for her escape.

Picking up the bag, she walked into the darkness. Violent visions of what she would do to Enrique, and that Ramirez woman played through her mind. She would have her revenge on them, and the others too! Greta walked north on the sidewalk and spotted a waiting taxi near the airport entrance. The red tinge coloring her vision subsided. She thought of the roughly quarter of a million U.S. dollars that she must now have in her bag, and smiled.

■■■

Captain Alvarez sat in a navy staff car parked unobtrusively behind the cargo containers near the customs office. He realized he had erred in selecting his vantage point. The containers blocked direct view of the custom office. That shouldn't matter though he had a clear view of the customs freight area tarmac. He watched the Venezuelan business jet through binoculars as it idled on the tarmac. He felt sure that this was Fuentes' planned means of escape. Ruben Avila had provided a full description of the aircraft, the containers and customs area just south of the terminal. It was a pity that few people would know what the small band of college students had done for the country.

Alvarez wanted Fuentes to board the aircraft before making his move. After a few minutes passed, a figure came down the stairs, appeared to stare into the darkness, and ran back up the stairs. The aircraft started rolling forward, turning back onto the taxiway. Something was wrong! Fuentes had not boarded.

Alvarez picked up a handheld radio. "Now! Intercept the plane now!"

He didn't worry about creating an international incident. Venezuela wouldn't want to do anything that might make public their culpability in the attempted coup. They, more than anyone, would want the incident buried in secrecy.

He retrained the binoculars toward the aircraft. The scene was dimly lit by the peach glow of the airport's sodium vapor lights, aided by the light of the moon which had risen above the buildings. He could see a large personnel carrier, with Honduran Air Force markings, charge up the taxiway toward the accelerating aircraft. The vehicle pulled across the pavement in an attempt to block the airplane's path. A half dozen Air Police armed with M-16 rifles poured out of the vehicle. But they were too late—the Gulfstream G200 turned onto the runway, accelerated with a piercing roar of its engines and lifted off into the night. Alvarez swore to himself.

A Note from the Author

I hope you enjoyed reading The Honduran Plot. Independently published authors rely on recommendations from readers and word-of-mouth advertising. Please rate this book on Amazon.com and write a short, honest review. If you feel so inclined, please make recommendations to your friends on Facebook or other social media. It would be greatly appreciated.

Visit http://www.facebook.com/honduran.plot, my author's page on Facebook, for interesting photos, book recommendations, useful information and insights, or lessons learned in self-publishing. There will even be some interviews with the characters from the novel (if I can get them to cooperate.)

Please also check out my website: http://www.hortonprather.com where you can find more information on upcoming novels.

You are welcome to contact me anytime by E-mail at horton@hortonprather.com.

Horton Prather

Made in the USA
Lexington, KY
14 December 2013